THE LAST DAWN

Jez Wood

authorHOUSE®

AuthorHouse™ UK Ltd.
500 Avebury Boulevard
Central Milton Keynes, MK9 2BE
www.authorhouse.co.uk
Phone: 08001974150

First published by AuthorHouse 10/4/2007

ISBN: 978-1-4343-3307-0 (sc)
ISBN: 978-1-4343-3308-7 (hc)

Printed in the United States of America
Bloomington, Indiana

This book is printed on acid-free paper.

In Loving Memory Of

Cyrus

A Better Friend I Could Not Have Wished For

Miss You Buddy

Mum And Dad

(The Boy Done Good XX)

Acknowledgments

I mean when I say these are in no particular order, and with the combination of my goldfish memory and bad brain filing system, some people will have been missed, and for that I am deeply sorry, but you mean as much to me (and in some cases more) as any of the names listed below.

I would like to thank

Andy, for without him you wouldn't be reading this now (now hurry and get yours done dude).

Emma, her support and encouragement have got this lazy bum finally off his arse.

Tris, for sitting beside me for the last five years, and constantly having to put up with my incoherent mutterings and random shrieks of Ohhh and Ahhh, as new ideas formed.

Sean, for his constant nagging (ok, ok, its finished).

Lisa, whom although makes the worse cup of tea in the western hemisphere, has pushed me from beginning to end.

Vex, my insane American friend (Starship taken off yet mate?).

Julie, Sam and Charlotte, gone but will always be part of me xx.

Rachael, sorry for losing contact, but by the time you read this, you'll be free of those four walls.

Angie, Christy and Pete, hugs to all three of you.

Scaniabird, sorry for the nightmares hun.

Hja, now at last you have something to read.

Phil, erm why am I thanking you anyway? ;-)

All the old AC crew, I have never met such a bunch of @#&$'s in my life (I'm not wrong).

Every one at Pistonheads, especially when they would go out their to try and answer some of my more random questions.

Nervy and his anonymous friend (you did more than you can ever realize).

Keith, my surrogate father and supplier of tea on a Saturday morning.

My old poker buddies, Ian, Tracy, Sue, Mike, Bill, Roddy, Dave.

And now my friends from my pixilated world.

Ben(dick)Green, Lasttrain, Nathan, Cereboro, Vlad, Glave, Magic, Dan, Nobby, Balmung, Slip, Cani and soo many more. Spread the word guys ;-)

And lastly, but to me, most importantly, any reader who doesn't know me personally, I thank you, and sincerely hope you enjoy the following pages.

Jez xx

Contents

Prologue   The Last Dawn 1

Chapter 1   Let the Games Begin..15

Chapter 2   Shaken Not Stirred 33

Chapter 3   Serenity...71

Chapter 4   Beer, Banter & Beans..117

Chapter 5   More Questions Than Answers - Part 1..................143

Chapter 6   More Questions Than Answers - Part 2..................173

Chapet 7   To the Hills, to the Hills, and F**k the Indians -
               Part 1 195

Chapter 8   To the Hills, to the Hills, and F**k the Indians -
               Part 2...217

Chapter 9   Surprises Aplenty 243

Epilogue   The Last Dawn 277

PROLOGUE
The Last Dawn

Janus Brown WAS Mr. Average, average height, average build, even had size nine feet, probably the most nondescript person you could happen across, plain looking, no distinguishing features. He didn't wear flash clothes, a branded watch or expensive jewelry. He was the type of man you could walk right past and not even notice.

This was just the appearance our Mr. Brown wanted, the more inconspicuous, the better.

His eyes were an enigma though, they were, well, distant would be the best way to describe them, or cold even, if there is such a thing.

Maybe that's why they were mostly hidden behind a pair of darkened glasses.

Janus worked in an office, didn't participate in out of hours activities with the other members of staff. He kept himself to himself. Wasn't unpleasant to his colleagues, but just didn't seem interested in getting to know any of them better, which included men and women alike. Even though much to his own serene amusement, at one time, most of the women there had tried to crack the nut named Janus Brown.

His work was good, not exceptional, he rarely did any overtime, there were plenty of staff more than willing to take the extra pay. The only time he did work late was when he was rectifying a mistake of his own doing, and that wasn't very often.

Janus knew that his boss suspected that he could do so much better and that he wasn't giving anywhere near one hundred percent, but his work was more than good enough and he seemed happy at his present position, never caused waves, so his boss let him be.

Janus lived close to the office, didn't drive, and never invited any of the workforce back to his flat.

Only once did Mr. Brown cause a buzz around the office. About six months earlier a new member of staff had started work there; he could only be described as a slimeball and a bully.

You know the type; he would harass the ladies and intimidate the men. Janus being an easy target got it worse than most, he would never answer back or rise to the bait. The other staff there felt sorry for Janus, but never did anything to help; fearing the bully would turn his attention onto them.

When Mr. Intimidator finally got tired of the non-responses from Janus, he moved on to the hired help, the poor girl was on a work scheme, because she had some mental problems and the mind of a child. Even witnessing this, other members of staff still did nothing and the workplace had become a living hell for the poor girl. The bully would act all friendly towards the young girl then just as she got sucked in he would turn down right nasty calling her a mongrel and not worthy of being part of the human race.

Of all the staff working there Janus liked her the best, like is the nearest word to describe what Janus felt for her, no, maybe an affinity would be better.

When he looked into her mind, there was no selfishness, no hidden agenda and no ulterior motive. She was pure as anyone could be and believe me that was rare. She of all people didn't deserve the shit she was getting from this coward.

So, one morning after the hired help had left in tears purely due to the abuse of this bastard. Janus followed him into the mens cloakroom, locking the door behind him. The all American hero exited the cloakroom maybe five minutes later, his face was sickly yellow and the designer shirt was coated in his own vomit.

Within ten minutes he had quit his job and never came back for the monies owed to him. When Janus was pressed by his colleagues about what took place, all he would ever say with just the merest hint of a smile, those who play with fire WILL get burnt. No more information was ever offered by Mr. Brown.

Today was one of the rare occasions that Janus had to stay late, an important document had fell behind his desk and wasn't missed until the day was nearly over, it was work that only Janus could do, so he would have to stay and get it finished before morning. Not best pleased, more annoyed at himself at not noticing earlier, Janus worked solidly to get the piece finished before too silly an hour. Going at a speed which would have impressed anyone that worked there; it still took him until 11 p. m. to finally finish his work.

He was then faced with two alternatives; either take a taxi home, which to be realistic wasn't worth it, or to walk home as usual through the park. Normally it would be no decision at all, but the lateness of hour and the parks reputation of trouble at anything near dark, made the choice a hard one.

The deciding factor was that Janus hadn't even brought his wallet, so a walk it would be then. A decision that maybe he would regret.

Upon leaving the office, Janus nodded his goodbye to the security guard on the door. A dry smile crossed his face, I don't even know his name Janus thought, but his mind revealed his most sordid and seedy secrets to me. It's a gift that is with me always Janus mused, but then he couldn't help but laugh out loud, " gift" he said to himself, more like my albatross.

Stepping outside the icy breath of the night awoke Janus' senses. The night was wet, not because of rain but a heavy mist covered all, kissing everything it touched.

Pulling his collar up around his neck Janus made his way to the park, wondering if the horror stories he had heard and read about were true, desperately hoping they weren't. The spate of savage and brutal murders that had occurred recently worried everyone. There was no motive, no pattern, all the bodies had been mutilated horribly, men woman and children, and many were sexually tortured. No one had been brought to justice as yet, minimal information was known about the people committing these atrocities. What little that was known, was that a sect named the Devils Own which was springing up all over America was responsible and that only a few members had ever been apprehended. All of the captives, bar none, had taken their own lives while in custody. One prisoner choked on his own fist, preferring that painful death, rather than talk.

Janus tried to banish these horror stories from his mind, convincing himself that these things always happen to someone else.

Approaching the entrance to the park, Janus slowed, rethinking his options. Should he really risk the walk through the park or maybe it would be wise to take the much longer route around it, at least there were people and cars about on the road, whereas the park was a no go area for public and police alike after dark.

"Bugger it, I don't believe half of what I read anyway", Janus mumbled, thinking if it was that bad it wouldn't even be open. The nagging pain in his stomach seemed to be telling him that he was making the wrong decision.

Above the park gates, painted in blood red graffiti, was the legend, "Abandon all hope ye who enter here".

The voice in his head was screaming at him to turn back, but something, maybe a desire to know, pushed him on.

A discarded newspaper fluttered to his feet, was this one last taboo urging Janus to rethink his options, the headlines bright as day in the near dark night " Devils Own claim another family". Curiosity getting the better of him he stooped down and picked up the sodden paper. His keen eyes scanned the paragraphs, key words jumping out at him, RAPE, TORTURE and MUTILATION were three words that seemed to be repeated a lot. Even for a daily paper, it was disturbing reading, perhaps being overly graphic.

A photo of the doomed family graced the front page, a smiling proud father, a younger attractive wife, an early teen's boy and a tiny babe in arms.

Janus looked beyond the picture, seeing the American pie family at home, father tossing a baseball in the garden to his eager son, mother multi-tasking in the kitchen, cooking brownies, tending her daughter, watching the midday soaps and gossiping to her neighbours on the phone.

Knowing the fate that was to befall the family, Janus felt emotion, not pity or sadness but anger.

His minds vision switched from the happy family photo, to their last moments.

Father caked in blood, dirt and his own excretion, pleading for the life of his family. The children's mother futilely trying to protect them. Both children silent, not even whimpering.

Janus paused, not wanting to go on, but he needed to see more.

The suffering of the family, he owed them that at least, he felt he must share their pain.

As if he was an unseen spirit, Janus was back with the family, watching with invisible eyes.

The ill-fated family ringed by grinning monsters, wanting to hear the screams, the pleading, the pain.

The teenage boy was crying for his mother, the cries quickly turned into screams. The mother was surrounded by maybe ten people, men and women, some holding her down, some slicing her open with various surgical instruments, others just brutally raping her.

The father was forced to kneel, his eyelids pinned open. Having to watch the torment of his next of kin and ultimately, their death.

Janus's minds eye searched for the infant, but it was nowhere to be seen, unfortunately Janus knew its fate was no better than the rest of the family, maybe even worse.

As well as Janus, there was another figure watching the gruesome episode. A man dressed in black, his hair long and as dark as his clothes, his eyes were similar to those of Janus, cold and emotionless, his tight lips curled into a grin as he surveyed the atrocities taking place.

These were his people, possibly even his followers, all eager to please their master, the more sordid and disgusting the better. He directed them, controlled them, without voice or gesture, all of them knowing his wishes and desires as if part of him.

The darkened figure turned and looked directly at Janus. Even seemed to see him, although this was impossible, as Janus wasn't there. The stranger's expression yet seemed to change, a look of confusion on his face. For a reason he didn't know, Janus laughed and then broke from this nightmare.

Janus opened his eyes; he was still standing at the gates of the park. The night had now become cloudless and bright due to the nearly full moon. He now knew that the horrific stories in the media were accurate, even played down some, the panic would be immense if the public discovered the full extent of the atrocities taking place in the name of the Devils Own.

Surprising himself, Janus pulled up his collar, put on his sunglasses, (even in the dark, he thought it lended him a fictitious coolness), took a deep breath and entered the park. More afraid than he had ever been before, still not knowing why he was persisting in walking home this way. Conquering his fear was the most plausible answer.

" Who wants to live forever, or something like that" he muttered under his breath.

The park was still, no movement anywhere, not even the bushes rustling. Janus's keen ears detected no sound; no twittering of bird, no singing cricket, it seemed even his footfall was silent.

Everywhere he looked ghosts watched him from the shadows, darting about avoiding his gaze.

Bloody gremlins Janus mused, and doing a good job of spooking myself considering I have no imagination. Keeping to the path walking maybe slower than he should be considering the circumstances, Janus began to feel secure, even chuckling to himself at his earlier paranoia.

All of a sudden his heart nearly left his body.

The hum was unmistakable, reverberating from every direction. How long had it been there? Why hadn't he heard it sooner? This wasn't a natural sound; Mother Nature never made a noise like this.

All his worse fears and then some were about to be realized. Torn in two minds, not knowing whether to run forward or back the way he came. Fuck 'em if the shits going hit the fan, let the bastards come to me.

Dutch courage on the face of it seems very brave but in reality can be a foolish trait. Once again surprising himself, Janus couldn't believe his actions, being the original cowardly lion.

"Good job I am wearing my brown trousers huh!" he said in a voice that was more akin to a soft bark.

The hum had become louder but as yet no one had shown themselves, Janus had to admit though that the sound was very eerie and intimidating. Well bugger this if they aren't coming I shall continue on my jolly way, Fucking cowards he thought.

Continuing along the path the haunting voices grew louder, as if he was walking directly into the parlor where the infamous spider was waiting. Not being able to remember if he was still breathing Janus took an almighty gulp of oxygen; he even tasted the bitterness in the air. Trying desperately not to use his given talent but not being able to help himself, Janus's mind searched the blackness, instantly returning with the inane chatter of other souls. He was not alone.

"Wish I had bloody gone the other way now, this isn't doing my ticker any good. Ah, but still you have to laugh".

After what seemed like an eternity Janus's worse fear finally raised its ugly many heads from each direction and every corner. Emotionless faces now surrounded him, Janus turned, but all around him his way was bared, darkened figures slowly closing in, and still the humming was becoming unbearable. Unseeing eyes watching him, then finally stopping, ringing him about ten feet away in all directions. In a moment of lucidity, Janus calmed and did a head count, at least twenty he could see, but sure that there would be more hidden in case he tried to flee and managed to break through. All bar none had the inverted cross crudely sliced into their left cheek, no mistaking the sign of the Devils Own. Knowing it was them long before seeing the symbol etched into their own flesh, Janus was now afraid, more afraid then he thought it could be possible. Death was inevitable, of this he was sure, but how he would die and how much torture and pain he would have to endure first?

Starting to quiver Janus said the first thing that came into his head.

"Look I don't want any trouble"

"Oh but we DO" the voice in his head whispered to him, Janus could even imagine its sneer and amusement at his situation.

The ring around remained unmoving, empty eyes not even blinking; it was becoming too much.

"Well say something you bunch of Batty boys, I haven't got all day," he screamed at them.

Abruptly the humming stopped, and as if by remote control a section of the swarm parted and two shadows entered the circle. One figure Janus instantly recognized, it was the man from his earlier vision. Looking even colder and more evil in real life, an original bastard child of the Marquis de Sade. He was tall, maybe 6' 3, slim and apart from his eyes would be classed as attractive or charismatic at the very least. His high cheekbones weren't scarred like the others, he was pale, a true creature of the night. By his side a stood a young man, obviously in thrall to his mentor, also as yet his cheeks were clear.

Unable to control his *gift*, Janus jumped into the mind of the man stood before him, but for the first time ever his touch was repelled as if a barrier was up. More than a barrier though, it seemed his probe was being forced back into his own mind, not sure what to make of this, Janus immediately closed his own mind and broke off his investigation. No mind of a man had ever done this before, was this merely a man? Or something far more sinister and evil.

"I am Mr. Smith and unfortunately for you, you have stepped into my world," the tall man hissed.

"I am Mr. Brown and I'm a fucking alcoholic" Janus replied removing his sunglasses.

It almost looked like there was a hint of recognition on the face of Mr. Smith upon seeing Janus's full features.

"You seem to be a very brave and foolish man Mr. brown, but within the hour you will be begging for me to end your life, of that I can guarantee. You are very fortunate for tonight we are going to initiate the newest member of our family" with that Mr. smith laid a hand on the teenagers shoulder, who looked back with loving eyes.

Slowly Janus could feel what courage he had left starting to ebb and could feel his legs shaking.

"An hour is a long time and I don't care what you and your gimp have planned for me, I'll never beg and grovel to you" Janus spat, not believing his own words.

"Ah, well if I had a dollar for everytime I heard that I would be a rich man" Mr. smith chuckled. " And your first name is? This feels so informal"

"Janus"

"Janus huh? What an intriguing name, I like it."

"Yeah I fucking chose it myself, but tell you what I'll make you a deal." Was Janus clutching at straws now?

"A deal" Mr. smith's eyebrow lifted.

"Yeah, just let me walk away now, I don't give a shit about you or your weird buddies, and there will be no retribution on my part" worth a try Janus thought.

The circle of followers were laughing now, cackling like coven of witches.

"Let me think about that, " laughed Mr. Smith laughed showing the first signs of any emotion.

Knowing all this was futile Janus considered trying to run, his eyes possibly giving away his plan because as he thought about it the circle visibly tightened.

"No point in running Janus, my children are like rock and we would never let our prized toy get away so quickly, no doubt you have heard about us and read the stories in the papers. Everything you have read is true and our motives are none of your concern. Mercy is not a word known to us, and your last minutes will be utterly miserable and hellish," said Mr. Smith in a voice that could freeze water.

The time is coming, thought Janus and he could feel the color draining from his face.

"But I will honor you with the prior knowledge of your fate, I think we owe you that much at the very least. My newest disciple here will slice you open, while my children hold you, he will then fuck you in the hole he has made, another will then cut you etc etc."

"Fuck you, fucking perv's" Janus gasped his ears not believing what was hearing.

"No Mr. Brown fuck you and due to plenty of practice we know where to slice to keep you alive for the longest time, even your eye sockets will be violated while you still breath, we shall dismember you and make you eat your own penis. That is for my enjoyment more than anything, a man has to have some pleasure in his work".

"Well make sure you use protection, I don't want to catch anything from you diseased bastards."

With the smallest of nods, Mr. Smiths young companion stepped forward and faced his idol, then with no more than a glance, Mr. smith opened his long leather coat, carefully placed his hand inside and pulled out something that looked metallic in the moonlight. Then as if it was an ancient ritual, slowly and very cautiously passed it to his disciple. Feeling his mouth go dry Janus saw what the item was; it was a blade, not like any blade he had seen before. At a guess it was about eight inches long and curved. Along the curved edge it was heavily serrated, a type of weapon that would be excruciating as it entered flesh, but the pain would be unimaginable as it tore innards and alike as it was pulled out. Feeling his legs giving way at seeing this and finding it hard to hold his bladder, Janus lost all his earlier bravado and could no longer speak. Mr. Smith and the afore mentioned disciple stepped towards Janus, and the ring of followers tightened their circle. Now only a foot or so away Janus could feel the sobbing welling up inside of him and thought to himself how long it would take him before he too was begging for his life like the inhuman Mr. Smith had predicted. Making things even worse Janus still knew nothing of the reasons or motives behind his forthcoming fate, nothing was explained or justified to him, he couldn't, wouldn't die not knowing.

"Any last words Mr. Janus brown? Sorry to rush you but we have a busy few hours ahead, ah mind you, you will be here for most of it anyway." asked Mr. Smith more for his own amusement again.

"……." Trying to speak but to no avail, Janus just hung and shook his head, feeling a gut wrenching wail building up deep inside of him. No longer being able to think straight or rationally he could feel his shirt being ripped open exposing his bare flesh.

The night became deathly silent, the only noise that could be heard was a snarling of dogs nearby, strange that Janus would only hear that sound with the fate that would soon befall him, but the grumble some how comforted him, at least he wasn't alone.

Looking up through his tear filled eyes, the grinning teenager stood before him, holding the dagger like it was an extension of his hand, no more words were spoken, and with eager enthusiasm he plunged the blade deep into Janus's belly, twisted it to make the hole bigger still, then slowly withdrew it. Janus began to sob, he had not been used to pain and the heat that now coursed through his body engulfed him. Every muscle and sinew crying out for relief.

Mr. Smith and his juvenile disciple were looking at the dagger, confusion clearly on their faces. Both were examining the knife, incredibly even though it had obviously burrowed deep into their sacrifice's body, it was still as clean and untarnished as it had been, before the ghastly act took place.

"What the fuck have we got here, I have heard of anemia, but this?" Mr. Smith said in a whisper.

Sobbing uncontrollably now, Janus looked at the two standing in front of him, he now lifted his head and stood tall, but being only of average height couldn't quite understand why he was looking the much taller Mr. Smith directly in the eye. Another moment of stillness, and the snarling of the dogs could now be heard by all.

Mr. Smith felt uneasy, something was wrong; unexpectedly he realized that Janus wasn't sobbing at all, but the cries he had been hearing were cries of laughter. The twisted and distorted face of Mr. Brown was no longer in anguish but was smiling, his laughing becoming louder, for the first time in his life, Mr. smith was afraid.

Not liking what was happening Mr. Smith called for his followers to join him, not the ones in the circle but the others hidden away, waiting in case Janus tried to escape, but there was no response, no movement. Where the fuck are they? My children would never desert me. Being a tall man he craned his neck and looked over the heads of his people, what he saw froze him to the spot. His circle was now itself ringed, not by man though but by dogs, a breed he had not seen before. The most vicious and frightening animals he had ever witnessed, if the hounds of hell had a form then this was it. Some were still licking their bloodied chops; the people hidden away would be no help, for they were already dead.

Faster than was humanly possible Janus moved, his hand covering the face of the baffled teenager. The boys eyes and tongue tore themselves from his body eager to embrace the flesh of Janus, even if he still had a tongue he wouldn't have been able to scream, his own heart, lungs and intestines were jammed in his throat also trying to escape his body.

Grabbing the knife Janus, like liquid moved to the next nearest disciple, slicing his face clean off before his body erupted spraying blood, guts and shit everywhere.

At the precise moment that Janus attacked, so did the dogs taking the hypnotized members mainly unaware. The first one having his spine ripped from him as the massive canine pounced from behind, another, his head crushed like lemon in the dog's giant jaws.

Mr. Smith couldn't move, only watch as Janus and his allies massacred his children, what he was seeing was horrific even for a sadist like himself, it was unearthly even. Almost faster than the eye could see Janus was moving from victim to victim, none that he touched lived for more than a millisecond, their bodies exploding from the merest of contacts. Any he missed the dogs would be upon them, tearing them apart like a rag dolls, the speed was such that no one had time to even scream. Running out of victims the dogs were attacking in pairs, literally tearing the not-so poor souls in half.

As suddenly as it began, the carnage was over, the whole episode probably only took a couple of seconds but felt like an age to Mr. Smith. Janus stood majestically before him, looking down at him; he was now a good 6 inches taller. The slice in his belly was gone, his clothes not even splashed with blood.

"I warned you and yours to let me be" Janus said in a growl, his eyes almost glowing red.

Not knowing what to say Mr. Smith just stood transfixed to the spot.

"You have awoken a wrath in me which I haven't known for many years, I will not sleep until everyone of your despicable cult is no longer breathing the same air as me. You shall live for a short time and will tell me everything I need to know, of that there is no doubt."

Mr. Smith didn't doubt for a minute that what Janus spoke was the truth.

"Who.. who are you?" he said weakly.

With a wicked grin, Janus replaced his sunglasses and lit a cigarette.

'You call yourself the Devils Own, well within a very short time all of your dirty troop will come face to face with *the Angel of Death.*"

"Now you and I have a lot to talk about and its getting a bit nippy out here, so me thinks its time to go home and you shall be my honored guest, well for a while anyway." Janus said with more than a touch of mirth in his voice.

The dogs had vanished, as had what little remained of the earlier crowd. Then seemingly as if on cue, the heavens opened and the downpour started, washing any traces of blood, gore and vile away.

Two figures soon exited the park; one bowed and scared, the other tall and confident, whistling happily to himself, a tune that sounded remarkably like the classic by Frank Sinatra, I Did It My Way.

Chapter 1

"Let the Games Begin"

The two figures didn't encounter anyone else, which wasn't unusual considering the time of night. Mr. Smith thoroughly broken just followed Janus, all thoughts of escape banished from his mind, fully resigned to his forthcoming fate. Mr. Brown was no longer the meek, cowardly man he had first encountered, nor was he the monster that moved and killed so efficiently less than an hour ago.

"Ah nearly home, there is a decent bottle of red with my name on it, which is begging for me to drink it"

Mr. Smith merely grunted, he had seen this man in action and knew there would be no point going for the sympathy vote or trying to make friends.

Janus felt surprisingly good; maybe the time was now, the millennia of patiently waiting over. There had been false alarms before, but this felt different, lets hope Mr. Smith can shed some light on past, present and future events.

Even though Janus was quite pleased with the nights events, he had the sneaky feeling that he was being observed, eyes burning into the back of his skull. No number of probes had sensed anything nearby though, but that didn't mean an awful lot, when an apparent weakling like Mr. Smith had learnt or been taught to keep himself closed.

They couldn't be on to me this quickly Janus mused, its been less than an hour. Looks like I will have to work fast on Mr. Smith, unless.., a plan formed in Janus's mind.

Finally the two paused and then entered the foyer of a long stay hotel; the place would be best described as squalid or sleazy. The man at the desk gave Janus only the merest of glances as they walked passed. It was the kind of place where people on welfare or alike lived, drug pushers, wife beaters, bums. Mr. Smith noticed all the doors had at one point been kicked in, some still hung on their hinges, children's' broken toys littered the stairwell, and the smell of urine was rife.

Janus lived on the top floor and as Mr. Smith half expected, the whole floor was spotless, no damaged doors, no graffiti and no ghastly smell. Walking up to the door furthest away from the stairs, Janus just casually walked straight in; incredibly his place wasn't even locked.

Once inside, the paradox that was Mr. Brown continued, the room was exquisite. This man had expensive tastes, which would be hard to believe by looking at his clothes and his earlier demure. Mr. Smith did notice however that there was nothing personal in the room, no photos or nik naks. A tasteful leather couch graced the center of the room; a large screen television was also prominent, as was a very full wine rack.

"Sit" Janus barked pointing to the settee', while he walked over to the wine rack, carefully choose a bottle, opened it and sat it on the table.

"You have to let them breath you know, good wine that is. Pity I will have to leave it all behind soon." Janus was talking to himself now as much as he was to his guest.

"You wont get anything out of me, they already know what's happened" Mr. Smith blurted out.

"Well that's one bit of information you have already given me, so thank you for the advance warning. So tell me, how do they know so much?"

Thinking to himself Janus knew that he spoke the truth, but how much information *did* these people know. Do they know my true calling or have our paths crossed accidentally?

"Who or what the fuck are you anyway, your not fucking human that's for sure."

Janus casually poured a glass of wine and sat down on the large recliner facing Mr. Smith.

"Not human? How observant of you, " Janus replied quietly, sipping his wine, savoring it.

"And what's this angel of death shit, I don't know who you think you are, but you are on the wrong side. There are tens of thousands of us, and growing everyday. The world will soon change forever, and you can't stop it"

"Maybe, maybe not, we shall see, so tell me the name of this false god you rate so highly" Janus was smirking now, but the numbers, if true, troubled him, this was bigger than he expected.

"False god? How dare you, he will make you pay for your blasphemy, I have looked into the eyes of Satan and he is humanities future." Mr. Smith was getting angry, Janus didn't mind this, an angry man often says too much.

Raising one eyebrow Janus leaned forward his piercing eyes looking directly into the other mans soul.

"Satan" Janus growled, " If I only tell you one truth it would be that your leader or whatever he calls himself, is not the Lord of Darkness. Did he tell you that he was?"

"No, he didn't fucking tell me, but I have seen him, felt his touch, his evil is absolute and will overwhelm all that lives and breathes. One man, whether human or not, cannot stop him."

Janus emptied the glass and poured another, slowly leaning back in his massive leather chair. A smirk forming on his tight lips.

"One man, Mr. Smith? I don't remember telling you that I was alone. Or are you presuming again? Once already tonight you have presumed wrong about me and it will ultimately cost you your life when I have finished with you."

"You mean those fucking dogs? Yeah, very clever trick but you will need more than a few mangy hounds to tip the balance, I think you overestimate yourself" Mr. Smith was laughing now.

His laugh died in his throat, he could feel his windpipe being slowly crushed by an invisible hand. He tried to move, to get up, but he was powerless to even move a muscle.

" The next time you laugh Mr. Smith, will be the last time you breath, don't try my patience. I don't suffer fools gladly, but with you I am making an exception all be it not gladly. And as for those fucking dogs as you so eloquently put it, they are merely my pets."

Janus finished his second glass of burgundy, carefully placed the glass on the table and stood up. Very clever Janus thought, trying to make me angry so I tell more than I should too. Coincidence, or is Mr. Smith still being controlled somewhat, maybe they don't know that much about me. Ah!! Questions questions. As yet though still no answers, time to take a gamble me thinks.

"Right, young Mr. Smith, this wine has given me an appetite, so I shall pop out for a short time and fill my grumbling belly. So, if you please I would be grateful if you stay put and don't break anything while I am gone, I shall see you shortly," Janus said, whilst already putting on his jacket.

He didn't even look back as he left the room.

"Stay put my arse," Mr. Smith shouted but not until he was sure Janus was well out of earshot.

Slowly and cautiously, he got up from the settee, massaged his neck and without further ado walked towards the door. Before getting within two feet of door, he was thrown back and what felt like an electric shock coursed through his body. It was many minutes before he could move again and when he did so the pain was still immense.

"Tut tut tut," an unseen voice boomed making his very bones rattle, his minds eye could see a giant incorporeal finger wagging at him. " Please don't defy me again."

Leaving the hotel Janus casually shook his head, some people just don't listen he thought.

The drizzle now was the annoying sort; the type that gets you wet very quickly, but is almost invisible.

"Should have brought me brolly" Janus chuckled to himself, surprised at his excellent mood.

Checking his watch, it was the early hours of the morning and in this part of town the streets were deserted. Only brave men and fools would walk these streets at night, which am I? He wondered.

The feeling of being watched was still there, now even more so, but this time as well as minds that Janus was unable to read, there was one that was defiantly shielded, hiding from him.

Of course Janus was right, there was at least one watching him. Hidden in the shadows, following, stalking, waiting for the right moment.

"Its been a long time Mr. Brown, and I see you have company" the figure whispered only for himself to hear.

Janus stopped, lit another cigarette, and looked at the long dark ally that lay ahead of him.

"A man might get mugged walking down there, an ideal place for an ambush even, be a shame to disappoint my concealed guests."

And with that Janus entered the ally.

The spectator watched Janus disappear into the unlit alley, and quickly moved to another vantage point, where he could see the forthcoming events, if any, unfurl.

Only the keenest of observers would have noticed that since leaving the hotel, Janus had grown, all be it very slowly, but his size was now a good six inches taller then it was when he first left.

The ally was dark, that posed no problems to Janus, day or night he had twenty twenty vision.

The shadows on the walls skitted too and fro, like madmen dancing to a silent tune. Janus had stopped breathing, his ears ever alert. Then finally he slowly turned around.

As half expected, four shadows slid down the wall, along the floor and in one fluid motion, they all took the shape of a man. The form was undeniable but they were all featureless, where a face should be was nothing, complete darkness, threatening to suck in your whole being. A mere mortal man would have died of fright, the nature of what had just occurred would be incomprehensible to the human mind, the brain would have simply shut down. Janus wasn't human, yes he was surprised but that was all.

Clasped in the hands of each was a sword, three foot long and a blade black as their faces.

Swords? This could be more serious than I thought, enough of the games.

"Four of you and just one of me and I see you are all armed, these odds are unfair. So I would be grateful if you come back when there is at least ten of you, make it more worth my while," as Janus spoke he was slowly moving back, readying himself for the obvious onslaught.

Catching even Janus by surprise, one of the four moved at a speed that was incredible, raising the sword as if to strike down on Janus, diverting his attention, then kicking him squarely in the chest, knocking flying backwards. While Janus was falling back, he twisted his body, timing his landing. He hit the ground with his back to them, rolled once and was back on his feet. Without even thinking, Janus ran at full speed to the end of the ally. Not running away like a coward, just giving himself enough time and space between them to decide his next move.

"You weren't expecting that were you? Now lets see how you deal with them," the unknown watcher whispered.

Fight fire with fire Janus decided; find out your enemies' strengths and weaknesses.

With no more than a thought, a sword also materialized in Janus hand. About time to even up the odds.

The four now walked toward him, in a perfect line, shoulder-to-shoulder, slow and purposeful. Right on cue a lonesome dove circling overhead, and gave one of the four a present of his own, only for a moment the blackness was speckled with brilliant white, until that also was swallowed up by the liquid darkness.

Janus stood tall, with his own sword in hand; drew an imaginary semi circle on the ground in front of him, sparks flew as he marked his boundary. The four continued on, no words spoke between them, they moved as one, their own swords held in front of them, without doubt this would be a fight till the death.

When his as yet, unidentified foe was ten feet or so away from his boundary, Janus pounced, hoping to catch them napping. He moved like a cat, faster than any eye could see, leaping over his attackers in one bound, turning quickly, he plunged his sword deep into the buttocks of the nearest and with inhuman strength, tore the weapon through its body and it exited at the shoulder. The phantom had disappeared before his dead body hit the ground. The remaining three didn't pause as their comrade fell, they surrounded Janus immediately, all Janus could do was parry their blows. The celestial weapons making no noise as they clashed. One would strike and as Janus parried the blow the other two would strike his blind side, twisting and turning, Janus was getting nowhere, he had to regain the advantage. Jumping again to get some distance, he was caught badly in his thigh, the burning pain shooting through his body.

"Fuck" Janus growled, maybe for the first time realizing that he could be hurt even killed.

The three regrouped instantaneously, and moved to attack again.

"Well you have finally managed to piss me off, " as Janus spoke another sword appeared in his free hand.

With a cry of rage or madness like a Berserker from old, Janus ran too his opponents. Now attacking with both weapons, beating them back, his speed was incredible. His blows just too strong, they were weakening, Janus could now see gaps, and they were leaving themselves open. While slashing one with his left hand, the defender managed to block the strike but simultaneously Janus's right arm was sweeping in an arc aiming for the unprotected midriff, like a hot knife through butter he was cut clean in half. Not even slowing Janus was on to the other two again, they were fighting well but Janus was obviously too skilled and powerful. His arms a blur, slashing, stabbing, hammering, within seconds the penultimate one fell, Janus's sword still trapped in his ribs, as he collapsed, the sword disappearing with the body. One on one, the final combatant was no match for Janus, but he didn't give up nor make a sound, Janus played with him for a bit cutting here, stabbing there until as if weary, Janus spun and in one fluid movement beheaded the final challenger, screaming at the top of his voice.

"THERE CAN BE ONLY ONE, " Janus laughed.

The alley echoed with the sound of clapping, Janus spun, sword back in hand.

"There can be only one? You watch too many movies," said the watcher as he entered the ally.

The sword in Janus's hand disappeared and a broad grin spread across his face.

The man that approached Janus was immense, when Janus was *angry* he was large but this man was bigger still, weighing at least five hundred pounds. He had flaming red hair and a beard that hid most his face. In his hand was a walking stick, even though he didn't seem to need one.

The two men stood face to face, said nothing for a moment then embraced each other, the large man nearly crushing Janus.

"Hey, did you pinch my bum then?" Janus laughed as he pushed the man away.

"Aye, I have to admit I did, well you being so good looking and all. "

The two men laughed and walked out the ally as if nothing had happened.

"I know of an all night diner nearby, where we can talk, " Janus suggested, his colleague nodded in agreement.

No more words spoken, the two walked in silence, the large mans cane rhythmically clicking on the sidewalk.

The diner was empty apart from a disgruntled looking over weight man behind the counter, chain-smoking himself to death.

Janus and his companion sat at the cleanest table they could find, the large man taking up two seats. The owner/waiter wobbled up to them, it was clear from his face he was hoping they wouldn't want food at this time of night.

"Two coffees, black, " Janus ordered not even looking up.

They both waited until the coffee was served before either of them spoke again.

"Well, well, well, Solomon Grundy, it's been a long time old friend, " Janus couldn't help but smile every time he said his friend's name.

"Still tickled at my choice of pseudonym I see, " the big man beamed.

"And as for the Scottish accent? You never cease to amaze and amuse me, in the nicest way of course"

"Well you know me Janus, I'd rather laugh than fight. "

"Its good you haven't changed, so what have you been doing with yourself, still working with kids old friend?" Janus asked.

"Yep, love the little people, currently a janitor at a kindergarten, children don't shy away and make false assumptions because of my size, innocence is a gift unfortunately they nearly all lose." Solomon said with just the faintest hint of unhappiness in his voice.

"Anyway we will catch up on old times later, lets get to the more serious matter in hand, I presume you saw what happened in the ally?"

"Yes I was there Janus, tough little beggars huh, I noticed you still held yourself back somewhat. "

"Well I don't want to show my full capabilities, not yet anyway. You can guarantee you weren't the only one observing the events. And why didn't you help me you old goat? " Janus said more in fun than in an accusing way.

"Och you were doing ok old friend, plus I wasn't far away if you really needed me, but to be honest if you couldn't deal with just four of them, we would be in trouble. "

"Yeah, suppose you have point" Janus said sipping his stale coffee.

"Anyway I think it was more of a distraction rather than an attack."

Janus then told Solomon about the earlier happenings and Mr. Smith.

"You think he's gone?"

"I know he is, while I was fighting they took him, my hold on the room was weakened, while I fought, I could have held him, but thought it wiser to let him be taken."

"Mind you I don't think they meant you any great harm by only sending four of those things."

"What do you mean only sending four?" Janus was a little confused.

"They sent eight of the bastards to get me and I think they were trying to kill me"

Janus was taken aback; this was the last thing he had expected to hear.

"What do you mean? You have already come across them?" this worried Janus, if they have found Solomon, they must know where the others are, and maybe even.. Janus couldn't help but fear the worse.

"I'll tell you about it later, seriously Janus, do you think that this is our time?" Solomon asked looking Janus straight in the eyes.

"I really don't know Sol, but I don't like it, especially now you told me that you have already been found by them, have you heard from the others?"

"No not a word and it is apparent that you haven't either, don't worry about them, they can take care of themselves," Solomon tried to lighten the mood.

"Yes I know they can comrade, but if they weren't expecting an attack, they could be vulnerable."

"Oh, come off it good friend, god help anything be it human or not that crosses the paths of the others, maybe you should try and contact them."

Janus nodded his head not entirely convinced, but Solomon's words did reassure him some.

"Yes I will do, as soon as we get some privacy, but right now I think you should tell me about your encounter before we decide our next move," Janus suggested bleakly.

"Yes you are right, were shall I start?"

"Well at the beginning of course, you have to make things sound so dramatic don't you" Janus couldn't help feeling a little better, Solomon could find the light in the darkest of situations.

"Ok ok, well it was twos day ago," Solomon started.

"Two days ago? Why the hell didn't you come to me directly after?" Janus interrupted, his lightening mood vanishing quickly.

"Yes two days ago, I have been here ever since, kept myself hidden, in case you needed me, I thought if you knew I was here then maybe so would they. Now let me continue." Solomon was eager to tell his story.

Janus sat back in the chair, closed his eyes, let Solomon tell his story and witnessed the whole thing as if he was there.

"Well, I have worked at this school for ten years now, even live in a small flat in the basement it isn't much but up until now its been home. There is plenty to keep me busy, be it painting or just some basic maintenance, I enjoyed the job and the life, must be getting soft in me old age huh Janus." It wasn't a question that needed an answer so Solomon continued.

"Anyway, as we all do, I have been keeping an eye on the news, papers etc. ever since this Devils Own cult sprang up, I have had a bad feeling in my gut. And my gut large that it is, is never wrong, I haven't the precognitive gift of Nathan but something wasn't right." Solomon voice became grave and serious, a trait that didn't suit him.

"The morning of two days ago started as any other, you know the usual problems, a burst pipe, a blown light bulb, nothing to taxing for a man of my many talents. But something just wasn't right, its hard to explain but it felt like a mist followed me wherever I went, I am sure the kids picked up on it too because they weren't their usual happy playful selves, and more than usual came to see the big old janitor saying they were afraid. When the day finally ended I was more than relieved, at least the kids were gone, out of any danger, if there was any." Solomon paused, drank more of his cold coffee before going on.

Janus shifted his viewpoint, now he was seeing the events through the eyes of Solomon.

Solomon was working in the boiler room, trusty cane by his side and massive wrench in his hand. Solomon then stopped, cocked his head, he could hear something.

"Hello! Is someone there?" Sol shouted, putting the wrench down, and picking up his cane.

The noise was a rhythmic hum, coming from all directions, and at the same time coming from nowhere.

"Janus is that you?" Solomon asked, he was moving slowly now, every muscle and sinew alert.

What the fuck is this Sol thought, I have to get out into the open, and it's too cramped in here for my liking. Time to get out FAST. Moving at a speed that belied his bulk, Solomon moved like a cat, dodging pipes and boilers ran up the stairwell, out of the nearest fire exit and into the yard.

Outside it was dusk; Solomon walked to the center on the concrete arena, and sat down crossed legged.

Let the fuckers come to me; I doubt they know whom they are dealing with.

Suddenly the humming stopped, Solomon casually rose, stood with his head bowed, both hands placed on his cane.

Like demonic weeds, black shapes grew from every corner. Solomon lifted his head, eight featureless figures surround him, each one with a sword as black as their non-exsistant faces. In Solomon hands was no longer his cane, but he too now had sword, a colossal one, easily as big as a normal man and probably a lot heavier.

"Come to me then!" Sol demanded, spiting as he spoke.

Obligingly the eight ghosts closed their circle, edging ever nearer to the giant. Solomon began to swing his sword, a huge deadly arc protected him, spinning faster and faster, Sol moved, confused by this tactic the phantoms stopped the encroachment. Within seconds Sol was onto two of them, both made a futile effort to block the gigantic blade, but their weapons snapped like twigs, almost instantaneously their bodies followed the same fate. As suddenly as he started Solomon stopped spinning, tossed back his head, his red hair like a lion's mane blowing in the breeze.

"Now things are a little more even, let's fight," Solomon chuckled, god I have missed this.

The dance that followed would have put even the Russian ballet to shame, seven figures moving in an artistic frenzy, that a human eye could scarcely follow. Solomon wielded the massive sword as if it was a toothpick and his skill was incredible for one of his size. Due to his style of combat, Solomon took hits, he was cut from a multitude of places, his pace didn't let up one bit. One by one, even the seeming unthinking attackers, tired and grew frustrated; this is when Solomon came into his own. Laughing like a banshee the colossal warrior stepped up his pace, a thrusting his broadsword into the face of one opponent and in the same movement, slicing the head off another. The three remaining had extraordinary skill and worked well together, but the odds were against them, how do you fight a man, that is prepared to get hit, doesn't slow and wouldn't never yield. They fought on though regardless, even with limbs missing they fought bravely, still silent, not even breathing. The end was an anti climax; Solomon swept his steel in a huge figure of eight attacking pattern, connecting with all three, who were mortally wounded and disappeared instantly.

"What the fuck was that all about? I might be behind with my taxes but that's a bit extreme." Solomon said allowed his body and mind still on yellow alert in case there were more of them nearby. Cane back in hand, he scanned around before returning into the school. His wounds already healing.

Janus opened his eyes, it took him a second or two to get his bearings, and remember they were still in the diner.

"Well that's about it, I left my note of resignation, along with the keys to the place and came straight here"

"You had no more trouble on your journey?" Janus asked.

"No, nothing, but I kept myself heavily shielded I don't know if they penetrate our shields, but so far its worked," Solomon offered.

"Lets us not presume anything about these creatures, we know nothing about them or their capabilities, so until we know more, lets think they know everything and keep alert at all times."

"So what's the next move?" Solomon asked.

"Lets get out of here, there's a motel just a couple of blocks away, we can talk some more there and I'll try and contact the others," Janus was already rising, he threw down enough coins to cover the cost of the coffee, not leaving a tip. The big man followed suit, and they both left the flea bitten diner.

Solomon hated walking in silence, so he made small talk with Janus who seemed distant.

"So what have you been doing with your self old friend?"

"Well up until yesterday I worked in an office, just a normal mundane job, something to do more than anything, its good to keep in contact with people, I don't crave attention like Cyrus or solitude like Nathan, would you believe at times I even forgot who is was."

"I do believe you Janus, I am like you in that sense, it was always you and I that tried to live as normal as possible, I loved my job. The old days are long gone, the crusades, the battles, the world has changed.

"Very true Sol," Janus agreed " but for the better?"

"In some ways yes, but not in others, this can be a very brutal place too. As you know I work with kids Janus, and some of the things I have seen and heard, made me sick and at times I wished I could impose some of my own retribution on certain people."

"Again I have to agree with you, it can be hard to stand back and watch sometimes, mind you once or twice I didn't stand back." Janus was smirking now.

"Aye, well if I had to be truthful I would admit that maybe I didn't always stand back too." Solomon laughed.

The two fell silent for a bit, both lost in thought, finally, Solomon spoke up.

"So any female in your life per chance old buddy?"

"No, been there and bought the T-shirt, relationships don't work with people like us Sol, and I can't be like Cyrus, fucking anything that moves." Janus felt uncomfortable, knowing what the next question would be.

"Erm, talking about Cyrus, how are things between the two of you?"

"Same old, same old, I haven't heard form him in ages, he's in Monaco or somewhere, we talk, we would still die for each other, but things can never be the same between us." Janus said quietly, he couldn't help thinking of the past and how he was hurt.

"If you don't mind me saying friend, it was hundreds of years ago, I know he did wrong, but cant you forgive him by now?"

"Forgive maybe, but I will never forget, I have only loved once in my life Sol and Cyrus took that from me, if he loved her too then maybe I would think differently, he used her and dropped her, that I can never forget." Janus replied bleakly, he breathed a sigh of relief when he saw the lights to the motel just up ahead.

No more words were exchanged, until they entered the hotel. Janus got two adjacent rooms.

"Did you see the look on the receptionists face when we booked together, och poor girl didn't know where to look." Solomon was clearly amused.

"Come to my room in half an hour Sol, let me freshen up first," said Janus clearly not in the mood for merriment.

"No problem boss"

Janus entered the basic but functional room, took off his coat and had a long shower.

Have to buy some clothes first thing tomorrow, my room is a no go area now, Janus decided before sitting prone on the bed and shutting his eyes for a bit.

A loud knock awoke Janus with a start. He opened his eyes, and let down the invisible barrier protecting the room before answering.

"Come in Sol, its open."

The large man entered and virtually filled the room, seeing nowhere suitable to sit, he plonked himself down on the floor with a sigh.

"Is the room secure again," Solomon asked.

Janus merely nodded his head.

"So what's our next move?"

Janus just sat in thought for a bit before answering.

"First thing to do is try and contact the others, bear with me for a minute while I try," and with that Janus shut his eyes again.

It seemed like an age before he opened his eyes, and shook his head bleakly.

"Nothing, they are either shielded or dead."

"Dead, you cant mean that Janus, surly we would know," there was panic in Solomon's voice.

"I honestly don't know if we would know or not Sol, none of us have ever been in this situation, I do think its highly unlikely that both of them have been got too, without contacting us first though, so chances are they are both shielded, but we cant rule out any possibilities." Janus merely spoke the truth.

Solomon was clearly shaken; the prospect that his friends might be dead was not one he had considered.

"Is it possible, that something is blocking the probes we are sending out?" Solomon asked.

Janus turned to his companion, and stroked his chin.

"Now that is something I haven't thought about, I suppose that could be the case, this means we will have to rethink our options."

"What do you mean?"

"Well I was going to suggest that you and I do nothing, just keep our shields down so the others could find us, but if we are being blocked, obviously that idea wont work."

"I have another question."

"Go on Solomon," Janus knew what was coming.

"Well you said that the others might be dead. So you mean that it's possible that those creatures we have already encountered can kill us?"

Janus had to think carefully of the answer, none of them before had ever faced death; he wasn't sure how his friend would take it if he spoke the truth.

"If there is enough of them, then I would have to answer yes Sol, purely hacking us to pieces would do the trick. On the plus side, that wouldn't be an easy task, nor have they seen us yet in our true form."

"Hell, being immortal isn't all it's cracked to be anyway." After a long pause Sol started to laugh.

"One thing troubles me even more though."

"Which is?" his laugh died in his throat.

"Those creatures, phantoms or whatever they are that we have so far encountered are only soldiers. Lieutenants probably, the thing or things controlling them must be very powerful and far more sinister."

"Stronger than us Janus?"

"Again that I cant answer, but when the four of us are together, I would find that hard to believe, maybe that's why they are trying to keep us apart, if just one of us is dead, we become considerably weaker."

"If that is the case, why have they only sent soldiers and not tried to destroy us themselves?"

"We can only speak for our experiences Sol, we don't know what happened to the others, for all we know, the controlling entity, has already paid them a visit."

"This is worrying me now Janus, don't you have any idea what we are up against, or even if it's possible for us to destroy them."

"I have no clue as yet Sol, but one thing I do know, we have been here for a long long time, and the reason we are here is to stop the destruction of free man. Armageddon as it is universally known, its what we were designed for, whoever placed us here knew what we would be facing and had faith in us. So lets do our job." Janus's voice was cold and it sent a shiver down Sols' spine.

"So what are our options?"

"The way I see it we have three choices, 1. We do nothing, keep our shields down and let the others find us, but if like you suggested they are blocking us, the others would never find us, or they could be dead already, we still wouldn't know. 2. We split up, try and find the others separately. That isn't really an option, the chances of finding the others especially Nathan, are near impossible, plus it would be safer if we stayed together. 3. We try and find the others together, Cyrus should be the easiest to find, and by his very lifestyle he normally leaves a trail behind him. If he has been found and is on the run I am sure he would leave us some bread crumbs."

"So its option three?"

"Looks that way, the main problem with it is, it's always possible that the others are trying to find us, if that's the case, we could miss each other, but that's a risk we have to take."

"Well whatever you decide Janus, I shall follow you unquestionably, your judgment has never let us down." Solomon didn't have to say those words, but he wanted Janus to know that he trusted him fully.

"Thank you Sol, my old friend, let's just hope my judgment is still good huh." Janus's attempt at a smile wasn't a good one.

"We could always go to the meeting place."

"No Solomon, that's a last resort, if we cant find the others in lets say two weeks, we will go there but I don't want to give its location away yet. So I suggest that you go back to your room, get some sleep for what's left of the night, but keep the room protected. I would think we are safe for now but we can't be too careful."

"Ok fair enough, we move tomorrow?"

"Yes, have you got a valid passport?"

"Sure have boss, even bought it with me."

"Good, I would rather travel by public transport if possible, we should be untroubled that way, for the time being at least."

Solomon rose and headed for the door, he turned back before leaving.

"Your worried aren't you Janus?" Solomon said softly.

"Maybe a little, friend, its healthy not to underestimate your opponents, now get out and let me sleep." Janus said lightly, in his mind he was thinking yes I am worried Sol and more than a little, although he kept that thought to himself.

Once alone Janus shut his eyes, he knew sleep would elude him, but at least he could rest his body. It won't get any easier from here on in, Janus pondered. All these years of waiting, now finally the time has come, for one night and one night only I shall be afraid. The whole fate of mankind rests on my shoulders; they at least deserve me to fear for them. After tonight, my fear will be gone for good, that's my vow.

Janus let his mind shield down for a moment, with all the mental force he could muster, Janus screamed " GLOAT IN MY FEAR UNTIL DAWN, BUT SOON, ITS YOU THAT SHALL BE AFRIAD."

CHAPTER 2

"Shaken Not Stirred"

The silken sheets had long since fallen to the floor. Marie had never before felt so naked; its seemed her whole body was being touched, caressed, kissed.

"Mmmmmmm Cyrus" she moaned.

He kissed her forehead, her eyelids, briefly touching her lips with his. Moving lower still, gently kissing her slender neck, Marie's body arched involuntary. Her nipples were hard, demanding attention; Cyrus's tongue quickly found them, his teeth lightly nipping her. Moving down again, soft kisses tracing a path to her ultimate ecstasy. Feeling his warm fingers slowly moving up one inner thigh and down the other, so nearly touching her THERE. Marie's body was ready to explode, she could feel his hair between her legs, he teased, tasted, probed her.

The bed was drenched, a night of passion had made it so, but Cyrus continued on, knowing exactly what she wanted, and more than willing to oblige.

Turning her onto her belly and lifting her hips, Marie moaned in anticipation of what was coming.

33

"Tell me what you are" Cyrus demanded.

"Your Slut" Marie whispered, as Cyrus entered her from behind.

"I cant hear you" Cyrus said in a stern voice, pushing his manhood deep into her.

"YOUR SLUT" Marie cried, pleasure and pain, melting into one.

Marie had lost count how many times Cyrus brought out the woman in her, no man could do it like him, how she wished she could have him solely for herself, but Marie know that would never happen. She didn't think that there was one woman in her clique that he hasn't had, he made love better than any man did, but as for giving love, Cyrus was incapable of that. Marie knew that some of the most beautiful and richest woman in the world had begged for his hand, as yet no one had even been close to snaring him.

Morning came to soon for Marie; even the thick drapes couldn't keep out the suns' affectionate touch.

Marie knew what was coming, she had heard it many times before but it never seemed to get any easier.

"Its about time you left," Cyrus said coldly as he got up from the bed. "Your car will be waiting for you as usual, if you need to freshen up before you go feel free to use the bathroom." Cyrus nodded to the large left-hand door beside the bed. Then without so much as a backward glance, the naked man left the room by another door on his side of the bed.

Marie was now alone. Part of her hated Cyrus, his love making was unsurpassed, but by morning he always grew cold and uncaring, at fist Marie thought it was her, but now she knew he was that way with all he bedded.

It was nothing more than an addiction to him, the need to have sex, pure and simple. He could be gentle and passionate, other times brutal and hard, never crossing the line though and physically hurting her more than she wanted, Marie trusted him completely which is one thing that she couldn't do with many men.

Silently Marie gathered her clothes, freshened up in the bathroom and left without seeing her previous night's lover again.

Cyrus stood, still naked in his bathroom, looking into a large ornate antique mirror, that dominated the room.

"An addiction huh Marie?" he whispered to himself, " if only it was a simple as that, most addictions can be cured". He pondered unhappily.

Cyrus was an attractive man, well over six-foot in height, his blond hair was always immaculately kept. Hypnotic swirling blue eyes, that could melt the heart of hardest person. A body that was tanned and nicely muscled without being vulgar. The only flaw in his Adonis type body was a large scar across his chest. Probably about a foot in length, starting just above his left breast and finishing where his appendix would be. It was well healed by now and Cyrus would never offer any information about how got it no matter how hard he was pressed, to most it just added to his mystique.

His age? Well that's wasn't easy to answer, most people accepted he was in his early forties, but he could effortlessly pass for someone in their twenties. Anyway no-one really cared, his company was enough and his parties were legendary, it was more than an honor to be invited, just by being there would open previously closed doors for people if that was what they wanted. People whispered, that even the local royal family was jealous of his status and stature, but unlike most rumors this one was actually very true.

So how to describe the man? Playboy, gigolo both was correct. A professional gambler, again true. His wealth was unknown. Many believed that he could possibly be the richest man alive, his fortune handed down from generation to generation, as well as the astute business deals he made on the side.

His penthouse was immense; it was the whole top floor of Monaco's newest and largest casino. Of which the bulk was owned by Cyrus, he agreed to finance the building of it, when young croupier came to him with nothing more than a head full of ideas and empty pockets. Cyrus Draig listened long and hard to the plans and dreams of the young man, and after careful consideration agreed to finance the whole operation. The local aristocracy thought him a fool; none said so to his face mind you

The land was purchased and the casino was built quickly, Cyrus promised large bonuses to the contractors if they finished ahead of schedule, and they did. The croupier already had detailed plans made and knew what he wanted; working hand in hand with architects the operation ran smoothly. All Cyrus had to do was sign the checks. Within six short months the masterpiece was finished, even Cyrus had to admit that he was impressed and also a little proud. The opening of AVALON was a grand affair, world famous celebrities, royalty, even professional gamblers were present, and they rarely had time for such occasions.

Cyrus took no part in the day to day running of the casino, the only stipulation he made was that penthouse suites would be his and his alone and for the young man to pay him back in full, interest free, whenever he could.

Much to the surprise of most, that would be earlier than anyone could have imagined, all apart from Cyrus of course, whose complete trust and faith looked like to pay off once more. The casino was a gold mine; by far the most popular in Monaco or the nearby Monte Carlo, its reputation for splendor and ingenuity was celebrated the world over. The young man ran it well and would be wealthy in his own right in a very short time, this pleased Cyrus. Its always good to give someone a chance especially if they grasp it with both hands and try to make it work, it didn't always, but as long as they did their best, Cyrus would be happy.

Another intriguing fact, was that AVALON had no crime to speak of, which again was unusual for a large casino, normally the case would be that a local Mafia are involved somewhere down the line be it, rigging the odd table. Finding which room affluent guests are staying and stealing any valuables even petty pickpocketing was run by them, but no-one not even an organization as powerful as theirs crossed Cyrus.

Apparently when Cyrus first made his home in Monaco, he was paid a visit, as most new residents are, but more that that is not known or why they gave him such a wide berth.

• • • • • • • • • • • • • • • •

MAYBE TWENTY YEARS EARLIER.

The Guinevere pulled into harbor in the dead of night, punching through the fog like an awoken Marie Celeste, almost silent and near invisible in the moonless night. She was a big ship, even by Monaco's standards, measuring over three hundred-foot in length. Only the seriously wealthy could afford a toy like this. Once moored, the harbormaster, who was despicable, short and grossly overweight went down to greet his newest arrival. He wasn't kept waiting long.

Slowly descending the gangway, was a man, impeccably dressed, his long coat swirling and dancing behind him. Sapphire blue eyes pierced the near darkness and long blond hair glowing, almost phosphorescent.

"Mr. Draig?" the harbormaster stuttered, beads of foul smelling sweat mockled his brow.

"I am he" the stranger replied.

"Your crew? Will they not be joining you?"

"NO, their quarters are more than adequate. So what do I owe this pleasure?"

"Erm. Just greeting our new guest, how long do you plan on staying, if you don't mind me asking?"

"Well I have paid the harbor fees for a year in advance, so to be honest it's none of your business." Cyrus said coldly, already knowing the real reason for the welcoming.

"But if this place is to my liking, I might very well stay here." Cyrus added.

"Of course, of course, sorry for prying, curiosity killed the cat and all that huh," the unlikable man said wearing the fakest of smiles.

"May I ask where you are staying, only I might have to contact you that's all."

"I am in the presidential suite" Cyrus growled brushing the man aside and not even turning back.

"But of which hotel?" the harbormaster shouted, but to no avail, the tall man had melted into the darkness.

The black Mercedes and its two occupants, who watched the whole encounter from the nearby rise, also melted into the darkness when there was no more to be seen.

The harbormaster rushed back to his office, his fingers feverishly dialing a number even before he sat down.

"This is Jules the harbormaster, let me speak to Tony" he panted.

"YES, it's fucking important, now go and get him."

After a few moments silence, " this is Tony."

"Tony, he's here,"

"Yes we know"

"You told me to let you know as soon as he turned up, he's a mean looking bastard mind you"

"Everyone's a mean looking bastard to you Jules, you fat fucking coward. Did you find out where he and his crew are staying?"

"He said his crew are staying aboard the ship, have you seen the size of the fucking thing? It must have thirty crew at least. I didn't even see one soul, apart from that Draig fella, gives me the creeps, I'll tell you that for nothing."

"Hmm, interesting, now where's this Draig staying?" Tony was growing impatient; he couldn't stand the money-grabbing leech.

"The presidential suite, that's all the fucker would tell me."

"Ok, wont be hard to find him, you let me know if any of his crew leave or the situation changes"

"Tony! What about my money?" But the phone was already dead.

• • • • • • • • • • • • • • • •

Stubbing out a cigarette, Cyrus materialized, stepping from some nearby shadows.

"You truly are a slimeball aren't you, how many other unsuspecting travelers have you betrayed for thirty pieces of sliver? Unfortunately for you, I will be the last." Cyrus quietly snarled, smoke still emerging from his lips.

• • • • • • • • • • • • • • • •

Tony replaced the handset in its cradle and debated whether to wake his boss at such a late hour. Knowing his boss better than anyone, Tony decided it wise to let him know what he had just learnt.

The villa was luxurious but tasteless; having pots of money didn't mean you also had good taste. If Carlos liked something he bought it or had it stolen, he had no morals and was feared in all of Monaco. No one crossed Carlos Manconi and lived. He had the police and judges on his pay roll, so if Carlos wanted someone to disappear, they did, pure and simple.

Tony walked up to the large oak doors of the master bedroom, as usual Luigi, alert as ever was stood ready to engage whoever was approaching.

"Its ok Luigi it's only me, I have to wake the old man"

"He won't be happy Tony, can't it wait till morning?"

"Not really, you know how he hates to be kept in the dark"

"Ok then, fair enough, on your head be it. I might as well grab a coffee while you are with him then, you know where I am if you need me."

"Thanks Luigi, I'll let the old man know that you weren't happy about me waking him."

Once the large bodyguard had left, Tony took a deep breath and knocked loudly on the oak doors, hurting his knuckles in the process.

"CARLOS ITS ME TONY, WE NEED TO SPEAK." He shouted, then waited patiently.

After maybe four or five minutes, Tony heard Carlos say it was ok to enter.

Now the bedroom was tasteful, Tony couldn't help but admire it every time he entered, which wasn't very often. The late wife of Carlos decorated it and as a mark of respect Carlos wouldn't let the room be touched. The old man was sat up in bed, already smoking a Cuban cigar and pouring himself a drink. Knocking on seventy years old now, Carlos was still remarkably fit and had a good few years in him yet, Tony knew that he would eventually take his place, but the old man treated him well so he was more than happy to wait till, god forbid the old man died. Carlos also knew this that's why he trusted Tony. In fact the only two people Carlos did trust were Tony and Luigi.

"Never trust more than two people" the old man told Tony many years ago, "that way you will live to a ripe old age." Tony never forgot that.

"Sorry to wake you boss" Tony said still a little nervous about how his mentor would take being woken.

"That's ok Tony, you wouldn't wake me unless it was important, anyway once you get to my age you don't need much sleep anyway." Carlos said gruffly, taking a pull from his cigar. "So what's the problem Tony?"

"Well I don't know if it is a problem yet, but remember a stranger booked a harbor space for a year in advance." Tony said unsure about whether or not to sit down.

"Hmm yeah, go on and for gods sake Tony sit down, your pacing back and forth is making me seasick," Carlos was waking quickly.

Somewhat relieved and a bit more at ease Tony sank into the large lounger facing Carlos.

"Well he's turned up, a couple of our boys watched him dock, and that insect Jules has spoken with him."

"Did Jules enlighten us with any new information, and what have you found out about him?"

"Well our boys have done some digging and crossed a few palms with sliver, but we don't know a great deal. This man didn't exists five years ago."

"Didn't exist?" Carlos replied unable to hide the surprise in his voice.

"Yeah, five years ago there was no Cyrus Draig, we can't find any record of birth or family anywhere."

"Hmm interesting, sounds like he has changed his identify"

"My thoughts exactly" Tony had by now pored himself a drink and sat back down.

"If that's the case it will work to our advantage" a sly smile crept across the tight lips of Carlos.

"It will? How?" Tony raised an eyebrow.

"You said one thing that you did find out was that he is incredibly wealthy"

"That much is true, his ship alone, was once owned by an oil baron, every fixture and fitting is gold, would you believe? No one knows how much he paid for it but the rumors suggest upwards of fifty million."

Carlos rarely looked surprised, but at hearing this he was obviously taken aback.

"Fifty fucking million, Jeesus, are you sure that he does own it?"

"That was one of the few things that checked out, yep it's bought and paid for and in his name, but we couldn't find any records of any other property though."

"Well he had done a fucking good job of changing his identity then, if we cant even find anything. Which means he has got something to hide. When we put the squeeze on him I think he will be more than willing to cooperate, in case we find out his true identity."

"Want us to keep digging?" asked Tony.

"Oh yes, and when we do found out from what he his hiding, it will give us a full deck. Did whatshisname find out anything?"

"You mean that lizard Jules, no nothing apart from his crew are staying on the ship and he seems to think that there could be upwards of thirty of them, but he didn't see a soul."

"That's a shame, I would have liked to check the ship out, and maybe check the cargo decks."

"So boss, do you want me a couple of the boys to pay him a visit?" Tony was getting excited now despite the lateness of hour; he was a hands on kind of guy.

"You know where he is staying?"

"He told Jules the presidential suite, a couple of phone calls will tell me where."

"Yeah have him watched and followed tomorrow, then in the evening take three boys with you and give him our regards." Carlos couldn't help but laugh, knowing what giving his regards would entail.

"Three boys? I don't need to take that many boss." It was Tony's turn to be surprised.

"Yes you do my Son and go packing heat too, we don't know enough about this man yet, so lets just err on the side of caution." Carlos said putting out his cigar and finishing his drink.

Tony could tell that the old man was getting tired now, and he knew better that to argue with him.

"Ok boss, no worries. We will talk some more tomorrow."

"Yes we will Tony. Now let an old man sleep."

Tony said his goodnights and left the room, for some strange reason he had acquired a dislike for this Cyrus Draig before even meeting him. People Tony didn't like tended not to live very long, and besides he had always fancied a ship.

Cyrus awoke early, he hadn't had much sleep due to lateness of hour that he got in, but Cyrus didn't need much if any sleep. He hadn't requested room service, he preferred to get to know his surroundings and decided to eat out. The room was everything you would expect for the presidential suite, overly extravagant and far too large for one man, but money was money, so the hotel was more than happy to accommodate him. One quick shower later, a clean pair of clothes and Cyrus was ready for breakfast.

Looking at his Rolex it was eight a.m.; plenty of places would be open serving food by now. Before leaving the hotel he deposited some cash etc. in the hotels safe. He wasn't afraid of getting mugged or anything but thought it wise to try and fit in and look as normal as possible. Plus even in the best of hotels, the housekeepers had wandering hands.

The morning was bright and warm, and it didn't take Cyrus long to find a nice pavement café that served breakfast. One continental breakfast and two cappuccinos later Cyrus was ready to see what Monaco had to offer and see if the town suited him. He was eager to settle down, for too many years now he had been a drifter. If there was anywhere on the planet he was sure that Monaco would be the place to complement his lifestyle. The rest of the morning entailed updating his wardrobe, Gucci, Armani, Versace all benefited from Cyrus's spendthrift.

Cyrus was more than aware that his every move was being watched and recorded. In fact the peoples tailing him were very good, switching from person to person regularly and never being too close. Even the most experienced in these matters would have had a job spotting them. No matter how well they melded with their surroundings and swapped places, one thing they couldn't mask were there thoughts and intentions. Like the brightest of beacons Cyrus could home in and read them as easy as a book placed before him.

"Well at least my evenings entertainment, is already planned for me," Cyrus said aloud to no one in particular.

Cyrus had considered purchasing an apartment, but decided against it. It would be so much easier having a hotel room on long term lease. That way all his cleaning, washing and food would be done for him. Money being no problem, that seemed to be the best option. The suite he was currently in was his for up to a month, it already being booked after that. So plenty of time to find somewhere suitable. One thing that did please Cyrus was the distinct lack of ugly women, nearly all that he had seen so far were very attractive, some over done maybe, but none the less, pleasing to the eye.

Already he could feel his hormones jumping and dancing in his body, screaming to be satisfied. It was hard but not impossible for Cyrus to banish his urges for the time being, knowing he had some important work to do first.

Working up an appetite after a hard day leading his new found friends a merry dance and getting to know the area. Cyrus thought he would sample the hotel cuisine. Boasting five stars and apparently the best food in all Monaco, he eagerly wanted to fill his grumbling belly. Since he was going to be here for a while

Cyrus thought it wise to eat in the restaurant, get his face known and all that.

Getting back to hotel suite to change before dinner, Cyrus was pleasantly surprised that most of his earlier purchases were already unpacked and laid neatly on a spare bed. Everything except the made to measure items which would of course take a few days to be completed.

Washed and feeling refreshed Cyrus changed into a suit and headed down to the restaurant. His plan being after eating to go straight on to the casino, get very drunk and lose a lot of money.

The meal was superb, as was the wine that complimented it. The only distracting factor was the waitresses, wearing their tasteful but very tight uniforms. Cyrus couldn't help himself and looked into their minds. They found him very attractive and what a few of them wanted him to do to them wasn't helping his situation. In the end all he could do was laugh to himself, at his lack of self-control, which had got him into a spot of bother more than once, usually with non-to-pleased husbands.

"Fucking hell Cyrus you're like a dog with two dicks today." Again speaking quietly to himself.

Tipping well, very well, Cyrus left the restaurant and headed down to the casino, which fortunately was part of the hotel. Being a guest at the hotel, his credit was already cleared and not even an eyebrow was raised when he sat at the roulette table with two hundred thousand dollars worth of chips. For ease of use most the casinos still used dollars, the high spending Americans liked things simple.

Cyrus excelled himself and lost spectacularly. The Dom Perignon flowed like water; Cyrus and all around him were getting very very drunk. The casino didn't mind this at all and was happy to keep glasses full at all times, Cyrus was paying and losing, the casinos perfect guest!

Cyrus was well aware that his every move was being scrutinized, so he made a big show of losing without a care, and acting inebriated. He was going to be paid a visit tonight, this much he already knew.

The usual casino gold-diggers had latched on to Cyrus, pretending to be his newest friends, but hoping for a share of any winnings and enjoying the free drink. One of them Cyrus knew to be a plant, put there to keep an eye on him and inform those nearby exactly of his state and maybe any plans for the rest of the evening.

Finally Cyrus was cleaned out, he had lost everything, granted during the night he had won some but lost it again quickly. No surprise though, his hangers on had one by one left, once they realized that the big win wasn't forthcoming. During the night Cyrus had slowly and carefully changed his appearance. Completely out of character he made himself look unkempt, disheveled and decidedly unattractive. This night of all nights he didn't need unwanted attention, especially from the ladies. There would be time for that soon enough. With all of his chips now gone the only person left with Cyrus was a young man, who to be honest was just far to drunk to move, even the girl set to watch him had left.

Meanwhile sat in adjacent hotel room to Cyrus's was Tony and three of his henchmen. During the night Tony had received regular updates, about the misfortune of Cyrus. A few times Tony himself had gone down into the casino merely to size Cyrus up and see who he would be dealing with.

"Mean looking bastard my arse," Tony laughed to one of his heavies " that Jules is a fucking paranoid coward."

Tony had phoned Carlos earlier in the evening and let him know what was going on and the plan for the rest of the night. Tony explained how much he was losing and how drunk he was getting, but for some reason Carlos remained uneasy.

"Just be careful Tony, and for fucks sake stay sober" Carlos warned him.

"No worries boss, I haven't touched a drop, it will go smoothly, trust me," Tony said, telling the truth about the drink, he neglected to tell Carlos that he was high as a kite on cocaine.

Tony had just been informed that Cyrus was cleaned out and looked to be returning to his room soon. On hearing that, Tony and his henchmen left their room and with the pass key they were giving by a chambermaid in their employ, entered Cyrus's suite and made them selves at home while they waited for him.

"Shit boss, this room is bigger than my house." Said one of the big men, heading for the fridge, heavily scared and with a boxer's nose, this man looked nasty.

"Yeah well, if you have the money you can afford a place like this. Now fucking sit down Frankie, you're here to work not drink." Tony growled, *starting to get a little twitchy. He always did before a confrontation like this so he wasn't unduly worried.*

"Sorry boss." Frankie replied plonking himself down on a large lounger. He too was itching for some action and found it hard to keep still. The other two men were professionals and kept quiet, knowing their place.

Downstairs in the casino Cyrus was in fact finishing up, all of his chips gone now and no more vintage champagne in the cellar; he was ready to retire to his room. Getting up from the table, he tipped the croupier extremely well and giving him some extra told him to make sure that the one man left with Cyrus, who had finally passed out gets home ok. Seeing the amount he had been given, the young man thanked Cyrus and did indeed promise to make sure the other man got home safely. One thing that struck the croupier as a little odd was that Mr. Draig who had been drinking all night and was clearly drunk for the best part of it, seemed sober all of a sudden, but he paid no more thought to it and diverted his attention to getting the other poor soul home like promised.

Cyrus made a good job of staggering and stumbling towards the elevator, even belching once or twice for good measure. He pressed the call button and waited resting his head on the doors, nearly falling in headlong when they did finally open. Cyrus examined the panel, found his floor, pressed the appropriate button and the doors closed.

"Get ready, he's on his way up." Tony said replacing the receiver of the phone.

The doors to the elevator open and out strode Cyrus. The change was remarkable. Gone were the red eyes, blotchy face and unkempt hair. The earlier ill-fitting suit now fitted perfectly, he walked tall and confidently. At some distance from his room he could see light escaping from under the door, he had definitely switched the light off when he left.

"Ah my welcoming party awaits." Cyrus said quietly, smiling.

Hardly even pausing when he reached the door quickly twisted the key in the lock and sauntered casually in.

Not so much as looking as his guests, Cyrus walked past the four, up to the fridge, pulled out a bottle of Smirnoff Black from the freezer compartment and poured himself a glass.

Tony was taken aback, not only by this mans nonchalant attitude but the report he had got merely minutes ago was that this man could hardly stand, but the person here now was clearly as sober as the proverbial judge.

Trying his best to look unfazed, Tony stood, faced Cyrus and addressed him.

"Cyrus Draig I presume." It wasn't a question. Tony wanted this man off guard.

Cyrus very slowly lifted his head and looked Tony directly in the eye, sending a shiver down his spine.

"Tony Vincenzo" Cyrus replied in a monotone voice.

That was the last thing Tony would have expected Cyrus to say, unable to hide his astonishment, Tony continued on the best he could.

"Ah, well if you know my name, then you will know my reputation." Tony said feeling a little better, his reputation was well known and if this man had found out his name then undoubtedly he would know the kind of man he was.

"Hmm, your reputation" Cyrus said slowly, "yes I do know that Tony, your reputation for preferring the company of young boys precedes you."

Tony felt the blood drain from his face, no body knew his sexual preferences or so he thought. The three heavies just glanced at each other not quite knowing what to do, but their hands inching towards their guns nonetheless.

"WHO THE FUCK DO YOU THINK YOU ARE, SPEAKING TO ME LIKE THAT." Tony screamed, starting to lose control.

"I am Cyrus Draig, but you have already informed me of that," said Cyrus, grinning and sipping his vodka.

"If you weren't going to be so lucrative to us, I would have put a bullet in your head by now, any more of your shit though and I'll do it anyway." Said Tony through gritted teeth, really wanting to kill this cocky bastard.

"Lucrative? I think not. You bore me now so it's about time you all left, oh and close the door on the way out." Cyrus turned and started to walk towards the bedroom.

Tony couldn't believe what he was seeing and hearing, fuck what the old man would say; he is going to murder this fucker anyway.

"Stay where you are, no-one turns their back on me and lives" Tony said, pulling out his gun and pointing it at Cyrus, the three henchmen also followed suit, all be it a little confused. Things weren't going to plan.

Slowly Cyrus turned and faced the four men. He looked at the three henchmen, having already been into their minds, they had done plenty to deserve to die but this wasn't their fight. Making eye contact with all three, each one thinking he was looking directly at them, Cyrus spoke.

"If you want to live, leave now, this is your one chance, if you stay your blood won't be on my hands." Cyrus said softly, clearing meaning what he said.

The three men glanced at each other, honestly not knowing what to do, Tony was shouting at them but they couldn't hear it. Cyrus wanted them to make their own decision so he blocked it out. All three considered leaving but in fairness to them they stayed. If they had left and something happened to Tony, Carlos and his boys would have found them and killed them anyway, and the odds still looked good here.

Cyrus slowly nodded his head, "I have to commend you on your loyalty, it's just a shame that the man you are about to die for is a worthless child molester and wouldn't die for anyone himself. For three of you I will make it quick, that's the least I could do."

Tony and his heavies stood facing Cyrus, their guns drawn, unable to comprehend how the man before them seemingly unarmed, had threatened their lives so confidently. Within seconds, surely he would be dead, riddled with bullets; it was too late to stop the inevitable.

Four fingers depressed four triggers but the hammers never struck home. Darkness engulfed the room, instantaneously and almost simultaneously, three blood curdling screams bit into the air. Then silence for a moment, until finally movement could be heard, then a pitiful simpering. It was Tony.

"Oh my god, pl.. pl.. Please no more. Have mercy" Said Tony, crying like a child.

"Like the mercy you showed those innocent children." Was the replying whisper.

The moans and agonizing cries continued on until finally there was a tearing sound, and what sounded like a tongue less scream in a mouth filled with blood.

Abruptly the cries stopped.

Carlos Castelli awoke from his nightmare, his bed drenched in sweat.

"Fucking hell, thank fuck that was only a dream." Carlos said, his mouth dry, as he reached over and switched on the bedside light.

"AHHH.. JESUS CHRIST." Carlos screamed as his hand brushed past the severed head, placed neatly on the pillow beside him.

"LUIGI LUIGI!!, GET IN HERE QUICK." Desperation and fear in his voice.

"He can't hear you," said Cyrus, stepping from a darkened corner of the room and into the light.

"Who the fuck are you?" Carlos stammered " you, you murdered Tony!"

"The answer to your first question is, my name is Cyrus Draig." A look of comprehension dawned on the face of Carlos.

"And yes I did kill Tony, but not before he was about to kill me. Nice touch putting the head in the bed, don't you think? I saw something similar in a film once." Cyrus said a wry smile spreading across his lips.

"LUIGI, WHERE THE FUCK ARE YOU?" Carlos shouted.

"Luigi can't hear you, so there is no need to shout."

"You murdered him too?" Fear in the voice of the old man.

"NO, he isn't dead, he just can't hear you."

"What do you want from me? Money?" said Carlos, hoping that his man did want only money.

Laughing now, Cyrus replied "no I don't want your money, nothing as mundane as that."

"What then? Are you going to kill me?" Carlos was now afraid; he considered reaching for the nearby draw, where he kept a gun.

"No I am not going to kill you and don't even think of going for the gun, you won't make it."

"How the fuck.."

"I am here purely to show you something, nothing more." And with that Cyrus stepped into the center of the room.

"What you are about to see, no human has ever seen before and lived. Count yourself privileged."

Unable to move, Carlos could only stare at what unfolded before him. Cyrus stood, arms crossed, hands placed on each opposite shoulder, head bowed. Then the metamorphosis took place. Before his very eyes, the man standing before him, grew, his clothes seemingly melting away, bodily hair was sucked away. Arms became elongated, hands turned into talons, fingers into deadly claws. Every artist's impression of Satan, through the millennia was here in some form. Horns sprouted from a diamond shape skull, a wolvine jaw complete with oversized fangs. A tail tipped with a spiked ball of bone. Large leathery wings folded neatly against its back. Plates of bone protecting areas of vulnerability, the chest, shoulders and face. The villa had a high ceiling but this abomination had merely centimeters to spare.

"IL Diavolo" Carlos managed to whisper, already having soiled himself, his graying hair had instantly turned white.

Carlos's brain wanted to give up and die, but Cyrus kept him conscious, wanting him to remember what he is witnessing.

"NO I am not Lucifer, I am far worse, for I still exist." Said unmoving lips in a voice that could freeze blood.

An invisible hand lifted the shaking naked man from his bed; urine ran down his leg. Brought closer and closer, until an inch away from the mouth of hell, slavering jaws gaped more than capable of tearing a man in two. Recessed deep in a helmet of bone, two piercing blue eyes looked into the soul of Carlos, a booming voice reverberated inside his skull.

"NEVER AGAIN CROSS THE PATH OF ME AND MINE." Carlos was sure his head was going to explode. " IF I EVER HAVE CAUSE TO VISIT YOU AGAIN, I SHALL TAKE YOU TO A PLACE WHERE NOT EVEN GOD WILL HEAR YOU SCREAM."

"DO YOU HEAR AND UNDERSTAND ME, CARLOS CASTELLI?"

"Yes yes, oh my god, yes" Carlos cried, waking himself in the process. Moments of confusion followed, his brain taking its time to catch up. Was it all another nightmare?

While still trying to gather himself, Luigi burst through the door, gun drawn.

"BOSS, what's wrong? Holy mother of Mary."

The site before Luigi was a puzzling, as it was horrific. His boss, Carlos Castelli, sat facing him; unbelievably his hair was snow white. Soiled sheets surrounded him, and a severed head placed neatly on the pillow next to him. It took a few seconds to realize that the head was that of Tony, his death mask one of pure torment.

Carlos came to his senses. What had taken place was no nightmare, feeling the bile well up in his throat he screamed at Luigi.

"GET OUT, GET OUT NOW."

"But boss" Luigi protested, " what's going on?"

"FUCKING GET OUT, NOW."

Luigi still unsure what to do, turned on his heels and left.

"I'll be just outside the door when you need me," Luigi said closing the large double doors, taking one last look at the butchery.

Strangely after all that had happened, Carlos was glad to be alone. The night's events burned deep into his soul. Sitting up, still shaking somewhat, Carlos wept.

A quick glance at his watch showed it was three thirty A.M.

"Hmm the night is still young, still one more errand to complete, then hopefully my work is done." Cyrus said cheerily to himself, lighting another cigarette with his antique zippo, then turning into the path that led down to the harbor.

Jules awoke for the umpteenth time from his fitful sleep. He reached over and switched on the bedside lamp, the naked bulb blinding him for a few moments.

"Can't fucking sleep tonight, What time is it?" Jules said to himself, while rummaging through the over full ashtray to find a butt worth smoking.

The fat man lived in squalor. His one roomed shack didn't even have a bin let alone a cleaner. The floor was littered with half-eaten takeaways, unwashed clothes and many other revolting items. It was a paradise for cockroaches and rats, which was quite fitting considering the type of person Jules was. It wasn't that the harbormaster was badly paid, quite the opposite in fact, especially when you take into account the extra money he earned working for Carlos and his petty pilfering from innocent tourists.

Jules was an addict, not drugs or alcohol, but gambling. Every penny he earned was wasted on the impossible dream; the gamblers Valhalla, the one big win.

Jules owed a fortune, but that didn't stop him throwing his money away. If it wasn't for his connections and usefulness to Carlos, he would have long since been wearing a pair of concrete shoes at the bottom of the sea. That's what normally happened to people that didn't pay their debts. Many of the fat mans lowlife gambling associates had mysteriously disappeared after owing large amounts of money.

Living this close to the sea, the night was never silent, but Jules was puzzled at the extra sound that he could hear and not quite make out.

"What the fuck is that?" he said sitting up in his bed, his ears straining.

Then it dawned on him. There was something scratching at his door.

"Piss off you mangy mutt, you'll find no food here." Jules shouted, while looking for something to throw at the door.

The noise grew louder; it seemed the whole side of the wooden shack was vibrating, a thousand fingers trying to claw their way through.

"YOUR TRECHERY IS AT AN END JULES MOREAU. BON NUIT." Said a deafening voice seemingly coming from nowhere.

Before the fat man could answer, the filthy blanket that covered him was impossibly blown off and onto the floor, leaving the man feeling naked, vulnerable and very scared.

"Ok I'm sorry, I'll pay the fucking money, just quit with the games." Jules blubbered, but the noise increased, becoming earsplitting. Jules tried to get off the bed but found he couldn't move, he was paralyzed from the neck down.

Two invisible hands grabbed his corpulent ankles, forced his legs apart, and then pulled him down the bed. The same was done to his arms, first pulled above his head before being pushed open.

He was now lying prone on the mattress. His hands and feet at the four corners of the bed.

Spread-eagled in an unholy cross, the sniveling naked man could only lift his head and stare.

As if his eyes were pinned open, his unblinking gaze fixed on the door, while the noise built to a soul-numbing crescendo. Ever so slowly, Jules saw the key turn in the lock, then notch by notch, the handle turned.

Suddenly, unable to take the strain any longer, the door burst open.

Jules screamed, as the cause of the scratching was quickly revealed.

Wave after wave of crabs poured in through the now open door. Thousands upon thousands of the crustaceans fighting to get through the small gap.

"OH MY GOD NO, PLEASE NO."

The tiny minds of the crabs, impressed with one thought only, FOOD, and Jules was dish of the day. Like a light to a moth, the crabs couldn't help themselves, not until their hunger was satisfied.

The floor now alive, not an inch was left bare, a twisted pattern of death coming ever closer.

Already some had found him. His toes, fingers and genitals no longer visible under a blanket of red.

His cries and pleas going unheard. Within seconds, the majority had reached him. A man shape sculpture of crabs, eerily screaming from an unseen mouth.

Soon the wails became muffled, then silence.

It was finished.

• • • • • • • • • • • • • • • • •

Carlos died some eight years later and it was his faithful bodyguard Luigi that took over the mantle in place of Tony. As organized crime bosses went, Luigi was a firm but fair one. The legacy left by Carlos that Cyrus Draig wasn't to be so much as bumped into, Luigi continued. Never knowing though what happened on that night so many years ago, but Luigi knew it involved Mr. Draig and that Carlos was never quite the same, nor could he ever forget the agonizing last face of Tony, which he saw only the once but burned lucid in his memory for ever. Sometimes it was wise to let sleeping dogs lie.

In fact over the years the paths of Cyrus and Luigi had crossed a few times, at formal dinners etc. and Cyrus actually quite liked the man, although no more than small talk was ever exchanged. It was clear that they both respected each other, and that was enough.

Alone now in his immense apartment, Cyrus decided to retire to his private quarters for a while. Although of course the whole penthouse was his, the east wing was his personal and private domain. He never entertained in there nor had anybody other than himself been in there since it was built, not even the hotel housemaids had a key.

Dressed now in nothing but a toweling robe, Cyrus strode up to the door inserted the credit card type key the quickly punched in a ten-figure code in the adjacent keypad. The large metal door hissed like a woken snake as it slid effortlessly open.

The main, more public rooms of the apartment were in themselves superb, costing a fortune to decorate. With expensive carpets and priceless antiques and paintings throughout, but Cyrus's private quarters surpassed the main suites one hundred fold.

A marriage, no, orgy of harmony, old embracing new at every juncture. Modern, postmodern and relic's hand in hand, interwoven in a lover's embrace. Watching with seeing eyes from one corner of a room, a sculpture, remarkably similar to Antioch's Venus De Milo, but fully intact, her cream skin, unblemished and fresh. Another corner hosting a glass cabinet. On close inspection would reveal entombed within, a rough but more importantly a complete version of Schubert's Symphony in B minor. Asleep alongside Schuberts' child, something that to the layman read like a book of bible, the author not Matthew, mark, Luke or john but one named Bartholomew.

De Vinci, Van Gough, Monet, were all here. Throughout this private domain none of the masters were absent, including antiquities from the lost city of Atlantis, as yet still undiscovered.

Pride of place in the master room, adorning one wall was a sword, it would be hard to describe its beauty, even the word alluring wasn't even close. Its handle entwined with tiny golden snakes that would wriggle and dance when seen out the corner of ones eye, but frustratingly stop when looked at directly. Its blue, purple, no green blade, loved to play games, hypnotically enchanting any that dared to catch more then the merest of glances.

As usual, Cyrus stood before the great blade and addressed it, as if it was alive.

"Within these walls, I own the world. Nations would war, history be rewritten, age old beliefs quashed, if I let so much as a small portion of my treasures be found. I would gladly trade them all, to have you as mine, to hold you, touch you, wield you." there was a hint of sadness in his voice.

"But alas old friend, such can never be, I shall have make do with your company, even though it torments me so."

With that, Cyrus left the room of treasures and entered an altogether more comfortable room down the hallway.

Pride of place was mammoth leather recliner, oozing serenity to any fortunate enough to sit within her loving embrace.

Cyrus slowly sat down, closing his eyes for a moment, enjoying the peace.

After only a few minutes, he opened his eyes and reached for the remote control, which was in its usual place on the small Davenport coffee table alongside the chair.

One touch of a button was all it took for the room to explode into life. A myriad of sound accosting the eardrums from every direction. Facing Cyrus was a bank of at least fifty television screens, the whole wall animated in a collage of moving color.

News stations from around the globe, world stock markets, even a channel of rock music playing next to Beethoven's 5th, all fighting for Cyrus's undivided attention, and ALL getting it.

Watching them all simultaneously, Cyrus soaked everything in like a sponge. Even the casino close circuit cameras were patched through here as well as the hidden cameras in the many bedrooms of his suites.

At times he liked to be a voyeur, watching others writhe and squirm in the oldest of dances.

Above the clamor of noise, that to anyone but Cyrus would be intolerable, his ears picked up another sound. A soft padding, that would be virtually undetectable even if the room was silent.

Smiling now, Cyrus leaned forward to greet his guest at the same time turning off the volume on his wall of sound.

"Come to me my boy."

The door opened and cautiously at first, in strode a magnificent panther, black as a moonless night.

"Ah, Cheech my son, I should have known it would be you. One day your brother will get here first and surprise me." Cyrus couldn't help but chuckle as he roughed the fur on his adopted child.

"Hope I didn't disturb your sleep old boy," a quick glance at his watch confirmed that he probably did, as it was the height of the day in their habitat.

"I do believe that Chong has decided to grace us with his presence."

Striding lazily in, was a creature equally as splendid as the first, in fact more so even. Almost identical to his brother, except his pelt was white as snow, but unlike most albinos though, his eyes weren't pink and pig like, but as black as his siblings coat, giving the animal an august allure.

Chong padded nonchalantly once around the room, giving his brother a welcoming lick on passing. On leaving the room, Chong turned and gave Cyrus what could only be described as a *dirty look*, and then was gone.

Unable to contain his mirth, Cyrus laughed, scaring Cheech a little in the process.

"Oh that brother of yours, I have never met such a cantankerous beast in all my days. He seemed in a particularly foul mood today, must have been about to give one of his feline bitches' a good rutting. He's probably back in the jungle sowing his oats already." Cyrus paused for a moment before continuing.

"Well old friend, I can see that you're not in a rush to get back, not quite so hot here, huh?"

Cyrus lent back in the huge chair and closed his eyes, contented and asleep at his feet was the majestic cat, purring like a kitten.

Cyrus awoke maybe an hour or so later, Cheech was already gone.

"Ah alone again," he said softly to himself as he got up from his chair.

Reaching for the remote and just about to switch the TV's off, when something caught his eye.

One of the casino monitors had picked up a young girl, obviously the operator also had an eye for the ladies, as he panned here and there, watching her every move.

Cyrus had to admit that she was exquisite. The one quality that stood out more than any, was innocence.

"Well hello my pretty little thing, it's about time that we had some new blood here." Cyrus said aloud, making himself laugh in the process at his unfortunate choice of words.

"Listen to me, I sound like a bloody vampire, tut tut tut."

As far as Cyrus was aware, vampires were a thing of the past, and not from this world. In all his millennia on earth, he has never come across a true one, but he didn't rule out the possibility. Well after all, he exists, doesn't he?

Cyrus washed and dressed quickly, feeling a little happier now that he had something or more precisely someone to occupy his time for a bit.

Stepping out of the elevator, Cyrus had to raise his shields somewhat, purely to make himself a little less recognizable. He didn't want the poor girl scared away or feel intimidated, with all and sundry coming over to make small talk with Cyrus or just even to shake his hand.

It didn't take him long to find her, she was sat alone at the bar sipping what was by now a warm and flat coke. Wisely she had already shunned the advances of the local vultures who quickly moved on when they realized that she didn't want to play their type of games.

As usual Cyrus probed her mind a little, not going too deep, just enough to see if she was what she appeared to be. Hurt, confusion and betrayal were all there, Cyrus would have to tread softly with this one, it looked like that she has had a hard time of things of late and deserved a smooth ride for a bit.

"Come on lets get you something to eat, you look famished." Cyrus said softly, startling the girl a little in the process.

The young girl spun round with all intentions of telling him, thanks but no thanks, but when she saw his liquid blue eyes and friendly smile, she couldn't, her mouth opened but no words came out.

"Oh I do apologize, let me introduce myself, the names Draig, Cyrus Draig," and with that he offered her his hand.

The girl took his hand, it felt nice and warm to her touch, already she was feeling a little more comfortable.

"I'm sorry, my names Gail Harvey," she said in a delicate English accent. As if on cue her stomach gave a ghastly rumble, somewhat breaking the ice and making them both laugh.

"Right that's it, I wont take no for an answer, you are joining me for breakfast, come on there's a free table over there."

Slightly hesitant for a moment, while she pondered, Gail was unsure what to do, but she was very hungry so her belly won out.

Like the gentleman he was, Cyrus pulled back the chair for her, and then when she was seated, joined her on the opposite side of the table. To make her feel a bit more at home he also changed his accent, almost matching hers, but Cyrus could tell that she was still a little uncomfortable about something and it puzzled him as to what it was.

After a minutes silence, Gail leaned over, and said in a voice that was barely a whisper.

"I am afraid that I can't pay for breakfast, I only have a little money left."

Cyrus laughed, but in a nice way, that was all that was making her feel ill at ease.

"Oh my sweet, I wouldn't expect you to pay a penny towards it, even if you could. Now choose what you would like, for I am hungry too now."

"And in return, what do you expect from me?" it was a question that Gail had to ask, yes she was young but she wasn't stupid.

"Your company is more than enough, and it seems to me that you could use a friend right now."

Gail simply nodded, feeling a little ashamed at what she was implying earlier about his motives, and yes she could use a friend.

"So lets eat, then we can talk." Cyrus said cheerily.

Even though Gail had forgotten the last time she had a proper meal, she tried her best not to embarrass herself by wolfing the food down and eating like a pig, but DAMM it tasted good.

After the meal, they decided to have coffee and that was when Gail opened up to Cyrus, telling him her story.

As it goes, her tale wasn't an unusual one.

She was nineteen, soon to be twenty. Her parents, who were fairly well off, were both killed in an ill-fated light aircraft flight. She was left quite a hefty inheritance, which her boyfriend quickly wasted for her by shooting most of it up his arm, but still finding time to beat her regularly.

When the money was gone, so was the boyfriend. Luckily for Gail, her parents' estate etc. wont be hers until she reaches twenty-one, otherwise the snake of a boyfriend would have sold that too. So with a little money that she had hidden, Gail bought a ticket to Monaco, in the hope of finding a job, until she was twenty-one at least. She had been here many times with her mother and father when she was younger and always remembered it to be a lovely and friendly place, but as is so often the case, childhood memories rarely live up to adult expectations.

So here she was broke, homeless and jobless.

Cyrus listened quietly and intently to her story, but instead of having to imagine and picture the various scenes, he actually saw them through the mind of Gail and felt her pain. Even before the story was finished, Cyrus had already decided to take a quick trip to England one afternoon and pay her ex boyfriend one of his special visits, but that he kept to himself.

By the time Gail had finished, it seemed as if a vast weight was lifted from her and she felt so much better, telling her story was what she had needed.

"You have been very strong Gail, others would have withered and died," Cyrus told her, meaning what he said.

"I don't feel strong, just stupid for letting myself be taken in that far."

"We all make mistakes angel, and at times love can be an evil thing if it isn't shared by both people, trust me I know."

"Yes you are right, and thank you."

"No need to thank me Gail, if you could wouldn't you do what I have just done for you if you were in my position?"

"Well yes I think I would, but still thank you anyway." With that Gail leaned over and kissed Cyrus gently on the cheek.

Gail was a beautiful woman and her kiss felt as sweet as nectar to Cyrus, but the emotion Cyrus felt confused him for a moment.

Normally he wouldn't think twice about bedding someone as attractive as her, nor was her age a problem, he a slept with far younger, but for the first time ever, he didn't have the urge to fuck her.

All he wanted to do was protect the girl, father her. Incredibly, not even Cyrus could believe it; he had a paternal instinct!

"Right come on, you go and freshen up quickly, and then we'll go shopping."

"Shopping? But Cyrus, I haven't even found a job yet or somewhere to stay, and as you know I don't have any money."

"A job isn't a problem Gail, nor is somewhere to stay, I'll have sorted both out for you by the end of the day, I promise, and don't try to tell me that you don't need any clothes or erm woman's things." Cyrus was actually a little embarrassed and he hoped it didn't show.

"Oh Cyrus, you're so sweet, and yes again you are right, I do need some clothes and *women's things.*" Gail whispered the last part of the sentence, and then burst into a fit of giggles, making Cyrus also laugh in the process.

"Ok ok, I'll quickly go to the ladies room" Gail started to rise but then sat back down again. " I have just thought Cyrus, you virtually know my life story already, but I all know about you is your name. Tell me about you?"

"Have you got a couple of thousand years free?"

"You are funny Cyrus, I am sure you will tell me in your own time, right give me five minutes," and with that Gail got up from the table and practically skipped to the bathroom.

Cyrus signed for the meal, and then sat for a moment lost in thought.

Something wasn't right, this much he new. Never in his life before had he felt this way, but he had only met the girl literally hours ago. He even considered the possibility that maybe he could be her father, he spent a lot of time in England, going there at least four times a year, but he knew that it was impossible for him to father a child, so dismissed the idea quickly.

"Come on Cyrus, this isn't like you at all, snap out of it."

It couldn't be something he had eaten, nor was it drink or drugs having an adverse effect on him, he was immune to both.

No matter what he considered, the answer just wasn't forthcoming, but something was niggling him and he couldn't put his finger on it.

"Maybe you're just getting old." But he didn't believe that was the answer either.

"Sorry did you say something Cyrus?" now it was his turn to be startled, he didn't notice Gail's return.

"No, no, please forgive an old mans mumbling, when you get to my age you don't even realize that you are doing it."

"What do you mean old man? Your not even twice my age Cyrus, you are far from old and you look fitter than people nearer my age anyway, so stop talking crap." Gail said in her best headmistress voice, but still unable to suppress a smile.

"YES MISS." Said Cyrus, failing miserably at his schoolboy impression.

With that, he got up and they both left the casino.

The rest of the day consisted of the two of them, exploring the less well-known but in many ways superior-shopping bazaars of Monaco. Granted the big overpriced boutiques weren't there, but second hand and small family run shops were a plenty and that's where the bargains were to be had.

Not for the first time today, Gail surprised Cyrus, her taste in clothes was exquisite, not caring about name etc. whereas nearly all the other ladies in Monaco didn't care what something looked like as long as the right label hung from it, and the more extravagantly expensive the better, no matter how garish the outfit.

"I intend to pay you back Cyrus," for once Gail was being sincere.

"I don't doubt it for a minute angel, and with plenty of interest I hope."

"Well I am not sure about that, maybe I'll cook you dinner, how does that sound?"

"I'll think about it" Cyrus was smiling now.

"Good, I'm glad that's settled."

"Hey! But.."

Cyrus was enjoying the day immensely, he could honestly say that he hadn't enjoyed the company of another like this for a long long time. He was a little disappointed when he realized that the days outing was virtually over and evening was drawing in.

"Join me for dinner?"

"I'd love too Cyrus, but I still haven't sorted out a job or somewhere to stay."

"Gail, I told you that it wouldn't be a problem finding you a job, as long as you don't mind working in the casino, but there a variety of jobs there, I am sure you will find one to suit. Your French is very good too, which will help. Tonight I would be honored if you'd be my guest and tomorrow we will find you a permanent place to stay."

"I cant thank you enough Cyrus, and yes I'd love to be your guest tonight, but so far you have given me so much and I have nothing for you in return."

"Spending some time with you is more than enough for me, and I mean that. Now I don't want to hear another word on that subject again, ok?"

60

"Ok." Gail was close to tears now; no one before had done this much for her without expecting something in return, normally something quite sordid at that.

"Great, we'll get back to the casino, you can wash and change, and I'll sort dinner out."

Cyrus did a quick mental check, just in case he had made other plans for the night, but he hadn't, well nothing he couldn't put off anyway.

It didn't take long to get back to the hotel, while Gail was busy sorting out her various bags, Cyrus quickly popped to the reception and told them that if he had any calls, they were to make his apologies and say he was away. All of the various receptionists had heard this before from him and knew what it normally meant, and when the young man saw the attractive young girl waiting patiently, he smiled and winked at Cyrus.

Now this actually annoyed Cyrus, but he bit his tongue, again his reputation preceded him, nor was the youngster to know that his intentions were for once, honorable.

The two entered the elevator; Cyrus inserted a key into the control panel and depressed the large " P ".

"You live here?"

"Yes, I thought I told you Gail."

"Cyrus, you haven't told me anything about you, maybe its about time you started."

"I'm sorry angel, but it totally slipped my mind, you know with having such a great day and all, I promise to tell you anything you'd like to know over dinner."

"Good, why do I have the feeling that I might not like all I am going to hear." Gail didn't mean it in a nasty way.

"Hmm, well we all have skeletons in the closet, maybe I have a few more that most."

"True, true, as long as they don't come back to haunt you."

"Oh I doubt that," said Cyrus smiling.

Within a few seconds and with virtually no feeling of motion, the doors opened and top floor was reached.

Gail could only gasp at the sight that met her eyes as they stepped out the elevator.

"Fucking hell." she whispered.

"Now, now, that's no language for a lady." Cyrus was used to this reaction from newcomers to his home.

"I know, but, I have never seen anything like this. I feel like a trespasser in a world I don't belong." Gail meant it to, her parents were fairly well off, but she had never seen splendor and affluence before. Kings didn't live this well.

"Don't talk rubbish Gail, what you see is a front more than anything, you know an image. Did you not enjoy my company when you didn't know about this?"

"You know I did Cyrus."

"Well that's why I purposely didn't tell you about me, whether or not you admit it, you would have acted differently towards me."

"Maybe," Gail was a little irritated, thinking that Cyrus thought her to be so shallow.

"Please Gail, it's not that I think you shallow or anything, if I did you wouldn't be here now. It's just that I wanted us to start off on an even keel, get to know the real me without any distractions."

"Once again you are right Cyrus, you always seem to know what I am thinking." Gail felt a little embarrassed.

"Oh, didn't I tell you that I am psychic." Cyrus said smiling, lightening the mood.

"It wouldn't surprise me in the least." Gail was only half joking, but felt better already.

"Fancy a guided tour of my humble abode then?"

"Love one."

"Great, but don't touch anything," there was silence for a moment before Cyrus added "joke." and with that they both fell about laughing like a couple of school kids.

For the most part of the tour Gail was genuinely speechless, she had long since lost count at the number of bedrooms there were, each one must have cost a small fortune to furbish. Four-poster beds, silken sheets, a host of antiques in every corner. Paintings adorned the walls. Gail didn't have to ask whether or not they were originals, she already knew the answer. One thing that surpassed the number of bedrooms was the number of bathrooms; every bedroom had one, some even having two, as well the others throughout the penthouse. She saw two swimming pools, a games room, consisting of a bowling ally and its own cinema. There was a stunning banqueting hall come ballroom. One wing even had a nursery for when the guests didn't want to leave their little treasures at home. The list went on and Gail was sure that Cyrus still hadn't shown her everything.

"What's in there?" Gail pointed to what seemed to be the only door that didn't fit in; it was plain and painted, unlike the turned oak doors of the other rooms.

"Oh, nothing special, just little trinkets really, you know stuff that you don't really want but cant throw out, come on I'll show you what I mean." Cyrus opened the door and switched on the light. For the second time tonight Gail swore.

"Well fuck me, Cyrus, you don't even have a lock on the door!" the sight that greeted Gail reminded her of the childhood stories she used to love, the ones with Aladdin, Ali Baba and so forth.

It took a few moments for Gail's brain to take in all that she saw, and when it finally did sink in completely, she felt a little stupid. It wasn't quite the treasure trove filled with silver and gold that she had thought at first glance. It was merely a trophy room. The word merely was the wrong word though, for it was still a very impressive sight.

"They are mostly worthless," Cyrus said casually and matter of factly.

"Monaco archery champion, five years running?" said Gail looking at a large silver plate.

"Erm. Yeah a misspent youth in Nottingham, England, many years ago, that's where I learnt to draw a bow. I was quite good as it happens."

"Seems like you haven't lost your touch. Fencing, tennis, croquet, is there anything that you aren't good at?"

"Yeah I am sure there is something." Cyrus said pretending to be deep in thought.

"Modest too I see."

"Of course."

"Well I notice that there quite a few second place trophies here too, that doesn't seem like you, I thought you would play to win."

"Ah well, I ended up sponsoring allot of the tournaments, it seemed a bad show for me to win them as well, don't you think?"

"Oh, that's very noble of you. You really are one of a kind Cyrus."

Cyrus caught himself checking out Gail's perfect figure out of the corner of his eye. The light summer dress she was wearing hung in all the right places. It was almost see-through in the bright artificial light. She wore no bra.

Starting now to become aroused, Cyrus moved a little closer as lustful thoughts filled his mind.

Suddenly, a wave of nausea hit Cyrus, literally knocking him back a few paces and actually making him feel physically sick.

"Excuse me a moment, I have to use the bathroom," Cyrus said weakly, leaving the room, not waiting for a reply.

"Sure." Gail half answered, she was somewhat distracted herself. A few of the dates on the trophies puzzled her; they couldn't all be Cyrus's then, so why did he keep them?

Once in the nearest bathroom, Cyrus vomited. He had never done that before and it made his head spin.

"What the fuck is going on?" Cyrus said to himself in the mirror. He had always been in perfect health; not even a simple cold had troubled him before. Confusion, angst, worry, were emotions alien to him. Cyrus had to get a grip of himself, and quickly.

He even seriously considered contacting Janus, but his childish pride reared its ugly head once more.

The scream that shattered the silence was unmistakably Gail's'

Cyrus was at the trophy room within seconds, all bilious feelings gone, as was Gail.

Cyrus's mind reached out; she was no-where in the penthouse. He widened his scan, nor was she in the hotel or casino.

This was impossible, she had cried out less than five seconds ago, even if she was dead Cyrus still would have been able to locate her, for few hours at least.

Cyrus nearly started to panic but managed to catch himself in time. He took some deep breaths, then evaluated to situation. His newly found paternal instincts struggling for dominance, but with allot of will power Cyrus pushed them back. He needed to think straight and lucid.

Standing still, head bowed and eyes closed, Cyrus let all around him engulf his mind, hoping for some clue. After what seemed an eternity, he slowly raised his head and opened his eyes.

"The Guinevere." he growled.

Cyrus had ways of getting to places quickly, very quickly, when he needed to. As long as it was fairly close and very familiar.

Moments later he was on the pier. It wasn't yet dark, the suns' red fingers were still clinging to the sky, trying in vain to hang on for a little while longer, like a young child not wanting to go to bed.

As he half expected the Guinevere was gone. Cyrus knew his " special" crew wasn't aboard, so whoever took it must have come well prepared.

Looking out onto the horizon, the unmistakable shape of the Guinevere could be seen, it didn't look to be moving, but it was hard to tell at this range.

Before making the next jump, Cyrus took a minute to take stock of the situation.

"Hmm, I know what the proverbial fly felt like now, before entering the infamous parlor." Cyrus said quietly before adding, " but this fly has a deadly sting."

Then he was gone, and pier was once more deserted.

Emerging on the deck of his ship, Cyrus could tell that the engines hadn't been used and it was anchored. The old girl sat in silence, waiting obediently for her master to bring her to life.

Gail's' terrified scream filled his head once again, her horror and fear was obvious.

She was in the ballroom, that much Cyrus knew, and without a second thought for his own safety, Cyrus was there.

The immense ballroom was in darkness; anyone other then Cyrus would be blind in the near pitch black, but the site that greeted him was clear as day. Darkness was no hindrance.

Standing in the center of the now unfurnished room, Cyrus slowly turned on his heels, surveying the situation. Lining the four walls, standing erect and unmoving were a multitude of near faceless figures, only their soulless eyes could be seen, seemingly looking out into oblivion.

At the far end of the ballroom, flanked on both sides and being held up by two of the unholy creatures was Gail. Thankfully she had passed out.

Standing tall and majestically behind them was a caped silhouette. His near liquid form dancing with the darkness, invisible eyes burning deep into Cyrus.

Stranger still though, two more intellects were present, unperceivable to Cyrus's eyes, but he knew they were there, silent, unseen, deadly.

"Welcome Cyrus, all be it to your own ship." said the hooded figure, his emotionless voice reverberating from wall to wall.

"Let her go, " Cyrus hissed, he could feel his rage building to an unstoppable finale.

"And why would I do that, she is such a pretty thing and I know you care for her oh so much."

Things started to fall into place for Cyrus, he now knew who or what was the cause for his new found paternal instinct. Managing to keep his anger in check, Cyrus spoke slowly and calmly.

"Give her to me, or you will have no hope of getting what you want."

"How very astute of you, but I will get what I want Cyrus whever you decide to join me or not."

"Join you?"

"Well of course, you don't think I would have gone to all this trouble just to kill you. That I could have done at anytime." There was no lack of doubt in his voice.

"Keep talking." For the first time in an age, Cyrus felt uneasy. Whoever he was dealing with here was very powerful, possibly more powerful then himself. He had to get as much information as possible before making his move. Getting Gail safe was also a priority; she doesn't need to be involved in this world.

The cloaked apparition stepped forward, then glided towards Cyrus, stopping maybe ten foot shy. His translucent form becoming more and more dense as he moved, by the time he came to a standstill, he was whole. His head still hooded and his face shrouded in an unending night, hiding what lay beneath. His hidden minders moving also, staying ever close to their master.

"The time of darkness is close. This world has bathed in light for long enough; soon it will be our turn. We have been preparing and recruiting for a long time now, my disciples are ubiquitous, our armies are ready." He paused for a moment, making sure his words had sunk in.

"How prepared are you and your three friends Cyrus?"

"Well enough " Cyrus answered coldly, unfortunately his mind was filled of the last millennia, wasted on stupid games and mindless quests. He couldn't help but wonder how prepared they really were and how this entity standing before him knew about the others.

It was time to contact Janus.

Closing his eyes for only a nano-second, Cyrus let his essence transverse time and space, automatically seeking it's chosen target. For the first time ever it found nothing, like an unhappy puppy unable to find its favorite stick, it returned, dejected.

"You're wasting your time. We have taken care of them, they are incapable of hearing you." The voice behind the hood said in a matter of factly way, bored even.

Cyrus hated to admit that he was out of his depth, right now he needed space, but the unconscious Gail kept him from just turning and running. It was a clever ploy using her, even if his feelings towards her were unreal and manufactured, but knowing this didn't help him. Cyrus couldn't leave her to these monsters.

"Don't tell me the others are dead, if that was the case you wouldn't need me. Why *DO* you need me anyway? And what makes you think I would be interested?"

"I never said the your friends were dead," impossibly the invisible face smirked. " So please don't put words into my mouth. You are a gambling man Cyrus, that much you cant deny, I am purely giving you the chance to be on the winning team that's all. Not that you and your friends pose more than a minor irritation to me, but I could do with someone like you in my New World."

"So its nothing to do with breaking up the chain of four then?" Cyrus said contemptuously.

The echoing laugh of the shrouded figure pounded deep into Cyrus's brain.

"Very good Cyrus, very good, like I said earlier you and your friends are no more than an itch to me, but yes, you joining me would make things a little more uncomplicated that's all."

"Well I am listening and I am still here, but as a show of faith, give me the girl."

"For the time being while we talk, I shall grant you your wish, but as I am sure you realize, the girl is my little bit of insurance, and I am also sure that you have no doubts what inhuman atrocities we could do to her if you try anything."

Cyrus knew he spoke the truth. He had to get Gail away, and quickly.

After the merest of nods, the two wretched creatures holding Gail brought her forward and she fell into the arms of Cyrus.

Ever so gingerly, the tendrils of Cyrus's mind entered Gail's', bringing her back to sentience.

"Where am I? " Gail slurred, thankfully her memory was sketchy.

"It's ok angel, it's just bad dream and it will soon be over." His soothing words filling her with warmth.

Cyrus was now ready to jump, and get the pair as far away as possible.

Nothing happened.

"DO YOU THINK I AM STUPID?" There was outrage in the voice the darkened presence. " Merely seconds ago I warned you what would happen if you tried anything. It's obvious that you don't take me seriously Cyrus Draig. Watch now, while some of my children defile this pretty flower. It will be bad enough for the girl, but nothing like the living hell she will experience if you try to defy me again."

"LIKE FUCK I WILL,   YOU WON'T LAY A FINGER ON H ER." The heat was building in Cyrus; the uninevitable was drawing closer.

"And how do you propose to stop us, not even *you* can defend yourself and her, we are too many. Let the girl get what is coming to her, then it will be over, but I have to prove to you that I am not one to be disobeyed." With that the sentinels lining the walls all stepped forward.

Gail lifted her head and looked up to Cyrus, fear and confusion in her eyes, her mind not sure what was going on, but she knew it wasn't good.

Cyrus held her tightly, softly stroked her hair. He filled her mind with joy and happiness, an ecstasy she had never known. Her loving eyes looked into his and she saw a single tear. He leaned forward and kissed her gently on the forehead. For a moment her life was complete.

It was during that instant that Cyrus cleanly and swiftly snapped her neck.

Even before Gail's lifeless body had hit the floor, Cyrus was in action. Jumping back, giving himself space, the compound bow already in his hand. Plucking silver arrows seemingly from thin air, his fluid motions no more than a blur. Gleaming darts fired at a speed that would put a Kalashnikov to shame. The sentries lining the walls barely had time to move before a hail of death engulfed them, but as one dropped another would instantly rise up and take its place.

"ENOUGH, " the hooded figure cried, having already melted into the background once things didn't go to plan.

The encroaching disciples halted immediately, once more inert.

Cyrus also stopped his bow gone, obsidian eyes full of anger and hate.

"Your a fool Cyrus, I came to offer you the word, and this is your gratitude."

"Fuck you," Cyrus hissed, "you tried to use an innocent girl to get me to do your bidding. You must need me. Well I ain't fucking playing."

"This is no game Cyrus. Admittedly, having you would have made things a little less troublesome, but that's all. I grow weary now, and I am not prepared to see any more of my children perish at your hands. So its time for you to die. Goodbye Mr. Draig."

Then, expeditiously the abhoration was gone, as were his so called children.

But Cyrus wasn't alone; he could feel two distinct presences. The minders had stayed.

"Show yourself, " Cyrus snarled his body morphing as he spoke.

Seeming, willing to oblige, the air shimmered with a bluey hue and within moments they were there.

Cyrus in his true form, which he was now, was barely half the size of these twins of Incubus. A detailed description at first was difficult; a liquid sculpture unable to choose which form it favored best. Until, finally settling on the one best suited for it's current quarry. Huge canine heads with undoubtedly razor sharp teeth adorned a body of natural armour. Long forearms with serrated barbs protecting the elbows, ending in pernicious talons. Immensely powerful legs ready to propel the beasts at a speed that surely belied their bulk. One thing was clear though, these miscreations had no intelligence as such, they were killing machines, pure and simple, and Cyrus didn't doubt for one minute that they excelled at their job.

" Hhmm, a face only a mother could love." The now demonic Cyrus whispered every muscle and sinew tense, nerve endings on fire.

He was ready.

Suddenly, moving at an impossible speed, one of the destroyers made its opening gambit. The deadly game of chess had begun.

In less than a blinking of an eye and with no more noise than a spring breeze, one of the assassins was behind Cyrus. Turning slowly, forcing the enemy to circle, Cyrus made his move. Crouching momentary like a tightly wound spring, and with a cry akin to a crazed banshee, Cyrus leapt. Not towards one of his opponents, but directly up, almost touching the ceiling, before crashing down. Increasing his mass as he fell, the mild steel ballroom floor offered little resistance, shattering like tinderwood. Continuing downward, the strengthened hull faired no better once hit by the living torpedo, giving away instantly.

Knowing their prey had gone and in the process scuttling the ship, the silent executioners saw no reason to stay, so they too disappeared. Leaving the old girl alone and silent, as the oceans' loving embrace quickly devoured her.

Unseen and unnoticed, taking place during the height of the commotion, invisible hands claimed the lifeless body that was once Gail Harvey. No trace of the unfortunate girl would ever be found. Cyrus *always* covered his tracks.

CHAPTER 3

"Serenity"

A Disney cartoon would have difficulty matching the beauty of this hidden nirvana. Situated high in the Himalayas, it was as if it was Mother Natures' *secret* place. Her loving and tender kiss was everywhere; even her own normally unbreakable rules didn't apply here. Although the climate was one of perpetual springtime, this didn't stop the trees in the orchard blossoming and bearing fruit all year round. Apples, oranges, grapes, the list went on, all manner of fruit was here, deliciously ripe and with a taste of pure ambrosia. The small vegetable garden told the same story. All that was seeded flourished, nowhere else on the globe would it be possible for such exotica to germinate then thrive, as it did here. The real beauty however, came from the flowers. As one walked down one of the many pathways on a carpet verdant grass, the first thing to assault your senses was the fragrance. An enchanting bouquet that changed with every step. Almost instantaneously followed by myriad of color. It was virtually impossible to keep your eyes on any one spot as your peripheral vision kept finding something even more wondrous. Thus steeling your attention, again and again. A living, growing Mobius strip, never ending and forever changing. The only thing missing in this scene of perfection was a newborn deer, with its proud mother gently nudging and encouraging her offspring to walk on unsteady legs. Undoubtedly though, if you stayed here long enough the afore mentioned scenario would assuredly play out.

This was a sacred place, a Holy place, a safe place. When man slept and the mind was free of the confines of the body, it was here it came. Unconsciously, it was a sanctuary that we all know, at one time or another everyone has been here. A fortunate few actually live here, or at least they did!

Lama Ngawang walked the gardens as he usually did at this time of day. Not one inch of this miraculous place was unknown to him. His footfall was steady and even as he negotiated the many twists and turns of this existent Elysium. All the more remarkable, considering he was blind.

Not as old as most Lama's, it was still difficult to place him into an age bracket. A small man, maybe only five feet four. He was dangerously thin, skeletal even, plus the fact his head was shaven probably made him look older than he was. The traditional Buddhist robes hung from him like sackcloth, exposing pointed elbows and visible ribs through his near translucent skin. This sightless, delicate and fragile man however, was far from weak. He oozed an inner strength, a vehemence that all that met him could not help but feel. Part love, part reverence was the feeling he left you with after only the briefest of contacts.

Ngawang stopped momentary, turned then spoke in a gentle voice.

"Ah, my faithful attendant Tenzin. It always lifts my heart to have you nearby." He said with an affectionate smile. "Come, walk with me."

The elderly newcomer nodded silently and joined his master. He was clearly older than the Lama, and not dressed in Buddhist robes, but the garments of a peasant. Like his father and grandfather before him, the attendant didn't quite follow the Guru's teachings. Serving his master and living a clean life was more than acceptable to justify his place here.

"It isn't the same without the students, is it my trusty companion?" It wasn't a question that needed answering.

They continued in silence for the remainder of the promenade, until finally coming to rest in a small enclosed clearing.

"Please sit Tenzin," the Lama said in a voice akin to father about to have a *special* chat was his son.

Doing as he was told, Tenzin sat crossed legged on the soft grass, closely followed by Ngawang.

After some long painful moments, the silence was eventually broken.

"We have known each other for many many years, in fact, I would not be wrong in saying that you are my only true friend here."

"And you mine," Tenzin said quietly.

"But we have never spoken like friends, have we?"

"No Master, it's not my place, I live only to serve. It's all I know."

Which of course was true. The attendant had been groomed for his current appointment from a very early age.

"Well today, let us forget rules and etiquette, I want us a talk like the old friends that we truly are."

"I must admit Lama, that I will find that difficult." The old man only spoke the truth.

"I understand that Tenzin, but its vital that you try." It would have been simple for Ngawang to gently probe the mind of Tenzin and make things a little more acceptable for him, but he wanted the forthcoming events to be entirely natural.

"First thing old friend, it would make me very happy if you called me Nathan."

"Nathan?"

"Yes Tenzin, it's a name I haven't used in a very long time, but none the less it my true and given name."

"I am still finding this very hard Lam.. sorry Nathan."

"It's ok," Nathan said in a soft soothing voice, while lightly and affectionately placing a hand on his friends' shoulder. "Of course it will seem strange Tenzin, I would never normally expect this of you, but time is of the essence."

The old man nodded; finally he began to understand.

"Let me try and make it a little easier. Imagine, speaking hypothetically of course, that today is our last together. Now I know as a matter of factly that your mind is full of questions. So please ask what you would do if this was our last meeting."

"But you aren't speaking hypothetically are you Nathan?" Tenzin's voice was sorrowful and somber.

"No."

Another awkward silence ensued, which Nathan let be, until finally Tenzin spoke. His words were direct and to the point.

"Are you a God?"

The question was a valid one. Maybe not a Buddhist, but Tenzin's beliefs were still very much polytheistic.

Even so, Nathan's laughter echoed around the garden, startling Tenzin in the process. In his many years here, he had never once heard his Master laugh.

"Oh my dear friend, please forgive me alarming you." Nathan was still smiling. It was true; he hadn't laughed in an Eon. "No, no, no, I am not a God. Far from it in fact. Tell me, what makes you ask that? "

Decades of ice at long last broken. Tenzin found he could finally speak freely.

"To be perfectly honest Nathan, I don't know where to start."

"Well just tell me your suspicions that led you to your conclusion."

"Ok," the attendant seemed lost in thought for a moment before continuing. "There's this place for a start." The two men instinctively looked around. "As you very well know, I have left here infrequently, but even an uneducated man like myself, is more than aware that the climate, the perpetual flowering, even the manner of things grown here are all unnatural."

"Uneducated? That just isn't true my faithful companion, you are one of the wisest and astute people I have ever met." Nathan meant what he said. "But as for this Eden, as much as I'd like to, I can't take credit for it. It has always been here and I deeply hope it always will be. I merely inherited it. Once I am gone, it will pass to another."

"I too hope this place remains." There was a tinge of sadness in his voice. He didn't seem convinced.   "Now though, back to you. I have served you for over fifty years, before me, it was my father and grandfather before him. In fact more generations than is recorded of my family have attended you. How long have you been here? "

"To be precise, I am not sure, but it's nearly five hundred years. I was a broken man when I first came here, the keeper at the time nurtured and looked after me. So the early years are not clear, but I will tell you what I do remember later. Let us concentrate on one thing at a time."

If Tenzin was suprised at the answer he was just given he didn't show it.

"How old are you Nathan? "

"Hhmm, that's harder to answer than the last question. The best I can do is say that I am as old as intelligent man. Sorry its abit vague." Nathan was genuinely apologetic.

This time the old man couldn't help but raise an eyebrow, but he quickly got back to the subject at hand.

"Again, as long as records have been kept, there is no account of food passing your lips. Have you fasted all this time? "

"More or less, yes. As have already mentioned I was sick, both physically and mentally when I arrived. I was fed then, until the time was, that I was my own man again. It was my own choice to fast." Nathan paused before asking softly. "I know this is allot to take in, how are you coping? We can stop if you want."

"I am fine, plus I now know the importancy of this to you, and the urgency."

"Thank you." The relief was clear in Nathan's voice.

"Your blind, but you see better than a mountain hawk. Before now, I have witnessed you deviate from the path you are walking, just to pick up an injured chick hidden in the undergrowth, and place it back in it's nest."

"Yes, once again you are correct. Granted, I *do* have perfect sight and am fully aware of my surroundings. Also if I wish I may look through the eyes of those around me." Nathan's tone changed slightly. "This wasn't always the case, on my arrival here I was truly blind and lived in the darkness. Until, however, I was ready to let in the light."

Tenzin didn't press that avenue any further; instead, he continued with the friendly but difficult interrogation.

"Once a year for twenty eight days, you lock yourself away and see no-one, not even I may disturb you. Until now I presumed it was for meditation. I am wrong aren't I?"

"Not entirely no. What was left in my quarters was only my body, no more than a shell, my erm. . essence was elsewhere."

"Can you explain?"

Of course, we have no more secrets." Nathan shifted slightly before continuing. "I have known for some time that eventually I will have to rejoin civilization. But technology, language, even dress, changes oh so quickly. Not even electricity was invented when I first arrived here." Nathan laughed. "So for four weeks of a year I leave my body, and live in the mind of someone in the Western world. Just as an observer, at times a voyeur. I lived as they lived, felt what they felt, learnt what they learnt, but never interfering. I have to be prepared for my return; otherwise I would be no better than a caveman lost in a city. Ahh, Tenzin, I wish you could have seen the things I have. Over the years I have delivered babies, taught eager school children, found cures for diseases. I have flown a plane, dived the oceans, even sang on a stage." Nathan paused uncomfortably once again. "Not all my hostings were wondrous and enjoyable. I have been addicted to narcotics, sold my body for money, beaten my wife and siblings. I have learnt much, and forgotten nothing."

"Are you ready to return?"

"Being ready or not is unimportant. The timing of my reappearance was never in my hands."

"Soon then?"

"Yes."

Another long silence ensued. Nathan could tell his faithful attendant was upset. As much as he didn't like to see Tenzin this way, unfortunately there wasn't much he could do. The forthcoming events had already begun, and time was short.

"Anyway old friend, correct me if I am wrong, but I do believe it soon to be dark. So let's retire to the relative comfort of the monastery. We still have much to discuss." Nathan said in an all-together lighter tone, whilst already arising. Tenzin also rose, somewhat slowly and took up his usual position, which was one full step behind his mentor.

"Please comrade, it would make me happy if you would walk alongside. Now is no longer the time etiquette or tradition."

The old attendant did as he was asked, although it felt awkward. A lifetime of habit was a hard one to break. He also made a real conscious effort to find a brighter side to what was now occurring, but no matter how hard he tried he couldn't lift the feeling of gloom that he felt.

"Come, come Tenzin, things really aren't as bad as you think."

"*Can he read my mind?*" Tenzin thought to himself.

"The answer to your question is, yes." Nathan paused. "But the truth is I never have. You have always respected my privacy, so it was only fair that I respected yours."

Tenzin didn't doubt it was truth. Over the years there were many things Ngawang/Nathan hadn't told him, but lie he did not.

As the two men rounded the corner and made their way down the final drag towards the monastery, Tenzin couldn't help but gasp in awe. The sight that he now beheld, a sight he had seen a thousand times, was incredibly, more wondrous than usual.

Maybe it was the unusual stillness. Never before in living memory had this place been so devoid of life as it was now. All the students gone, leaving only the duo that momentary walked side by side, shoulder to shoulder. Both silent, one lost in thought, the other briefly and involuntary speechless at a beauty he had till now taken for granted.

Or maybe, as the sun said its final good-byes to all that listened. Dragging behind him a rose colored cloak, saturating the sky, making the perfect backdrop for the living canvas that was the monastery.

The words to describe the beauty before him haven't yet been invented. More than words even, it was a feeling. Akin to a mother seeing her newborn child for the first time. Like the saying goes, "there is only one beautiful newborn baby in the world, and it belongs to EVERY mother."

Well, the monastery belonged every mother.

The basic structure of the temple was no different to the thousands of others dotted around the globe. Multi tiered and very similar in shape to a Japanese pagoda, but altogether on a much larger scale. What made this building wholly unique however, was like the rest of the garden, the monastery was *alive*. Not one inch of wood, stone or whatever else was used in the original construction could be seen under the floral cladding.

At this time hour, to compliment the terracotta sky, the blossom was a liquid gold. It's molten form rippling with pride. Whereas at sunup, she would be a soft lilac, making sure she was easy on the student's still blurry eyes. More precious than any metal, rarer than any gem, the temples wallpaper was of incalculable worth.

The two men, both still silent, finally reaching the anterior of the temple, walked slowly up the two steps that encircled the building, before stopping briefly on the veranda.

Nathan turned, at first his unseeing eyes seemingly looking over the garden, then further afield at the colossal Himalayas that flanked them at all sides. They were the protective mothers, ever watching their unknown child.

"Magnificent, truly magnificent." Nathan whispered, shaking his head. "I genuinely believe I am the luckiest man alive to have been a part of this place for so long. God I will miss it Tenzin." There was an unhappy pause, before Nathan added, "you have seen me laugh today old friend; I don't want the indignity of you seeing me weep. Come let us go inside."

The two mammoth oak doors opened silently at the merest of touches, happily inviting the pair in. Strangely though, they were the only part of the temple untouched by bloom. Undecorated, but far from plain, the many eyes in the knotted wood could tell a thousand stories.

The room was immense, encompassing nearly all of the ground floor. It could, and normally did hold hundreds of students. Totally bare, apart from the wooden supporting pillars, many scented candles and one whole wall a devoted shrine to Buddha. This room was used only for prayer. The many levels above housed the student's dormitories, kitchens (including the grain store), extensive library, places for meditation as well as *special* training rooms. No part of the monastery was left fallow.

Nathan's' quarters was a small annex, through a nondescript door, on the west wall facing the shrine. It was there the two men entered after bowing briefly to an ever-smiling Buddha.

The tiny room made a prison cell seem cluttered, consisting of two painfully thin mattresses (one for sleeping on), a plain wooden table, and somewhat of an anomaly in this part of the world, a western style rocking chair, probably English and definitely very old. There were no shelves, no trinkets, no personal momentous, not even a book decorated the room. A Buddhist, even a Lama had no craving for comfort or luxury, simply, this is how they lived. Following the path for spiritual enlightenment was the only importance.

Nathan gestured for Tenzin to sit on the spare mattress. He obliged, his old bones complaining until finally he was seated, crossed legged in the usual fashion.

Nathan followed suit, slowly easing himself into the battered chair.

"Arthritis getting worse old friend?" An unfamiliar half smile spread across Nathan's lips as he spoke.

"No, no, its not too bad, just old age catching up with me." Tenzin would never admit how bad it really was or the true pain he was in.

"Ok, even though I am not convinced that you are telling me the whole truth. I am sorry to sound cold, but we will discuss your problems later. Right now, time is of the essence and we have much ground still to cover."

"Of course," Tenzin nodded understandingly.

"Before we continue, would you like anything to drink?"

"I am fine, thank you."

"Good, good. Let us resume, I know you still have many questions. I must apologize once more for putting you through this, but it must be done and finished today."

"No need."

Tenzin paused for a moment, thinking, until he asked. "I know enough to realize your teachings here are not from one of the four schools of Buddhism, and yet, all the Lama's from the various schools send only their best students here to train. Even the Dalai Lama himself, comes here and requests to see *you!* I have always found that very confusing."

"Hmm, yes." Nathan had to ponder for many seconds. "Good question, difficult to answer, but good none the less. I shall try my best. Buddhism is probably the only religion where the truth is more important than what is written. For instance, if Allah showed up on earth proclaiming that the Muslim faith was the only true one and that there is only one god, even with the undeniable evidence put before him, a catholic would still argue until blue in the face that his religion is the still only true one. Are you with me so far? "

"I think so, please continue."

"Anyway it was my good fortune, or perhaps even fate," Nathan said lifting one eyebrow slightly, "that I ended up here. Quite exactly how I got here is still unknown to me, so I cannot answer any questions related to that part of my life, I am sorry."

There was another thoughtful pause before he continued.

"Please excuse me, I digress. As I have already mentioned, on my arrival I was a broken man, an empty shell akin to a newborn infant. The keeper at the time, Lama Shepa, took me in, looked after me, nurtured me, taught me. Finally, after many months, I was my own man again. That was when I decided to tell him of my purpose for existing. The old Lama just smiled at me and said he already knew." Nathan said laughing kindly.

"Your purpose for existing?" Tenzin queried.

"Yes, yes old friend, but please, one thing at a time, we will get to that."

The old attendant nodded, and let him continue.

"I held nothing back, all that I could remember I told. Even, everything about the *others.*"

Tenzins' mouth started to move, but then he thought better of it and remained silent.

"Once I had finished my story, the keeper wasted no time. He summoned the Dalai Lama and some of the nearest Lama's, all of whom came within two days. When they had all arrived, I repeated what I told Shepa. After a lengthy discussion it was decided that even though it greatly went against the Buddhist teachings, that they would help me, as long as I followed the path to my best ability. In fact, for them it was a simple choice to make, what good would Buddhism be, without anyone to practice it." Nathan eased back on his chair, letting it rock slowly, then added. " Hence the reason for the temple to be run the way it is and the students from the four schools being sent here. Like I said, I was lucky to have ended up here, for *no* other religion would have put themselves second, but of course my existence isn't common knowledge, only the chosen few know the truth."

The two men stared at each other for some time; it was Nathan that broke the spell.

"That hasn't really answered your question, has it? " Nathan said smiling.

"Well no, but...."

"The next question, the one you are dyeing to ask, will do however." Nathan interrupted.

"You mentioned existence, others, purpose. What is your purpose Nathan? " The question was straight and too the point.

"Well Tenzin, quite simply, with the help of three others, when the time comes, to try and stop the destruction of mankind." Nathan's answer was also straight.

"And the time is now?"

"Soon, yes I believe so." There was no trace of doubt in his voice.

"Destruction by what?"

"More of a case by whom, old friend."

"Whom? I am sorry, I don't understand." Tenzin couldn't hide his confusion.

"I know this isn't easy for you and still allot to take in, here, I will explain the best I can. The one constant that all the religions of the world have is that they all speak of a savior. One that is either still to come or that has already been."

Tenzin, listening as if his life depended on it, nodded in agreement.

"But there is also another constant, which, I am sure you have guessed by now is, there is always a Dark Force trying to gain ascendancy. It's the Ying and Yang of the universe, and with time not being important, it stands to reason that eventually the darkness will win."

"Will win? So you are saying that your purpose is pointless?"

"No, no, far from it. We were created to stop this happening, and Buddha willing we will."

"But you are not sure?" There was the slightest of trembles in Tenzins voice.

"I cannot be sure, the future isn't written."

"You talked about fate earlier, if you believe in fate doesn't that mean that the future *is* written?"

Once again Nathan's laugh startled the aged attendant.

"You don't miss a thing my wily old friend. This is also hard for me to put into words. Let's just say that fate does exist, but only in the smaller picture. I could have told you many things that would happen before they did, but they are all trivial and would not affect our ultimate destiny." Nathan took the briefest of breathers before adding. "Understand?"

"Erm. Yes I think so."

"Please don't worry, I don't expect you to take this all in and comprehend everything in one go. I am just giving the facts for now, understanding will come in time."

"Let's hope we have time." Tenzins said in barely a whisper.

"Time you will have plenty of, that is one thing I can assure you."

"But?"

"No buts, all I ask is you to trust me."

"You know I do."

"Thank you."

"You say that you and three others were created. By whom? Was it by a God and if so which one?"

Nathan's lips curled into the slyest of smiles before answering.

"That is one question I cant *or* won't answer. Some things are meant not to be known."

"Yes, I accept that. It was silly of me ask. So how are you and the others going to stop what is coming, and are the others the same as you?"

"Again I cant be sure exactly what *is* coming, so I can not tell you how we will try to stop it, but there is more to me than meets the eye. The others are like me yes in many ways, but we are all individuals. Once we were inseparable."

"What happened?"

"Two of the others fell out over a woman, would you believe. So one of us left leaving three. I had always felt to being the outsider and once we became three, things were no longer the same, so after some centuries, I too left. I know that it might sound a long time to make up ones mind to follow my own path, but you have to remember that days, years, centuries, in fact *time* means little to us."

"Something happened to you once you left, something bad. That's why you ended up here, didn't it?"

"Yes."

"Do you want to tell me?"

"Yes Tenzin I do, that was one of the main reasons for our chat today. Are you comfortable, this may take some time."

The old attendant had already noticed a marked change in Nathan, not physically of course, but more of a case of his whole persona was different. It was no longer the demure, quiet man that he had grown to love sitting opposite him. This in itself wasn't a problem now Tenzin knew what he did, but there was something else nagging at him. Something that he couldn't quite put his finger on, but he was sure it was to do with something Nathan had said. Then it dawned on him and he wasn't sure he liked it. This question Tenzin almost loathed to ask, but knew he had to.

"I am fine, but before we continue, there is something troubling me. It's probably nothing but may I just for a few moments, change the subject slightly?"

"Yes, Yes old friend, please tell me what's wrong." The concern was clear in Nathan's tone.

"It's not easy to put this in simple words but I will try to my best ability. You have told me that you are one of four, also, you have mentioned the destruction of mankind."

Tenzin paused briefly, and if Nathan knew where this line of enquiry was going, his body language didn't betray him, for only his lips moved.

"Go on."

"You speak of your 'purpose' and tell that you are as old a Man."

"This is correct."

"Well, my knowledge in Western Christianity is limited, but I do know a little. What you have told me so far has an uncanny resemblance to, I am not quite sure of the correct words, but if I remember rightly its the Four Riders of the Apocalypse."

"Horsemen." Nathan corrected him.

"Ah yes, of course. Are you one of them?"

"Over the years and in many religions we have had many names. In answer to your question, yes, that is one epithet that has been used."

"I thought so, but correct me if I am wrong. Isn't it written that you will *cause* the destruction of mankind?"

Nathan laughed once more, this time however Tenzin was more annoyed than startled.

"Is this a laughing matter?" Tenzin didn't try to hide his irritation.

"No, please forgive me. I shouldn't have laughed, especially since you don't know the true story. You see, my friends and I have been the victim of the ultimate bad press."

"Bad press? I am sorry I don't understand." Irritation was quickly replaced by confusion.

"Sorry, I wasn't thinking, it's a western saying, there is no way you could have known it. It will be simpler for you to understand if I put it this way. It has always been a source of amusement for myself and the others, knowing that we walk the earth amongst *normal* people, yet, the whole of Christianity believes us to be their destroyers. All because whoever originally wrote about us, misinterpreted the vision, sign or signals they were given. How he or them even knew anything about us is beyond my understanding, but I can assure that what is written is wrong."

"How can you be so sure?"

"I'm sorry?" It was now Nathan that showed a little annoyance. " I have never lied to you Tenzin and I know *exactly* what my reasons for being here are."

"No you misunderstand me Nathan. I do not for a second doubt what you have told me. What I am trying to get at is, say the person that made the predictions wasn't wrong."

"Now it's my turn to be confused, am I missing something?"

"You tell me a Dark Force is near and you and your friends are going to try and stop it taking ascendance, but what if by your interference you involuntary *cause* mans demise?"

Nathan leant back on his chair and nodded.

"Ahh, I see what you mean now. When I said that you are one of the most astute people I have ever known, I wasn't wrong. I can honestly say that your theory had never even crossed my mind, but what I do know is the Dark Force I told you about, is pure evil and has to be stopped."

"Is there no other way to stop it?"

"No. The reason the time is now is because man is weak. Faith in goodness is at an all time low, the timing is perfect. We have to try to stop it. The alternative is worse than the darkest nightmare for any that are left. I am sorry Tenzin, but knowing the outcome if we don't succeed, I can't believe your theory no matter how valid it sounds." Nathan's words were full of conviction.

"That's good enough for me, and I wish with all my heart that you triumph, but you understand I had to air my trepitations."

"Yes of course and I shall mention it to the others when once again we assemble."

The two men sat in silence for many moments. Nathan hadn't been prepared for the last part of the conversation, so he needed a little time to let Tenzins observation or warning even, to sink in, before composing himself and continuing where they had left off.

"Right! So where were we before we went off track? And please don't worry about changing the subject briefly, I am glad you told me of your fears."

"Thank you. I think you were about to tell me the story of how you ended up here." The relief was clear in the old mans voice, knowing Nathan understood.

"Ah yes, I was about to tell you the story of place now known as *Roanoke*. Please bare in mind that the memory has been locked away for a long time now, so some minor details might be incorrect, but the basics of the story is as true as I remember. So if you are ready," Nathan paused, made himself comfortable and checked Tenzin was also the same.

"Then I shall begin."

My narrative is from an era long ago past, a time gone by of nearly five hundred years.

The world was in a period of great change, adventure and discovery. New lands, cultures and freshly acquired knowledge were beginning to assimilate into every day life.

My existence was nomadic, a simple drifter, traveling from place to place.

As I am sure you can imagine, a man with my talents can turn his hand to many things, so as long as my belly was full, I was content. In fact, it was one of the happier periods of my life.

Eventually I ended up at Plymouth, England. There was an excitement and bustle in this harbour that I hadn't experienced before. You could almost physically feel the electric anticipation as a ship docked. The normally impossibly clamorous town would fall almost silent as everyone held their breath, waiting to see what new treasures would be brought ashore.

Being no more than a keen observer however, I became increasingly troubled that the setting reminded me of a meddling child continually trying to open Pandora's notorious box,(the horrific Black Death being a case in point), but it wasn't my place to interfere.

That was when I decided it was the right juncture for me to move on again, so I gained passage on a ship headed for the New World.

The ships' name escapes me although it may have been The Tyger, and the fleet consisted of four or six vessels, but trivial details like that are unimportant, and from little I can remember, the journey was mostly uneventful. I thought the easiest route would be to become a ships hand to pay for my voyage. Work on a ship back then was a profession with an extremely low life expectancy, due to constant danger and malady. So finding a Captain willing to take me wasn't difficult, in fact, I could have had a choice of vessels. One small but not at all unexpected problem was the way the paid and veteran crew treated newcomers like myself. They would never put any of us in any real danger, but the distaste and sometimes even hate for any of the "part time" crew, was as clear as day on their faces. They knew that a ship couldn't function without our numbers, but bullying was still rife and not just from the crew.   Not only were the passengers made up with a contingent of gifted civilians, such as craftsman, scholars and alike. There was also small garrison of soldiers aboard headed by an odious and bitter man named Ralph Lane. General Lane he insisted on being called, although any military history he had was quickly glossed when over brought up. Anyway, Lane (I refuse to call him General) took an instant disliking to me. It didn't unduly trouble me as it was something I was long used too. Being small in stature, quiet and preferring my own company, I had always been an easy target, especially since I rarely had any friends to back me up or fight in my corner. My steadfast refusal to pander to Lanes' hugely inflated ego (the title of General should be earned, not bought) didn't help my situation. In fact it was my stubbornness that ultimately was responsible for the tragic event that later followed. Pride can be a perilous thing.

Here, let me digress for a moment. I made a vow to myself a long long time ago to live as an ordinary man, to let my talents lie dormant as much as that would be possible. A task easier said than done. Imagine if you will, a drug addict trying to kick his foul habit by keeping a small amount of his chosen poison always close to hand, his misguided logic is one of, if he knows he can satisfy his craving if he really must, therefore he never will. Surprisingly, the theory behind this is a sound one, but what theory cannot account for is that an addict is an addict, and even the slightest of temptation, nearly always ends in disaster. Even though I strived to live as normal a life as possible, I was still the fore mentioned addict, knowing my talents were always with me no matter how much I tried to pretend otherwise. Because of this, no matter how much the quiet loner I craved to be, I invariably oozed a confidence many misconstrued to be arrogance. Hence I made enemies as easy as I made friends, most likely even more so. Someone as self-conceited as Lane, it was unacceptable in his tiny mind to have the likes of me within close quarters. Hate and more dangerously jealousy quickly made me his biggest enemy.

I must apologize for straying a little there, and I shall continue forthwith, but I need you to understand me as much as possible, including any mistakes I have made, whether subconscious or not.

Back on the Tyger, the soldiers under the command of Lane also knew of his loathing for me, which suited them. He could be an evil and despicable man to any he took a disliking too, so while he was focused on me, the rest of the garrison had it fairly easy. For that reason alone my voyage was made doubly difficult, most of the men were happy to keep a low profile, stick to their duties and not get involved. However, unsurprisingly a small contingent of equally small-minded officers DID get involved. Scrabbling and scrapping like hogs in a sty, grateful for any snippet of favor tossed to them by Lane. Everything began innocently enough, with me always being assigned the vexatious and unpleasant chores. Admittedly I probably didn't help matters though. All the tasks given to me, I completed, never complaining, quicker and to a higher standard than anyone else could have managed. All the while keeping the faintest of sly smiles (which my old comrades used to say, I did so annoyingly well) upon my face as I toiled. Unable to crack me or my spirit, the foul tasks soon became physical ones, to be completed by me alone, even when it was clear two or more should labour together. Mindless duties that served no purpose other than to break me. At this point things changed ever so slightly for me, some of the other passengers and crew began to sympathise with my plight. Still no help was offered, (Lanes' wrath wasn't worth the risk), but a small few would give me the odd nod of encouragement and sometimes I would find a handful of extra rations tucked into my bedding. It's always good to know that there's some trace of humanity left, no matter how small.

A turning point came, with a solid oak table of all things. Now I had traveled to many strange and wonderful lands, met some amazing people and cultures, but at this point in history, the British were the most arrogant and pompous I had ever encountered (and that is saying something).

They truly believed that the known world was theirs for the taking, and that it was their right to rule over all. No matter how idiotic or inconvenient it would make things, they insisted on taking whatever luxuries they could fit in the space available. Why on earth a colossal solid oak table would be needed on a voyage of discovery to the new world, is beyond me. Purely, a foolish extravagance, nothing more. Even with the journey drawing to close, Lane was resolute that he wished to change cabins from the bow to the stern of the ship, (and believe me they were deceptively large vessels). It was a futile exercise that served no purpose other than to once again try and break my sprit. As tempted as I was, I made sure that nothing was broken or damaged in any way. I refused to give the man any ammunition to blacken me even more. All that remained in his now vacant stateroom was the absurdly expensive and tasteless table. An impossible task lay before me. I would not be beaten, but I could see no way how I could transport it the length of the ship. Inch by painful inch, I slowly dragged the monstrosity through the bowls of the ship. A vessel not designed for easy transport of this future antique.

"Enough is enough," a kindly voice said behind me.

I turned to see a friendly looking well dressed man, slowly shaking his head.

"You take one end and I'll lift the other, we'll do this together."

"Thank you, but no, this is my trial and there is no need for you to get involved, I can manage."   "Nonsense my good man, you're a man not a beast and this is the last straw. Don't worry if you are thinking I shall get in trouble with Lane, it's ok, I am sure I can handle the likes of him." The fellow said with a glint in his eye.

"Excuse my rudeness, my name is Annanias." With that he struck out a welcoming hand.

I was literally taken aback for a moment by this stranger's clemency. Not because of just the offer of help, but I instantly liked the chap stood before. I also felt a little embarrassed that I had been too busy in my own little world to have noticed or acknowledged him earlier.

"Sorry, I'm Nathan, you really don't have to do this," I replied, but he just grasped my hand and shook it vigorously.

"Don't be silly, now come on, time waits for no-one and this eyesore wont move itself."

Even with two, it was still a momentous undertaking. We worked in silence, but it was a comfortable one, both of us fully focused with the job in hand. Prior to the last push before we reached the deck, something dawned on me.

"It was you that left the extra food in my bunk?" I said feeling strangely humbled.

"No, no friend, you have my good wife Eleanor to thank for that. You'd be surprised how many of us are appalled at your treatment."

"Well I shall of course thank her personally at the first opportunity. I must admit though that I do feel somewhat ashamed I haven't observed either of you earlier." I meant what I said.

"Please don't Nathan, my wife has not been in the best of health for the journey and stayed in our cabin most of the time, and I of course tended to her, so the chances of seeing us would have been slim at best. We still have friends aboard and are kept up to date with the day to day happenings, including the disgraceful treatment of your good self." The sorrow was clear in his voice.

It was obvious to me that this was a good person with a large heart and even though I hadn't met her, I knew his wife was equally as virtuous.

"Sick you say? Is there anything I can do? I might not look much, but you'd be surprised at my talents, especially in the field of healing (as well as numerous others)." As I have mentioned earlier I made a vow to myself to live a normal a life as possible, there would always be certain situations or occasions where I would break it. If she was ill and I could help her, then it would be done.

"I hardly know you Nathan, but I believe you entirely. Already you are turning out to be a happy conundrum and I am genuinely sorry for not making your acquaintance earlier, and for that please forgive me. But I am sure you realize that my priorities had to be with Eleanor, as you obviously know some woman can be so demanding." Annanias said with a smile, somehow turning what could have been a grave conversation into a lighthearted one.

"Thank you however for your kind offer, but there is really no need. The uneven motion of the ship is mainly to blame, as well as couple of other factors, which will become clear soon enough. When the time comes I am sure your services will be called upon, as neither of us have much faith in the talents of the ships drunken necromancer."

A silent nod then passed between us, no more words were needed.

We only had to negotiate a vexatious staircase before reaching the deck and some welcome fresh air. Finally we did it. The table was set down while we rested. The kiss of the sea's breath was a passionate one, which made us both feel lightheaded for a moment in a narcotic stupor.

" Come on my friend, lets get this thankless task finished, I have built up quite an appetite and would like you to join Eleanor and I for dinner, she is eating again at last."

It was a kind and genuine offer, which I couldn't accept but before I had a chance to decline, the thing I was dreading happened.

"STOP RIGHT THERE!" a familiar voice boomed from behind me. I turned to see Lane standing there red faced, surrounded by his entourage of jackals'.

"HOW DARE YOU." He literary screamed.

"Is there a problem Lane?" Annanias calmly asked.

Before Lane could answer, Annanias walked towards him and stopped slightly in front of me, as if shielding or protecting me.

"I gave that man a job to do, alone. You have no reason sticking your nose in where it's none of your business." Lane had somewhat composed himself now.

"That man, as you so eloquently put it, has a name, and it is Nathan. If you speak of him again, use his name, is that clear?"I am not sure whether it was Lane or myself who was taken aback most by the way Annanias spoke.

"You don't tell me what to do." Lane growled.

"Nor do you tell me what to do, and I shall stick my nose where ever I see fit. Do you have a problem with that?"

I was becoming increasingly uneasy with the situation brewing, and by now the whole ships crew had diverted it attention to the scene playing out to what could only be an unhappy conclusion. Unusually for me, I was at a complete loss at to what could be done to diffuse matters.

"If it wasn't for your father in law."

I later discovered that Annanias' father in law was John White, the already named governor of any permanent settlement founded and in overall charge of the fleet.

"I would never hide behind my father in laws cloak, and you know that Lane, you just use him as an excuse because you fear me, isn't that right? Annanias took a step towards Lane, who in turn followed suit.

Before any blood was shed, and I am sure that would have been the inevitable outcome, the ship lurched and came to a sudden dead stop. It had run aground and now was leaning at a dangerously obtuse angle. Every man standing was thrown violently to the deck, most landing in an undignified heap. Everybody's eyes had been on the exchange between Lane and Annanias including whoever's job it was to watch for potential hazards like the one we just encountered. I pitied the poor soul, for he would be in a whole heap of trouble.

After myself; Annanias was the first to his feet, closely followed by Lane. Thankfully I noticed Annanias was unhurt, but so was Lane, mores the pity. The table had crashed into the port bulwark, luckily not crushing anyone, unfortunately, that too was undamaged.

"Are you ok Nathan?" Annanias asked genuinely concerned.

I did look the fragile type, so he did have grounds for his anxiety. I merely nodded.

"Good, please excuse me, but I must check on Eleanor."

"Yes, yes, do go, I'll see you ashore."

Annanias gave me a somewhat quizzical look, turned, and hurried off.

The commotion on the ship was deafening, orders being barked from all directions, cries of injured shipmen, the events from only moments ago already forgotten. I could see that the shore was less than a mile away, and knowing the vessels few longboats would only carry about twelve. It was obviously going to be a long process to ferry everybody off the ship, and that I would be left till last, if at all. So I made the easy decision to make my own arrangements. With everything going on, I was ignored and unnoticed. So in less than a blink of an eye, I lifted the damned table with one hand, threw it over-board, closely followed my good self.

It was good to feel ground under my feet again, the soft sand felt as true as the hardest of marbles. The Suns' rays welcomed me with warm fingers and the softest of motherly kisses. The silence was sublime, broken only by the intermittent conversations of the jungle's native dwellers. Their curious chatter focused on the strange looking newcomer.

I sat in the sand and lay back, eyes closed, savoring the short-lived tranquility.

As predicted, it wasn't long before I could hear a muffled murmur coming from some distance away.

I sat up and slowly opened one eye, my blurry vision taking a little time to focus. The three longboats belonging to the Tyger were making their way to the shore, powered by some very in adept oarsmen by the looks of things.

As they drew closer, the first distinguishable sound was one of heavy laughter, and I instantly recognized its source, Annanias. I also had a sneaking suspicion that I knew what caused him such merriment. With both eyes now open, I focused properly, to the point where I could have been stood on the bow of the boat. Lanes' back was to the shore, but he must have been confused at Annanias's amusement, so he turned. It took a moment for what he saw to sink in, and when it did his face became a perfect mixture of incredulity and enragement. Seeing me sat happily on the deserted beach was bad enough, but to rub salt into his wounds, gleaming in sun looking newer than ever beside me, was the table.

Once they reached the shore, Lane disembarked the Longboat and stormed past me, trying (unsuccessfully) not to make eye contact with me. Then he proceeded to order what soldiers he had brought to start making a defensive perimeter. A paranoid gesture in my eyes, but I was unaware that this wasn't Lane's first visit to the island.

I strode to the waters edge, eager to greet Annanias once again. He spent a few moments being the perfect gentleman and helping whom I assumed to be his wife off the boat and carried her to the shore. The pair being very much in love was obvious, just by the way he carried her and the way she nestled her head close to his body. Also the reason I haven't seen her aboard and her sickness was crystal-clear, she was heavily pregnant. To many, the wisdom of bringing someone in her condition on such a long and dangerous journey would be questionable, but to me it just showed the unbreakable love that they shared for each other, unable to be apart for more than a few hours. Such a thing was rare in a time when marriage was seen mostly as a way of gaining wealth, land or a peerage.

Annanias lightly and carefully let his wife down, safely away from the gentle lapping waves, but before he could make any formal introductions, she marched over and embraced me tightly like I was an old friend. I was stunned to say the least (and that doesn't happen often). I caught Annanias's eye and he just smiled, no hint of surprise whatsoever on his face.

"Nathan, its so good to finally meet you." She said in a divinely hypnotic voice, still gripping my hand tightly.

It was now for the first time that I had a proper look at her. It wasn't just her voice that was angelic, she was truly beautiful.

During my nomadic existence over the past few millennia I have had encounters with many attractive woman, but the Venus before me, surpassed them all. A beauty that continued right down as far as her soul. In any surroundings she would be like a diamond in the dust.

Rivaling even, the Jezebel that tore us apart, yes she was beautiful, but sadly her soul differed by being mostly crepuscular.

I just stood there, mouth open like a village idiot, mesmerized by the bluest of eyes.

Eyes that reminded me of an old friend.

She spoke once again, breaking the spell I was momentary under.

"I must apologize, I haven't formally introduced myself, but I am sure you have gathered that I am Eleanor, Annanias's better half, and here to keep him out of trouble." She said with a playful taint in her voice.

"Now come, let us find shelter from this baking Sun." Eleanor announced, whilst interlocking my arm and marching with purpose up the beach, deftly collecting Annanias on the way.

I happened to glance back, and didn't like what I saw. Lane was watching the three of us; the look on his face was a worrying one. A grotesque leer, primeval lust directed at Eleanor.

His thoughts must have been very powerful, because unwittingly I caught a brief snippet of them. He was forming plans for Eleanor (and Annanias), and they weren't pleasant.

One detail was clear though; Lane was completely insane.

The intervening few weeks passed swiftly and without incident. Mainly because, originally unbeknown to me, Eleanor's father was John White, the man in overall charge of this whole venture and governor of the now named Cittie of Raleigh.

Incidentally, I also learnt this wasn't Lane's first visit to the island, but the reasons behind his hasty retreat were shrouded in secrecy.

As a father, John White had lot to be desired, but as an organizer and leader of men he was remarkable. He was a formidable and imposing figure, his word was law and everyone knew it. He showed no favoritism and didn't suffer fools. If one was given a task, it was done, pure and simple. Annanias was his right hand man, because he excelled at his job and for no other reason.

During that first month we split into two separate small communities, craftsmen and soldiers.

We were the builders and farmers of this new world, where as Lane and his troops who (for reasons that were beyond me) outnumbered us nearly two to one, did nothing but endless drills and patrols. Not even when an extra strong pair of hands were needed would they help us, but they still expected us feed them.

There were natives on the island, they kept themselves hidden and too my knowledge we had nothing to fear from them and maybe a lot to gain by making contact, but Lane forbade this and surprisingly at this time, John White agreed.

They were however watching us, that much I could sense, and their focus seemed to be mainly on Lane and one other, although I could not fathom why.

The other of course, was me.

" Nathan, Nathan, please come quickly, it's Eleanor." Annanias was clearly in a state of panic as he ran towards me.

I barely had time to drop my spade before he was upon me.

"Please try and be calm my good friend and tell me what has happened." I said holding his shaking body. "It's, it's Eleanor, she has taken a fall in the canteen." Annanias was sobbing uncontrollably.

"Blood, so much blood Nathan, I pleaded with her to take it easy. She's going to die, the baby is going to die, and it's all my fault."

"Look at me Annanias, no one is going to die, now take me to her quickly." I said with a confidence he can't of believed.

Annanias ran like a man possessed and I struggled to keep up, he burst through the canteen doors with me hard on his heels.

The sight before me didn't look good; Eleanor was unconscious on a makeshift bed and deathly pale. The poor excuse for the settlements doctor and the well meaning but inept midwife were hovering over her without actually doing anything. There was a trail of blood and water from where she must have fallen, leading to the bed, and her undergarments were claret.

The doctor turned, looked at us both and shook his head.

"Annanias, I am so sorry, but there is nothing. . . . . ."

"All of you, out, NOW." I said forcefully, cutting the doctor off in mid sentence. There wasn't time for niceties.

"I must protest, there is nothing you can do for her, this just isn't proper," was all the shocked doctor could manage.

Eleanor didn't have time for this, so I faced Annanias who was clearly in a state of shock.

"Do you trust me?"

"Yes, Nathan," he replied without hesitation, distraught as he was, I knew he spoke the truth.

"If you want your wife and unborn child to live, I need to be left alone with them. Now quickly please, and don't return until my say so."

I had got through to him, Annanias walked over to the doctor and midwife and literally grabbed them by the scruff's of their necks and almost carried them out. Their feet scrabbling on the floor and their loud protestations falling on death ears.

Then finally, we were alone.

Since the luxury of time was the one thing Eleanor did not have (and I could do with some myself), I would have to give her some.

I slowed Time down as much as I could (or did I just speed up? I could never quite work out which it was. My friends were convinced it was the latter, but being an old romantic at heart I preferred to look at it the other way) to give us both breathing space.

Awakening facets of me that have happily slept for many many years I thought would be a bit of a shock to the system. I was wrong; it was no more of a shock than slipping on an old pair of comfortable slippers that I haven't worn in a while. Maybe, parts of me weren't quite as dormant as I had liked to believe.

In the short period we had been here, Eleanor, Annanias and I had become the closest of friends, they were good people, always putting others before themselves without a second thought and expecting nothing in return. I would do everything in my power to try and pay back some of the kindness they showed the stranger that I once was to them.

I knelt beside Eleanor's lifeless body and looked deep into her soul. She was a fighter, and a wave of relief washed over me as I detected the faintest spark of life. It would be just enough; the baby however, was dead.

I shut my eyes and let part of me enter her very being. In her present state she was defenseless, so it didn't take me long to find the barely glowing embers of life that she so defiantly clung on to. I softly blew on those embers, lovingly nurturing them until they became a dancing flicker of flame. It was only then when I could safely stop for the time being. Something as delicate as this could not be rushed.

Eleanor deserved some dignity, and looking at her now, she had none.

Thoughtfully the midwife had brought nightclothes and some essentials. So I undressed Eleanor and carefully hand bathed her, washing away all trace of the matted blood from her legs and inner thighs.

I then dressed her and brushed her hair till it shone like a morning sunrise.

That done, I got on my hands and knees and scrubbed the floor till it was also spotless.

Once finished and happy with my work, I jumped back into "normal" time and went back to the now sleeping beauty that was Eleanor.

It gladdened me to discover that the weak dancing flame had become a raging fire and that she was fighting for consciousness, but I wouldn't let that happen just yet.

I stole a lick of flame from her and placed it in the inanimate child. It would not be anywhere near enough to give back life, but I had made a promise and intended to keep it.

Inside me burnt a white-hot inferno, which could probably bring a rock to life, so I was confident that my word would be good.

I borrowed a little from me and mixed it with hers, the result was instantaneous. The unborn infant lived, and wanted out.

I would have to induce labor and do it quickly. To spare Eleanor of any pain, I kept her asleep and took control of the parts of her needed for childbirth. Thankfully, there were no complications and it only took a few moments. I cut the cord, but there was no need to slap this newborn, it was already eager for life. I quickly washed the infant and wrapped it in swaddling.

In my arms, looking at me with unfocused eyes, smiling a huge smile, was the most beautiful baby girl I had ever seen (of course, I may have been slightly biased).

It was now time to arouse Eleanor, I gently let my grips on her conscious fall away, it didn't take long for her to stir.

"Annanias is that you? I am so sorry my love, I was only trying to help out." Eleanor whispered.   "Eleanor, its me Nathan, please, you have nothing to worry about, now sit up and open your eyes." I commanded softly.

Her eyelids slowly opened, it took a moment for her to realize what it was that I was holding out to her. "Here, take her, she's your daughter."

97

"I don't understand, I had an awful dream that she was dead, I remember nothing of the childbirth, where's Annanias?"

"It was just a nightmare, you had a fall and was in shock, that's why you don't remember, Annanias will be here shortly, now take her, she wants her mother."

As soon as I passed the child all questions were forgotten. The bond between mother and daughter was firmly sealed, and due to the special circumstances, this link would be stronger than any other.

The few blissful moments of serenity were shattered by a commotion outside, quickly followed by the door bursting open.

In strode a wrathful John White, flanked by the doctor, a sneering Lane complete with a handful of troops. Amongst the throng I picked out Annanias's deathly pale visage, all fight in him gone, afraid to look, but knowing he must.

"WHO THE HELL DO YOU THINK YOU ARE? AND WHAT DO YOU WANT WITH MY DAUGHTERS BODY? The man was enraged; if he were close enough he would have surely torn me in two.

No words were needed of course, I just smiled and stepped aside, letting what everyone saw speak for itself.

"Father, come and see your granddaughter, Virginia." Eleanor almost sang.

John White glowered at Lane, and then eagerly went to embrace his daughter.

Lane turned to the doctor and whispered something, I am sure it wasn't anything nice, because his face began to drain of color, just as Annanias started to get his back. Joy, relief and many more emotions soon made him tearful and crimson red. He pushed through everyone to join his father in law, wife and babe, he was sobbing now, but still managed to mouth the words "thank you" as he passed.

I was also joyous, it was a good outcome, but I still considered my debt to them far from paid.

This was now a personal time for the family and I had no right to be here, so I turned to leave.

"Wait," all fury gone from White's voice. "I am not sure I understand what has happened here today, or ever will. But, I do know young man, that owe you a debt of gratitude that I can never hope to repay. Tonight there shall be a celebration, a feast, everyone shall attend, and you," He quickly looked at Eleanor and she said something. "Nathan, shall join my kin on my table. From this day forth, I shall consider you as family."

When one has lived as long as I have, seen what I have and can do what I can, it never ever occurred to me that I could feel the vehemence that I felt now. I could honestly say, this was the happiest day of my extensive life.

"Good, glad that is settled. Lane! Make the necessary arrangements, I want us all to eat like Kings." White boomed with a proud taint to his voice.

As I sauntered passed a dour faced Lane, I could not resist giving him a cheery wink as I went on my way.

As much as it galled me, I had to give Lane credit for the spread he laid on. It was magnificent, roasted pig, a milking cow sacrificed for its beef, an array of vegetables, and what seemed like an endless supply of wine and ale flowed. Spirits were high; the air was filled with playful banter and out of key singing by some that had drunk a little too much.

Seated at the head table (which ironically was Lane's beloved oak table, which White had commandeered as his own shortly after arriving here) were myself, Annanias, White, Eleanor and a good as gold sleeping Virginia.

Tables to the left of us, had seated Lane and his mob, while the ones to the right accommodated everyone else. Fires roared in the center giving us welcome heat and light. Once our bellies were full and the evening was drawing to a close, not unexpectedly John White stood up to speak. The hush from nearly one hundred and twenty people was immediate, even the fires, wanting to listen became almost silent.

"Friends, as you are all aware, today has been a momentous day."

A huge cheer broke out, and John White waited patiently until it died down before continuing.

"Virginia," he glanced briefly and the cot and still blissfully sleeping newborn. "is a special child." He quickly raised a hand before another cheer erupted. "Not only because she is hopefully the first of many grandchildren for me, but special because she is our first infant born at our new home, and for that reason she will forever go down in history.

So we should all be proud because we are ALL going to be part of that history." With his hand still raised he turned to me. Surprisingly I felt my cheeks redden. "One of our small community, turned what nearly was a dark day into so far, the most joyful. So it would mean a lot to me and my family if you all rise and join me in a toast."

There was a brief pause, even Lane made the effort to stand.

"TO NATHAN"

"TO NATHAN" echoed across the clearing by all, but one.

As I don't relish attention of any kind I breathed a sigh of relief when White lifted his hand once again.

"BUT, this day is also somewhat tinged with sadness." The silence was once again instant. "For in a few short days, I shall be returning to England." Whispers and murmurs were everywhere.

"There is no need for alarm, and nobody wants too go back less than me, especially with my daughter and grandchild here. But the reason for my return is testament to our success here. We have proved that we can make this our home, so I am only going to collect supplies and some more settlers. Then, like you, I shall be here for good, on that you have my word." From his tone of voice, no one doubted him.

"I have spoken at length with Annanias, and he has agreed to take the place of temporary Governor in my absence. If there are any objections, let me hear them now." There was none, but I could tell that Lane was not happy (did he seriously imagine that the post would be offered to him?), although he said nothing, he made a show of getting up, nodding to White and leaving, following like puppies were a handful of his men.

"One more important thing." People held their breath. "I PROMISE, to be back before the ale runs out." Whoops of laughter and much banging of cups on the tables, all but signaled the end to a most satisfactory day.

The next few days were strange ones for me; I had gone from being a virtually nameless nobody to becoming someone that everyone knew. A small contingent that still believed the myths of witches and alike, steered clear of me, but most people sort me out when suffering any pain or malady. I just explained I knew nothing of medical matters, it was only because I was the eldest of ten brothers living on a remote farm and I had to deliver four of them as no doctors lived close, so I knew a little about childbirth and nothing else. That seemed to satisfy most.

As Annanias was Whites right hand man, on his departure I unwittingly became Annanias's. Many times I tried to explain to him that I didn't want nor enjoy the responsibility but he would just laugh saying I was being my usual overly modest self and anyway, people liked me and that I was doing an excellent job.

Even the normally despicable Lane seemed a changed man; he had no problems with Annanias and myself in charge and was always willing to help. In fact he was being nice, a little too nice.

Impossibly Eleanor was more beautiful than ever, motherhood suited her and it was a running joke that Virginia would smile whenever I was nearby. I was asked to be godfather; it was an honor that I gladly accepted.

Things were going well, but something wasn't right, there was a storm brewing, I could sense it and it made part of me very uneasy.

Then early one morning, it began.

I didn't need much (if any) sleep, so I was taking my usual barefoot stroll along the shore watching the sunrise when I heard Annanias.

"Nathan."

I turned to meet my friend.

"Good, thought you would be here. I shall be gone for the day, so I'd like you to take charge in my absence."

"Of course, may I ask where you're going?"

"I am going to make contact with the chief of the natives."

Now that was an answer I wasn't expecting.

"I'm sorry?" the surprise was clear in my voice.

"We have been here a while now Nathan, I think it's about time we broke bread. I am sure we have a lot to offer and learn from each other."

"Hhmm, maybe, what does Lane think about this?"

"Actually to was his idea."

Alarm bells started ringing in my head.

"Pardon?" I didn't hide the suspicion in my tone.

"It's ok Nathan, I think he finally realizes that he's been in the wrong in this matter. He is really keen to be honest and you have to admit that he's been much more amicable lately." Annanias didn't sound too convinced to me.

"That may be, but I don't trust him Annanias, a leopard cant change its spots, he was dead against the idea a few weeks ago. There is something behind this, I am sure of it. I am coming with you."

"No. If there is the slight possibility that you're right, then I want you here with Eleanor and Virginia. I will be fine my friend. I am going only armed with wine. Their leader and myself can get drunk long into the night and hopefully break down some barriers, language being the main one."

"You're going alone, without any troops?" it was obvious from my voice that I was imploring him to stay.

"Yes Nathan, it's a visit of peace. Soldiers will not be needed. Our scouts have given me precise co-ordinates, I leave immediately."

"At least wait until John White gets back, please Annanias." I held him by his shoulders, trying to get through to him.

"No my brother, we both know it could be quite some while before he is able to return. My mind is made up. Just give me your word that you shall keep my loved ones safe and then I shall be gone."

I had no choice but to agree, so I nodded in defeat. Annanias embraced me, turned, and left.

The day was a busy one, and I am embarrassed to admit that it wasn't until late in the day that my thoughts turned to Annanias. At that precise moment I could feel eyes burning into the back of me, and I knew whose they were.

I spun round and sure enough, Lane was standing there across the camp, and that half smile/sneer was back on his face. He whispered some words, but with my keen hearing he might as well of shouted them at the top of his voice.

"It wont be long."

That was all I needed. In less than a blink of an eye I was onto him, pinning him to the floor like a captured animal. With no time for niceties I jumped painfully into his mind, oblivious to his screams, I then saw the truth.

Last time Lane was here, here personally executed the chief of the natives for supposedly stealing nothing more than an empty cup. His thinking was the remaining inhabitants would bow down and accept Lane as their new leader. He was wrong. They came for revenge, outnumbered and afraid, Lane and his band retreated quickly. That was the reason so many troops were brought on this journey. Annanias had been sent to his certain death.

I was up and running before any one knew what was going on, Lane's screams still behind me, reverberating around the camp. Speeding faster than the wind that was trying so desperately to keep up. Like an impossibly fast bloodhound, I tracked Annanias's scent, hoping against hope.

The half a day trek I completed in minutes, skidding to a halt on the outskirts of the natives tented village. Now all but deserted bar a drunken old man wearing a fathered headdress dancing and singing around a painted wooded effigy.

Hanging by his wrists from a wooden frame was Annanias. His beaten and tortured body swinging in the breeze. His head impaled on a stake, eyes still pleading for the mercy he never got.

Tears would have to wait; my only priority now was Eleanor.

I spun round and was once more running, praying to any that would listen that I wasn't too late, again. I slowed as I neared our village, fearing to see it up in flames, thankfully I had made in back in time.

I could hear a commotion in the square, it seems Lane had taken charge. Guards were posted everywhere, obviously for me, but little did they know that I was the least of their worries. With no time to be hindered, I became a shadow, slipping past unseen until I reached Eleanor cabin. Without knocking I walked straight in. Eleanor didn't seem surprised to see me.

"Nathan, what's going on? Lane and an angry mob have been here looking for you."

"No time to explain Eleanor, please just listen. You must take Virginia and leave, now!!"

"I don't understand. Leave to go where? What about Annanias?"

The clock was ticking, so subtleties had no place.

"Annanias is dead." I had readied myself to sooth her mind if she became hysterical, but unsurprisingly she did not.

"We both shall grieve later Eleanor. But the last thing Annanias made me do was to promise to keep you and Virginia safe. There are people, bad people coming here, and there is something about them that is different, so while your still in the camp I cannot be sure I'd be able to keep my vow."

"Where do I go?" Eleanor said calmly, babe already in her arms, a small bag slung over her shoulder, and a lone teardrop running down her cheek.

"South, just keep following the shore southwards, don't stop or rest until you can walk no more. I shall come and find you once the events of this night have played their course."

"What's going to happen here tonight Nathan?"

"Nothing good." I said somberly. "But I can almost guarantee Lane will finally get what he deserves."   Eleanor walked to the door, paused and turned.

"Goodbye Nathan."

Then she was gone.

Once I was sure Eleanor was safe and away, I made my way to the beach and sat down in the soft damp sand. My back to the camp, was my way of washing my hands of all that resided there. I cared not what would happen to any of them, soldiers or farmers, young or old, I would aid none.

Even with Annanias's last tortured screams ringing inside my head, I placed no blame on the natives. The two men responsible still lived and breathed. One would surely be dead by morning, and the other would always have to live with the knowledge and desolation that he let his best friend walk to his death.

I had only been lost in my thoughts for a short time when the tender breeze stopped and hid, the air became clammy and the chanting began.

It was then I recognized why these peoples seemed different. I had heard very similar choruses before.

A very small number of cultures had links to the "other" place and a limited ability if all the ingredients were correct to summon an undesirable for a short period. It appears that tonight this tribe had all the elements needed for such an undertaking.

As the ubiquitous chanting increased in intensity I could the feel abomination burgeoning, taking its nourishment from the darkness, until whole.

Devoid of any compassion, stricken by grief, consumed with anger, I wanted to witness this macabre episode at first hand. So I watched through the nether beasts eyes.

The monster's vision was keen and the darkness posed no handicap, so I could clearly see the ensuing panic the eerie melodies from unseen foe was causing. Lane in the center of the village, ordering his men to defensive positions and sending civilians to their quarters. The Grendel must have had some intelligence for it furtively circled the camp before making its first silent and bloody kill. The young infantryman was stationed at the outmost post. He was alone and afraid, his pike planted next to him and his sword still sheathed, (not that it would have aided him in the slightest). The creature approached silently from behind, its size must have been quite impressive, as it had to look down some distance at the shivering trooper. With a speed that would have rivaled my own, it pounced. With no finesse or subtleties its gigantic jaws enveloped the mans head, crushing it as easily as one would pop a grape, embracing the poor soul from behind, razor sharp claws opened his chest and with very little effort virtually turned his torso inside out. Not that he would agree (if he could from beyond the grave), but that soldier was the lucky one, he saw not what attacked him and felt no pain due to the swiftness of his demise. But the others in the camp would not be so fortunate.

If the natives had some degree of control on the demon, it was gone now. It had tasted blood and wanted more, lots more. Literary, hell was about to break loose, and I was glad.

My morbid piggyback ride took me from trooper to trooper; hardly any had the time or voice to scream, and none put up any resistance, (which would have been futile anyway, an army could not have stopped this tornado of death). The efficient machine let no one suffer for long, making sure a vital organ or alike was crushed or devoured before moving on to the next kill. I have no idea what shape the beast took, but I would gleam snippets of the fresh organic jewelry its barbed limbs collected in its ever-decreasing circle of extermination.

I know not whether by coincidence or design, but it pleased me to see that Lane would be the last to die. His entourage of hangers-on already long dead, most had their spineless backs to the beast as they ran away.

With none others left to slay, the beast finally slowed and approached Lane who stood alone in the square, which was at the heart of our village.

Lane continued to surprise me, this time by defiantly drawing his weapon. What use such a small dagger would be was laughable to say the least. It must have dawned on the beast and myself simultaneously that Lane had no intention of defending himself, but only to plunge the dagger deep into his own cowardly heart. Before he even got close, one of the monsters claw like appendages shot out, grabbing Lanes arm and snapping it with a satisfying crack. For no other reason than to satisfy its idle curiosity, it broke Lanes other arm and was happily rewarded with a similar musical note. It soon became no more than a cat toying with a mouse. Giving him freedom for a stark few seconds before pulling the crippled man back and maiming him some more.

Eventually I grew bored of watching this torture, and it seemed Lanes nemesis grew wary also. It held aloft Lanes shattered body by his ankles, showing his trophy to the invisible audience before effortlessly pulling his legs apart and neatly splitting him in two, the crescendo being a spectacular fountain of blood.

Job done, the beast disinterestedly tossed aside Lane's spasmodic remains, eager to return from whence it came.

I had had my fill and was about to withdraw, but I could not understand why the chanting intensified once again.

The fiend was also confused, its head was cocked and it started shuffling from side to side, its time here was done, so why was it not going back?

Then its keen bat like hearing picked up the faintest of muffled sounds, it spun quickly on what I loosely describe as feet, searching for its source.

Its origin was the canteen, the very same one where I delivered Virginia.

It was then that I had the horrible feeling in the pit of my stomach. Of course, I had forgotten about the settlers.

With a purposeful lope, the beast made its way to the wooden building, and incredibly, slowly opened the door.

Inside I could make out maybe seventy people crammed into the tiny space. The men bravely shifting themselves, so they were in front of the women. I knew at once that the place that barely a few days ago had given life, was about to become a location of horrendous death.

I had no wish to observe any more, granted, I no longer cared what happened to those that lived here, but they didn't deserve this. Unable (or unwilling) to help, I decided to pull myself out and walk away, some things are best left to kismet.

But I couldn't pull out; in fact, I was immobile, all motor function gone.

I would have no choice but to witness the slaughter, and be tortured inside this living iron maiden.   Just at the precise moment I screamed out "NOOO", the beast let out a blood-curdling cry and struck.

The sheer ferocity of the attack was unneeded and upsetting, no quarter given, no mercy shown. These people posed no threat to the Goliath cutting them down, some of the men tried to bravely fight back, even knowing it would be futile. Terrible screams from the dying settlers filled my head as each and every one was brutally torn apart.

All I could do was watch and weep.

Thankfully and finally after what seemed like many lifetimes, it was over. All dead, none recognizable as even being once human. Not one body was whole, severed limbs and such, decorated the entire interior like a gruesome shrine to Hell.

The eerie chanting stopped when the last heartbeat did, it was then, and only then when I could finally close my eyes.

The escape I wanted to achieve eluded me however. The blood, pain and pleading would not go away, it was a movie on repeat, again and again I watched them die.

I needed to get far away from this cursed place as swiftly as possible, so I opened my eyes with the intention to run.

First, disorientated; I wasn't seeing what I expected too.

Second, puzzled; I was standing in the canteen.

Third, horrified; the blatant truth hit me harder than any physical blow.

Afraid to look down but knowing I had too. My hands, arms, legs and torso were soaked in blood. I could taste the flesh of people that once were my friends.

The natives hadn't summoned a beast from the nether world; they had merely used me as a puppet to do their dirty work.

It all become clear, murdering Annanias had been the catalyst. It left parts of me vulnerable, the very portions they needed to use me.

I was a fool, the signs were there all along, their strange interest in me was one, and if only I had spent a few moments to have a closer look at that effigy the old man danced around. It would have looked very familiar, probably enough so for me to understand what was occurring.

All these innocent people dead by my very own hands, blame and guilt consumed me.

The screams continued on in my head, visions of the once smiling faces burned my eyes.

I stumbled out of the canteen and fell to my knees.

Oddly, I remember seeing the word Croatoan carved into the palisade, and thinking what it meant.

In fact, it was the final coherent thought I had, and the final thing I saw, before the distressing visions came back, stronger than ever.

Unable to take any more ,the pain too great, I plunged my thumbs deep into my eyes.

Thankfully, the relief was immediate, and my world turned black.

"And that old friend, is my story."

Tenzin looked around for a few moments, unsure of his surroundings.

"It's ok, you will feel strange for a couple of minutes." Nathan's calm voice soon brought his companion coherent once again. After a brief silence, the still shaken Tenzin was the first to speak.

"That was an experience I have no wish to repeat, but thank you all the same." The quiver was clear in his voice.

"Yes, I am sorry if it was a bit much. But with so little time I couldn't really prepare you. It was something that you had to see however."

"See, touch, taste and feel. It seemed as though I was actually there. Is that how it truly happened Nathan?"

"More or less, yes, I had to change the language spoken and update some of the terms used. I also censored the more gruesome parts." Nathan said with a hint of sorrow.

"Good grief! That was censored?"

"Very much so Tenzin, some of the horror that occurred on the final night should never be witnessed by anyone."

"It wasn't your fault Nathan."

"Thank you for your heartfelt and kindly words comrade, but yes I know there was nothing I could have done. It took me a long time to come to terms with that, and the guilt."

Old man Tenzin was uneasy.

"Questions?""A few, do you mind Nathan?""Not in the least, you have a lot yet to learn before we go our separate ways." Nathan said sadly. "Now please ask away.""Difficult really to know where to start." Tenzin mused for a moment before continuing. "How did the peoples of that place use you in the way they did?""Straight and to the point I see. The natives are what are widely now known as Red Indians, and in the days before technology clouded people's minds, it all started to change once electricity was invented and widely used. Before then, the populace of the entire globe was much more in tune with nature, as I mentioned there were many tribes that had the limited know how to do such things. Maybe deep in the rainforests etc there are still some with the knowledge, the last few that I am aware of still using the dark art live on Haiti. Such information was also used for good, but unfortunately that

mostly wasn't the case." Nathan paused a moment. "Sorry, I was going a little off track there, but I am just trying to make you aware of as much information as I possibly can do. Anyway, I guess the Indian's shaman read the signs he was given and maneuvered events until they were perfect to act upon. They lived a simple life, but that did not make them stupid. I lay no blame on them for the actions they fashioned that night; I was merely a tool, a weapon to be used. Only a bad leader would fail to use the very best instruments available to them."

"So what are you Nathan? The man before me now or the beast I already fear?"

"Most definitely the man, you don't really fear me do you old friend?"

"Until the day began, no, but a lot has happened and I have learnt so much since. You aren't quite the same man I thought I knew yesterday and the story I have just lived, terrified me. Sorry, but I am only being honest."

Nathan rested a comforting hand on the upset Tenzins shoulder before he spoke.

"Be me man or beast Tenzin, I am still the same person you have known for so long. What happened that night was beyond my control, and it could never happen again."

"How can you be so sure?"

"At this juncture in time Tenzin, it's probably the only thing I can be sure off." Nathan said it with so much conviction, Tenzin had to be satisfied.

"Eleanor and the baby, what became of them?"

"I know not." Nathan's body language changed slightly. "After all these passed centuries the only regrets and guilt I still carry with me are the ones concerning those two. I broke a promise Tenzin, that's something I had never done before or will ever do again. By the time I finally regained control of myself and my sanity, they would have been dead for many years. Haunting visions of Eleanor, forever waiting, maybe even until the day she died, still trouble me now." Nathan said with more than a touch of melancholy. "I should never have broken down the way I did, I was weak. With my responsibilities, I should have been much stronger."

"So how was it, you ended up here?"

"Unfortunately, I cannot answer that question. Its not that I don't want too, believe me when I say, no one would like that mystery solved more than me."

"You just turned up here with no memory?"

"Worse than that Tenzin. I have no recollection from the time I blinded myself, to when I awoke at this place. I couldn't even tell you how long it was, days, months, years even. Lama Shepa told me I was discovered collapsed at the edge of the garden. It was weeks before I even regained consciousness, then a few months more until I was lucid."

"Is that why you carved the word CROATOAN into the oak tree, to help you remember?"

"I didn't." was the surprising reply.

"Excuse me? I don't quite understand Nathan."

"According to Lama Shepa, he told me that the word was engraved into the tree long before I came. It's been there as long as anyone can remember."

"But you saw the same word, who did it, was it a sign, does that mean that the true name for this place is Croatoan?"

"Tenzin old friend, I have asked those very same questions a multitude of times, and the only definite answer I have is that this place is not called Croatoan. Which creates even more queries. It's a mystery I have never solved, and not through lack of trying."

It appeared Nathan had more to say, but he cut himself short. He turned his head slightly and seemed to sniff the air. His next words were somber ones.

"It's time for you to go Tenzin."

"Go? Go where? I thought it was you that was leaving."

"Yes, I shall soon be. But first I would like you to go down to the village and bring widow Dolma back here."

"You know about her?"

"Of course, it's nothing to be ashamed of."

"I am not ashamed." Tenzin said rather tersely. "What has she got to do with any of this?"

"I apologize Tenzin, that came out wrong. I have always been very happy that you have a platonic friendship; it's good that you enjoy each other's company. It's only a pity that your ages restricted it being anything more. She has nothing to do with this my friend, but if things don't go our way, this could be the only safe haven left on the planet, so I presume you would want her here."

"Just her?"

"No, no, if you can bring the whole village, try to convince as many peoples as possible."

Tenzin finally understood how grave things could become.

"I'll try, and thank you. You'll be gone when I get back wont you?"

"Sadly, you already know the answer to that. I truly wish we had more time, but you really have to leave now. I still have much to tell you, so I shall walk you to the boundary and we can talk some more." Without warning Nathan leapt from his rocking chair, instinctively from years of servitude Tenzin followed suit.

Nathan was now smiling.

"Well?"

"I'm sorry Nathan?"

"That was a little cruel of me, but please, tell me how do you feel?"

Tenzin was clearly confused and a tad irritated with this strange behavior.

"Fine and a bit puzzled."

"Hhhmmmm." Nathan's annoying smirk was back.

"Is this the time for games Nathan?"

"Please indulge me for a moment old friend, you sprang from the mattress like a cat."

"I was startled, it was a reflex action. What's the point of this?"

"The point is Tenzin, cast your mind back to the difficulty you had to sit down."

Tenzin thought for a few seconds; then the Archimedes moment happened. He flexed his fingers, bent his knees, twisted his head from left to right, and for the first time tonight, smiled.

"My arthritis, it's gone!" Tenzin said in hardly more than a whisper.

"Yes it has, now look at your hands."

He did as he was asked, his wrinkled leathered skin was now tanned and tight.

"If I had a mirror I would love to show you your face, it appears I can no longer call you old my friend." Tenzin slowly reached up and touched his new visage; his young fingers examining every feature.

"You did this?" Tenzin was close to tears.

"As much as I'd like to, I can't take credit for that. You have the garden to thank."

"The garden?"

"Yes, you are now it's new keeper, and it's how it shows its gratitude. It will look after you and widow Dolma for as long as you want the position it has offered you."

"I love this place, you know that Nathan, I would stay here forever if I could."

"Then it seems the garden has chosen well, I foresee a long and successful partnership ahead."

"But I don't know where to start or what to do?"

"Worry not; we have the utmost faith in you and your abilities. More than ever, this place will need a father figure to teach and tender.

Without a shadow of doubt, you are perfect. Now come let us walk, there is still more to learn."

Nathan carried a heavy heart as he walked slowly back to the temple alone. Saying goodbye to someone you truly love is never an easy task, but he was also gladdened knowing that the garden would forever protect his time old companion. The garden would keep a promise that Nathan once had not. Not wishing to dwell on the past any longer, and with Tenzin gone, Nathan finally gave himself the luxury of a new pair of eyes. Knowing he would soon have to integrate back into society it was the prudent thing to do. He waited until Tenzin had gone because the poor man had more than enough shocks for a lifetime, let alone twenty-four hours.

"It's good to see again through eyes that are my own." Nathan said to nobody.

But the garden heard him, and delighted itself in swamping Nathan's newly regained sense in an impossible visual cabaret.

"Thank you." Nathan quickly remembered what tears felt like.

As he neared the immense oak doors they opened for him, even a garden could show affection.

"Soon then?"

The unmistakable click as the doors locked behind him answered his question.

Nathan entered his room and walked up to its new addition, slowly he opened the large suitcase that was now on the mattress where Tenzin had sat. He then undressed, respectfully folding his robe and carefully placing it into the case. Next he put on more suitable western attire, finishing off by tightening his belt to the very last notch.

"I need to put on a few pounds."

Upon leaving he couldn't resist a farewell glance at the quarters that had been his abode for so long, the suitcase of course had already vanished.

Nathan made his way to the center of the immense hall, once there, he sat down crossed legged, closed his eyes and composed himself for a few moments before speaking.

"Let them in."

With eyes still shut, Nathan could feel the room fill with static electricity, for a few seconds there was a loud crackling noise, then silence.

In no rush, Nathan unhurriedly opened his eyes.

"Coward." He growled.

Stood before Nathan was the cloaked figure, he was flanked on both sides by six of most abominable creations he could ever have dreamed up.

"Ah, the infamous Nathan. Not a coward, just not stupid." An icy voice said from within its hood.

"So you send just a mere apparition of yourself, I notice the Village People you brought with you a real enough though."

"You childish humor has no effect on me."

"And nor do your scare tactics on me." Nathan said blankly.

"Scare tactics? Oh no Nathan, you have got me all wrong. My children are here to rip you apart, tear every limb from your body and then feast on them. But it seems I vastly overestimated you."

"Really? Do tell."

"Well frankly I am disappointed, you don't seem half the man Cyrus was, and he ran away like a little girl from just two of my beloved. There isn't enough meat on you to feed even one."

"I am not Cyrus."

"Yes that's true, he didn't slaughter one hundred innocent people."

The figures' throaty laugh was curtly cut short when the walls of the great hall started to vibrate, and then emit a low frequency pulsating sound, similar to that of a heartbeat.

Nathan raised his hand and it stopped as abruptly as it began.

"Going to get this overgrown allotment to fight your battle I see." Sneered the darkness.

"Far from it. As you are aware, this place could crush you and yours in the blinking of an eye, that's why you're too afraid to come here personally. But for one time only, I have given the garden instructions not to intervene, if your handsome spawn defeat me, they will be allowed to return from whence they came."

"And I have your word?"

"Yes."

"From what I hear that doesn't mean much."

The whole building shook violently for a moment, showing its disapproval.

"OK OK, his word is good." Shouted the faceless voice.

"Satisfied?"

"Yes. I am looking forward to watching your painful demise."

"That may well be the outcome, but unfortunately for you, it's a sight that you shan't be privy too. Ringside seats are invitation only, and I am afraid your not invited."

"You cant do that! You gave your word."

"And my word still stands, I never agreed to giving you an audience however. Goodbye."

"Noooooo." His cry faded out, just as his apparition did, leaving only his six thralls.

Even without their master, the six children of Satan knew their task in hand and quickly surrounded Nathan. His barely five foot frame was dwarfed by these ten foot monstrosities.

"Best I even up the odds a little, me thinks."

Nathan morphed into something unrecognizable from the form he was moments before. His basic shape could be best described as that of the mythological centaur, but one protected by razor sharp diamond edged scales, hands and hooves replaced by deadly claws with malleable appendages. An evil tail, terminating in a spiked ball that had impossible mass for its size and weight. Its other extremity housed an armored triangular head, with slavering gaping jaws and silver fangs. As large as this equine creature was, it still didn't quite match up to the size of bloodthirsty opponents. With a cracking of joints, sinew and muscle, it now stood steadfastly on its hind legs. Nathan had now become something akin to a lethal Vishnu. Each of his four arms held a sword with blades darker than a moonless night.

"Lets play." Said a voice that was very wrong for the entity that it emanated from.

As if that was the cue they had been waiting for, silently and simultaneously the six creatures attacked.

CHAPTER 4

"Beer, Banter & Beans"

Situated in a small village in the heart of North Wales, The Stag was a locals' pub. Any strangers that had wandered off the beaten track were quickly made ill at ease and unwelcome, so they never stayed for long. Farmers were an unfriendly bunch at the best of times, but Welsh farmers perfected the art. Devoid of any pool table or jukebox, the musical note was supplied by the native tongue of its patrons, a guttural language that only the inhabitants of this district could understand. The nationwide ban of smoking in public places was ignored here; these were hard working men, ale and a smoke was part of their tradition.

If you peered through the thick smoky atmosphere you would notice two men sat in a booth who were most definitely alien. One could only be described as a man mountain, a huge figure with fiery red hair, he easily took up two seats on his side of the table. The other however, couldn't have been more different, he was only noticeable due to the company he currently kept, otherwise he would have just blended into the background. The only anomaly he processed would be the pair of darkened glasses he wore.

Somewhat surprisingly the mismatched duo were largely ignored, even being honored with the occasional nod when eye contact happened to be made.

"Nice and friendly place you found here Janus."

"Sarcasm doesn't suit you Sol." Janus replied with no hint of malice.

"Only kidding old chum, you have to admit they're a mean looking bunch though."

"Sadly, in this part of the world they are a dying breed. The closure of village shops due to supermarkets that import most goods mean British farmers have a hard time existing."

Solomon just nodded.

"Anyway, we aren't here to talk politics."

"True."

"This place more than adequately suits our purpose, we shan't have any unwanted intrusions from strangers, and the locals will leave us be."

"I have utmost faith in your powers of perception my friend, but how can you be so sure after they have had a skin full?"

"Oh I think I can be sure, I know the owner well, in fact, he speaks very highly of you."

"He does? Who the hell is he?" Solomon said raising one eyebrow.

"Me."

"You?"

"Yep, yours truly, I have owned this quaint drinking house for over a hundred years, under various guises of course."

"Well of course."

"Always handy to have a few bolt holes dotted around the globe, and it actually pulls in quite a good income."

"It doesn't surprise me to be honest, you and Cyrus were always the type to invest and prospect. Where as my own good self, came here with nothing and shall leave with nothing."

"I am fully aware of your charitable lifestyle Solomon, I also have done my bit and give my fair share."

"I know you do Janus, and believe me I wasn't having a go at you. Now before this conversation turns needlessly sour, lets get back to this place. So you're known to the locals then?"

"Not in the slightest, but I had the foresight to phone ahead and asked them to prepare four rooms, so word would have slipped out."

"Four rooms? Your expecting Cyrus AND Nathan?"

"Cyrus yes, as for Nathan, your guess is as good as mine."

"It would be good to see the wee chappy again, it's been a long time."

"Too long old friend."

The conversation was brought to an abrupt halt by the sound of a powerful sports car skidding to a stop outside.

"Here we go," Janus said bleakly.

A sharp dressed man breezed into the establishment, wearing an expensive suit, which was entirely out of place for the current setting. All idle chatter stopped and every pair of eyes was on the stranger as he approached the bar. He paused, cleared his throat, and spoke in a voice that was altogether a tad too loud.

"Does dim het ar fy Asyn."

Uncharacteristically the place erupted into laughter and there was much shaking of heads.

Janus and Solomon just groaned.

"Did he say what I think he said?" Solomon asked.

"Afraid so, he just announced to the whole establishment that his donkey has no hat."

Obviously the newcomer got his second attempt right at mastering the language and walked over to their table with a freshly pulled pint of real ale. Once the locals realized he was with them, they quickly reverted back to their private conversations about crops, livestock and taxes.

"Janus."

"Cyrus."

Nothing more than a strained nod that wanted to be so much more, passed between them.

He then turned to Solomon, but the big guy was already on his feet. He clasped his arms around Cyrus in an embrace that would have easily killed any normal man.

"Wayhey, ease up big fella, it's good to see you too. Erm. . Weren't you Black last time we met?"

There was a short uncomfortable silence and a blushing Solomon tried not to look directly at Janus.

"It's ok Sol, I have known all along that you and Cyrus kept in touch, and had the odd clandestine meeting. I always thought it a good thing, and if I am brutally honest, I must say I was a little jealous."

"Jealous?" Cyrus and Solomon said in tandem.

"Of course, what's past is past. We all had a bond stronger than kin, and I was weak-minded in letting myself fall for someone, who in turn was envious at what we had. It soon became an age-old cliché, she turned ever more bitter and twisted, I was blinkered and wouldn't listen to anyone. She slept with you, and blamed you, thinking I would take revenge, but her mischievous hatchings didn't quite go to plan. She did succeeded however in dividing us. Foolish pride then infected us both, and sadly, the rest is history. "

Cyrus just nodded, unsure at what to say. Janus stood up and spoke first.

"Cyrus, I am sorry." And he offered him his hand.

"And I also." Cyrus replied, taking the outstretched hand in both of his.

"Well about bloody time." Solomon boomed happily. "It's taken the pair of you over a millennia to say those few small words. It's worse than having kids I tell ya, I should have banged your thick heads together a long long time ago. And another thing. . ."

"Yes, yes Solomon, we get the point." Janus cut him off mid sentence. "Now lets just back up a bit, you were black??"

"Och aye, but first will you two stop holding hands and please sit down. I am as open minded as the next man, but frankly you look a bit gay, and I do have my image to think about."

Laughing, the two men did as were told.

"But yes, for nigh on a hundred years I lived in the deep south of the United States of America. Prejudice and racism made me sick to my oversized stomach. So I lived as a Colored and tried my best to help where I could. It was a very upsetting time for me, and a dark part of American history. I could write a book about those evil years, and one day I will." Said an unusually solemn Solomon.

The grudge that had lasted for more than a thousand years was instantly forgotten, and the trio sat down and talked just like the old friends that they truly were.

"What news do you have of Nathan?" Cyrus asked.

"Sadly, none." Janus replied.

"None? For how long?"

"More than five hundred years." Solomon interjected.

"Jesus!! I thought he was just pissed at me, apparently not it seems."

"I don't think it was a case of him being pissed at any of us Cyrus, probably more like he just simply became bored, so left us to sort his head out."

"But no contact in such a long time, I know he was always more of the loner, but are you sure he's ok, and as much as I loath to say it, still with us?"

Janus paused for a moment to take a sip from his beer before continuing.

"If it was you or Solomon that I hadn't heard from in such a long time, then I would be genuinely worried. But as you both know, Nathan can more than adequately look after himself, better than the three of us put together in fact." The other two nodded in agreement. "As I see it, it can only be one of two things."

"Go on."

"Well, either as we mentioned before he purely had enough of everything and wanted or needed to shut himself away for a time, and if that is the case, I have no doubt he will be with us when the timing is right."

"Or?" Cyrus already had an inkling at to what was coming next.

"Or, he has been a victim of a tragic accident and is longer with us."

"You don't really believe that, do you?"

"No I don't, but that doesn't mean we can't rule it out."

"So what exactly are you saying?"

"We have to continue under the premise that he won't be joining us."

Solomon and Cyrus were clearly shocked at this unexpected answer.

"You can't really mean that?" Solomon whispered.

"Sorry Sol, as much as I would like to think otherwise, it's the only thing we can do. You know how I think, always prepare for the worse case scenario, that way nothing can surprise us."

It was Cyrus's turn to jump in.

"But can we win without Nathan?"

Janus's shrug answered the question even before he spoke.

"Win against what? I don't even know what we are dealing with. The only things I have come across are infected people, turned by him, and human shaped entities that are most defiantly not of this world."

"Aye Cyrus, I have had dealings with them too, tough little bastards but far from undefeatable."

Cyrus then stood and collected up the three empty pint glasses.

"I think I can maybe shed a little more light on what we are dealing with, here let me fill these and I'll tell what I know."

A few minutes later he was back with a tray containing four freshly pulled pints.

"There you go big guy, two for you as you seem to drink a little faster than us two."

"Erm. . It's my glands." Was his sheepish reply.

Cyrus once again took his seat before continuing.

"I have had a face to face encounter with the being, individual or whatever you want to call it, and the bastard forced me to sink my ship, which really pissed me off, I tell ya."

"Ship? I'm confused, what does that have to do with anything?"

"Sorry, went off on a bit of a tangent then, I'll tell you what I know."

"Please do." Janus said patiently.

"Firstly to make things less longwinded, I shall call our nemesis a Him, until we know more ok." He took a moment for another gulp of the amber nectar.

"Well, the form he took was standard fare B-movie scare tactics, shimmering hooded figure, face hidden in a swirl of blackness etc. Mentally however, he was very powerful, he managed to manipulate me like a marionette, granted I was unprepared so caught by surprise, I doubt he could do that again."

"Possibly." Was the only input Janus would enter at this juncture.

"Not only that, but he was also able to block me from contacting you and stopped me from jumping."

"Hhmm. . . Did he speak at all?"

"Oh yes, I must admit he seemed very confident about the final outcome, saying we were no more than a minor irritation, and that we couldn't stop him etc. He even offered me the opportunity to switch sides and join him."

"Interesting." Janus mused.

"So what do you think boss?" Solomon asked, already on his second pint.

"I think we are in trouble Sol. But I also surmise that Cyrus is correct in saying that he wouldn't be able to manipulate us, I doubt very much he would bother even trying again."

"But if he's that much of a threat, why did he try an recruit Cyrus?"

"I'm sorry Sol, but for no other reason than purely to piss me off I think. The spectre is supremely confident in his task in hand and in its eyes we pose no threat whatsoever. We are no more than an amusing distraction."

"Can we stop him Janus?" Solomon asked with a worrying tone, not liking what he was hearing.

"Honestly, I think we have one chance and one chance only, and that will involve him being a victim of his own arrogance."

"Erm. . There is one more thing." Cyrus interrupted.

"Go on." Janus groaned.

"You and Solomon spoke of human shaped entities; his soldiers, sentinels or whatever you want to call them."

"Yes?"

"Well, he has something altogether a tad more dangerous."

"Such as?"

"When he paid me a little visit, he had shadowing him, hidden at first, two creatures which can only be best described as us in our other form, but without any sentient intelligence as such, bred purely for killing."

"To be honest, that doesn't surprise me, I knew he had to have something more of a threat to us to be so confident, how many he has is the question."

"Like I said, he had a pair of the drooling creatures with him, maybe that is all he has."

"I doubt that very much, he wouldn't risk his only two Aces so early, just for you to obliterate them."

"Erm. ."

"You DID destroy them, didn't you?"

"No, I ran away." Cyrus said curtly.

"RAN AWAY!!" Solomon snorted loudly.

"Do you have problem with that Solomon?" a nasty edge was creeping into Cyrus's voice.

"We don't run away from a fight Cyrus." Said the normally good-natured Solomon.

"I am not as big and stupid as you though. Look at the facts Solomon, I had been played like a puppet, I couldn't contact anyone or make a jump and I had no idea with what I was dealing with. Since it was only myself in danger, I thought it prudent to retreat with what information I had gathered."

Solomon was about to speak but Janus raised his hand to stop him.

"And you did entirely the right thing, a good General would never go into battle until he had acquired as much intelligence as possible."

Solomon knew he was right.

"Sorry Cyrus, speaking before I think again. That's why Janus is the boss and I'm just here to smash heads."

"It's ok buddy, trust me it wasn't an easy decision to flee, especially in doing so I had to scuttle The Guinevere."

That name brought an uncomfortable silence and a mixture of contrasting memories for the seated trio.

"I'd really like to know how many of those beasties he has. That information is going to be one very important factor regarding our chances of success. It could be two or two hundred, we have no way of knowing." Said a somewhat deflated Janus.

"Well he has six less than what he started with." A voice piped up from the adjoining booth, closely followed by a casually dressed smiling Nathan stepping from his hidden sanctuary.

Janus, Cyrus and Solomon were literally dumbstruck.

"I take a short sabbatical and you virtually write me off as being dead, well some friends you lot are." Nathan said jokingly.

It was Janus that found his voice first.

"A short sabbatical?? You call five hundred bloody years short? How long have you been sat there for anyway?"

"It's good to see you too Janus by the way. And I was already here when you came in, I am parched I can tell ya." With that, Nathan finished Solomon's second pint.

"Of course sorry, it's great to see you, it's been a long time old friend."

"Too long." Solomon added.

"Err. Who's this?" Cyrus said with a wink.

"Sigh, if I knew this would be the welcome I got, I wouldn't have bothered, I don't even get offered a drink."

"Aye, I'll soon change that my wee friend." Solomon said, as he pushed passed Nathan, giving him a hearty slap on the back that would have knocked any normal person half way across the room, the demure Nathan stood rock steady.

Janus waited until everyone was finally seated with their glasses full before speaking again.

"So you also have had a visit than Nathan, can you shed any more light on the situation?"

But before Nathan could answer Solomon jumped in.

"Whoa, hang on a minute! We are now just sitting here like four friends having their weekly pint down the pub, I don't about you two," Solomon looked at Janus and Cyrus, "but I am bloody curious to know where you have been Nathan for the last half millennia?"

"I think Nathan will tell us that when he is good and ready Sol, right now there are more pressing matters at hand."

"Don't worry my big friend, I will happily tell you all when the time is right, and if things go well for us I will even take you, I have a feeling you will be quite taken with the place."

"Yes, you're right, please continue. It just feels so good to have us all together again, there must be so much to hear and learn, and you know how I love a good story." Solomon said sounding a bit like a child denied of something he was looking forward too.

Nathan patted the big man's hand and continued.

"The Being we are dealing with calls himself Ahriman."

That name completely changed the atmosphere, any lightheartedness was gone and things became instantly serious.

"Ahriman." Janus whispered, it was name hidden deep in his memory.

Up until now Cyrus had said nothing. " Could it really be him?"

"Possibly, or maybe it's just the sobriquet he's using, I think it matters not."

"You don't think it matters??" A taken aback Solomon could hardly believe his ears.

"If you had let me finish I was about to say what is of much more consequence is what he can do."

"Ah."

"He has the ability to infect people."

"With?"

"The worse and most contagious disease ever to face mankind." Nathan paused briefly. "Evil."

"You can't contaminate Man with Evil Nathan, we all know that, it has been tried before if you remember." Solomon argued, but Janus and Cyrus stayed worryingly silent.

"In that respect you are right of course, but what if he can amplify even the tiniest trace one hundred fold. How many people can you honestly show me that have never had dark thought, even if it is locked safely away deep in their forgotten conscious.

Can you imagine the scenario Solomon; every living being wakes up with their mind full of villainous and depraved thoughts, any balance that have until now kept them in check, now gone. Who is going to keep any resemblance of law and order when EVERYONE is infected? No sense of right or wrong, only wrong, morals will be a thing of the past. Malevolence will feed humanity."

"My God, what about the children? They will be the true innocence left."

"I'm very sorry old friend, but they will suffer the most. And the few that survive, with all the abuse, suffering and torment they endured will bring evil to an impossible new level."

"We have to stop him." Said the big man, choking back tears.

"We can't." Was Nathan's flat reply.

An upset and angry man often says things he doesn't mean, Solomon was no exception.

"WELL, FUCK YOU NATHAN." Said the man mountain rising from his seat. "What the fuck do you know? You ran away and hid for five hundred years because you wanted to find yourself for fucks sake.

Looks like to me the only thing you discovered, is that you're a fucking coward. If we can't stop him, then why the fuck do we exist Nathan? In fact, why did you even bother turning up here?"

"SOLOMON ENOUGH, now sit down." Said Janus removing his shades, his piercing gaze was one that Medusa herself would be proud off.

The big man did as he was told and Janus turn to an impassive Nathan.

"Sorry Nathan, Solomon's outburst was uncalled for, but you have to admit he had a point. I have always trusted your word when you've seemed to know things that for the life of me I could never comprehend how you became privy to such knowledge. But this time are you sure we can't stop him?"

"Yes and no."

A loud snort could be heard from Solomon's direction, which was swiftly cut short after a sideways glance from Janus.

"You are what you are Nathan, but please, less of the riddles. Could you be a bit more specific for us lesser men."

"I'm sorry Solomon, Janus, Cyrus, it's been a long time since I have interacted in such a way with friends, forgive me please."

"Of course, now tell us what you can."

"The problem we face is that he only has to infect one carrier, which he hasn't done as yet by the way. The said carrier in turn infects all he comes into contact with, via touch alone. Those infected also become carriers, and so forth. Within days, the world is populated by six and a half billion people that make the Marquis de Sade look like a children's entertainer."

"Is there a cure and will destroying Ahriman or whatever he is calling himself reverse the process?"

"Sadly no cure, nor killing him will make any difference once the wheels have been set in motion."

"A grave situation indeed then, but you say he hasn't infected anyone as yet, what is he waiting for?" Janus asked.

"Us."

"Us?" It was Cyrus's turn to sound surprised.

"Yes, he's giving us one chance to stop him."

"How?" Then Cyrus added, "why?"

"The why is easy, as Janus has already mentioned, he is arrogant and over-confident, he also resents us being here, so he wants to utterly destroy and crush us in a huge spectacle."

"And how is he planning to do that?"

"Simple, in battle."

"In battle?" Cyrus's voice went up an octave.

"Yes, our army versus his." Nathan made it sound like this was an everyday occurrence.

"We have a slight problem then."

"We do?"

"Of course we fucking do Nathan. First I presume when you say battle, you mean like the good old days?"

Nathan merely nodded.

"That was over a thousand fucking years ago Nathan, I don't know about you, but I am a bit rusty. And secondly."

"Go on, surprise me."

"Last time I looked, we don't have a fucking army."

"I think you meant to say, YOU don't have army. At least one of us has been preparing it seems."

"How could we prepare for an eventually which we didn't know what form it would take. Why didn't you step down from your hidden ivory tower and warn us?"

"Because up until a few days ago I didn't know either, I just hedged my bets and kept my options open that's all. So out of interest, what exactly have you done in the last five hundred years?"

Things were starting to become heated, so Janus stepped in once more.

"Come on guys, arguing and snide remarks are getting us nowhere. What we have or haven't done is not important right now. We need to concentrate on whatever resources we have at hand now. At least we have some hope now, whereas a minute ago there was none. So please, no more bickering and lets be thankful, agreed?"

"Fine by me." Nathan answered first.

"Agreed." Said Cyrus, closely followed by Solomon.

"So Nathan, any idea how big his army is?"

"No sorry, I'm afraid not, could be two thousand, or could be two hundred thousand."

"Is it possible he has that many?"

"Oh yes, quite easily I should think. Lets look at the facts. He has all the humans that have already been turned but are not yet carriers. Pick up any paper and you'll see reports of cults and increased levels of violent attacks everywhere. Added to them, he has those sentinels that you mentioned earlier, again, numbers unknown. And finally we have his demonic puppies, once again, numbers unknown."

"Ok, thank you Nathan. Realistically I think we have to presume his army is in the hundreds of thousands. What does your infantry number Nathan?"

"Against the odds we face, no more than a drop in the ocean unfortunately. Minimum a thousand, maximum maybe five or six."

"Good, that's a start at least."

"How are you getting five thousand people armed with swords through customs Nathan? You can't even carry a toothpick on a flight any more." Cyrus asked.

"I have a container ship docking any time now, all weapons are on that. My men will be making their own way across the water, and they are going through customers armed with nothing more dangerous than a ham sandwich."

"Good thinking." Cyrus admitted.

"Right guys, we need a break for a few minutes. There is still much to discuss and it's going to be a long night. Solomon, fill the glasses."

"Solomon do this, Solomon do that. It's like being a Colored all over again." The big man muttered under his breath as he made his way to the bar.

It already must have been late into the night as the pub was now all but deserted, only a couple of die hard old boys were left, making sure they drained every last drop of ale purchased with their meager pensions.

The trio sat in silence, all three lost deep in thought while waiting for Solomon's return.

The brief tranquility was shattered by an unnecessary loud crash as the disgruntled Solomon slammed down the tray full of drinks, spilling most of them.

"The landlord is asking if its ok for him to lock up and retire to his room once the last two have left, and if we could turn the lights off once we have finished down here."

Janus made eye contact with the barman and nodded.

"On a health spurge Sol?" Cyrus asked jokingly.

"I'm sorry?" was the confused reply.

"Just curious as to why to bought an orange juice, watching your weight?"

"I didn't," but sure enough mixed in with five pints, was an out of place glass of orange. "He must have misheard me when I placed me order. Not to worry, it all goes down the same hole." Said a now slightly better spirited Solomon. His lifted mood didn't last.

"Did you feel that?" Solomon asked, after an uncontrollable shiver.

"Feel what Sol?" Cyrus asked.

"I'm not sure, but it's really strange, up until a moment ago I still had hope that we would succeed. But just then when I sat down it felt like a physical wave of dread and failure hit me. I have never experienced anything like that before."

"It's ok big guy, you're afraid, we all are. Nothing to be ashamed about my friend."

"Hhmm, maybe, I am sure it was something more than that though."

What Solomon didn't know was the other three all had the same icy shiver run down their spine, but they all kept the feeling of hopelessness to themselves.

"Ok, lets all settle down, first thing we need to do is come up with a rough number of the force we can expect to gather to stand against him. What kind of timescale are we looking at Nathan?"

"Seven days, from dawn tomorrow."

Solomon's mouth began to open, but a raised eyebrow from Janus soon shut it.

"Fair enough, where?"

"Death Valley, California."

"Predictable, America would also be my choice to begin the fall of mankind. Also Death Valley being one of the most inhospitable places on the Earth, is an ideal place for the final battle."

Almost comically, Solomon started to raise his hand.

"We're not in school Sol, what is it?"

"As you know, I am not the sharpest mind around, and this may be a stupid question, but what's to stop us marching up to the Whitehouse and asking the President to nuke the bastard. Or turning up at the battle with the US Army in tow, complete with air strikes etc."

"Not a stupid question at all old friend, but it's a no go all the same. We have to abide by his rules, and he holds all the aces. And if it means, no outside influence, no guns, tanks or napalm, we have no choice but to bite the bullet, so to speak." Nathan paused only to half drain his glass. "Don't forget, he could infect the world tomorrow if he so pleases, and there is nothing we can do to stop it. This battle is only being fought for his amusement, and to boost his already over inflated ego."

"Looks like we're fucked then." Solomon's briefly lifted spirits took a downward tumble.

"Don't be like that Sol, lets just be thankful that we at least have been given a chance. Plus, we never expected it to be easy old friend." Were the only words of comfort Janus could think of.

"S'pose."

"So, what kind of numbers can we rustle up Janus?" Cyrus asked.

"Hhmm, difficult to say really. We are going to have to awaken the knights here and at the Blanik Mountains of course, but there number is only four hundred or so in total."

"Bloody Hell, I had all but forgotten about them." Solomon chirped. "But will they be mentally up to it Janus? They have been in stasis now for over one and a half millennia. This world will be alien to them; it would be something similar to a caveman walking into a shopping mall, can you just imagine his confusion."

"Good job we aren't taking them shopping then hey Solomon." Cyrus interjected.

"Ha bloody ha."

"Don't worry Sol, I'll have Cyrus fast track their minds and subconscious, so by the time he wakes them, they will fit right in. can I leave that with you Cyrus?"

"Sure, no problem Boss."

Janus was taken aback for a brief moment, he would never have expected Cyrus to call him that. It showed that everyone was more worried than they let on.

"And don't forget Solomon, those men were/are the best mortal fighters ever to walk the Earth, that's why we put them to sleep, even though I sadly hoped we would never have to awaken them. Even with our erm advantages, any of them could give us a bloody good run for our money."

"Speak for yourself." Nathan said with a smile.

"Of course I didn't mean you Nathan, you have always been abnormal." Janus returned the smile; happy to see some of the friendly banter was coming back.

"We do have the slight problem of the logistics involved to get them across the Atlantic, any ideas guys?"

"I can also handle that Janus, I own an airline, passenger and freight, it's going to be a tight squeeze but I can't see it being a problem. Getting the three hundred fully kitted out Knights from the mountains in the Czech Republic to the airport, is going to be the hard part, I sort it though. I also have at our disposal a private jet on standby, when the time comes, you three can use that, and I'll come over with our ancient hooligans."

"Why aren't I surprised, forever the playboy." Janus said with long overdue genuine affection. "Best if you take Nathan with you, it's too much of a handful even for you Cyrus. Agreed?"

"Agreed" was the resulting chorus.

"It's good to see things already coming together, now who said this was a hopeless cause."

There was a moment's silence in the now deserted establishment, totally unnoticed by the quartet the last couple of stragglers have long since left, and the barman had locked up and was by now happily visiting the land of nod.

"Guys, do you mind if we continue this tomorrow?" Nathan asked.

"Of course not, is there a problem Nathan?" Janus asked with just the slightest of concern in his voice.

"Not at all, everything's fine. I just need some sleep that's all."

"Sleep? Since when have we needed sleep?" Concern became surprise.

"Strictly we don't I know, but are you telling that once a week or maybe even a month, you don't like to lie down, shut your eyes and totally relax for a few hours."

"Well yes of course we do Nathan." Cyrus added.

"And the last time you did that was?"

"Not sure, fortnight ago or so Nathan."

"It's been slightly longer for me."

"How long Nathan?" concern was back in Janus's tone.

"About five hundred years." Was Nathan's blank reply.

"Fuck Me, you must be shattered."

Nathan, Cyrus and even Janus couldn't help but smile at Solomon's amazing powers of reasoning.

"Yes, of course, you get your head down for a few hours."

"Will do, oh, I have ordered three breakfasts for the morning, so I'll see you then."

"Three? Who's not getting one?" Cyrus enquired.

"All of you, they're for me."

"Don't tell me you haven't eaten either Nathan?"

"Not important, night guys, speak on the morrow." With that Nathan turned and left.

"Three breakie's? Pah! I've ordered five." Solomon added.

"Well you do have your fabulous figure to maintain Sol." Cyrus said with a smirk.

"I do, I do. Takes a lot of hard work to look this good"

"Oh I can quite believe it Sol. Perhaps it might not be a bad idea for you to get some rest as well, tonight will probably be the last chance we get." Cyrus suggested.

The normally slow on the uptake Solomon immediately picked up the hint in Cyrus's voice, he wanted to be alone with Janus it seemed. And after how far they went back, and how close they once were, Solomon could wholeheartedly respect and understand his wishes.

"Aye, not a bad idea, I'll see you both on the morrow, and no talking about me behind my back, ok."

"Goodnight Sol."

"Night big guy."

The long since departed souls that once inhabited the ancient establishment, carefully watched the two shadowy seated figures; urging one of them to break the tense silence.

It was Janus that obliged.

"Full marks for your lack of subtlety there."

"Have you ever tried being subtle with Solomon? It's like banging your head against a brick wall."

"He's not half as daft as he makes out."

"Oh I know. He does it on purpose, that's why he can be so infuriating."

"I wouldn't have him any other way."

"Amen to that." Said Cyrus raising his glass.

Surprisingly to the pair of them, the ensuing small talk wasn't in the least bit uncomfortable, and both secretly wished they had made up an eon ago.

"Nathan being here was certainly a turn up for the books, what did you make of him?"

"That's the $64,000 question. It was a surprise to see him, but I wasn't "surprised" if you know what I mean."

"Oh Lord, give me strength, I don't believe you just did that."

"Did what?"

"Held up your hands and did that idiotic quotation thing with your fingers."

"Fuck Off!!" Cyrus replied laughing.

"Seriously though, something's not right with him, I just cant put my finger on it."

"I agree, Nathan's always been somewhat of an enigma, but this time he has definitely changed. He oozes a new confidence that I haven't seen before, but have also you noticed that dark edge he has somehow acquired?"

Janus nodded.

"Back in the day, when he turned, he was a always handful, but I have a feeling that the new Nathan is going to virtually unstoppable when the time comes. Thank fuck he's on our side is all I can say."

"I'm with you on that one." Agreed Janus.

"There is something he's not telling us though."

"Yes, he is hiding something, I am sure of it."

"Do you think we should just ask him straight out?"

"No, I don't think that would be wise. If it is something we should know then he will tell us when the time is right."

"And if its bad news?"

"I'd rather not know to be honest."

Cyrus pondered for a brief moment.

"I suppose your right. Refill?"

Janus looked down at his empty glass.

"Please, I think I might let myself get slightly inebriated. It's been a long time and tonight as good as occasion as any."

"And I'm happily going to join you."

Cyrus left the table, leaving Janus lost in thought and with the ever-increasing cloud of despondency being his only companion.

Janus soon returned, with two glasses and a bottle of Macallan 25 year old.

"If were going to pretend to get pissed, we might as well do it in style."

"I hope your intending to pay for that."

"Stop being such a gloomy Gus. Anyway, to lighten the mood, I have brought you a present."

"Oh joy, my heart is filled with anticipation."

"You were always the master of sarcasm, even long before the word was invented. But I think you will like this gift." Cyrus was in unusually high spirits all of a sudden.

"Surprise me."

Cyrus cleared the center of the table with a childish enthusiasm, and plonked an overly large hold all (which Janus was sure he didn't enter the pub with) on the table.

"Open it."

"Yeah right, do I look stupid?"

"Trust me."

Janus raised one eyebrow.

"Please Janus."

"Hhmm, since you said please, but I am sure I am going to regret this."

Cyrus sat back, poured himself a tumbler full of malt and watched the man standing before him tentatively open the zipper.

"Don't worry, it's not a bomb."

But Janus didn't hear him, his knees buckled and it took most of his strength to stop himself from falling, as a multitude of memories almost physically hit him, most good, some terrible.

"How on Earth? Where did you?" Janus whispered as he slowly drew from the bag the most intricate and magnificent sword ever created. Thousands of minuscule golden serpents eagerly embraced Janus's hand as he grasped the hilt, forming a metallic gauntlet, running half way up his forearm.

"To be honest, it was a foolish idea to recover it. I nearly drowned, and the burns on my hands took an age to heal."

"But I had just banished you, so why did you even try? You must have hated me."

"I have never hated you Janus. It was me in the wrong, not you. Retrieving the sword was something I had to do, it was my penance. The placement of it, and with you being the only one able to wield it, was all done for a reason. And I think at last we have finally found our reason."

"Do you know why I cast it away, so it would be gone forever."

"I always presumed your mind wasn't straight due to grief."

"No, quite the opposite in fact. I threw it away so I didn't kill you with it."

"You nearly did once, it's the only scar that has never healed."

"The second time I would not have stopped myself." Janus said truthfully.

"I'm sorry."

"It's ok, all three of us were to blame. We live and learn old friend."

"True, true."

"Anyway, enough of this gloomy talk. I already feel a tad more optimistic. Plus you have saved me from getting wet." Janus said with a returning smile.

"Get wet? You mean you were going to recover it anyway?" Cyrus's voice raised a pitch.

"Well of course, we don't stand a cat in hells chance without it."

Cyrus muttered something under his breath, the only words Janus could make out were "hadn't bothered". Janus had to admit, he hadn't laughed so hard in a long time. His newly reclaimed sword already disappeared, safe and ready until the time comes for him to wield it once more.

The two men spoke well into the small hours, again feeling like the best friends they once were. Both agreeing and realizing their own stupidity, in that it had to take such grave and dire circumstances for them to finally reach this happy point. So lost in conversation the duo were, they didn't realize it was morning until an interrupting cough came from the landlord, prompting them to turn around.

"Bore da, wyt ti eisio brecwast?" he asked.

"Dim diolch, dim ond coffi." Janus replied.

"Dim problem." The landlord said, turning about and then entering the kitchen.

Soon returning with a steaming pot of fresh coffee, that smelt divine.

"Diolch." Said Cyrus, thanking the landlord in his native tongue.

The coffee was good and strong, the chat once again flowed nicely, and plans were formed.

"Look at them, like a couple of long lost love birds, sickening I tell ya." Solomon said to Nathan as the pair walked into the snug and sat down.

"That breakfast was out of this world," Nathan said rubbing his stomach. "Beans, eggs, sausage, toast, mushrooms, hash browns, fried tomatoes, black pudding and buttered bread to mop it all up."

"I'll second that, haven't eaten so much in an age, I am nearly full."

Cyrus looked at Janus, no words passed between them, but it was obvious they were thinking the same thing.

Janus made sure he caught the landlords' eye while he was busy preparing the bar ready for opening in a few hours time.

"Would it be too much bother to rustle up a couple more breakfasts over here my good man."

He merely smiled, nodded his head and returned once more into the kitchen, happy that his culinary skills were being appreciated.

"A wise choice." Solomon admitted. "So what's the plan for today?"

"Cyrus is going to see the Duke of Kent and tell him the time has finally come."

"Hang on a mo, why him and what's he got to do with this? and isn't he royalty? You can't just waltz in and see the likes of him you know."

"I have no intention of waltzing anywhere Sol, he is flying up here by helicopter later this morning."

"Oh," said a slightly deflated Solomon.

"And as to why him, c'mon man you cant be serious."

"Erm."

"Well, in laymen terms, I would say he ultimately works for us."

"Err."

"Oh for fucks sake Sol, not even you are that dense. You explain it to him Janus, I'm going for a piss."

"Right Solomon, I'll break this down as simple as I can for you." Janus began.

"Ok."

"The Duke of Kent, is also the Grand Master of the United Grand Lodge of England. Which in other terms means he's the head of the Freemasons."

"Right, Gotcha."

"The origins of the Knights Templar back in the early twelfth century are surround in myth and legend to most. Very few people on the planet have ever known their true calling."

"Aye, now that brings back some fond memories. The best and most skilled warriors I have had the pleasure of fighting with. Remember how they used to ride into battle on those colossal horses, sat two up and back to back, so they could defend themselves from all quarters. A sight to behold I tell ya."

"Yes Sol, we were there remember."

"Yeah, yeah, I was just saying."

"Anyway, by the eighteenth century the Freemasons became more or less a known organization, which of course included the Knights Templar."

"I am with you so far Janus, but aren't now they just a bunch of wealthy fancy dress wearing men? All pomp and ceremony, but no substance. You can't seriously expect a group of middle aged accounts and bankers to fight with us."

"If you let me finish Sol all will become clear. Since the conception of the Knights Templar's and then the Freemasons, either Cyrus or myself has paid a visit to the overseer, which in this day and age is the Grand Master of the United Lodge of England. We explain our reasons for being here and then show them some undeniable proof that we are genuine." Janus paused momentary as Cyrus returned and took his seat. "When a Grand Master steps down and a new one is about to be appointed, one of us is called in to approve the nomination. If he isn't suitable for whatever reason, we wipe his mind of any details he has been privy too and choose another."

"Yes I know and understand all of this, but it still doesn't answer my question."

Janus ignored the hearty sigh that emanated from Cyrus's direction.

"Ok, as you rightly pointed out, the masons is now a social organization, meeting monthly and doing charitable work etc. but at our behest there is still a small contingent of highly trained soldiers within the loop."

"Ah, now all becomes clear. Why didn't you just say all this in the first place?"

But before anyone could answer the landlord coming in unrudely interrupted them, complete with two of the largest plates Janus had ever seen. Space was quickly cleared before the poor man dropped them under the weight.

"A feast fit for a king, thank you kind sir." Janus said, and Cyrus echoed those sentiments.

"Now if you'll excuse me, I'll be down the cellar for a while cleaning the pipes and changing the barrels. Just shout if you need me."

"No you carry on, and once again, thank you for being so accommodating."

He turned and left, leaving behind the heavenly aroma of freshly cooked fare and two men with eyes nearly the size of the plates it came on.

"Please don't think I am being rude if I ignore you all for five minutes, while I heartily shovel this down before it gets cold." Said Janus, knife and fork in hand and already attacking an escaping sausage.

Barely two mouthfuls had been devoured before the air in the pub turned icy, and like a scene out of a B horror movie a ghostly figure floated in through the locked front door. The shimmering apparition halted some six feet away from the seated quartet.

"You've got a bastard nerve, I'm going to enjoy cutting you in two." Said Solomon already on his feet, sword in hand, about to strike before Nathan rested a hand on his forearm.

"Sit down Sol, it's nothing more than a projection, you can't harm it."

"Yes Nathan, you are of course correct. I just thought I would show my face, in the loosest sense of the word." Chuckled the figure. "Well just look at the happy crowd, have to say you remind me of the four musketeers." He paused. "Hang on, don't tell me, Dumas based his book on you didn't he?"

A nonchalant shrug from Cyrus was the only reply he got.

Janus still hadn't even bothered to look up, and continued to eat his breakfast with the same gusto he began with.

"You're a bunch of hypocrites, you look at me with hatred and distaste in you eyes. Yet, you all have enough blood on your hands to fill a lake. Attila the Hun, Alexander, Genghis Khan, Leonidas, Richard and William, I could go on."

"We deny nothing, and your point is?" Cyrus questioned.

"My point? My point is, you have always been behind the biggest tyrants and murders the world has ever known. So don't play your holier than thou card with me."

"It seems you don't have all the details after all."

"Really? Pray, do tell."

"I'll gladly educate you. You are correct in saying we were behind the great men you mentioned, and yes in many cases we steered them down the paths we wanted. But the vital bit of information your lacking is that there were many other warriors and generals, just as tyrannical and almost as successful. But they made the fatal mistake of entering one battle too many, and remember the winning side writes history. We fought on both sides, and when the commander reached the point that we wanted him to be at, or became too greedy, that's when his rule ended. The world was a brutal place, and if it wasn't for our guidance it would still be in the dark ages, and much more innocent blood would be spilt."

This time it was that cloaked figure that shrugged. Janus still hadn't bothered to look up and was currently mopping up his plate with the bread provided.

"Anyway, what the fuck has this got to do with anything?"

"The four of you are warriors, it's part of your design. Modern day war has no place for you. You stand against me in a battle you cannot win. I would have thought, my new world of chaos would be perfect for you."

"You just don't get it do you? Battle's used to be fought for reasons, be it land gain, or justified beliefs. Soldier's fought for a cause, aggressors and defenders, fighting for King, country or family. War was fought with honor, and you are right in saying modern day war has no place for us. The invention of the firearm saw to that, when the first man was killed by a projectile fired from a musket, honor died with him." Cyrus shot Janus a sideways glance, wondering when he would decide to say his piece or at least acknowledge the apparition before him, but he still seemed to be a world of his own. "We will do everything in our power to prevent your fantastic new world. A world of chaos and anarchy, we will play no part in. Every man woman and child consumed by hate, fathers slaughtering their daughters, sons raping their mother. Don't you EVER compare us to the likes you."

"Whatever, be prepared to die then." He sneered, but Janus's disinterest finally caused him to snap. "IS THE OH SO GREAT JANUS SO AFRAID, THAT HE WONT LOOK HIS VANQUISHER IN THE EYE, I SHALL HAVE YOU BEGGING FOR MERCY AT MY FEET."

His plate now spotless, Janus swallowed his last mouthful of food and slowly lifted his head, he spoke no words but his eyes burned brighter than a star going into supernova. For a spilt second, impossibly the faceless figure looked worried, and then was gone.

With a blink, Janus's eyes were back to normal.

"If you aren't going to finish your breakfast Cyrus, it would be a crying shame to waste it." And with that Janus swapped plates and noisily began to eat once again.

CHAPTER 5

"More Questions Than Answers"
Part One

"Is that it?" Solomon said incredulously.

"Sorry?" Janus replied with a mouth full of food.

"We have just had a visit by that arrogant prick, and all you give a fuck about is whether or not you can get a whole sausage in your mouth."

Solomon had to wait a few moments for his answer while Janus swallowed what he was chewing and drained his coffee mug.

"First thing Sol, as Nathan pointed out what, came here was no more than a projection with no substance. Added to that, he told us fuck all and nothing new was learnt. With those being fact, I wasn't going to waste my breath or even give it the satisfaction of acknowledging it."

"When you put it like that, suppose you got a point." Solomon conceded. "But why do you think he keeps his identity so guarded."

"Dramatic effect probably, but to be honest I really haven't got a clue. Any ideas Nathan?"

"Could be something, could be nothing."

"Not the most helpful of answers, any chance that you might elaborate?"

"It's pure speculation of course, but you might not like what I have to say."

"That's ok Nathan, we're all big boys here, I am sure can take it."

"Ok, I'll try. The most probable answer is as Janus already pointed out, he looks the way he does purely to boast his already over inflated ego."

"But?"

"I think it could also be entirely possible that he is from a different plain, so to speak. A dimension we know nothing off, and that would explain him having no corporal form here."

"So why would he come here?" Solomon asked.

"He feeds of evil, so perhaps he has already consumed all from his place, until it became barren and dry. Or maybe he was banished by forces unaccountably more powerful than himself. The present karma of the world's populace is at an all time low, just ripe for a leech such as himself, to suck humanity dry. Hell, Earth would have been like a magnet, doubt he could have resisted."

"But there's another possibility isn't there Nathan?" Janus prompted.

Nathan inclined his head, grimaced a little and half nodded in Janus's direction, similar to a child who's secret had been discovered.

"Yes there is, and don't shoot me down for this."

"Go on."

"It's briefly crossed my mind, that He is actually one of us."

"BOLLOCKS!" was Solomon's predictable response.

"Shut up Sol." Cyrus said coldly. "How could that be? Are you saying one of us is a traitor Nathan?"

"I don't mean to imply it's any of us from now, but from a time yet to come."

"DOUBLE BOLLOCKS!"

"It most likely is bollocks Sol. I am just looking at all the options, that's all."

"To satisfy my idle curiosity, how could you possibly come to that conclusion?" Janus asked calmly.

"Ok, what if sometime long into the future an event takes place with catastrophic consequences, and the only way to prevent that is to virtually wipe out Man, and start a fresh."

"Hhmm, isn't what could be happening in a weeks time catastrophic enough? And if sadly you are right, I am sure there would be a less horrific way of achieving it."

"If I may, I'll answer you second question first. As much as it loathes me to say it, his method of extinguishing Man and starting again, is a near perfect one. Turning the people against one another with no organization or design, just pure hate, means they will tear each other apart with their bare hands, literally. Buildings etc will remain intact. No chemical or nuclear weapons will be used, so there won't be any radioactive contamination, which in turn means land will still be fertile. Also, our co-inhabitants, from insects to elephants shall suffer not from our extinction."

"And the first question?" Cyrus asked bleakly.

"If we fail in seven days time, the results will be catastrophic and horrific, that I grant you. Although sometimes you just have to look at the bigger picture, I know it's been said before, but no matter how tragic the consequences, the needs of the many, outweigh the needs of the few."

"How can you call six billion deaths, a few?" said Solomon sourly.

"Six billion in what context Sol? How many inhabited world are there in this universe? As well as those we alone know of at least four different dimensions all containing life. The total number of sentient beings could well be incalculable. If the existence of everything is going to be somehow at threat, the death of six billion would be a small price to pay. But like I said, don't shoot me down here guys, I am merely playing the devils advocate and looking at all possibilities."

"It's still bollocks. If it was one of us, which it isn't, don't you think he would reveal himself to us, talk to us and explain the situation."

"You think? Hi, it's me Nathan from the future; do you guys mind doing nothing while I destroy all of humanity? Get real Sol."

It was time again for Cyrus's input; Janus just sat back and listened.

"Correct me if I am wrong, but wouldn't killing the four of us battle, which if I am honest, with the odds we are facing is a very real possibility, also mean he would fail to exist?"

"Quite simply, I have no idea. Paradox's I know nothing about, in fact, no one does due to the fact that there has never been one. But it's a scenario I am sure he's aware of and would have put the appropriate wheels in motion. His own death so to speak would be a small price to pay, if it achieves the outcome he needs."

Nathan was now getting weary with the constant questioning, but the other two didn't seem like letting up any time soon.

"You say no carrier has been infected yet. So the answer is blatantly obvious than."

"Go on, surprise me then Cyrus." But Nathan knew what was coming next.

"Simple, the four of us commit hara-kiri, and end it all now."

"I give up, you haven't listened to a word I said have you." Nathan sighed shaking his head.

Before things became unnecessarily heated, Janus decided it was time to speak.

"And if Nathan is wrong Cyrus, we are all dead, along with any hope mankind has."

"Erm."

"Anyway, before this ends in a needless argument, can I ask what led you to that conclusion Nathan?"

"Just something somebody said, that's all."

The other three waited in silence for Nathan to elaborate, but it didn't seem he was going to, not without prompting anyway.

"Come on man, you've piqued our curiosity, you cant leave it there."

"Ok then. I was telling a friend about us and.."

"Did you just say you were telling a friend about us?" Cyrus interrupted.

"Yes."

"I don't know what to say, quite frankly I am astonished. I can't decide which is the most incredible; the fact that you go round telling any Tom, Dick or Harry about us, or that you have a friend."

"Fuck off Cyrus, that's one more true friend than you've ever had."

"Ignore him Nathan, you have me intrigued, please continue."

Nathan nodded a quick thank you before speaking again.

"For your information Cyrus, I had good reason to tell him, and in many ways the responsibility and burden I left upon his shoulders, is greater than ours." Nathan paused briefly to see if Cyrus or Solomon had anything detrimental to say, wisely in this instance they remained silent. "I explained how we were the ultimate victims of the earliest case of bad press, and how whereas mankind believes us to be the cause and not the cure for global destruction. As always he listened intently, mulled over things for a short time, then said maybe the predictions were correct all along."

"TRIPLE BOLLOCKS."

"Shut up Sol!" and Janus meant it. "I apologize one last time for the children, they wont interrupt again, that I can assure you. Please I'd like to hear more." The look Janus gave the other two assured there would be no more imprudence.

"There's not much more to tell really, his thinking was along the lines of, is it possible our inaction or actions unwittingly precipitate Armageddon."

"Interesting."

"Yes, but I have looked at just about every possible scenario where we stand back and do nothing, and the outcome each time is, that carrier is released, therefore Man is doomed. There is no way he can be right, that's when I came up with the possibility that Ahriman is one of us. It's the only thing I could think of that made the slightest resemblance of sense."

"Your friend is a very astute fellow Nathan, and makes a valid point."

"Yes, I told him as much."

"But he is wrong." Janus said flatly.

"I know both of us have given Nathan a hard time, but only because we respect him and what he has to say, and to be honest, we were worried that he just might be correct. I really hope your right Janus, but how can you be so sure?" Cyrus asked.

"Because I also came to the same possible conclusion."

"Really?" was everyone's surprised reply.

"Yes. So whist I was ignoring his pathetic projection I was probing our minds, including mine. If he had been one of us there would have been a connection, even if he tried to conceal it. Deep down in the subconscious there would be a link, which would be impossible to camouflage. The four of us are definitely in the clear."

"Well, that's good enough for me, and it's a weight of my mind to say the least. It doesn't change the situation or the astronomical odds we are facing, but strangely makes things just a little easier."

"I know what you mean, I was dreading it being one of us. I don't know what I would have done if it had been. A truly impossible conundrum would have faced us."

The four sat in silence for some while, no words needed to be spoken, now was a time for reflection and preparation. Once again it was Nathan that brought everyone back from the little worlds they had absorbed themselves in.

"There is something else."

"Go ahead, questions and secrets must all come out, no matter how insignificant you think it may be."

"It's most probably nothing, but does the word Croatoan mean anything to anybody?"

"You mean this word?" and with that Janus slid a small laminated business card across the table. It was embossed with the word CROATOAN in large black letters, nothing more.

That was something Nathan wasn't prepared for, and it took him a little while to find his voice while he fingered the tiny pristine card.

"It's virtually brand new! Where did you get it? How long have you had it?" was the best Nathan could manage.

"This is where it gets a little strange, but that unremarkable little card is over forty years old."

"QUADRUPLE BOLLOCKS," Nathan couldn't resist saying. "But seriously, it looks no more than a few days old, any other man I would call a liar. Where did you get it?"

But before Janus could answer, like a street card trickster Solomon deftly flicked an identical tiny card in Nathan's direction, which without even looking up he only just caught between the tips of two fingers.

"Reflex's slowing down there, wee fella."

"Considering I am sitting less than two feet away I thought I did pretty damn well. So you also have one I see." Nathan said while comparing the two cards.

"Oh yes, and I think I can top Janus."

"Really? In what way?"

"Boss man says he has had his for forty years. Well I'll see his forty and raise it to sixteen hundred." Solomon smirked; glad to have something up on the others for once.

Three jaws visibly dropped.

"No disrespect big guy, but you must be mistaken, there is no way that this could be sixteen hundred years old, the materials, ink etc hadn't even been invented then."

"Oh, it gets stranger."

"How on earth can it get stranger?" Nathan's was now completely confused.

"Have you tried losing it?" Solomon asked Janus.

"You too then?"

"Yep."

"WHAT?" asked a frustrated Nathan.

"The card can't be lost or destroyed, and believe me I have tried. Every time I mislaid it, burnt it, cut it in two, low and behold the next day it turns up again somewhere visible."

"Same here." Janus agreed.

"For the first time in my life, I am totally out of my depth here and haven't got a clue what's going on." Nathan admitted.

"Well I haven't got one." Said a dejected Cyrus, feeling a little left out.

"Yes, for once Cyrus, your not the center of attention. I just can't get my head around this, these didn't exist sixteen hundred years ago, in fact even forty years ago is pushing it. Didn't you think it was strange at the time Sol?"

"I didn't pay it much attention to be honest, it simply became something that is always with me that's all. It was only in the last twenty years or so that I realized what it was."

"How to you acquire it Sol?"

Solomon took a deep breath and sat back.

"I'll tell ya, now there's a story. It begins with the time when I took a short sabbatical for about half century."

I was happily traveling about, going nowhere in particular, finding new places and revisiting old favorites to see if the years had been kind too them. My current blissful meanderings led me to what we now know as southern Turkey, and a large town named Myra. Due to the lateness of the hour the streets were deserted, my only companion was my faithful smiling friend, as ever, beaming down his comforting moonlight and showing me the path. The towns' beauty was breathtaking and long before sunrise I had decided that this would be my home for at least a little while.

When finally my consort and his subtle gift left me to guide another, and his bright and brash brother stepped in to take his place, my heart sank.

Not for the first time, the light of the moon was somewhat rose tinted, and the earlier beauty was replaced by dilapidation. Times were harsh, with crop failures and unusually inclement weather, the people tried their best, but obviously survival took precedence, aesthetics rightly came a poor second.

Because he had shown me what once was, and what could be once again, the moon had earned gratitude from two parties; one being my good self, for leading me here, and the other, the townsfolk (who sadly would never know to thank him), because, I had made the easy decision to stay and help them.

So, where to begin? Lodgings would have to be my first priority, and the local church is always a good start.

To my dismay, the once magnificent church had fallen into a state horrendous disrepair. The grounds unkempt and strewn with litter, the pathway to the entrance, overgrown and carpeted with dead leaves.

Did the bishop have no pride?

On entering the church, it was clear what the answer was, no he didn't.

The once white walls were weeping with age and neglect, there were large patches of discoloration where tapestries and paintings once hung, all that was left of them was their unhappy shadow. The roof offered no shelter; it was no more than a skeleton, with visible ribs devoid of meat.

Nothing of any value remained, any silverware had long since gone, even the good book and tin collection plate were missing, probably stolen or sold.

I could sense someone else present, so I bellowed out a greeting.

It was many minutes before a disheveled, unkempt man wearing unwashed and threadbare rags, appeared from a rear annex.

"There is nothing of any value here, please leave." The man said tiredly.

"Your Grace?" Was this truly the Bishop? Were times really so hard?

"Once, a long time ago, when people still had respect for me. But no one has called me that for many moons, nor is it a title that I am worthy of."

"I am sorry, respect or no respect, that's still no excuse for lowlifes and vagabonds to steal blessed items of value." I said looking around the sad building.

He mumbled something under his breath, in fact, it was obvious he begrudged me being there and didn't want too initiate in any more conversation.

"I am looking for lodging's, in the past the Church has always been most accommodating."

"If you have money, then the inn has plenty of rooms, otherwise, I'm sorry I can not help you. Good day."

As well as his faith, the man had lost any sense of charity it seemed.

"Oh, I have money, plenty of it. My parents were extremely wealthy and have recently passed on. I like my solitude, and the inn is a little too rowdy for my tastes. Oh well not to worry, and sorry to have troubled you." And I turned to leave.

With the hook baited, I barely had time to take one step before he bit.

"Money you say?" the bishop said in a tone that I had heard many times before.

"Plenty." And I plucked a bag of gold from a pocket and shook it, so he could hear the coins dancing inside.

"Well, as you can see, the church is in dire need of repair, so the money would help. I no longer use the vestry, so I could set up a bed for you there. Would that be acceptable?" He was actually rubbing his hands together as he spoke.

"Perfect, please do that, and I shall return later." I tossed him the bag before leaving.

As much, a force of habit as well as curiosity, when I decided to settle anywhere I always spent plenty of time exploring every inch of my new surroundings. And on more than one occasion, such familiarity has saved my hide or an embarrassing confrontation.

I whole-heartedly enjoyed my constitutional, although I was surprised at how few a people were about, but every one I did meet was surprisingly affable considering times were so harsh. Filled with pleasure and zeal at my interesting reconnoiter, I had lost track of time and it was already dusk when I returned to the church.

The place was dark and deserted, and the bishop was nowhere in sight. I soon found the vestry and sure enough, it was now furnished with a bed, table and a couple of wooden chairs. More than adequate for my humble needs.

As I sat on the bed, pondering about nothing in particular, a worrying thought hit me.

The very bed I was sitting on, was comfortable and well used, which could only mean one thing; it was the bishops.

I was quickly on my feet and investigating the other rooms of the church, sadly, it soon became apparent that I had just cause for my apprehension. The bishop had absconded.

It was at that moment I knew that the valuable church relics hadn't been stolen, but he had sold them, and foolish me had given him a bag of gold.

Losing the money wasn't a problem in itself, if truth be known; I could confidently say that I was one of the four richest people on the planet. I had always been generous, too generous and trusting many would say, but the one thing that really irked me was underhandedness. It's happened before and would no doubt happen again, but it still pissed me off all the same.

I was filled with pity more than anger, at how far the bishop must have fallen to stoop so low.

Some hours later I was lying on the bed, still seething at my own stupidity, when I could feel the presence of two people very close by.

"I hope for your sakes, your not here for what I think you're here for." I whispered quietly to myself, whilst tuning over on the bed, making sure my back was to the door.

Sure enough, the wooden door slowly creaked open, and then I could sense two afraid and unsure minds in the room with me.

I waited a few brief moments before causing the door to slam closed, that split second distraction was all I needed. Reflex reaction meant the two men had no choice but to look in the door's direction, when they turned back I was already standing before them.

"SIT" I growled.

They of course did as they were told.

"Now think very carefully before you answer. Why are you here?"

The braver of the two answered almost immediately.

"I sorry, we came steal some gold."

That honest answer had saved their lives. If I had thought they were true thieves, both would be dead by now, after I had shown them a new type of hell. I then realized, I wasn't the cause of the fear these men felt.

Now that piqued my curiosity, most the time I am a friendly giant, but if need be I can become more than a little intimidating, but something has scared them more than me.

"With no excuse for being here, or club to beat me to death, you can't be very successful thieves."

"Sire please, don't hurt us, we are not bad men. But our children are missing."

Of course, the one thing scarier then me; a parents fear for their offspring.

 I sat on the bed, all thoughts of intimidation gone.

"Please, call me Nicholas. Now tell me more." I asked in a voice more akin to my usual self.

I have no idea to this day why I chose the name Nicholas for this little adventure, it quite simply just sounded right.

"My name is Michael, and this is Peter, my son Martin and Peter's two sons Joseph and David have been missing since nightfall yesterday. Most of the townsfolk have been good enough to help us search, but as you know, we are in dire times and we cant expect them to lose another days pay by helping us."

"But why come here, I am sure you knew that there was nothing of any value left?"

"The sorry excuse for our bishop, got very drunk before leaving town, he bragged about a wealthy stranger staying here. I am ashamed to admit through sheer desperation, our plan was to steal just a few coins from you, enough to pay the townsfolk for their help. Once again, we are sorry."

I paused for a moment, thinking how to handle this situation, but time wasn't a luxury I had, so straight and too the point it would have to be.

"No need, now Peter, go home and fetch some of your children's warm clothes, enough for all three. Michael, I noticed a fire bell in the towns square, hurry there and ring it."

"But that will wake every one up and they will come to investigate."

"That's the plan, and we shall search through the night and not rest until we find them."

"I can't ask them to do that."

"Maybe not, but I can, and don't worry I shall make it worth their while. Now go and hurry."

Now they had been given just a faintest flicker of hope, the two stunned men, nearly ran out of the door.

This wasn't quite the way I had envisaged to introduce myself to the people here, my plan was to slowly integrate with the community until they accepted me as no longer the new comer.

But children being in danger took precedence over my original intentions.

The reason for asking Peter to fetch the clothing was two fold; one, obviously so they would have something warm to wear, not that it is cold, but they will probably be in shock. And two; to give me a link to them, having contact with an item that belongs to them, would make my job much easier.

Before I even had a chance to work out the best way to approach this predicament, the silence was shattered by the monotone clanging of the town's bell.

I opened my shoulder bag, which until a few moments ago was empty, and plucked out a large coat and a silken sack of money, then left the church.

By the time I reached the square, most of the townsfolk were already there and congregating in small groups, torches lit and not looking best pleased at being awoken at this hour, especially since there was no fire.

Michael was doing his best to placate them, but with nothing to offer and unsure at what to say, he was fighting a losing battle.

I purposely walked through the crowd, making sure all eyes were on this unknown stranger. Standing on the steps of the inn, which was the highest point available, I prepared to speak.

"Peter, please pass me those clothes."

The quiet man, still numb from shock and worry, did as he was asked.

"Tonight, two men, Peter and Michael, came to me, a complete stranger, and asked for my help." I had no reason to shame the men by divulging the true events of our first meeting.

"But why come to me, a newcomer, someone who has only just arrived? I asked them. And do you know what they said?"

The crowd remained silent, even though most already knew the answer.

"They told me that they were too embarrassed to ask the townsfolk, because they couldn't pay you." I slowly shook my head as I ended the sentence.

There were mutterings and much shuffling of feet in the gathered throng.

"TOO EMBARRASSED TO ASK THEIR OWN NIGHBOURS AND FRIENDS?" I bellowed. "What kind of godforsaken place have I come too, when a father, and it could be ANY of you, has to PAY the townsfolk, whom he had always considered to be his friends, to find his missing child." I then held up one of the child's items of clothing, making it look tiny in my huge hand.

Still no one spoke, so I put my free hand into one of the many pockets of my jacket, and pulled out the purse, I then threw it on the dusty floor, at the feet of the gathering.

"But I am not going to pay YOU a penny. That money is a gift to the town, a thank you for finding Peter and Michael's son's. SO ARE WE READY?" I had changed the townsfolk's mood, from guilt to enthusiasm. Everyone was starving, and they needed money to live, the way I worded my offer, meant they wouldn't feel bad about taking it, and could search for the children, without having the constant worry of where their next meal would come from.

But I now faced a problem.

During my big speech, when I symbolically held aloft the child's clothing, I instantly became aware of their whereabouts. They were close, very close in fact, but how was I going lead them there, without looking suspicious.

"Is the innkeeper here amongst us?" I asked, and was rewarded by a chorus of laughter.

"You must be joking, all he cares about is himself and his profit." A voice from the crowd shouted. Obviously the word irony hadn't reached these parts as I looked down at the bag of money.

"Does he have any children?"

Again there was more laughter.

"He hates children, because they have no money." The same voice replied.

"Hhmm, that's strange, when I arrived late last night, as I walked passed the inn, I heard a crying child in a backroom." I lied, but the laughter stopped.

"I smell foul deeds afoot, some of you go around the back and block any exits, the rest of you wait here. I am going to investigate."

Michael grabbed my arm.

"I am coming with you, the innkeeper is a nasty piece of work, and its my son remember."

"No Michael, please stay here, for a few moments at least, I don't want you getting hurt, and don't fret about me, I can take nasty to a whole new level." And I meant it. "But don't worry, your son is ok." I wish I could have said that with more conviction, but Peter still nodded and let me go.

The large wooden door was locked, but one shove from me soon solved that problem, and I was in. The large room was dark and empty but the smell of wrongness was rife. From under a door at the rear of the room I could see a faint light, I was across the room and through the door in less than a heartbeat.

The scene that greeted me was bad, but could have been so much worse. On the immense kitchen table, lay the three children, drugged and unconscious. The innkeeper had his back to me while he lifted the lid off a large barrel of brine, one of three in the room. A quick scan of his mind revealed his horrific scheme, unwilling to pay his suppliers increasing prices, he was going to drown the youngsters in the saltwater barrels, then serve their meat as ham, quite possibly even too their own fathers'.

By now, the innkeeper had turned around, and knowing he'd been caught red handed, was looking for an escape.

"You're going nowhere my man." I told him, as an invisible hand grasped his throat and painfully pinned him against the wall, his gurgling protestations falling on deaf ears.

I left him choking and flailing about like a bewitched marionette, while I quickly tended the children. To my relief, the children's comatose ness was no more than a deep slumber and they would suffer no lasting harm. It didn't take much to gently enter their minds and slowly awaken them.

The townsfolk could wait no longer, and by now they were streaming into the inn, Peter and Michael were first through the backroom door, so I quickly released my hold on the innkeeper and he fell to the floor sniveling and crying for forgiveness.

"Your sons are fine and unharmed." I said quietly.

What must have been the children's mothers' burst through the crowd and went straight too the confused and groggy little ones, and checked them thoroughly for any injury or malady.

Meanwhile, I ushered the crowd back out into the towns square, and explained the despicable intentions of the innkeeper, all the while he groveled for forgiveness on the dusty floor."

"HANG HIM."

"STONE HIM."

"DROWN HIM IN BRINE."

The people wanted blood, and they wanted it now.

"ENOUGH!" I said in a voice that ensured silence. "Appropriate justice shall be dealt, but not this night. He deserves all that is coming to him, but having a man's blood on your hands is something you have to think carefully about, it never washes off and lives with you until your final breath. We shall wait until the morrow, and then decided suitable punishment. AGREED?"

Tension and emotions were still high, but apart from a few procrastinators the townsfolk agreed.

"So until the morning, this sorry excuse for a man shall stay in my care in the church. Is that acceptable?"

Nobody argued.

"People, please go back to your homes, and get some sleep, we shall settle this tomorrow."

The townsfolk split and made their own ways home, many still hurling abuse at the innkeeper as they left.

"You know the way to the church, so have some dignity and walk, or I will carry you." The innkeeper did as he was ordered.

It wasn't long before we were in my room and I allowed the man sit.

"You saved my life, thank you." He sniveled.

"I saved you from a quick death, yes."

"Thank you, thank you, thank you."

"But I am going to give you a slow and painful death, and this way none of the towns people will have your demise on their conscience."

The man's sniveling stopped.

"At this moment in time, I can quite confidently say, you the unluckiest man alive."

It's true when they say you can smell a man's fear, the innkeeper reeked of it.

I calmly walked across the room and began to pour myself a beaker of water.

The innkeepers fear turned to confusion, he looked around not understanding what was happening. He was still sat in the same room, but now it was empty apart from himself, the chair and of course my good self.

"Constantine, yes I know your name, welcome to your dream world, or more appropriately, Hell."

Even in this in-between place, it is still possible to empty ones bowls, and he did.

"Although this is essentially "your place", here I am God, and it obeys my rules."

I paced slowly back and forth; terrified eyes watched my every step.

"Anyway, enough of the small talk; let us begin."

I clicked my fingers and instantly Constantine became a white-hot burning inferno, his screams were horrific.

I let him burn for a full minute before I snapped my fingers again, and the fire was gone. His skin, hair, clothes even were still intact, no physical damage was done.

The innkeepers' eyes sprung open, he was back in my "real" room, and I was still pouring my water, in fact the beaker wasn't yet a quarter full.

"Hello." I said smiling; Constantine mumbled an incoherent reply that I didn't understand.

"It would be rude of me not to explain the rules of "the other place", you feel every ounce of pain there as you would here, you cannot die or pass out, and five minutes there is less than a second here. Just thought it was only fair to let you know. Ready to go back?" I asked whilst sipping my drink.

"Please no, have mercy," he sobbed.

"Joseph, David and Martin, pleaded and cried for their mother when they were cold and afraid in your cellar. I shall show you the same mercy that you offered them. "

"But, but, I drugged them, I could have easily slit their throat with a knife." He whispered ashamedly.

"Do you take me for a fool? You intended to drown them in brine, so their meat stayed fresher for longer."

The innkeeper stayed silent, now knowing his fate was sealed.

"Ah, look where were are again."

But he already knew.

"So, any last words?"

"I, I, I'm sorry." Was all he could manage.

I clicked my fingers and the inferno once more began.

I returned to the real world, leavening Constantine burning in the other. To give the man a few grains of credit, he lasted nearly five minutes before he finally died, his face contorted into a hideous death mask.

I had neglected to tell him, that his heart would eventually give out.

"They always say their sorry when faced with the inevitable." I sighed to myself as I lay on my bed; with nothing more to do than wait for morning.

It was not long after sunup when where was a knock at my door.

"Come in Michael, but prepare yourself."

As expected, Michael entered, but I was surprised at the nonplus he gave the deceased innkeeper. Michael said nothing but merely raised an eyebrow and looked at me.

"He died in his sleep, would you believe."

"So it seems. I would have happily put a noose around his neck you know."

"Yes I know, and you would have had just cause to do so. You may find it hard to believe now, but at some time in the future, the fingers of guilt would grasp you, and they have grip that would last until your last breath."

Michael just shrugged his shoulders.

"At least justice has been served. Now, my main reason for being here is to thank you Nicholas, I didn't get a chance last night."

I was slightly confused for a split second; I had nearly forgot that I was using a pseudonym.

"Don't be silly my friend, no need whatsoever to thank me."

"Even so, thank you. I shan't ask how, but when you held aloft David's clothes, I saw the change in you, that's when you knew where the children were."

It was my turn to shrug,

"Like I said, its none of my concern. My other reason for being here is now a little defunct; I was going to ask if you could bring him to the towns square, everyone is waiting."

"Ah."

"Not to worry, what do you suggest we do with the body?"

"There's a cliff nearby, let the fish feast on his rotting flesh. He deserves nothing more."

"Agreed, no argument from me there. I was accompanied here by two townsfolk to escort Constantine back. If you don't mind, would it be acceptable if the three of you dispose of the body, in the meantime I shall return to the square and explain the situation, and when you have finished, meet us back there."

"Certainly, consider it done."

Michael left to apprise the others while I found some old sacking and fashioned a makeshift shroud for the innkeeper. When finished I then hoisted his body over my shoulder and left the church.

The two townsmen greeted me by name and seemed pleasant and affable as we made our way to the nearby cliff face.

Job soon done, and we continued to make happy small talk until we reached the town's square.

As I expected, it was filled with what I guessed to be nearly the whole town, but totally unforeseen by myself was the monumental cheer that erupted as I drew near.

Michael, who obviously had been nominated as the towns' spokesman stood at the forefront.

"Nicholas, I speak for everyone when I say we all owe you a debt of gratitude." Michael's sentiments were echoed by the nodding crowd.

He then walked towards me with something in his hand.

"We would also like to return the money you kindly offered, we appreciate the gesture, but we cannot accept it."

I held up my hand to halt Michael's approach.

"I refuse to take back the money, as I said last night, it's a gift for the town, and to get it back on its feet. I have been here for less than a blink of the eye, but already my heart feels like it belongs. So with my help, we shall make the town of Myra, the envy of everyone. The matter of the money is closed."

Another cheer erupted, and Michael turned to the people but was silently prompted to speak once more.

"We would also like to offer you the post of Bishop, since there now seems to be a vacancy."

"I am truly flattered, but sadly, it's a title that I cannot accept."

I had to hold my hand up once again as the townsfolk were about to protest.

"BUT, if you allow me to stay in the church for the time being, I will gladly offer consul and be a confidant to whoever seeks it. Also, once a week if you so wish, we can gather inside the church as a community, and will happily regale with tales that will restore your faith in the goodness of man. Until such a time when a new bishop is found of course. Is that acceptable?"

A third cheer went up, and I spent the next hour shaking hands and meeting the townsfolk individually, I was a little concerned by Peter's absence however.

Such was everyone's enthusiasm that I had lost track of time, when I felt a tap on my shoulder, I turned to see Michael standing there.

"Nicholas, please come with me."

My concern turned to worry as I made my excuses to leave and follow Michael.

He was leading me back to the church, and I soon discovered that my anxiety was unfounded.

What must have been all the town's children were in the grounds of the church, picking up leaves and tending the garden, supervised by a smiling Peter.

When Peter saw me approaching, he rushed over and embraced me like a brother.

"I have not had a chance to thank you personally, but I shall forever also owe you a debt of gratitude."

By now the children had stopped worked and were lined up at the church gates.

"Well, what do you have to say?" Peter prompted.

"THANK YOU NICHOLAS, FOR RIDDING US OF THE NASTY MAN." Came the chorus.

I winked at the two adults present, and walked over to the children.

"Right my little ones, best I learnt your names don't you think?" The wide-eyed children had no fear, as I towered over them. "So after three I want you to shout out your names, ok."

The eager children nodded in anticipation at this new game.

"Ready, one, two," I paused for a moment. "THREE"

The sound of over fifty kids shouting their names simultaneously would have been nothing more than an impalpable noise to any other ears than my own.

Then I amazed the children, and probably Peter and Michael, by repeating each child's name back to them, whilst pointing at the said child.

"Ok, ready to play a game?" A silly question to ask I know. "I shall turn my back, close my eyes and count to one hundred, you run off and hide and the last person I find, shall get a special gift."

As the stealth less giggling kids ran to find the best hiding places, I faced Peter and Michael.

162

"Well, you seem to be in your element Nicholas." Michael said.

"Can't argue there my friend."

"Is it ok to leave them in your care for a short time, we have some business to attend too."

"Of course, I'll be honored to look after them, but I shall have to send them home in a couple of hours, there's a violent storm brewing."

The two looked up into the sky, then back at me with a slightly doubting look on their faces.

"Ok, thank you Nicholas, we shall see you later."

The duo left and I continued my loud counting, making sure I kept getting the numbers wrong, which rewarded me with muffled laughter nearby.

After nearly two hours of enjoyable play, it was time to send the kids home, I could sense the storm was nearing and I wanted them safely tucked in bed. So I sent them on their way, with promises of more games tomorrow, and if they behaved, maybe even a story or two. And unbeknown to the little ones, I ensured that each left with a couple of coins hidden in their pockets.

With night drawing in, I sat in my room, thinking up activities for the next day, and listening to the growing winds concerto as she played in and out of the exposed rafters.

"Come in Michael." I said just before he knocked.

He entered looking windswept and cold.

"Sit down man, this no night to be out."

"I am sorry Nicholas for coming at such an hour, but something is on my mind and is troubling me."

"My door is always open, for you or anybody. Please tell me your problem my friend."

"Not my problem as such, but a member of our community, who shall remain nameless, has come to me sick with guilt and worry."

"Go on."

"Well, he fears that he may have to sell his daughters into prostitution."

"Excuse me?"

"He has three daughters, who in turn are very much in love with three brothers, but as we all have nothing, he cannot afford a dowry."

"And the brothers insist on this? I thought you said their love was shared both ways."

"No, the brothers have no interest in the dowry, but the family is equally as poor and cannot afford to lose their only three sons without one."

"Ah, now I understand. Don't worry Michael, leave it to me."

"May I speak honestly Nicholas?"

"I would feel insulted if you didn't." I wasn't quite sure where this was going.

"Thank you. I mean it from the bottom of my heart when I say we are all grateful for your generosity."

"But?"

"But, although yours is a lovely gesture, you might as well given us pebbles from the shore."

"I don't understand Michael."

"We ALL have nothing, so what good is money and gold? I truly apologize for being so blunt, but we can't eat coins."

"Of course you can't Michael, this is a sea port, so I gave the money so everyone could buy what they needed when the next ship docks."

"There is no next ship." Michael said sadly.

"Pardon?"

"All the captains know we have nothing, and haven't docked here for nearly two years."

"I see, I am sorry, I should have realized that. Please fret not my friend, leave everything to me. Now best you get home quickly before the storm really gets its wind."

"How are you going.."

"Not important right now." I cut him off.

"Why are you doing this Nicholas?"

"I'll see you tomorrow Michael." I said with a smile.

"Goodnight, and thank you again." Michael replied, knowing his was getting no further answers from me.

He left, but I could clearly make out tears starting to well up. Seeing a man, who spoke for the all in the town, nearly start to cry because a stranger had offered them some small glimmer of hope, made me doubly certain that my decision to stay was the right one.

I waited nearly a full hour after Michael had departed before I stood up, donned my coat and hat, but realizing in this wind, my hat wouldn't last long, so I begrudgingly took it off.

"Busy night ahead big man, best we get started." I said only to myself.

Upon leaving the church, it seemed the wind took umbrage to anyone that dared test her strength, so she showed me her temper, and the wind increased.

Walking through such weather, which would have taken any normal man clean off his feet, troubled me not, especially knowing that this would be simple in comparison to my later task.

Although Michael hadn't named the man we spoke about, I knew exactly whom he met. Upon meeting the townsfolk, this particular man was the only one with three daughters. Because by shaking his hand, I had made physical contact, so finding his house only took me a few moments.

Even from the outside, I knew that the household was all asleep, which was quite an achievement considered the noise of the storm.

I entered quietly through the front door, for a larger man I could be very light of foot when needed. The girls all shared a room and bed, which made things slightly easier. At the foot of the bed were three neatly folded piles of clothes, and upon each one I placed a small bag of gold, an ample amount for a dowry.

I then left the house as silently as I entered.

"One job down, one to go."

Next I made my way through the winding streets, and down towards the shore, the wind chasing me all the way.

I looked out onto the boiling ocean, the sea as rough and angry as I had ever seen it. The Forty-foot waves parodying immense gaping jaws, tipped with huge white teeth, devouring one another in a never-ending cycle.

Far out, invisible to most, I could make out a ship, anchored down and riding out the tempest.

A small rowing boat lay sleeping high up on the shore away from the oceans wrath. Turning the vessel over I was happy to find its oars secreted beneath it. I slowly dragged the craft towards the waterline, her old timbers groaning in protest.

"Don't worry old girl, I'll keep you safe." I said to myself as much as to the boat.

Once in the water and fighting every forward inch, I came to the conclusion that in all my centuries of existence, this has to be top of my stupid ideas list. I had to call upon many of my special talents, and even then, I was damned lucky not to sink or capsize. After the longest three hours of my life I finally reached the moored ship.

The poor soul that for whatever reason must be out of favor with the captain, to be assigned the unenviable duty of being the lookout during this storm, nearly fainted as a sopping wet me clambered over the rail.

"Take me to the captain." I asked, blunt and to the point.

"I think he may be asleep." Replied the still gob smacked deckhand.

"I wasn't asking." I previous few hours had dampened my mood somewhat.

"Follow me." The deckhand was intelligent enough to realize someone insane enough to be out in this weather, let alone in a tiny craft, wasn't going to take no for an answer.

He led me to a door at the rear of the ship.

"I'll take it from here boy, best you return to your duties."

The lookout shrugged and left, and I banged on the door.

"Come, and this had better be good." Came the muffled reply.

I entered the cabin; the captain was up and sat behind a desk, scrutinizing the charts laid out before him.

"Who the hell are you, and what are you doing aboard my ship?" Asked the captain, unable to hide the astonishment in his voice.

"My name is Nicholas, and I represent the town of Myra, tell me, what cargo are you carrying?" I wasn't in the mood for small talk.

"Well Nicholas, I am sorry to say your perilous trip was a wasted one. My hold is full to the brim with livestock, grain and building materials, but alas, all is already sold at my next port."

"Superb, just what we need. I'll take it all."

"I notice your foolhardy trip has damaged your hearing, everything is sold."

"My hearing is fine, and I shall say only once more. I'll take it all."

The bag of money I threw onto the desk, would have covered the price of the cargo three times over.

"We shall dock at Myra tomorrow, once the storm clears." Was the captains response.

"Good, now there are two conditions."

"I had a feeling there might be, go on."

"You tell the townsfolk, that due to the storm, you have missed your deadline and your original customer no longer requires your cargo. And you will sell them your goods at ten percent of the normal value."

"And you want the ten percent I presume?"

"You presume wrong, that money is also yours."

"Ok, and the other condition?"

"Once you are unloaded, you return from whence you came, stock up your hold once more, and make Myra your first port of call. Trade will then be conducted at a fair price."

"Agreed."

"I have your word?"

"You do." And the captain thrust out his hand sealing the verbal contract.

"One more small detail, please make no mention of me."

The captain nodded, understand what I meant.

"I can find you a bunk for the night, and you can return to shore with us tomorrow, and don't worry, my crew shall say nothing."

"Thank you for the offer, but I shall have to decline."

"So be it, I must say you're a strange one Nicholas, and this has been the second strangest encounter I have ever experienced?"

"Second?"

"Oh yes, many many moons ago, when I was a young deckhand, a shadowy figure boarded the ship I was crewing on, and said if I valued my life, it would be best I left. His tone was one that I did as I was told without a seconds thought. The horror stories I later heard, about the events that took place that night, are now stuff of sea legend. In fact, nights such as this very one, are still known as Cyrus's Fury."

"Well he always had a temper. Right, I shall bid you farewell and look forward to meeting you again in the morn."

"Until then."

I turned to leave, but just before I reached the door, I realized I had forgotten to mention something.

"Ah, one very last minor detail."

"Yes?"

"If you cross me in any way; there shall be another sea legend to rival that of Cyrus's Fury."

And with that I was back out into the torrent and soon on my little boat that had faithfully waited for my return.

Thankfully, my return journey was much easier, it seemed a truce had been called between the battling elements, to allow me safe passage back.

The Sun was just beginning to awaken from her slumber, and was lazily rising by the time I reached the shore. Although exhausted, I dragged the staunch little rowboat back to her resting place, so she could enjoy the repose she richly deserved.

I could now safely return to the church, rest a while and then watch the coming days events unfold.

As promised and true to his word, the ship did indeed make port at Myra the very next day, and with the captain virtually giving his wares away, the townsfolk cleared him out and emptied his ship before nightfall, and he was gone on the next tide.

(That day, saw a new beginning for Myra and it's people, and much to my embarrassment at the time, the community held a meeting and decreed that, this date shall be known as Nicholas Day, and unbeknown to me at the time, we way we celebrated it, began a tradition that is still observed the world over, and hopefully will be for a long time to come.)

The very next day after the ships departure I was out with the children, taking them on a walk and teaching about the wondrous things that grew and lived on the outskirts of the town and down on the shore. And when I returned I could see that the church was bustling with activity. Curious as to what the problem could be, I headed straight there. My heart lifted and I couldn't stop myself from smiling when I realized what the problem was, it was the church.

The town's many craftsmen, who until now lacked the materials needed to continue their given talent or skill, now had plenty to spare, and they made the church their first priority, even before their own homes.

Roofers, carpenters, painters, everyone had something to offer; even the women began to wind new tapestries. Within a week, the church impossibly surpassed its former glory, and was once again the pride of the town. Its first official duty was to house the wedding of a particular man and his three daughters, which I was asked to oversee in my stand-in role as patron, I of course happily accepted.

The next year was hectic and wild to say the least, once word had got out amongst the sea captains that Myra had money and plenty of it, we become the first port of call along that route.

Michael became the new innkeeper, which in turn became the second most popular landmark in the town, and I have to admit, I probably spent a little too much time there myself, but never to the same extent as the old and now long forgotten bishop.

The one thing that gladdened me the most, was the fact that the people never forgot they had been blessed with good fortune, they never became greedy or arrogant, and always gave newcomers a warm and heartfelt greeting.

The years turned into decade's, the children grew up, and in turn had little ones themselves, Michael's son Martin, left to study and train and one day hopefully become a true bishop. I altered my appearance to age along with everyone else, and it was a sad day when I decided my work is done, and it was time to leave.

The catalyst came one evening when I was sat outside the inn watching the sun go down with an elderly Michael for company.

"We're getting old Nicholas."

"Speak for yourself old timer, I still feel twenty five." Which of course was actually true, but Michael laughed in the throaty way only an old man does.

"It's your special day tomorrow, where do the years go my friend?"

"Not my day, you know I have never been comfortable with it being called Nicholas day."

"Comfortable or not, the naming is right and well deserved, everyone here has a lot to thank you for, and we shall never forget it, even long after we are gone."

"Hhmm, I must admit, I helped a little to start with, and planted the seeds, but how they grew and how the people nurtured them, was nothing to do with me, and nor can I take any credit for."

"Again, I am not so sure, so on that point, we shall agree to differ."

"Agreed."

"I haven't got long left on this Earth Nicholas, so may I ask you something?"

"Don't be silly, I am certain you will out live me you old goat. So what's on your mind?"

"Who are you really Nicholas? Even to this very day, I still remember clearly, hidden in the shadows and watching you on the night of that awful storm, pushing out the small boat, and rowing off into the distance. And then conveniently the next day and ship pulled into port, with a story full of holes as to why they had to sell us their goods cheap."

"Good grief man, you waited all these years to ask me?"

"It was none of my business, and I am sure that at the time you would have denied it."

"You're right, there would be no point in denying it now. Funny thing is, that night of the storm, I had a feeling somebody watched me, and I am glad it was you Michael." I had a quick sip of my wine before continuing.

"My true name is Solomon, and I like to think myself as an adventurer, I have many gifts and talents, which I use to help people, or sometimes judge."

"Like the innkeeper?"

"Yes."

"That's all you going to tell me isn't it?"

"Afraid so my friend. Anyways, what's the news on Martin?"

"Thank you, for telling me that much at least, I am glad you decided to help us."

"And so am I, I have enjoyed every day of being here, and that's no lie."

"Martin will be home tomorrow for the celebrations, as always, and he is soon to be ordained."

"That's great news, it's about time the church had a true bishop."

"No, no, he wouldn't dream of coming here. We already have a bishop, maybe not in name, but we still have one none the less."

"Your very kind Michael, but it's time for young blood don't you think?"

"Maybe."

The night was drawing in fast, so I drained my cup and stood up to leave.

"Time to get back, I'll see you tomorrow Michael." I said, but my voice didn't conceal what I really meant.

Michael got up, his creaking old bones shouting their protestations, and then embraced me with a tear clearly in his eye.

"Goodbye Solomon."

My journey back to the church, I carried with me a heavy heart. Hearing my true name again after such a long time, brought back so many memories, and the fact that Martin would be returning tomorrow, meant it was the right time for my departure.

I detoured from my usual way home, lost in thought and trying to work out the best way to leave. The people I had grew to love and watched mature, deserved more than moonlight escape.

Skirting the outskirts of Myra, I stumbled across the body of a traveler; the poor man had died from exhaustion, and was beyond any help I could give him.

But the poor unfortunate soul could help me.

I carried his body back to my room still in the church, careful not to be seen by anyone. I stripped and washed him, dressed him and placed the man on my bed.

"Sorry I couldn't help you, but at least you shall have a decent and proper burial."

Using a trick I have utilized many times in the past, I made it so anyone who looked upon this poor ill-fated traveler would see my peaceful cadaver.

I had one last look at the place that had been my home for the last four decades, and then I left.

There was one final task for me to complete, not a necessity, but something I wanted to do all the same.

Since it was Nicholas day in a few hours' time, and it was part of our tradition to give small gifts to friends and loved ones, especially the children. So I made sure everyone had something and no one was forgotten, then and only then, could I leave, still heavy in heart but happy at the thought of their smiling faces come morning.

Upon leaving the town for what I knew to be the final time, I in avertedly glanced at the very spot where the traveler had fallen. Like a three-dimensional shadow, the bent and broken grass still carried the mans shape.

Then a glistening object, dancing in the ample moonlight caught my eye.

I walked over to the said spot, confident in the knowledge that I left nothing when I lifted the man from his eternal slumber; I had the piece of mind to check at the time. But lying neatly, as if placed, on the flattened pasture was. . "

"This." Solomon said, plucking the card form the table and spinning it around his fingers.

The other three just looked at him, with the dictionary definition of "Gobsmacked" on their faces.

"What?" Solomon asked, unsure at what the problem was, and was greeted by the trio's synchronistic chorus of.

"YOUR SANTA??"

CHAPTER 6

"More Questions Than Answers" Part Two

"Well yes, in a roundabout way. Myths and legends have distorted the facts somewhat, but what I told you is how events actually transpired." Said a slightly embarrassed Solomon. "Anyhow, I thought I had told you all that story before and you knew all about it."

"Erm, no Sol, I think we would kinda remember if you had done. Fucking hell buddy, they even made you into a Saint." Cyrus couldn't hide the admiration in his voice.

"Yes, patron saint of children, sailors, merchants, coopers and pawnbrokers, if I recollect correctly." Embarrassment now became pride.

"Pawnbrokers?"

"Yep, what's the universal emblem of a pawnbroker?"

"Three golden balls." Cyrus had to think for a moment. "I know we are all special, but I can virtually guarantee that you're gifted with just two testicles, and I am fairly sure that they are both pink in color."

"Ho fucking ho, it's was three bags of gold I left for the sisters, but with the way Chinese whispers twist the truth, somewhere along the way they became balls."

"Ok, but I do have a serious question."

"Yes?"

"Can I have a mountain bike for christm.."

"FUCK OFF." Solomon interrupted before Cyrus could finish the sentence, and it brought a volley of laughs all round.

"So much for us keeping a low profile." Cyrus jokingly chided.

"Like Cyrus's fury?" Nathan decided to help Solomon out a bit.

"Ah."

"Yes, I am also quite curious about hearing the story behind that one." It was now Janus that spoke.

"Curiosity killed the cat." Cyrus taunted.

"But satisfaction brought it back." Was Janus's retort.

"Touché, smartarse. Tell you what, in eight days time, when this business is settled, I'll treat you all to a meal, in the restaurant of your choice, anywhere in the world, and then I'll tell you all about it. Deal?"

Everyone agreed, although the mood once again became somber, each knowing that quite possibly, it would a date that maybe one or all of them, may not be around to keep.

"So Nathan, what is the significance of these cards, or more importantly, the word Croatoan?" Janus had the break the melancholy silence.

"I honestly have no idea, I'm totally at a loss. It must mean something and it has to be important, but with less than a week to go, sadly we can't devote any time to getting to the bottom of it."

"I'll have to concur with you there, one thing however, someone or something has gone to a lot of trouble making us aware of it, and I cant see it being for no reason, so I am sure all will become clear when the times comes." Was the best Janus could offer.

"I hope so."

"How did you procure your shinny gift, Boss?"

"Unfortunately Sol, its nothing as glamorous or earth changing as your fabulous tale, quite mundane in fact."

"Well, come on then, you cant leave it at that." Cyrus was still a little aggrieved at not being part of the Croatoan gang.

"Ok, if you insist."

The day that small brown envelope fell out of mailbox and onto my doormat, I had nothing to blame but my own stupidity.

I opened it with the usual disinterest that you do when you presume its just another bill.

"*Fuck.*" I groaned, although no one was present to hear.

The inconspicuous buff sheath contained my draft papers. The identity I was using at that time, was a fairly legitimate one, I had social security number and paid taxes, which meant I was part of the system.

I spent the best part of the morning and four pots of coffee trying to decide the best course of action.

Changing my persona, wouldn't be a problem, I had done so a thousand times in the past. But my heart was one of a warrior, and although modern day war had no place for the likes of me, the pull was too strong, and my mind was made up.

I would soon be playing a part in the Vietnam War.

Landing in the camp at Bien Hoa, the first thing that struck me was the organization, or lack of to be more precise. The place was an open-air asylum; a brood of headless chickens, would have had more coordination and synchronicity. I have fought in battles and wars a thousand years earlier, with tribes that did not even speak the same language, but were brought together by a common cause, even they were better disciplined and more unified.

Airborne surveillance photographs, two-way radios, helicopters, jeeps and the now infamous M16, gave the Americans a superiority complex, that, entwined with their inbred megalomaniac attitude, was responsible for the unnecessary deaths of many guiltless and innocent young men.

Orders and objectives from plush office bound Generals; passed down the chain of command, until landing in the lap of a twenty year old platoon Captain. The said Captain, convinced of his immortality because he survived a tour of duty unscathed, in most cases though, sadly, they were proved very wrong.

The camp CO was a battle-hardened veteran at the ripe old age of thirty-five. Thankfully, he was a good commander, even with the disinformation fed him and lack of resources at his disposal, he tried very hard to look after his men, and when he wasn't stuck behind a desk signing papers and deciding on mission parameters, he tried his level best to personally meet everyone in the camp.

I had been there only a few hours before he found me.

Pretending to act like a frightened twenty year old (which of course I wasn't), was easy enough, even safe in knowledge knowing that is was entirely within the realms possibility that I might be the only one in the whole camp that survives the war unscathed.

Confused in my tent, listening to the torrential cleansing on the canvas, unsure at what to do when the drenched CO entered.

I was on my feet, and adopted the only thing I had been taught so far, standing to attention.

"At ease Richards, please sit." And he motioned to a bunk.

I did as I was asked, still slightly uncomfortable, you can never be totally at ease when the CO is present.

Surprisingly, he also sat on the facing bunk.

"Janus? Curious name." It was a rhetorical question. "I'm William." With that he struck out his hand and shook my own.

Taken aback twice in as many minutes, forenames just weren't used in the military, and a CO being so forthcoming was unheard of. I just sat there like a moron, mentally double checking my identity, making sure I hadn't I left any holes big enough to warrant this mans involvement.

"Nothing to be worried about Janus." Was I really that transparent? "I know its not SOP, but this is my camp and I'll run it the way I want. Any other time, I am your CO, but if we ever have a tête-à-tête like this one, unless it regarding military affairs, I am no longer your Commanding Officer."

"Sir?" I couldn't bring myself to call him William.

"There are six hundred men here Janus, but at times, this will feel like the loneliest place on the planet. If you ever feel you can't take any more, I want your word that you will come and see me. My door is always open, and during times like that, I am no longer your CO, I am your father, mother, best friend." He paused briefly to let his words sink in. " I am not going to bullshit you son, I have given this speech hundreds of times, but hear me when I say, I mean every word. Understood."

"Yes Sir." And he did.

"Good man, war is a terrible thing, but thinking one of my man couldn't come to me, is something I cannot accept. I am proud that this unit has the lowest suicide rate, in this whole damned hellhole, and I plan to keep it like that." He then stood up, his piece had been said.

"So back to your duties Richards, and be careful out there man, always watch out for yourself and the other members of your platoon."

And with that he was gone, off to find the next new recruit.

William had earned my respect, that was a nice gesture he performed, and to a lot of frightened teenagers, it was probably just the thing they needed to hear. I shall be keeping an eye on William Dean.

The weeks turned into months, and as morbid as this may sound, unlike most wars I have been involved in, this one held no joy for me. It was a dirty and rotten conflict.

I simply kept my head down and did as I was asked. The platoon were a disorganized joke, led by people who thought they knew more than they actually did, which in turn meant they were normally the first to die, be it by booby trap or sniper. The rest of the infant platoon would then fall apart, and on most occasions, join the in their Commander's misfortune.

More than once, I returned to the camp alone and unscathed, where possible, I brought any wounded back, I firmly believed in the adage of not leaving anyone behind, but if truth be known, had I been a "normal", I would have died many times over along with the rest of the platoon.

I quickly earned the nickname of "Bird", based on the seaman's albatross, charmed for some, ill-omened for others. I was loved, hated, avoided or embraced in equal measure throughout the camp.

One dusk, returning from an uneventful patrol, the camp was buzzing with whispers and rumor. A platoon had broken the army's cardinal rule, and left a man behind; apparently the CO hit the roof, and went out alone to recover the solider.

As more information filtered down, it was obvious that the men weren't entirely to blame. They were part of a division known as the "Tunnel Rats", which without a shadow of doubt, was the worse and most godforsaken job in the whole war. Only the very brave or clinical insane requested that post, even I would baulk at doing that job. Spending hours upon end, underground, in miles of pitch-black tunnels, large enough to only crawl through, and littered with deadly traps, wasn't something I was prepared to do.

Apparently, a newly found tunnel had collapsed, leaving one man cut of from the rest, the others understandably panicked, frightened that the Vietcong could return at any time. Even with his muffled pleas, begging his comrades not leave him down there, but in all reality they had no choice. They did the right thing by going straight to the CO and telling him what had happened, but he was foolish in going after the man on his own, emotion can cloud a mans judgment and thinking.

Settling debts was one of the few rules I lived by, and I owed the CO one, paying me a visit on the first day here, had quite possibly saved his life, if I get there in time.

I sort out and found one of the returnee's, a quick scan of his now very mixed up mind gave me their last location, and I left immediately.

I was soon there, and I found the tunnel entrance quickly enough, forty feet west of the said entrance, you could clearly see where the tunnel had collapsed. It would be fruitless entering there, but thankfully all of these subterranean networks had more than one way in, or out.

The CO was nowhere to be seen, so obviously he had found one. Following his unseen trail, it didn't take me long to locate it.

I could sense no Vietcong nearby, so we had a little time at least.

"Fuck it." And I was in.

Even knowing where I was going, and safe in the knowledge, that no harm would come to me, being down there was one of the most claustrophobic and uncomfortable experiences I have ever encountered. The clammy, un-circulated air was tainted with hate, and embraced you like an enemy.

I had no intention of hanging about, and crawled as quickly as I could through the damp underground maze, homing in on my quarry's life-force. Within a few minutes, that felt like hours, I found the CO, dragging the now unconscious soldier inch by painful inch, and clearly lost.

"Follow me Sir, I know the way out." Straight, and to the point.

"Bird, is that you?" he managed to ask, even with a small flashlight in his mouth.

"Yes Sir, quickly we haven't got much time." I lied, but I had already had enough down there.

"How the hell can you see where you are going man, its pitch black down here?"

I normally try to cover all the bases, but in my haste to get this task done, taking a flash light didn't even occur to me, not that I needed one, but I always try to be as inconspicuous as possible, and never do anything that would raise too many questions.

"Dropped my torch Sir, but I have always had very good night vision." Was the best I could do.

Wanting to get out of there as much as me, no more questions were asked and minutes later, and not a moment too soon, we were out and breathing fresh air again.

The comatose soldier had apparently been bitten by a snake tethered to a wall in the tunnel, a simple but highly effective booby-trap. I offered to carry him back, but the CO would have none of it, even in his exhausted state. I just hoped that he wouldn't also collapse, and I would end having to carry both of them, because that would raise just too many eyebrows.

But in all fairness, I had to give William Dean credit, he carried the fallen soldier, and never stumbled once, he was a tough man, in more ways than one.

As we neared the camp, I fell back somewhat, and as soon as the CO was spotted, what must have easily been half the population there, came to help and greet.

In the commotion, I effortlessly sloped off and returned to my bunk, with a smile on my face, mission accomplished.

The next day, as I expected, I was summoned to the CO's office.

Upon nearing the prefabricated cabin, I was shown straight in.

"At ease, and sit down please Janus." First name terms and saying please, wasn't quite what I was expecting.

"I have a hundred questions, but I have a feeling that you already would have realized that, and have all the right answers that I want to hear."

Which was true, why was I there, how did I find them, and many more besides; I already had prepared the suitable response's ready.

"I haven't got the time or energy for verbal ping-pong, so I'll cut the crap and skip right to the end. Thank you solider."

"Just doing my job Sir." I inwardly cringed at how lame that sounded.

"Quite. However, I have found a way to repay you."

I could hardly explain, that I only helped him to repay a debt, but now he intended to pay me back. The way this was going we would be owing each other ad infinitum.

"I am giving you carte blanche over your next posting."

"Sir?"

"Just tell me where you want to go, what you'd rather do, and I'll sign the paper work. Hell, you can be an army cook if you so desire."

He effectively was giving me a "get out of war" card, but I wasn't quite ready to leave yet.

"Reconnaissance."

"I'm sorry Richards?"

"Lone reconnaissance, that's the posting that would suit me best Sir. I have an aptitude for it, and I work better alone."

"Jesus H Christ man, I offer you a chance not to see another days combat, and you want to jump into the lions den, alone."

"Yes Sir."

"I'll give you until morning to think about properly, I sadly have to admit though, it would be something suited for you. If tomorrow you still wish to proceed, I draw up the relevant paperwork." I detected a touch of sorrow in his voice, but my mind was made up.

"And the other solider?"

"Physically he'll make a full recovery, but mentally he may never heal, arrangements have already been made to have him on the next transport back."

I honestly didn't know what to say, it was one of those moments where words were useless.

"Oh, one more thing. Just a quick heads up, a certain division, now holds you in very esteem, and are going to make you an honoree Tunnel Rat." The look on my face was impossible to hide. "But don't worry, you'll never have to step foot in one of those hell holes again." My relief was equally as transparent.

"I hope you don't mind me saying Janus, I cant quite put my finger on it, but there is something about you, that's, well, different."

"My mother always said I was special Sir."

"Amen to that Janus, amen to that." The CO laughed.

I have to say that I am a little ashamed to admit, I actually quite enjoyed the passing few months.

I came and went as I pleased, but still brought in good results, so that non-procedure was tolerated. In many ways I helped both sides of the conflict. During my nighttime reconnaissance's, often I would discover villages, some were Vietcong nests, and others were innocent dwellings. Although it was my duty to report any and all I found, the innocuous ones always slipped my mind when giving my briefing of the nights findings. Even though they posed no threat, it was army procedure to check them out; gung ho soldiers and frightened screaming people, was normally a recipe for disaster. I did however find plenty to do for the Tunnel Rats, and incredibly they always thanked me for it, what a strange breed they were.

I was well liked in the camp and got on with most people there, and very uncharacteristically for my usual self; I readily took part in the camps banter and jovial activities. But with the way of Ying and Yang, for every new friend you make, quite often, an enemy is similarly created, and here was no exception.

Be it by luck or design, there was one platoon that only contained the camps' dark minded few, undesirables in every sense of the word, totally suited in the role they excelled at, Special Forces, search and destroy. They hated everyone and trusted nobody (not even each other), they also enjoyed being here, but for very different reasons than my own, and people like them were one of the reasons why my report would always contain some missing intelligence.

Every army in every war had units such as these; battle has an odd habit of bringing the best out of some people, and the worse out of others. They eat alone, lived in their own small section, and if they thought they could have got away with it, bullying would be their bag, but here they had to make do with arrogance and snide remarks.

Everyone gave them a wide berth, me included, not that I was intimidated by them; I just couldn't be bothered with the hassle that's all.

Then one bright humid night, I was deep in the jungle, in a grid location I knew to be safe and clear from Charlies', when I picked up the faintest of sounds at least two klicks west. I immediately froze, straining my already heightened senses, two klicks would be a large deviation from my current path, and I had to be sure I wouldn't just be investigating a noisy rodent.

Immobile, eyes closed, breath held, heart stopped, after nearly five minutes my patience was duly rewarded, the sound was definitely human.

I covered those two kilometers quickly and silently, only slowing when a few meters short of my audio beacon. Camouflaged well in the dense undergrowth, it was soon apparent what the nature of the source was. The smiling moon aided me with her nocturnal spotlight, her powerful beam illuminating a large clearing.

"Well, well, well." I whispered.

I was hardly surprised to see the eight members of my least favorite platoon, but with one addition, a barely pubescent Vietnamese girl. I didn't need my unusual talents to know that the poor petrified child had a night of torment and torture ahead of her, and would never see the morning.

But luckily, whatever God's she worshipped, had answered her tearful prayers, and she would live another day at least.

My spirits already lifted, I was going to enjoy this.

I removed the magazine from my M16, and carefully placed the gun on the jungle bed, I then noisily stepped out from my concealed vantage point.

Seven semi-automatic weapons immediately pointed in my direction, the eighth man had his hands full and was busy holding down the gagged girl.

"Bird?"

I didn't even bother to justify them with an answer.

"What the fuck are you doing here? If it's a piece of her your after, well your shit out of luck, they'll be fuck all left by the time we're finished." Said the platoon commander, the rest of his motley crew laughed in eager anticipation.

I ignored them, turned to the girl and looked into her wide frightened eyes.

"Con dung lo, cha van binh an." I said soothingly.

"You can speak Vietnamese? What the fuck did you tell her arsehole?"

"I told her not to worry, and that she was safe now." Which was true.

Some of the confused troops looked around, worried that I might have been accompanied.

"Don't worry men, this prick always works alone." That still didn't convince everyone. "So how you gonna stop us then, Mr. CO's blue eyed boy? You don't even have a gun!" The laughter was slightly more nervous this time.

"Nope, but I have a big knife and a bad temper." I then unsheathed my matte Ka-Bar and the laughing stopped.

"He's fucking serious Sarge, what are we gonna do?" ask the youngest at least inexperienced trooper.

He ignored him, and gave just the slightest of nods, and his men surrounded me. To be fair, they were trained well enough, even to the point of making sure no-one stood directly behind me, I smiled knowing full well the reason for that.

"I don't know why your smiling motherfucker, coz your about to die."

And then he shot me twice in the chest, which pissed me off because I didn't have a chance to come back with my witty retort.

The M16 being a powerful weapon and at such a close range, the bullets would have passed clean through any normal man, hence my back being unguarded. This didn't happen of course, I stayed on my feet, in fact, I don't even think I blinked as they hit me.

"You're an idiot Jack." Using his first name, doubled his surprise. "A double tap to the chest? What were you thinking? Didn't you realize that when my body is found, two shots in such close grouping, is Special Forces S.O.P.? The Vietcong don't waste ammo like we do. You'd have been ratted out and discovered within days." A pointless speech, but it was more of the fact that I was still standing and talking as if nothing had happened, that spooked them.

"Now this is where you all line up and empty your weapons into me. So come on, get it over with, we haven't got all night."

Three men run away having seen enough, including the one holding the girl. I let them go, knowing they would only get as far as the jaws of some overly large, evil looking, hungry canine's.

The five now faced me, unsure at what to do, when a trio of dreadful and horrifying screams coming from the jungle pushed them over the edge, and as predicted, they emptied their guns.

Being shot a multitude of times, especially in the face, is not a pleasant experience, and it kept distracting my train of thought, because I still hadn't decided their grisly fate.

Finally they were done, and the guns fell silent.

"My turn." And I casually strolled over.

Two and a half hours later I stood back and admired my handiwork.

I had never before skinned a man alive, and unfortunately the first three died on me before completion, but I quickly learnt from my mistakes, and the two remaining lived, or they would for a short while at least. Metaphorically, the mind has many fuses or trip switches, when certain extremities of pain, cold etc are detected, a fuse blows and the mind shuts down leaving the person unconscious and no longer aware of the suffering, I merely bypassed the fail-safe's, leaving them with no choice but to endure every excruciating minute. They would survive for anything up to another hour; before my mental tweaking is in turn cracked, and their minds' finally go into melt down. I had long since shut off my ears to their screams, and the young girl with a little help from me, was sleeping soundly and would have no memory of the night's events once I revived her.

I hoisted her onto my shoulder; it was time to take her home.

It didn't take me long to find her village, at this hour most would be asleep, but I knew one hut would be full of very awake and anguished kin. Still unarmed, I walked straight in, the girls family were of course all there, and sick with worry, I explained in fluent Vietnamese, that she must have fallen and knocked her head and I had found her whilst on patrol. I reassured the startled inhabitants, that no harm had come to her, and at that point I revived her, and the strange American unarmed solider was instantly forgotten. Happily I turned and left.

Just as I was about to leave the village, I heard someone shout my name, which was a bit of a surprise, considering I never once happened to mention it.

I turned to see what must have been the girls' youngest brother, running towards me in that funny way that only small children do. He was barely old enough to talk, and yet here he was, waddling quickly towards me, saying my name.

I got down on one knee, ready to welcome my tiny companion, half cringing thinking he was going to fall over at any moment, but he reached me and still incredibly managed to stay upright. He then proudly thrust out his arm, and tightly clutched in his tiny hand was a small plastic card, which although confused, I took and thanked him for. Before he ran off home again, I tried to ask him how he got and knew my name, but of course that was fruitless. So I gently popped into his fragile mind for hopefully a clue, it seemed the little man was in a sense hypnotized, and when he saw my face he went into a kind of autopilot, with the task of giving me the card, no other details were available in there. In fact it was a good job I heard him, or the poor little mite would have chased me half way through the jungle.

With nothing else to be learnt, I left the village, totally bewildered and with a head full of questions, which I knew I wouldn't find the answers for.

Even before that bizarre little episode, I had decided that the war was over for me, but I had one final job to do before I left for good.

I knew on discovering my disappearance, the CO would waste resources he couldn't really afford too, trying to find me. I liked the man and wasn't prepared to let him do that.

Even at this hour, a camp such as ours is never completely asleep, but I still snuck in unseen, found his quarters and quietly entered. I knew men like him were notoriously light sleepers, so I made sure he wouldn't wake up while I was there.

When he would wake up, on the table next to his bed, he would find a note written by me, giving him a slightly abridged version of the nights events and where to find the bodies, and for him not to worry I was safe, but would not be coming back.

"Goodbye William." I said quietly, and then was gone.

"And that's my story as to how I acquired my little gift."

"Bravo, what a great story." Solomon said cheerily.

"I was in Nam." Cyrus piped up.

"Really? Where and doing what?" Janus asked.

"Black Ops, can't talk about it, classified." He said with a wink.

"Fuck off." Janus laughed, soon joined by Solomon when he realized Cyrus was kidding.

Nathan however wasn't laughing, and seemed lost in his own little world whist staring at the card in his hand.

"Nathan?"

"I'm sorry Janus, I just can't seem to get my mind off this. Its like a puzzle, but the vital piece is missing."

"I understand what you are saying my friend, but we really don't have the time to worry about it. If it's a important as you say, I am sure the answers will come to us when the time is right."

"I know, I know. Are you sure you have nothing like this Cyrus?" Nathan couldn't help but ask.

"Well, there is something."

"Really?"

"Yes, but its probably nothing."

"Come on man, spit it out." It was Solomon's turn to join in.

"Ok, if I must. About fifty years ago, I purchased an old country house. The previous owners had refurbished and modernized it, to the best standard of the day. But the place always felt wrong to me, but I could never seem to put my finger on it. I rattled around the big old house for a couple of weeks, but I couldn't help but feel uneasy all the time." Cyrus paused to have a sip of his cold coffee.

"Then one cold, winters night, as the wind was howling outside, trying its best to get in through any cracks or gaps, I could hear a bell, ringing in one of the other rooms upstairs. So I went to investigate."

"Go on." Solomon prompted.

"Well, the winds relentless probing, had finally found a weak spot, and she had blown open a window in one of the guest bedrooms. As I entered, the unchained wind played around like a mischievous poltergeist, and it was causing the little brass bell above the door to dance along with her. That's when a thought struck me."

"What?" Janus was now also hooked.

"All the bedrooms had these tiny bells, or the framework at least, above the doors. Which many years ago, would have been used by the butler, to let the sleeping guests know that it was time for breakfast.

"Of course, a few of my properties have had something similar." Janus added.

"Yes mine also, but it dawned on me that this house didn't have any servants quarters."

"Ah."

"Quite. So even at this hour, I had to get to the bottom of it. Back downstairs, not quite sure what my next move would be, when I noticed the painted wall under the staircase was slightly a different shade to the surrounding area."

"The previous owners had bricked up the entrance to the servants quarters below the stairs?" said Nathan, his mind briefly off the business card.

"Exactly. I was like a foxhound that had caught a sent, that wall was coming down, and it was coming down tonight. Lost in the moment, I didn't even bother trying to find a large hammer, a couple of well-placed shoves and the wall was down. I was hit by an unearthly icy breeze, something that had been trying to escape for a long time. A shiver went down my spine; it felt like cold fingers running up and down my back. I poked my head into the hole, and saw the beginning of a wooden staircase, until it was devoured by darkness. Part of me wanted to wait till morning, but there was no way that was going to happen. So I slowly descended into the gloom. As you know, we have perfect vision even in the darkest settings, but down here I was almost blind. I was sure I could hear whispers, and my peripheral vision kept catching glimpses of movement. For the first time in my life, I was afraid."

"I bet you were, I am getting spooked just listening."

"Hush Sol, let Cyrus speak." Nathan said quietly.

"I could sense something was down here, something not right. My sight improved slightly, my world had become grey. The large room seemed full of old junk, chairs, tables etc, but I was being drawn to a far corner, it was a pull I couldn't resist. Unable to stop myself, I inched closer and closer, the corner was a magnet, I had no choice. A door slammed somewhere in the house, I wanted to run, but my feet were leaden. After what seemed like a lifetime, I reached the said corner; under a fallen bookcase was a large chest, I knew straight away that that was the beacon that was calling me. It wanted me to open it, and I had no choice, even though I knew I was going to open Pandora's box. I heaved the bookcase out of the way, and the chest sighed with relief. I undid the clasp, and slowly lifted the lid, I nearly screamed when I saw a skeleton in there. I stepped back, unable to take my eyes off the poor soul, when something in his ribcage caught my eye. Carefully I neared once more, the house and wind now silent, I could now clearly see a small metallic object, wedged between the ribs. Slowly I reached out, expecting at any second the lifeless bones to become animated and try to stop me. But no, I was allowed to proceed, and soon I had the small round object in my hand. The whispers started again, urging me to read the inscription, I rubbed of the surface rust, held it close to my face, and read the words. My eyes widened and my mouth opened."

"What did it say?" Nathan whispered.

"1812, Norfolk Hide and Seek Champion."

"OH FUCK OFF" Solomon shouted. "Cyrus you are a bastard and a wind up merchant." But he still couldn't help but laugh, infectious as it was Janus soon joined in, quickly followed by Nathan who held out as for long as he could.

It was nearly a whole five minutes before any of them could speak again.

"Thanks Cyrus, I think we all needed that." Janus said wiping a tear from his eye.

"No problem Boss, been looking for an excuse to tell that story for ages. And on that note, I had better shoot, I have the meeting with the Duke in a couple of hours."

"Good point, take Nathan with you, that way you can get straight on with the other business."

"Do you mind if I pick Nathan up tomorrow?" Cyrus asked more to the pair of them.

"Fine by me." Nathan replied.

"Yep, ok, do you mind if I ask why though?" Janus enquired.

"No, not at all. The orphanage I am patron of, is having its annual charity dinner and auction tonight, I'd like to be there that's all, and I have some business to attend to at the same time."

"Yes, that's fine, to be honest it's a good thing that we carry on as normal as possible. Have a good night and we'll see you in the morning."

"Hang on a minute handsome." Solomon said, also rising. "Let's have a look at this flash motor of yours."

"Excuse me? I'll have you know; I don't do flash, I do stylish." Replied Cyrus, pretending to take umbrage.

The two men left, trading playful insults all the way to the door.

"So, you ok Nathan?" Janus asked, sounding like a cross between a parent and a headmaster.

"I am rested, fed and apart from our little conundrum bugging the hell out of me, I'm fine."

"It wasn't your fault you know." Now completely sounding like a father.

Nathan knew exactly what he was talking about, and wasn't going to insult his friends' intelligence by playing dumb.

"You knew then?"

"Yes, all along. It truth, I have lived four lives as much as I have lived one."

"And you didn't even try to make contact, come to me or console me?" Nathan was literary taken aback.

"No." Janus's admission wasn't a happy one.

"But why?"

"My job was only to observe; just in case."

"In case of what? I'm not sure I understand." And Nathan didn't.

"Ok, let me put it this way. What do think my greatest fear has been for all these millennia?"

"Apart from what we are up against now, you mean."

"Yes."

"I have no idea, one of us getting sloppy maybe, and the populace discovering that there is an immortal living amongst them."

"Close but no. My biggest worry has always been that one of us would lose their mind, and go rogue. Can you just imagine the possible mayhem and destruction left in the wake?"

"And you thought I would be the one most likely to suffer from the said dementia?"

"God no, you were always the least of my worries, but I still had to keep tabs on you on the less."

"Are you saying that one of us was actually close to losing it?"

"Oh yes."

"Do you mind if I ask who?"

"Not at all. Me." Janus said flatly.

"You?" said Nathan, unable to hide his surprise.

"Afraid so my friend."

"But you have always been the sensible one and easily the most level headed."

"And that is where the problem lay."

"Ah."

"Yourself, Cyrus and even Solomon are all slightly "touched", but not in a bad way. Whereas, I was the normal one, the unofficial leader of us, a calling I was never comfortable with."

"Rubbish, you were always the right man for the job, the other two would both back me up on that."

"Maybe once I was, when we were together I always had something to do, battles to be fought, kings to advise, keeping Cyrus out of trouble etc, but once we spilt, I was lost. I still had the pressure of keeping an eye, somewhat covertly, on everyone. I went into a deep depression, and at times a small part of me wanted one of you to lose the plot. Then I realized the very fact that I was thinking thoughts such as those, meant I was the one losing it." Janus had a melancholy pause. "And the last century has been a nightmare, with mans progress, and the advent of modern technology, this world no longer had any place for me."

"Don't talk crap Janus, you just have to adapt that's all."

"A week ago, I was working in fucking office, for fucks sake. One of the richest, most powerful men in the world; a nine to five slave. I very nearly went home Nathan."

"Why the fuck didn't you say anything Janus?"

"Because I would have sounded weak, I know that sounds stupid now, but at the time, that's how I felt."

"You need a woman mate."

"Been there, done that. She caused the problem in the first place."

"I don't wish to sound harsh, but that was a fucking thousand years ago. Let me ask you something."

"What?" Janus replied curtly.

"Do you have a race car license?"

"What kind of question is that?"

"Just answer it."

"Well yes I have, but I don't see what that has to do with anything."

"Can you scuba dive?"

"I'm a PADI qualified instructor, but I still don't understand what you're getting at."

"You can skydive, ski and you're a low handicap golfer I presume?"

"Yes, yes and yes." Janus sighed.

"You can play a concert piano and the electric guitar."

"So?" Janus was getting tired of these inane questions.

"My point is; of course you can do all those things I mentioned, plus many many more no doubt. You have the resources, and one of our talents is that we pick things up very easily, and then normally excel at them, that's how we have remained undetected for so long."

"And?"

"For fucks sake, do I have to spell it out?"

"Yes, humor me."

"Go out, and fucking enjoy doing them, rather than miserably brooding in your office. Your world is your playground, so play in it."

"I cant."

"Why on earth not?"

"Because what the point in doing any of this if you haven't got friends to share it with?"

"Jesus H Christ man, make some bloody friends."

"People like us don't have friends." Janus said sadly.

"Don't talk crap Janus, I bet Cyrus has plenty of friends, and he lives life to the full."

"Yeah, but me and him are very different."

"Bullshit, what about the men we are waking tomorrow, weren't they our friends?"

"You can't seriously compare them, they are from a different era, an honorable age."

"So you're saying there is no honor left anymore?"

"Yeah, pretty much."

"Again you're wrong. I have spent the last five hundred years with nothing but honorable men, and each and every one I was proud to call my friend." Nathan said with conviction.

"Hhmm, I suppose."

"No suppose about it good buddy. Now when all this over, promise me that you will go out enjoy your life, and the multitude of adventures out there."

"Ok, I'll try." Janus tried to sound like he really meant it.

"Good man, because I am going to be there with you. I've got five hundred years to catch up on." Nathan smiled at last.

"Ok, ok, you've got me, both of us shall learn how to live once more." Janus returned the smile.

"Anyway, it's all a mute point now, the four are once more together, and we have the next week to get through." Janus said changing the subject.

"Ok, but when this over, promise me, if you ever feel like that again, you come to me, right?"

"Will do Boss." Janus tried half a smile.

"Don't call me that my friend; you're the boss and always will be. But can I ask you something?"

"Sure, fire away."

"What happened to me after Roanoke? And how did I arrive at the Garden?"

"I don't know."

"Excuse me?"

"Honestly, I haven't a clue. I lost all contact with you and didn't get it back until you and your mind awoke, and that's the truth."

"Actually, that doesn't surprise me. Its linked with the Croatoan strangeness, I am sure of it."

"I'd have to agree, but I do have a question, if you don't mind."

"Sure, ask away."

"What IS the Garden Nathan?"

"You don't know?"

"I wouldn't ask if I did, and don't answer a question with a question, its bloody annoying." Janus laughed.

"I am not entirely sure to be honest, I have a fair idea, but I might be way off the mark."

"Which is?"

"Phew, Erm. Ok, I am not being awkward for he sake of it, but it's nigh on impossible to explain."

"Have a go, please."

"I really don't know how, and that's the truth. It's one of those times when I know the answer, but I am buggered as to how to put it into words."

"That doesn't really help."

"Tell me about it, but because there is no scientific answer it's really hard. Case in point; ask a learned man how the Sun works and what it does for us, you'll get a pretty accurate answer, because physics, chemistry and math's are all used, but ask the same man to explain the how's and why's of love, to someone that has never heard or experienced it, he would be stumped, or even something as simple as asking him to describe the concept of left and right, try it, it's nigh on impossible."

"Right, I understand, I think. So what came first, Man or the Garden?"

"The Garden, most definitely, it's a phenomena that without it, Life simply wouldn't have evolved."

"Wow, that does surprise me."

"When you think about it, it isn't surprising at all really."

"Really, how so?" Janus was fascinated.

"As I am sure your aware, for Life to begin on any Planet, many many factors must be just right at certain given times, and the odds of it all coming together are virtually incalculable."

"That much I know."

"But for intelligent, conscious life to evolved one vital and exceptional element is needed."

"The Garden."

"Exactly."

"I am none the wiser, but now I understand a bit more, if that makes sense."

"Perfectly my friend." Nathan smiled.

But before the duo could continue that line of conversation, a noisy Solomon returned.

"Stylish my arse, he's still a flash bastard." Solomon proclaimed loudly, but with no hint of malice.

"Yep, that'll be our Cyrus, never one to do things by halves." Janus was glad Solomon was back.

"Sorry to mention this, but we have a slight problem guys." Nathan quickly changed the mood again.

"What is it?" Janus's sensible head immediately back on.

"Well, we aren't meeting Cyrus until tomorrow, so we have a day to kill. What the fuck are we going to do?" Nathan said smiling.

"That's easy."

"Really Sol?"

"Yep."

"Come on then man, don't be shy." Janus urged.

"Armageddon a week away, three immortals in North Wales, it's bloody obvious isn't it."

"For fuck's sake, spit it out Sol."

"Sometimes I wonder if I am the only one with any brains around here." Solomon was clearly enjoying this.

"If you don't tell us NOW, I swear I am going to kick the living shit out of Santa Claus." Nathan tried to sound menacing, which he failed miserably at due to the big smile of his face.

"Ok, Ok, we go fishing."

Janus and Nathan looked at each other, but no words were needed between them.

"Solomon my friend, that is such a stupid idea its brilliant." Janus admitted.

"Told ya." Said a proud Solomon.

The duo stood up, took their empty plates and mugs to the bar, Janus reached into an inside pocket and placed a large envelope on there also.

"What's that?" Solomon enquired.

"The deeds to the pub, already made out in the managers name. In all the years he has been here, never once has he fiddled me out of a penny, all the previous ones did. It's not like I ever needed the money, so it's just a little thank you, that's all."

"So you have got a heart then." Solomon said with a wink.

"Piss off, now come on, we got fish to catch."

CHAPTER 7

"To the Hills, to the Hills, and F**k the Indians"

Part One

It was already dark by the time Cyrus turned into the mile long driveway of the manor house. So far the day had been a successful one, the meeting with the Duke if Kent went well; he listened intensely and quickly understood the graveness and urgency of the situation. A straight up fellow, no bullshit and to the point, promised his small in number but highly trained men would be at the rendezvous, without fail.

Aided by a following wind, the avenue of ancient oaks bowed down in greeting to their revered patron, and the freezing damp road with its crystal's of ice forming atop, giving the impression under the bright headlights of a diamond encrusted highway.

The overflowing car park housed all manner motoring exotica, in monetary terms enough to settle the debt of a small country was easily the worth of the sleeping automobiles.

"Seems like a good turn out." Cyrus said to himself as he pulled into a space that no one had dared take.

He locked the car and with no wish to be out in the cold for a moment longer than need be, he nearly ran up the granite steps to the entrance. The young impeccably dressed hired doorman tipped his hat as Cyrus approached.

"Sir."

"Cold enough for you." Cyrus said with a wink as he was let in.

Barely in the warm for a minute before the ambitious and over eager Master of Ceremonies pounced.

"May I have your ticket please Sir?"

"Oh, I am afraid I don't have one." Cyrus was in a good but mischievous mood.

"With regret, I can not allow you entrance then."

"I see, well, would it be possible for me to purchase one?"

"No sorry, it's a private function, invite only, even with a ticket I would have to refuse you entry, there is a strict dress code. Sorry but you seem to have wasted your time."

"What's you name Son?"

The M of C obviously took umbrage to being called Son by someone clearly a lot younger than himself, and made a conscious effort to make eye contact with the plentiful security present.

"Please, I'd rather you didn't cause a scene. The people present do not wish to be hassled by reporters such as yourself. So before I have you physically escorted out, do the honorable thing and leave with your pride still intact." And with that, he made a motion with his hand to summon backup.

The head of security quickly appeared out of apparently nowhere.

"Do we have a problem." He asked.

"No problem, but could you kindly show this man the exit."

The tall well built man looked at Cyrus and smiled.

"Hello again Sir."

"Good evening James, how's Moira?" Cyrus replied.

"She's well thank you Sir, and the gift was a lovely gesture."

"Not a problem my friend."

"You know this man James." Asked the rather surprised M of C.

"Oh yes, he pulled a similar trick on me a few years back."

"Trick?" Now he was confused as well as annoyed.

"Here, let me introduce our distinguished guest." He paused for effect. "I give you Mr. Cyrus Draig."

The color clearly drained the other mans face; he was a professional and took pride in being bloody good at his job, yet he failed to recognize his own employer.

"Don't worry about it, in fact, it is I that owe you an apology. But I honestly couldn't resist the opportunity, and to be fair, you had no idea of knowing whom I was, so you did entirely the right thing."

"Even so, I feel a fool."

"Please don't, it seems your good wife will also be on my Christmas list now." And he winked at James. "Now if you don't mind, I had best change into something more suitable, but before I do, may I ask a favor from you."

"Yes, yes, of course, anything."

"I like my anonymity, and apart from a select few that might be able to identify me, I'd rather it isn't widely known that I am here."

"Certainly Sir, you can be assured of my discretion."

"Good man. Make sure you give Moira my best James." And with that, he left to go to the room, which is always kept for him upstairs.

On entering the plush room, as requested, a newly dry-cleaned and pressed tuxedo, lay ready on the four-poster bed. A bottle of Louis XIII and a box of the finest Cuban Cohiba Esplendido's both awaited on an antique dresser, all paid for from funds from one of his private accounts, he couldn't expect a charity, all be it his own, to purchase the little extravagances he enjoyed so much.

Cyrus had a quick shower to freshen up, and before he changed completely into his eveningwear he took a few moments to enjoy the pair of small luxuries that he had behest.

He filled the brandy snifter to its correct level, sat down in the large comfy chair and lit the cigar. Eyes closed, he savored the contrasting aromas and tastes for a few moments, until another presence in the room snapped him quickly out of his rumination. .

"Well, well, well, I am honored." Cyrus said with a huge grin.

The uninvited guest gave Cyrus a distasteful look, cautiously approached him, then gave his face an almighty lick.

"Whoa, big guy, what's up old chap? It's not like you to be so affectionate."

The immense snowy feline then pushed his head into Cyrus's chest; wanting nothing more than a good fuss.

That one act of warmth and caring from the normally irascible beast, really hit home the graveness of the situation that lay ahead. Up until that moment, Cyrus hadn't really been worried about the outcome of the futures events. Failure, hadn't even occurred to him, they were the Four and when together, nothing could stop them, but seeing Chong's big black eyes looking at him, full of anguish and sadness, filled him with doubt; an emotion that until now, he had never experienced.

"C'mon buddy, don't look at me like that. Everything is going to fine, have I ever let you down?"

But his words fell on seemingly deaf ears as a oversized white paw landed on his lap.

"Yes, yes, its good to see you too, but enough's enough. Off you go home, and I promise in eight days I'll come and see you."

The panther didn't budge.

Cyrus stubbed out his half smoked cigar into the remaining brandy, his taste buds gone sour.

"I shan't ask again you awkward animal, I haven't the time for this."

Still no movement from the beast.

Cyrus tried to get up, but the cats paw held him down, worry turned to anger, never before had his pet so blatantly disobeyed an order.

"CHONG, GO HOME." He shouted, and with that, sent the unhappy feline on his way. Its sorrowful mewing still reverberated around the room long after his departure.

Although he felt rotten for losing his temper and forcefully ridding the beast, another thing troubled him however.

Chong's behavior had showed that the possible catastrophe facing Earth, had spilled over and was known in the "other" place; and that can't be a good sign.

Cyrus physically pushed all negative thoughts from his mind, because he intended to enjoy the coming evening.

He arrived downstairs just in time to catch the start of the charity auction. He loved events such as these, watching the small minded middle-aged affluent, trying to impress their teenage brides, and always trying to get one up on a business rival or competitor whom also happens to be present.

As instructed by Cyrus, the items he anonymously donated were first under the hammer. He made sure he won them all back, not because they held any sentimental value, but the near ridiculous prices he paid, would set the standard for everything else.

He also picked up a gift for the Master of Ceremonies wife, and one for James's spouse. His little joke was becoming an expensive tradition, he laughed inwardly to himself.

Nothing else piqued his curiosity so he give instruction as to where to send the various items, then went in search of the bar, and was gladdened when he noticed they served his favorite tipple, Macallan 25 year old.

"Don't you ever fucking age?" Said a good-humored accented voice behind him.

Cyrus turned to see an olive skinned impeccably dressed man, maybe in his late fifties, but looking excellent for his age, standing there.

"Luigi, you made it, its great to see you." And Cyrus was genuinely pleased to see the man and happily embraced him, in the way they still do on the continent.

"And likewise you; I noticed the Guinevere has gone, so I was a little concerned."

"She's at the bottom of the Med I'm afraid old chap."

"Good grief! Is the crew ok? Is there anything I can do?"

"Thank you for you kind offer, but no. And there never was any crew Luigi." Cyrus smiled.

"Now, why am I not surprised." And Luigi returned the smile. "Do you want me to organize a team, and see if she can be raised?"

"Once again, thank you but no. She is now part of my ancient history and distant past, and my peace has now been made with my oldest of friends. So let her finally sleep."

Luigi of course knew, that Cyrus meant something a lot deeper that just his ship being sunk, but he learnt long ago, that there was no point in probing any further.

There has always been a mutual respect between the two, even maybe a friendship of sorts, and Luigi was genuinely taken aback at how open and warm Cyrus seemed; but there was a sadness undeniably lurking just below the surface.

"So how's business Luigi?" Cyrus wanted to change the subject.

"Good, excellent in fact. I wish we had gone legit years ago. Plenty of opportunities and money to be made, but without the slight inconveniences of breaking the law. Times are good."

"Superb, that's what I like to hear; mind you, you always had a keen eye and good business sense."

"Saying that, I'd still kill, not literary of course," Luigi laughed, thinking back to the bad old days, "for the same kind of profits that your place makes, it's a goldmine and that's for sure."

"Ah, I can take no credit for Avalon, my co-owner is good man, with a very astute business brain."

"Is?" Luigi's voice became somber.

Cyrus instantly knew something was wrong.

"What is it? What's happened?"

"I thought you knew, that's one reason why I am here today; to offer my heartfelt condolences."

"Condolences?"

"Yes, Paulo and his young family are dead." Luigi couldn't mask the sorrow.

"My God, how?"

"The police and coroners report said they were killed in a house fire." But his voice masked something.

"What really happened Luigi?"

"Come let's sit down."

The two men found a quiet table in the far corner of the room.

"I am so sorry to be the bringer of such grave news Cyrus."

"It's ok old friend, I'd rather in be you than an anonymous phone call to be honest. Now please tell me what happened."

"A local police detective, whom happens to be one of my nephews, received a phone call telling him to go to Paulo's address, and to take the coroner along with him."

"Who made the call?"

"Unknown, sorry. Worried that it might be a hoax, my nephew decided to investigate alone before alerting the higher chain of command. Upon reaching the fairly secluded hilltop retreat, the first thing he noticed was that the front door was open. So cautiously he entered. What he discovered is almost too horrific to describe. A poor

Paulo, naked and tied to a chair, his eyes pinned open, and his wife and two young daughters, tortured and worse before him. The tiny bloodied baby used as a paintbrush to daub an inverted cross on one the walls. It was the most disturbing and upsetting thing I have ever witnessed."

"You were there?" But Cyrus already knew the answer, for he now saw the same tragic scene.

"Yes, I was the first person my nephew rang. I told him not to ring anyone else and wait for me. I immediately dropped everything and with a couple of my most trusted men got there as quickly as we could. I went in alone, and wept at the sight before me. Once composed, I untied Paulo, carried his beaten body to bed, and did the same with the others, so at least they had some dignity. I then instructed my men to douse the house in petrol, and burn it to the ground."

"Thank you Luigi." Cyrus eyes were filled with tears.

"No need." He replied, touching Cyrus's hand across the table. "Paulo was a good man, liked by all. If I had left things as they were, every grisly detail would have been plastered all over the papers. He didn't deserve that."

"No he didn't."

"And I shan't rest until I find the ones responsible, no matter what the cost. And they shall pay, trust me on that."

Cyrus just sadly shook his head.

"Don't waste your time and money, they are long gone."

"You know who did this?"

"Sadly, yes. It pains me to admit, that I am responsible for his death."

"How so?"

"I refused to do something asked of me, and this is how I was punished. I didn't for a moment think anyone's life would be in danger, or I would have handled it differently."

"That's terrible, please let me aid you?"

"No Luigi, another kind offer all the same. There is something you could do for me however."

"Of course, just ask."

"And you promise to do it?"

"Yes, anything, you have my word."

"Take the next flight home, cancel all work engagements, and spend the next week with your family and loved ones."

"Your tone worries me Cyrus."

"Worry not, just please do that. And I vow to make the ones responsible suffer." It was the first promise he had ever made that he might not be able to keep.

"That is enough to satisfy me, I'll leave tonight. When will you be returning?"

"I probably wont be, not in a business capacity anyway. I'll put the wheels in motion to hand over the ownership of Avalon to you, I no longer want anything to do with it."

Luigi knew Cyrus well enough that would be no point arguing.

"That's very kind, may I change the name, with your blessing of course."

"Too?"

"Paulo's, and it will be the worlds first casino that every penny of profit goes to the needy. I shall make sure of that."

"You don't have to."

"I know, but I have more money than I could ever spend. Its something I'd like to do."

"Agreed then, I have one condition however."

"Name it."

"My private penthouse is to be left untouched. When the times comes that do return, I'd still like my own place."

"Of course Cyrus."

"But just a quick note; there are certain area's that are completely no go, and if anyone tries to get into them, well, lets just say that I have my own type of security in place." Cyrus's tone held a warning as well as his earlier request.

"Noted." Luigi answered.

"I have to say that I am truly sorry that our first proper meeting is under such circumstances Luigi."

"As am I."

"Once I have finished the task ahead of me, we shall meet up, get terribly drunk and talk of the old days."

"I'll hold to that."

"Good man, now if you'll excuse me. I have a long night ahead."

Cyrus stood up, as did his companion, they embraced once more, but this time as good friends, and Cyrus turned to leave.

"Cyrus." Luigi called.

He spun round.

"Yes?"

"Be careful."

Cyrus nodded and then was immersed in the crowd and gone.

He returned to his room, poured another brandy into a clean glass and lit one more cigar. He sat down, deep in thought; the day that had started so well, had now turned to shit.

Meanwhile, in a nearby room, not dissimilar to the one that contained a lugubrious Cyrus, a young mans day that started badly, had already culminated with a "pearl necklace", and it looked like things were only going to get better.

"My husband never fucks me like that." Said the attractive thirty-something as she slipped back into her sleek designer dress, making sure she smoothed out the worst of the crumples.

"You were wonderful." He lied.

"Your just saying that." She blushed.

"No, I mean it. You could teach me so much." Another untruth. "Come here, you have missed some."

She walked over to him, he spun her around, and slowly run his hand down her back, smoothing the creases she couldn't reach. His touch went lower, and lower.

"MMmmmmm, Steven stop, your turning me on again." She whispered.

"I know." He replied quietly in her ear.

"But I really must get back, my husband will be wondering where I am."

"Pity." He feigned dejection.

"Oh but fret not my sweet gigolo, I SHALL be seeing you again."

"Good."

"And if you don't mind, I have some friends that are equally as unsatisfied with their husbands performance. So if you don't mind not being exclusive, I am sure they would be very grateful. If you know what I mean." She said with a wink.

"Hhmm, I think there might just enough of me to go around."

"Excellent, as long as you remember that I always come first." She laughed.

"Oh trust me, whenever we are together, I guarantee that you will cum first." He teased.

"You're a bad bad man Steven." And with that she plucked a large wad of notes from her Louis Vuitton hand bag, and thrust them into his hand."

"Now, don't argue, and treat yourself to something nice."

Steven had no intention of arguing, but they were both expected to put on the show with each other.

"Thank you, but that isn't the reason I am here, you know that don't you?" His third lie.

"I know baby, do I look presentable?"

"Good enough to eat."

"Behave, I'll ring you tomorrow, I promise." She kissed him lightly and left.

"Result." Steven said to himself as he eagerly counted the money.

He had been alone for less than a minute before there was a knock at the door; he quickly hid the money under one of the pillows.

"Back so soon angel? No need to knock, come straight in."

Seeing a well-dressed man enter the room was the last thing Steven expected. The newcomer was impossibly handsome, and had one of those faces where he could easily pass for his early thirties, but there was something about him, that you just couldn't quite put your finger on, that belied his true age to be much older.

"Look, I didn't know that she was married." Steven blurted out defensively.

"Isn't that a contradiction in terms?" Asked the guest calmly.

"Excuse me?"

"Well, the very fact that you said that you didn't know she was married, proves that you did know."

"Oh." Steven felt foolish.

"It's of no concern to me what you and that slut get up do anyway, your both adults."

"Oh." Foolishness became worry.

"I'm here for an entirely different reason."

"Well I ain't go no money."

"Now, a double negative. You have a lot to learn young man; and no, I don't want the few crumpled notes concealed under the pillow." He laughed.

"Look, what the fuck do you want then?"

"I am sure you understand that this is a very special and exclusive evening."

"I got a fucking ticket." And Steven rummaged in his jacket, trying to find the said item.

"Yes I know; I sent it to you."

"What? Sorry? I don't understand."

"Of course you don't. Maybe I should introduce myself."

"Yeah, best you had huh."

"Cyrus Draig." And with that, he stuck out his hand.

An automatic response Steven shook the afore mentioned appendage. Still unsure of the situation, the name was a familiar one, but he just couldn't place it. But before he was about to show his ignorance once more, the realization dawned on him.

"YOU sent me the invite?"

"I did."

"But why? You don't even know me." This was becoming surreal in Steven's mind, and before long it would get much worse.

"Come with me Steven." Cyrus didn't turn to see if his new acquaintance was following.

"How would you like to be the richest and most powerful man in the world?"

"Yeah sounds good, and I presume you going to offer that to me?" He didn't hide his sarcasm.

"Not quite, but I shall offer you the tools to achieve it."

"Really? And tools would that be?"

"Immortally."

"Bullshit. Enough of the fucking games already."

"I offer you a gift of incalculable wealth, you could at least be bloody grateful."

"If the offer is one of such largesse, why don't you take it then?"

"I have no need for it, I am already immortal."

"You watch way too much TV mate, this is a fucking joke. Thank you for the invite, but I'll be on my way now."

"It's a one time offer, and if you leave, you'll never see me again. Now I understand it's a lot for you to take in, but I am pushed for time. Suppose you would like to see some proof?"

"Go on then, humor me."

"Look around, tell me what you see."

The two men were now stood in a large stately room.

"Erm, big posh room, with lots of pictures." Steven said disinterestedly.

"Ok, now, this orphanage has been funded by the Draig Foundation for nearly two hundred years. Go take a look at the portraits."

Steven did as asked, still not sure what the point of any of this was.

"All the men in the pictures look like you, big deal. Similarity genes get pasted down from one generation to the next. A couple of old painting's prove fuck all."

"One thing at a time, I have to ease you gently into the next revelation. Follow me again please."

"If I must, so when do I get to meet the ghost of Christmas pass?"

Cyrus didn't justify the young mans comment with an answer, and instead led him back to the room that had originally been made ready for him.

"Right, just let me warm you, from now on things will begin to get weird. Are you sure you want to continue?"

"You weirder than they already are? And yeah, as long as it isn't going to cost me any money, lets step into your twilight zone." Mocked Steven.

"So be it."

Cyrus open the door to the room, but held his arm across the entrance so Steven couldn't enter.

"Wait a moment, first tell me what you see."

"Looks like a room similar to the one I was just in, with a fancy bottle of something or another on the dresser."

"Good, good." Cyrus briefly closed the door, and then opened it once again. "Now tell me what you see."

"Fucking hell." Was the best Steven could manage.

The room could now only be described as something akin to a child's fantasy vision or a Hollywood version of the infamous tomb of Tutankhamun, the room was now filled with gold; statuettes, coins, plates and goblets.

"All that could be yours." Cyrus said closing the door.

(Did Cyrus actually fill the room with endless wealth, or did just make Stevens' mind see what he desired? I don't know myself, and I am writing this book.)

"Convinced yet?" Cyrus asked entering the again empty room, he sat down and poured two glasses of brandy.

"Neat trick, and I have no idea how you achieved it, but still not convinced yet, no." Steven replied, taking a huge gulp of cognac.

Cyrus either didn't hear, or just didn't bother responding to Steven's remark.

"Let me tell you, I have lived one hell of a life. I own countless houses, same with businesses; I enjoy the best of everything, I have a huge appetite and have loved many many women, I even had a brief affair with a famous singer of the seventies, and she wrote a song about me. Ahh, happy days."

"And that helps me how?"

"Sorry, was just reminiscing for a moment. It's going to have to be, the good ol cut my finger off trick; for you to be finally satisfied, isn't it."

"I have no idea what you are talking about, but I can tell you that I am not chopping anyone's digits off."

Cyrus sighed, before lighting another large stovey.

"I know it's an awful cliché, but all I have to hand is my cigar cutter, now watch carefully, I don't make a habit of this." And with one swift click, he lopped of his thumb from below its knuckle.

"Fuck this." Steven cried, and got up to leave. "Your insane, and I am out of here."

"You can't leave." Cyrus said, but seemed preoccupied with the remaining stump. "Feels really weird, its true when they say you can still feel it, fascinating."

Steven spent the next minute trying with of course no avail to escape, what for the time being at least, had become the worlds plushest cell. Eventually, he sat back down, defeated and deflated.

"Finished?" Cyrus asked, waggling about his newly grown thumb. But before Steven could answer, Cyrus's arm shot out at incredible speed and grabbed his hand.

"Your turn."

"Nooo." Steven whimpered, but his captors grip was one of rock and he had no chance of pulling free. There was another loud click and Steven's fattest digit fell to the floor.

"Your fucking insane." Steven wept.

"Stop whining you big baby. Tell me, can you feel any pain?"

Steven paused for a moment, now the initial shock had passed.

"Come to think of it, no."

"Now look at your hand." Finally Cyrus released his vice like grip.

Like a plant being filmed with a time capture camera, tiny tendrils grew and merged with each other, braiding and knotting until once more, the thumb was complete.

Steven vomited.

"Everything you told me was the truth, wasn't it?" He asked, his face terribly pale.

"Of course." Cyrus winked. "Now lets clean this mess up."

"Yes, I'm sorry, I'll fetch a towel." Steven started to rise.

"Sit down man, being immortal has many perks." Cyrus waved his hand, and all trace of sick vanished.

"And I'll be able to do all of this?"

"Yes, in time."

"Unbelievable; now I am convinced, but why choose me?"

"I have a rough week ahead, and I promised to do something, so here I am, since I might not get another chance."

"Rough week? Promises? I still don't understand what you are talking about."

"Don't worry, I'll explain later." Cyrus paused briefly. "Ready?"

"Ready for what?"

"Your first adventure."

"Erm. Yeah I think so, will there be any woman where we are going?"

"You've only been one of the elite for less than ten minutes, and your already thinking about sex. Not sure if I made a right choice choosing you now." Cyrus joked, but he knew that he had selected entirely the right person.

"A man has needs."

"Quite. Now, come on."

They left via a rear entrance, and Cyrus for his own reasons was glad they didn't encounter anyone along the way.

"Wanna drive?" Cyrus asked, already tossing the keys to a wide-eyed Steven.

"That's yours?" Steven squealed as they approached the yellow GT3, one click of the keyfob, and the indicators blinked, happily answering his question.

"This is one of the lesser cars from my fairly vast stable, but it's also one of my favorites as an every day hack. You can have them all, I'll have no use for them before long."

"Great." That was exactly the response Cyrus was expecting, pure selfishness, completely the wrong trait for any of the "special" ones; modesty, humbleness and a certain degree of intelligence are all vital to become prosperous and yet remained undetected for any length of time. Steven possessed none of the much-needed qualities.

"Right, where are we going?" Steven asked eagerly as he gunned the engine to life.

"Just drive, I'll tell you when we get there."

"Er, ok."

The yellow Porsche, left the car park in a flurry of spinning wheels, peppering the other cars in a hail of gravel, its heavenly exhaust note reverberating along the wooded avenue.

Cyrus wasn't in the mood for chat; unbeknown to Steven his mind had been gently steered and instructed, so he drove in silence directly to the destination Cyrus desired.

After a good two hours driving, the journey terminated down a narrow track in a dense forestry area.

"Here we are." Cyrus released the mild control on his companion.

"Wow, I enjoyed the trip that much, I hardly remember driving. Where the hell are we anyway?" asked an elated but slightly confused Steven.

"A very special place, come on." Cyrus got out of the car, quickly followed by an excited Steven.

The duo took a short walk and were soon in the heart of the woodland.

"Before we proceed, are you one hundred percent sure you want immortality?"

"Fucking A I do."

"So be it, now close your eyes."

Enthusiastically Steven did as instructed.

"Ok, open then." Cyrus said after a couple of seconds.

"JESUS H CHRIST." Steven said in awe.

The two men were now standing in a colossal cavern, Cyrus emitted a bright glow, a visible aura that more than adequately illuminated the wondrous underground chamber, complete with obligatory stalactites and mites in their never ending search for a final purchase. Variegated walls showed the many ages of Earth.

The hollow's contents could best be described as one would imagine a pirate's trove to look like, a hidden cavern filled to the brim with booty and riches, incalculable wealth, in this one place alone.

"You have more gold than fort Knox." Steven murmured, eyes nearly popping out of his head.

"Yes, that is quite probable. I have many of these inaccessible grotto's dotted around the globe."

"Inaccessible? But we are here."

"Here; is a mile underground, surrounded by solid rock, the chamber once carved by natures chisel; a long time dry reservoir."

"So how did we get here?"

"Once, long ago, there was a way in, but I permanently demolished and plugged any means of possible future entry, but the very fact that I have previously been here, means I always have a way of retuning."

"Superb, and I will be able to do the same?"

"No need."

"But why show me then?" Steven couldn't understand the point of all this.

"Because this is your new home." Cyrus's tone of voice changed, from amicable to unpleasant.

"Why? For how long?" Panic was clear in Steven's voice.

"Why you ask? But isn't this the fountain of wealth that you have been searching for?" Cyrus paused. "Like I said earlier, I made a promise, all be it to myself, but its one I always intend to keep. And as for how long? Well, eternity of course."

"You must have me confused with someone else, please, I beg of you, you can't leave me here." Steven sobbed falling to his knees.

"No Steven, I know exactly who you are, you are a victim of cause and effect, and now you are paying the price. I haven't been entirely truthful however about your immortally, there is a slight catch."

"Catch?"

"Yes, you life will be eternal, but if by the slimmest of chances this place is somehow discovered, upon laying eyes on any ephemeral being, you will instantly perish."

"Why are you doing this? I have done nothing to you?" Steven was sobbing uncontrollably now.

"Of course you haven't done anything to me, you prey on the weak and helpless."

"Who?"

"Looking into your greedy and despicable mind, I see many cases, but only one concerns me. Gail Harvey."

Steven didn't help his cause by not recognizing the name for a few moments.

"I'll make it up to her, I promise, I'll do anything she asks." He pleaded.

"She's dead. Goodbye Steven."

And with that, Cyrus vanished, along with the any light, leaving a screaming Steven in his eternal pitch-black penitentiary.

"That was a bit of a cunts trick mate." Nathan said leaning on the wing of the Porsche as Cyrus walked out of the thicket.

"Fuck him, he deserved it." Cyrus shrugged.

"What on earth did he do to warrant eternal damnation?"

"He pissed me off."

"Seems a tad harsh, but still, it's none of my business."

"Your not wrong, how'd you get here anyway?"

"Can we just get in the car? It's bloody freezing out here." Nathan said ignoring Cyrus's question.

"I'm with ya there brother, don't suppose you want to drive?"

"Do I look like pimp?"

"Cheeky bastard." Cyrus laughed as he got into the car, starting the engine and turning the blowers on hi.

"Seriously though, he'll go insane within a week down there."

"No he wont, I did a little mental re-wiring."

"Fucking hell Cyrus, you really can be a vicious shit."

"Maybe, but I was taught by the best. Wasn't I?" Cyrus said, looking Nathan in the eye.

"Ouch, a little below the belt there. That was a different age and lifetime ago." Nathan said sadly, thinking back about old memories.

"Yes it was, but still doesn't change the fact that I learnt everything from you."

"When did I EVER dress and act like a pimp?" Nathan chided, trying to lighten the conversation.

But before Cyrus could answer, just as he pulled the car out onto the main road, with the Sun being low in the sky due to it being early morning, the pair were blinded for a brief moment until Cyrus pulled down the sun visor, at which point something fell onto his lap. The yellow sports car skidded to a stop, but both its occupants already knew what the item was.

"Ha fucking ha." Cyrus's tone held more than a hint of sarcasm.

"Don't look at me, I had fuck all to do with it." Nathan replied, the genuine surprise in his voice proved he spoke the truth.

"How the fuck did it get there then? It wasn't there earlier, I had my wallet up there, so would have noticed. How long were you waiting for?"

"Five minutes tops."

"And you didn't see anyone?"

"Cyrus, am I a fool?" The normally serene Nathan was getting a little pissed off at his companions questioning.

"Sorry buddy, just got a tad caught up in the moment. I was down not much longer than ten mins, so they had a five minute window to deposit it."

"Ok, was that dirt track the only way in to the woods?"

"Yes, definitely."

"Well it took me longer than five minutes to walk up it, and no one passed me."

"You walked?" Cyrus joked; after the initial shock, good nature prevailed once more.

"Yes, unlike some people I know, I can "do" walk."

"I suppose, mind you, you've had five hundred years rest."

"Touché."

"Anyway, I'm just chuffed I got one, I'm a fully fledged member of the Croatoan club now." Cyrus said with pride.

"Doesn't bring us any closer to finding out what the fuck it means though."

"We've already gone over this mate, it will become clear when the time comes; otherwise what's the point."

"Hhmm, I hope so." Nathan didn't sound convinced.

"Everything will be fine. Where are we going anyway?" Cyrus asked as he started driving once again.

"Janus and Sol are in a roadside café about ten miles down the road."

"Excellent." Cyrus exclaimed, whilst putting his foot down.

The two men sat in silence for a couple of minutes.

"Erm, Cyrus."

"Yes good buddy?" His spirits lifted considerably.

"Ten miles; in the other direction." Nathan laughed.

"You're a cock." Cyrus laughed back; then quickly handbraking the car and scaring the shit out of Nathan (metaphorically of course), before heading back up the road at a fair rate of knots.

"Hang on." Nathan suddenly exclaimed.

"What now?" Cyrus braked again.

"Lets go back to the cavern."

"What the fuck for?"

"I've got a hunch."

"You think Steven is gone?"

"If that's his name, then yes."

"I bloody well hope not." Cyrus said in a pissed off type of way.

"Well I hope he is." Nathan countered.

"Why?"

"Lets just see first."

A few minutes later and a mile under solid rock, the two men now stood, both emitting a heavenly and incandescent glow, the still air was ripe with the unpleasant odor of excreta.

"You were right, the fuckers gone." Cyrus snarled.

"Good, I'd have been worried if he hadn't."

"How come? And stop speaking in arseing riddles."

"It shows that our silent watcher has compassion."

"Ah, unlike us heartless bastards you mean?"

"Speak for yourself, I was going to come back for him."

"Really? Even if it was against my will?" Cyrus half growled.

"Yes." Nathan paused. "Oh and Cyrus."

"What?"

"Next time you take that tone of voice with me; I'll rip you in two." Nathan wasn't joking.

"At last; your sounding more like the Nathan of old."

"Hhmm."

The drive to meet the others was an usually somber one, both men lost in their own little worlds for their own personal reasons.

"I don't think there's any need to tell Janus about what has just happened, he's got enough on his plate as it is." It was Cyrus that broke the false tranquility as he pulled in a parking space.

"Agreed, although he already probably knows as much as we do. So no point mentioning it, unless he asks."

"Sounds good."

The two entered the establishment, which was already fairly full; one of them dressed in completely the wrong entire for a place packed with burly truckers, a café such as this, has barely even seen someone wearing a suit, let alone a tuxedo.

"I always dress for breakfast." Cyrus said to one of the many people staring at him, which in turn rewarded him with a round of laughter and everyone got back to their own business.

"For fucks sake, stop acting the clown and sit down." Janus said, but only three other people heard him say it, because his voice was in their heads.

"Sorry Boss." Cyrus sat down as instructed, followed closely by Nathan.

"Successful night?" Janus asked, his tone revealing that he knew more than he should.

"So so." Was his truthful answer.

"As was ours." Solomon added, his mouth full of food.

"Really? What do you do?"

"Nathan didn't tell you?"

"No."

"We went fishing." Sol announced proudly.

"Fishing for what?" Cyrus was sure it was a metaphor for something more sinister.

"Erm, fish."

"Oh." Cyrus felt a bit of an idiot. "So what's the plan of action today?" He wanted to change the subject.

"When can myself and Sol fly out?" Janus asked, straight to business.

"Are you going legit?"

"Yes, we have valid passports etc."

"In that case, whenever you're ready. I can get a jet up to Manchester now, and by the time you get there it will be waiting with all the completed relevant paper work. It will just take a phone call."

"Do it."

Cyrus nodded and left the café to make the arrangements.

"So he's got one too now." Janus spoke to Nathan.

"Yes, do you know all that happened last night?"

The slight incline of Janus's head affirmed the question.

"What do you make of it?"

"You guys have lost me." Solomon added, feeling a little left out.

"Don't worry big guy, I'll explain later." Janus said amicably to his friend. "I have to agree with your summation Nathan, who or whatever it is showed some degree of humanity and sympathy, and that can only be a good thing."

But before any more could be discussed, Cyrus returned, complete with a new set of clothes, which confused most of the patrons, as to how he could have changed so quick.

"Talking about me?"

"Of course we are Cyrus, and we spent all of last night doing it too." Solomon answered.

"Piss off ginger."

"Yo mamma." Solomon countered.

"Ok, ok, you win." Cyrus laughed at being out-insulted by his normally slow on the uptake friend. "Everything is sorted, plane will be at Manchester within two hours."

"Excellent, it will take me and Sol about that long to get there, so we'll leave immediately. But before we go, are you two going to be ok? Can you foresee any problems that I should know about?"

"No, we'll be fine. Logistics shouldn't be too much of a ball ache, and that fact that the other guy's passports will be about fifteen hundred years out of date means our flight will have to go unrecorded, but its nothing we cant handle, is it Nath?"

"Walk in the park."

"Fair enough, I'll leave it in your capable hands then. Just try not to bring too much attention to yourselves, ok?"

"Boss." Cyrus and Nathan answered together.

"Catch you on the flip side. Come on Sol."

"Laters Boss." Cyrus said as the two men got up to leave.

"Well, there's no point us hanging about. How long does it normally take to get to Somerset?" Nathan asked.

"Normally about four hours driving."

"Sorry, I'll rephrase that question. How long will it take you to get to Somerset?"

"Two hours, give or take." Cyrus smiled.

"Thought so, just don't bloody kill us on the way."

"I wont, coz Janus would batter me if I did."

Five minutes later, the duo were already driving down the road at a speed with wasn't really appropriate for the given conditions and weather.

"What ARE you listening too?" Nathan just had to ask.

"Ice-T, he's the Godfather you philistine."

"I don't care if he's bloody God himself, turn off this awful gansta crap."

"Want, want, want; how's this then?" Cyrus asked, changing the cd.

"It's a terrible cliché, but perfect none the less."

The yellow Porsche was now doing well over a ton, with its two occupants were singing badly at the top of their voices; Bat out of Hell.

CHAPTER 8

"To the Hills, to the Hills, and F**k the Indians" Part Two

As predicted; the journey took a tad over two hours; it would have been quicker, if they hadn't been stopped for speeding. The policeman that pulled them over, strangely forget his reason for doing so by the time he walked up to the car, and after a bit of small talk he let them continue on their way, thus slowing them down for about ten minutes. However, the said law enforcer, would be in hot water when he returns to base and the in-car video footage is scrutinized (as it is at the end of every shift), the yellow car he gave instruction to pull over was clearly exceeding the speed limit by some margin, but no ticket given? The poor man would have no answer to the multitude of questions too follow.

"So Nath, what's the best way to handle this?" Cyrus asked.

"Don't call me that. We need to pull over as soon as we find a phone box." Nathan was relieved that the pace was at last, less of a white-knuckle ride and altogether more sedate.

"Now, now, no need to be touchy, it was said with affection." Cyrus joked. "But why do we need a phone box? This is the twenty-first centaury good buddy; and we have things called mobile phones."

"Oh yes, of course, silly me, we'll just cram one hundred and twenty burly knights into this two seated contraption then."

"Ok, fair point, but still why do we need a public phone box?"

"Don't they normally have a phone book and business directory in them?"

"Erm, I presume so, can't say I have ever had need to go into one, but why a business directory?"

"We need to charter a couple of coaches, a small local operation would be ideal."

"Ah, good thinking Batman." Cyrus exclaimed as the penny dropped.

One phone box and four phone calls later, they found just the thing they needed; a family run company, with two vehicles and only a few miles away.

Cyrus drove past the yard and parked his car a couple of streets away.

"Why you parking here?"

"We aren't coming back here, so best not leave the car on their premises, it will raise too many questions."

"True." Nathan said exiting the car.

"Be with you now." Cyrus called. "Good bye old girl, I'll miss you." He whispered affectionately, as he patted the top of the dashboard, lit a cigarette, and purposely left it burning on the flammable cloth Recaro.

"Did you just kiss your car than?"

"No." Cyrus answered, maybe a little to quickly to be convincing.

"Hhmm, ok, if you say so."

"Come on, we haven't got all day." Cyrus clearly wanted to change the subject.

The mismatched duo were soon standing in a drafty portacabin which housed a makeshift office, and although the small firm had bookings for the next few days, with a bit of mental persuasion they agreed to tender their services immediately, as a generous hard cash offer is always difficult to refuse.

Unbeknown to them however, no one would have any memory of the little mission that were about to partake in, all the more mysterious when they find ten thousand pounds in cash, secreted in their safe.

Another couple of hours later with only a slight hold up, when pulling out of the yard all traffic had to be redirected due to a nearby car fire, Cyrus and Nathan were standing in a cavern not dissimilar to the one they were in earlier in the day, all be it much larger however.

The scene before them was one of a bizarre second-rate backwards sci-fi movie; over one hundred souls, clearly in stasis, yet wearing the garb of a era long time past.

"Any idea about how best to proceed?" Cyrus asked his colleague.

"Well, my knowledge of the last half millennia at least, is through the eyes of five hundred entirely different people, the randomness and lack of consistency would be too confusing for them to take in." Nathan conceded.

"Fair point buddy, in that case they shall experience history through the eyes of the Magnificent Cyrus Draig." He announced loudly.

"God help them." Nathan replied, shaking his head.

"An abridged version, of course."

"Of course."

"Right, this may be a process of trail and error, so shall we make a start?"

"Knock yourself out."

"Anyone in particular to be our guinea pig?"

"Perceval?" Nathan suggested, for good reason.

"Oh yes, great choice."

A mere five minutes later, the Knight awoke from his protracted slumber. Cyrus and Nathan eagerly stood over him, breath held, awaiting the result with anticipation and intrepidation.

Perceval gingerly arose, took in his surroundings, then swallowed before speaking.

"Yo Dudes, how's it hanging?"

"Fucking hell Cyrus, you've created the hybrid bastard love child of Bill and Ted." Said an exasperated Nathan.

"Ah, erm. Well I do like me movies, and that one is a classic." Was the best he could come up with, briefly thinking back to one of his private rooms in the casino.

"Nah, just fucking with you guys." Perceval joked, then the large Knight embraced the two men. "But by God, it's good to see you again."

"As it is you, how do you feel Percy?" Cyrus asked.

"Great, like I have just woken up from a goodnights sleep to be honest. How the world has changed, it's unbelievable; speech alone is so descriptive, not stuffy and formal like it was. And my name now is Percy I noticed, but it's like that was always my name."

"Yes, we shall update or change everyone's name, but their new given cognomen should feel like second nature. Does it?" Nathan asked.

"Strangely yes. So why wake me first? Because I am most intelligent I suppose?" Which actually was true, Percy always was the most lateral thinking of all of them; so if the awaking process worked on him, it would undoubtedly be a success on the others.

"We thought we would try the one with the smallest brain first." Cyrus smiled.

"Pah, your just jealous because I was always better looking than you. Anyway I am just going to stretch my legs, you've got a long day ahead of you." Percy said, looking at the many comatose bodies, then turned and started to walk away.

"A positive result, don't you think?" Cyrus asked Nathan, but before he could answer, Percy turned to face them once more.

"I'll be back." He said in an awful Austrian accent, and then walked away.

"No comment." Nathan answered Cyrus, shaking his head.

Ten hours later, the cavern happily echoed with the sound of over one hundred voices, each man eager to get out and taste the kiss of fresh air.

Although all shared the same memories given to them by Cyrus, their individuality, identities and traits remained their own; but when Janus and Solomon appeared seemingly out of nowhere, everyone fell to one knee, head bowed, some habits were deeply ingrained and nigh on impossible to change.

Janus nodded to Cyrus and Nathan, whom of course remained standing; he then prepared to address his loyal and faithful men.

"Please stand." All obeyed. "This is a new era, but is my word still law?"

"Yes Sire." Came the loud chorus.

"Good, so hear and obey when I say from this day forth you no longer call me Sire. Times have changed, and you are awake and standing before me because you are the best of the best, and WE need you." Janus paused. "As you know, my name is now Janus." He quickly glanced at Cyrus, and the look he got back confirmed that his men had been updated fully. "And you will also be aware of the impossible odds that face us, but the one thing we ALL have in common is that we were bred to fight, and fuck me, we are going to give them one hell of a battle. So are you with me?" A huge cheer erupted. "I said, ARE YOU WITH ME?" The second cheer could have brought down the very walls of Jericho. "Good, now lets get you bunch of ugly bastards out of here."

For the time being, Nathan and Solomon were left with the task of transporting the men out of there, Janus needed a word with Cyrus.

"Safe to talk?" Cyrus asked.

"Yes, he can't probe or earwig this far down."

"You were right then?"

"So it seems. As per your instruction, the plane was to take off at the given time, whether we were aboard or not, me and Sol watched from the concourse for a whole hour after the supposed departure, but nothing. So the pilots must have been compromised."

"Sounds that way, people in my employ do as they are told, I pay them well enough. What I can't understand is why though? I thought he promised a truce until the final showdown."

"I am sure the armistice still stands, but he's just fucking with us, it's all a game to him. He probably would have redirected the jet to some obscure location or have it crash in the Atlantic, tem miles out from the shore, nothing critical, just time consuming and enough to piss me off." Cyrus conjectured.

"So we continue to use telepathy?"

"Oh yes, with any vital questions or ideas."

"But you think he'll try again?" Cyrus asked.

"I doubt it, but he'll be annoyed that we second guessed him at least. So to be on the safe side, I think it would be prudent to forego going to the Blanik Mountains."

"Four hundred is a big number to lose Janus."

"Against the odds and possible numbers we are facing, I don't think it will make much difference; we aren't going to win this one with brut force. Plus I have a feeling that we would find them dead." Cyrus said sadly.

"You think?"

"Fraid so, human life means nothing to him, and it would be his way of getting back at us, also it would do nothing for moral."

"True, good point."

"And another thing, by our inaction, we might just save their lives at least."

"So we continue as planned, but leave out the Czech Republic leg?"

"Yes. Now lets see how the other two are getting on."

To be fair to Solomon and Nathan, by evacuating ten at a time, there was only a handful of Knights now left to pull out.

"You've done well." Janus was speaking to both of them.

"Aye, we've only got John, Paul, George, Ringo, Derek, Rodney, Albert, Grant and Phil left. Percy went first so he could look after everyone topside." Solomon answered.

"You named them I presume?" Janus asked Cyrus.

"Guilty as charged." He laughed.

"If I find out you have named any of them Dopey, Sneezy and Bashful, I swear I will slap you."

"Promises promises."

"Right guys, lets get the fuck out of here." Janus announced.

On the surface and in the open air, the Knights were dotted evenly about: some swinging their swords in the moonlight, others doing basic exercises, and most in small groups discussing their newly acquired memories and experiences. The coaches were parked nearby, the drivers sat inside, in a daze of sorts but still able to function perfectly well, all be it in an autopilot capacity.

"Where too first Boss?" Cyrus asked.

"We need to get the guys new clothes for a start, leather and steal is very fetching but not practical if we need to blend in at any point, and then fed." Janus looked at his watch. "It's just past eleven; we passed a twenty-four hour Tesco on a near-by retail park, they'll have an adequate selection of outfits there, and chances are there should be somewhere open that serves food in close proximity."

"Your going to take the hoard to a public supermarket dressed as they are?" Solomon had to ask.

"Of course not Sol, I'm going to send you in alone to buy one hundred and twenty pairs of Y-fronts."

"WHAT??"

"Joking big guy, the place will be virtually deserted at this time night apart from the skeleton staff; its none of their business but if asked, our story is one that we are members of a battle re-enactment society, one of

our coaches was stolen, hence everyone is packed like sardines into two vehicles and they are dressed how they are."

"Of course, simple really; that's why you're the boss, and I'm just along for comic effect." Solomon added.

"And you've only just realized this?" Janus chided. "Lets get this show on the road; Nathan, you ride with me, and you two travel in one coach each."

"How come he gets to ride in the car?" Solomon asked.

"Because you smell, now stop being childish, and let's go. See you there guys."

"I know you hide it well, but at times, you can be a funny fucker Janus." Solomon replied, and then walked off in a pretend huff to join the others that were already boarding the vehicles.

The two remaining men got into the black Range Rover; Janus started the engine, selected drive, then sped off.

"I think you're wise avoiding Blanik." Nathan said, although his lips didn't move.

"Yes, it's a situation we don't really need right now, and like I told Cyrus, the missing numbers won't make much, if any difference." Janus's answer came from a face equally as unanimated.

"To be honest, there is no more we can really do now; so I just kind of want to get it over and done with now." Nathan said.

"I have to agree old friend. It feels like being in a dentist's waiting room; you don't mind the wait, even though you know you must go in and get it over with. Being sat there and not going in is great at first, but after a while you just think fuck it, just get it done will ya."

"Totally agree with you, and now seeing the guys again back there, sort of brings it home, knowing we can't turn back."

"We never even had the option of doing that, but I hear ya." Janus agreed. "I just can't shake the feeling that we have been here before."

"We have, remember?" Nathan reminded him.

"I know, I know, but Man didn't have our help last time."

"No. We were the ones that were the genocidal maniacs." Nathan said sadly.

"That was a long long time ago; a different world and life. My, how irony can be a strange beast."

"And we aren't?" Nathan laughed. "But at least, finally we get to pay our penance, and this time, the people have someone fighting for them."

"That they do; and no matter what we find ourselves up against, we are going to put up one fuck of a fight." Janus meant it.

"Amen to that, but I have to be honest when I admit, I am not just fighting for them."

"No?" Janus asked, a little curious now.

"Of course not, I am fighting for me. I love this place; here is where I call home. We have watched it grow from infancy, like fathers, we have subtly guided it somewhat, until we were no longer needed, and our children finally grew up and left home. But although we are nothing more than aged observers, I intend to be here till the end, and I don't mean in five days time. I'll think you'll find, Cyrus and Solomon feel the same."

"I agree, your right about the others." Janus answered, already knowing what the next question was going to be.

"And you?"

"Does it matter?"

"Not to me, but I think it might do to you."

"If your implying that I wont be fighting with the same heart and passion as you, then you are very very wrong Nathan. Although the reasons driving me may be slightly different to yours, the passion consuming me is anger; there is an inferno burning inside me at the gall and audacity of that Monster, thinking he can come here and destroy something that I had a hand in building." Janus's unheard voice was full of wrath.

"Sounds like to me that we ARE fighting for the same reasons then." Nathan said softly.

"Since this conversation is one of candor, do you mind if I say something?" Janus asked.

"Please do." Although Nathan also knew where this was leading.

"For us to have any chance of winning the battle, you are going to have to become something that you haven't been since we've been here. Can do that again?"

"No." Nathan replied.

"No?" That wasn't the answer Janus was expecting or wanted.

"Back then, I was nothing more than an animal; a brutal killing machine, with no conscious or soul."

"In some respects we all were. Cyrus did it for the spoils, me for the power, and Sol the least blameless, was just easily led."

"Maybe, but compared to me, you three were Saints."

"I wouldn't quite go as far as that."

"Well, at least the word mercy was in your vocabulary. Whereas, blood was my aphrodisiac, the sight, touch and taste, gave me the high I craved. It was an insatiable addiction, and my never-ending appetite kept me hungry until I had laid the plains barren and there was no one left to kill."

"None of us are blameless Nathan, and we all have plenty to be ashamed about. But you say you can't resurrect the beast you once were?"

"No, because now I am something much worse."

"Worse?" That answer did surprise Janus; because of course he knew Nathan's terrifying past history.

"Oh yes, although I am the same abomination I once was, now I fight with a sense of logic and have a purpose driving me, far more formidable don't you think?" Nathan smiled.

Although the question needed no answer, Janus noticed Nathan's eyes already had a taint to them, which scared the hell out of him.

"Looks like we're here." Janus said pulling into the nigh on deserted car park, a few presumably staff vehicles were dotted here and there, but otherwise it was empty.

"Best I go in ahead and appraise the manager of our situation, otherwise he'd probably call the police, and that kind of attention we could do without." Janus decided. "Coming in?"

"No, I'll just chill here if you don't mind." Nathan answered.

"Ok, catch you in a bit."

Janus got out of the expensive Range Rover, leaving it unlocked, but inwardly chuckled to himself, knowing it contained the worlds deadliest security system.

The manager seemed a happy and cheerful chap, and was more than willing to accommodate the forthcoming throng, and promised that he or the members of his staff present would gladly assist or fulfill any requirements needed.

Whilst the manager rallied his troops ready for the invasion, Janus waited outside, also for his troops, but those of a very different nature.

It wasn't a long wait before the two coaches turned up, the trailing bus was rocking from side to side and muffled out of tune singing could be heard from within.

"That'll be Solomon's." He laughed to himself.

Five minutes later he stood before his men, whom were eagerly awaiting his instruction.

"Right guys, you already know why you're here. Clothes are the priority, but none perishable snacks might also be a good idea; we have a long journey ahead, so anything that doesn't need cooking and has a sell by date of over a week will be fine. Cyrus has kindly offered to pay." Janus looked at his friend who feigned a look of shock. "Now, any questions?"

"Is it ok to buy beer Boss?" A voice shouted from the crowd.

"Yep, that's fine, but Paddy."

"Yes Boss?"

"Put the axe back in the coach, I doubt you'll be needing it in there." Janus couldn't help but smile as the large Irishman muttered loudly to himself, raising roars of laughter from everyone. "Now grab a trolley and knock yourselves out." Janus was happy; his men were in good spirits, which in turn brought his mood up a couple of well needed notches.

The comical CCTV footage of one hundred and twenty men mountains, clad in leather and chain mail, fighting against the worldwide enigma known as the wobbly shopping-trolley, would undoubtedly at some point in the future reach mainstream television.

226

The store also contained a couple of other patrons, that weren't part of Janus's assemble. Two acne encrusted teenagers, whom obvious to any observer had had maybe a little too much to smoke, and were down the aisle selling crisps, trying to make the near impossible decision of what type of potato based foodstuff would best satisfy their munchies. Seeing the place fill up with men like these didn't do their already battered heads any good.

"That's shit hot weed dude." One said to his wide-eyed, open-mouthed companion.

Just then they were approached stealthily from behind.

"Excuse me." A voice boomed, scaring the poor kids half to death.

"Ye Ye Yes." One of them managed to say, turning and facing the man now towering above them.

"Would you be Hobbits?" He asked in a very menacing tone, which was enough to put the poor stoners over the edge, and make them run at great speed out of the entrance, fearing for their lives.

"PERCY." Cyrus shouted, rounding the corner into the aisle after nearly being knocked over by the fleeing pair. "Behave, and stop scaring the natives."

"Sorry Boss, just having a bit of fun that's all."

It was then when Cyrus noticed something in Percy's already brimming trolley.

"Why the fuck have you got those?" Cyrus asked, plucking a box of Tampax from the said receptacle.

"Handy in case I go roller skating or cycling." He answered in a tone that said it was the obvious answer.

"I give up." Cyrus shrugged. "Now, come on, we are waiting for you."

Janus waited outside while there was a slight hold up because the checkout girl had not seen a black American Express card before, and wasn't sure if they could accept it.

"Close to you credit limit huh?" Janus joked.

"Ha, very funny."

"Have you seen what the guys have bought?"

"Yeah." Cyrus laughed.

"I see clothes and plenty of alcohol, but no snacks." Janus observed.

"You did say that they could buy beer."

"Yeah I know, and I can't berate them to be honest, but it's probably best we get them fed before they start drinking."

"What do you mean before they start?" Cyrus asked, as the noise that was obviously cans being opened could be heard in all directions. "So where we gonna eat?"

"There's a pizza restaurant just over there at the entrance of the park, and of my old eyes aren't deceiving me, it looks like they are just about to shut for the night, which is perfect, go and sort it would you please Cyrus."

"Which means I'm paying AGAIN I suppose."

"Do you want to borrow some money?"

"Piss off; get them to change into suitable attire then bring everyone over."

"Ok."

Cyrus walked towards the eatery and could see quite clearly through the many plate glass windows the various members of staff milling about, some cleaning down tables, others mopping the floors and what must be the manager cashing up at the till. He looked up and saw Cyrus approaching the door, thought briefly about ignoring the stranger, but realized it would be a futile venture since the man had already made an effort come that far.

"Can I help you?" He asked, opening the door slightly.

"Yes my good fellow, how many can your fine establishment accommodate?"

"One hundred and fifty comfortably, or maybe two hundred at a push." The manager knew the answer immediately.

"Excellent, in that case I would like to make a booking." Cyrus said cheerily.

"Certainly sir, please bare with me while I fetch the reservation book."

"You wont be needing that."

"I'm sorry? I thought you said you wanted to make a reservation."

"I do. I'd like to make a booking for about one hundred and twenty."

"Not a problem, when for?"

"Now."

"Now?" The man clearly thought Cyrus was taking the piss.

"Yes."

"I am sorry sir, but are closed."

"I see, I shall ask you one more time only. I have one hundred and twenty hungry people over there." He gestured towards the parked coaches. "Now, I will pay you in cash, an entrance fee of one hundred pounds per head, plus the cost of food and drink, also a two hundred pound tip for each of your staff."

"That is a very generous offer, but please do you mind if I ask my employee's first, because it's them that will be doing most the hard work."

The man just went up in Cyrus's estimation, most managers, being offered twelve thousand in hard cash would have snapped his hand off, and wouldn't give a fuck if it inconvenienced his staff or not. But judging by the much nodding of heads by the people inside and the fact that the extra money for a few hours extra work would come in very handy at this time of year, Cyrus was sure the outcome would be a positive one.

The manager soon returned to a waiting Cyrus.

"As long as you assure me that you'll keep your word about the tips promised to the staff, the restaurant is yours, but I have no interest in the extra money you kindly offered, thank you all the same."

"Excuse me? I think maybe you have me read wrong, the money is completely legitimate, we are not bank robbers or drug dealers, I am just a very wealthy man that has no problem paying well for good service."

"And good service you will get sir, but I cant justify accepting half my annual income for a doing couple of hours overtime. I firmly believe in karma, and taking your money would be nice at first, but I would worry myself half to death at the possible repercussions." The man spoke from the heart.

"You're a good man Paul, and one of a rare breed, but fear not, when I give my word, I always keep it." Cyrus promised; in fact, the manager had struck a nerve with him, and showed him that humanity was worth fighting and even dying for.

But before Paul could ask this stranger whom he had never met before how he knew his name, he could see a crowd approaching, so he opened the large double doors and left to ready his staff.

"Everything sorted?" Janus asked.

"Yep, fuck me, even Nathan is joining us I see." Said an astonished Cyrus.

"Only coz you're paying." Nathan answered.

One hundred and twenty large men traipsing into the restaurant, all wearing similar clothes all be it with only slight variations in color etc was a bizarre sight to say the least, and it got even stranger when they all requested exactly the same topped pizza's; because they only had Cyrus's experiences to go from, they of course ordered his favorite.

The mood was jovial, beer flowed, banter at times was side splitting and compared to the rambunctious banquets of old, the men were remarkably well behaved and hardly broke anything.

It was just as everyone was on their third helping of ice cream when Percy came over to Janus's table.

"I hope you don't mind, but the men have a request Sire." Percy just couldn't shake the epithet.

"Sure, what is it Percy?"

"Erm. They would like the company of a woman." Answered a now embarrassed Percy.

"Shouldn't be a problem, I'll have Cyrus sort it." Janus replied, it wasn't an unreasonable request and he'd been half expecting something along those lines.

"Thank you Sire, I mean Boss." Said Percy, he then turned to the others and gave them the thumbs up sign, which in turn brought a tremendous cheer from everyone.

"Cyrus will sort it?" Cyrus repeated.

"Yep, I faith in your abilities."

"How the fuck do you expect me to get over one hundred man laid?"

"Simple, do what you usually do, pay for it."

"Ouch, bit below the belt there buddy, but seriously, how am I going to do this?"

"Are you telling me that in the phonebook of your girly blinged up mobile, you haven't got numbers for a few well to do Madam's?"

"I might have, but one hundred and twenty is a hell of a big number."

"Sex is their business, make the call and let them sort out the numbers. Now whose the nearest?"

"Bristol." Cyrus answered after briefly flicking through his phonebook.

"Excellent, tell them we'll be there in two hours."

"It's one o'clock in the morning Janus!"

"Oh sorry, silly me, I forget whore-houses only open between nine and five."

"Ok, ok, I get the message."

"Good man. You pay for dinner, make the necessary arrangements with whomever, and we'll see you back at the coaches."

"You can be a bossy bastard Janus."

"That's why I'm the Boss." Janus winked, got up from the table, thanked the manager and left the establishment, closely followed by everyone else.

The vehicles were already boarded, Janus and Nathan sat inside the four by four; Janus dropped the window as Cyrus walked over.

"Well?"

"All sorted, luckily some people aren't quite as honorable as the good restaurant manager, and the offer of cold hard cash, gets you what you want."

"So where we going?"

Cyrus gave Janus the address, and he put it directly into the cars' SatNav.

"Got it, see you up there."

"Ok Boss."

Just over two hours later, the three vehicles pulled into another large car park, but this time, it was owned by what looked like an imposing members only casino.

"Of course, where better to have a high class brothel than in the upper levels of a casino; a place mostly full of inebriated wealthy businessmen with plenty of money to burn, along with any sense of morality." Janus admitted.

"Gambling and prostitution, some things never change." Nathan observed.

"Good, and maybe they shouldn't."

"You agree with whoredom?"

"In this environment yes."

"Hhmm."

"Oh come on Nathan, don't give me that holier than thou attitude. The woman are very well paid, they do it because they want too, there is no abuse, security is aplenty and if anything, the only exploitation taking place is by the woman themselves. Its not like we are outside a seedy back street massage parlor occupied by eastern European heroin addicted women."

"I'm glad that you can make a distinction."

"Oh fuck off, I can make the distinction, because there is one Nathan, so don't get all high and mighty with me." Janus didn't try to hide the pissed off tone in his voice.

"Yes, I'm sorry, there's a lot on my mind that's all."

"We all have, that's why we are here, to try and switch off for a couple of hours."

"You're going in?" Asked a surprised Nathan.

"Damn right I am, going to have a wee game of poker me thinks. Care to join me?"

"Erm. No thank you, but if you don't mind me asking, what's the point in playing a game such as that, when you know what cards everyone has?"

"Because I don't know what people have; when I play, I play an honest game and close my mind to any tells that aren't physical or visible."

"Yeah right."

"Sarcasm doesn't suit you Nathan, and don't confuse me with Cyrus." Janus was still annoyed.

"I seem to be doing a lot of apologizing tonight, sorry boss. You go and have a good time; best you try and win some money, because I think the night is going to be an expensive one for Cyrus." Nathan at last smiled.

"He can afford it." Janus replied as he stepped out of the car. "Oh, and Nathan."

"Yes?"

"Please try to stop worrying about Croatoan." And with that Janus was gone.

"Easy for you to say." Nathan said quietly to himself.

Janus met Cyrus as he stepped of the coach, carrying a large Samsonite briefcase. The duo walked up to the entrance of the impressive period building, standing there ready to greet them was a late middle aged oriental woman, whom was still very attractive, and twenty years ago must have been quite simply, stunning. Alongside her stood an impeccably dressed man, also of Asian origin, Janus guessed at Vietnamese, obviously her business partner, perhaps maybe more.

"Madam Suzie, looking as beautiful as ever." Cyrus turned on his usual charm. "You'll have to tell me your secret."

"And this coming from some who has seemingly tapped in to the fountain of youth." She joked. "It's good to see you again Cyrus." They embraced and he gave her an affectionate kiss on the cheek, before tuning to her companion.

"Peter, Peter, I know we say this every time, but its been too long old friend." Cyrus also embraced him.

"As Suzie said, its good to see you Cyrus, but first, my I offer you my heartfelt condolences, Paulo was a good man." The sadness was clear in his voice.

"Yes, yes he was." Cyrus gave Janus an "I'll explain later type look", before continuing. "Anyway, let us not dwell on what's past, he wouldn't want that. Its time to do business instead; I have a ruck of needy men behind me, so Suzie as agreed, you'll find two hundred and fifty thousand here." He passed he case over, which she handed to two men that seemingly morphed out of nowhere, unspoken they took it and disappeared into the building.

"A QUARTER OF A MILLION?" Janus shouted to his friend, although it was only him that could hear it.

"How much did you think it would cost? These aren't twenty bucks a bang girls, the going rate is normally a thousand per hour, so in fact, I have got a good deal." Cyrus replied, also silently.

"Jeesuss." Was all Janus could say.

"Please forgive me, it seems I have forgotten my manners." Cyrus spoke verbally now. "Peter and Suzie Chung, I would like to introduce my very good friend, Janus Brown."

Suzie also embraced Janus warmly, as if he was also an acquaintance of old.

"A friend of Cyrus is a friend of ours, if there is anything you need, please ask." She said softly.

"And I would like to echo my wife's statement Mr. Brown." Peter said as he shook Janus's hand.

"Thank you, both of you, that's very kind. And maybe you could help me Peter."

"Of course, name it."

"Would there, per chance be a small poker game on tonight?"

"I think I might have just the thing to accommodate you." Peter smiled.

"Excellent." Janus replied, already liking the couple; Cyrus had his bad points, but his choice of friends was normally spot on.

"Don't worry about us, we'll sit here all night." Said a voice from behind.

"Sorry Sol, didn't realize that we were taking so long." Cyrus replied. "Ready to accommodate our motley crew?" He asked Suzie.

"Always ready Cyrus. But is the big guy going to be trouble?" She joked, already falling into her role as Madam.

"More than you can handle." Sol answered.

"I can handle, much bigger than you." Her voice now had a gorgeous sultry tang to it. "Come on through guys." And she turned to lead the way.

"You going to partake?" Janus asked Sol, as he walked past.

"Och aye, I am no virgin you know." He replied without even slowing.

Janus and Cyrus shared a glance, after all this time, even their best friends could still surprise them.

After a couple of minutes, it was just the three of them left standing in the foyer.

"And you Cyrus?" Janus asked.

"No, no, shan't bother myself, I'll just share a bottle or two with Peter, while we catch up on old times."

"You go up to my office Cyrus, pour a couple of glasses, while I find Mr. Brown a seat. Oh, I don't have to tell you where I hide the good stuff."

"The good stuff huh? I am honored."

"I've got a bottle or two hidden away for special occasions, from the case you sent me. Now would you like to follow me Mr. Brown." Peter asked.

"Please call me Janus."

Due to the lateness of the hour and the day of the week, the casino was all but empty; it was still an impressive set up however. All matching period furniture, with décor to suit, roulette and blackjack tables closed, the staff that could be seen, were all immaculately dressed and took pride in their appearance. Although nigh on empty, security was still plentiful, but very professional and discrete.

"You fought in the war Peter?" Janus already knew the answer.

"Yes, you?"

"Briefly, until its futile nature sickened me, and I came home."

"Unfortunately I didn't have that luxury, I was already home." Peter said without malice.

"It will forever be a sad and unnecessary episode in the Worlds history."

"Yes, yes it will. Maybe one day when you are next this way, you'd like to come again, and I'll also open a bottle of the good stuff as Janus calls it, and we'll talk."

"I'd like that, and the fact that Janus paid for it, makes it even more inviting."

"Excellent, I shall look forward to that day."

"As will I." Janus sincerely hoped it would be a meeting he'd be able to keep.

"As I am sure you're aware, it's a quiet evening for us, but there is a private fairly high stakes cash came playing, I presume that would be acceptable?"

"Perfectly, may I ask the buy in?"

"Fifty thousands maximum, but unlimited re-buys, blinds five hundred and a thousand."

"Sounds good."

"How would you like to pay for your first stake, cash or credit card?"

"Credit card, but you still use cash? That does surprise me."

"Oh yes, in fact most transactions etc are done that way. Its how a lot of the local underworld organizations launder their money." Peter replied, obviously trusting Janus to be so candid.

"And you don't mind?"

"God no, we make a very comfortable living that way, because the house always wins." He joked.

"But what about the cash games like tonight, how do you profit from them?"

"Those are the exception, it's a service we offer to our most valued members. Tonights game is hosted by Ginny; now a word of warning Janus."

"Go on."

"She may look like an angel, but believe me when I say she's an ice maiden underneath. She is the best and most ruthless player I have ever seen, and never fails to make a profit. So be careful."

"Thank you for the heads up Peter, but I play purely for fun, and if she's good enough to take all my chips, then she deserves them."

"A noble attitude, I wish more patrons were like that."

The backroom room turned out to be a cordoned off area of the main hall, separated by a heavy velveteen curtain, which was dutifully slid open as they neared.

Janus had no trouble instantly spotting his esteemed host; Peter was right, yes she was stunningly beautiful, and her chip stack confirmed his other observation. Also, the fact that she was the only female on a table of six men, made Janus's Holmes' like deductions seem a little lame.

"Any objections to one more joining?" Peter asked Ginny, it was her table, so even if any of the men did protest, their opinions mattered not.

"Not at all, new blood is always welcome." Ginny replied, the tone in her voice showed an upbringing from very good stock.

"Thank you, please take a seat Janus, and a trusted assistant will be along to collect your credit card. Now you be gentle Ginny, he's a friend of mine." Peter joked, and Janus flushed slightly with pride at being considered a friend so soon.

"I'm always gentle sweetheart." Ginny countered.

Janus sat in the offered chair, and an assistant quickly came to take any drink order and relieve him of his plastic briefly. Janus ordered bourbon and placed his card on the small silver tray.

"We need your PIN number Sir." The assistant whispered quietly in his ear, as not to embarrass him.

It was then Janus noticed a pen and one slip of paper on the tray, obviously for him to write the needed details.

"Look at the card." Janus whispered back, returning the favor of not humiliating the young girl.

The girl did so and saw that the matt black credit card had the four-digit PIN number written crudely with what looked liked liquid paper in large figures on the front. Janus's adage was one of, if he was stupid enough to lose his wallet, then whoever found it, would be more than welcome to go on a month long spendthrift.

"Hi, I'm Janus." He introduced himself to everyone present.

"Intriguing name, is it the one you were born with?" Ginny was the only one that had enough manners to reply.

The question threw Janus for a moment; over the centuries he had used many pseudonyms and been known under various nom de guerre's, and although he always thought of Janus as true name, he honestly didn't know or couldn't remember if that was his given birth name. But before Janus had to give an answer, somebody else spoke.

"Are we here to talk or play poker?" One of the seated men asked in a heavy accented tone, Russian or surrounding countries Janus guessed.

"Now, now Nikolai, I am just being cordial, maybe you should learn the same manner." Ginny admonished, this was her game and she wouldn't stand for any nonsense.

The reason for Nikolai's poor mood was fairly obvious judging by his meager chip stack, and the fact that his own credit card was still on the table, meant he had recently re-bought at least once, no prizes for guessing which player probably had won the majority of his stake.

Janus's chips promptly arrived along with his credit card and a glass with a generous shot of Jim Beam Black, so he was all ready to settle down into his game.

As per his usual tactic, he started off playing slow and steady, not getting involved in ego fueled pots and making some calls where he knew he was the underdog, but seeing his opponents hole cards would give him valuable information for later on, getting a read on players is the most important factor of live poker. He steered clear of hands involving Ginny, her play was quite simply sublime.

Whereas Janus was happy stealing small pots here and there, Ginny only seemed to get involved in the monster pots, and she won each and every one. An onlooker would swear she knew what cards everyone held, of course any half decent player would know that she just had everyone's tells and give away mannerisms completely worked out; all the same, she was still an awesome player. The few small bluffs Janus tried, she called down each time, and when he did have the "nuts" she would always fold.

This went on for a couple of hours and a whole bottle of Jim Beam; Janus was up, most of the other players were down and Nikolai just became more and more agitated, having to re-buy twice more, his aggressive play was just losing him money by the truck load. He kept looking at his watch, as if he was late for an appointment, but didn't want to leave until he had recuperated his loses.

Janus was happy being something like a paying spectator, this girl had turned the game into an art form, and she was a living Da Vinci.

Never before had Janus been tempted to look into the mind of an opposing playing, but in this case he was fighting a battle with his internal demons, and he knew soon he would give in.

The curtain being noisily raped open sucked him quickly out of his unhappy dilemma.

Janus turned to see two heavily armed, masked men, and from the way they held their weapons, obviously ex military.

"You've gotta be kidding." Janus whispered, shaking his head. "This whole weekend is turning into a series of clichés."

Nikolai ignored Janus's mumblings and stood up.

"Security?" he asked.

"All taken care off Colonel, downstairs is secure." Replied one of the men.

Janus did a quick mind scan and discovered that there were twelve armed men plus Nikolai, which seemed a tad overkill for a normally deserted night, somebody must have tipped them off as to the increase in numbers present.

"Your going to pay you cheating bitch." Nikolai snarled at the still demure Ginny.

"Hang on a second, Boris, Ivan or whatever your name is." Janus wanted to deliberately antagonize Nikolai, so he would forget about the innocents briefly. "I presume this is a robbery of sorts, but what the fuck do you intend to steal? Our credit cards are no good to you and there is precious little hard cash here. It seems you're not just a fool at playing poker."

"Shut your mouth arsehole." Said one of the armed men as he leveled his automatic weapon at Janus.

"You have just signed your death warrant." Nikolai said coldly. "I know exactly how much money is here, and trust me its more than enough to make this worth it."

"Nathan, could do with your assistance here." Janus transmitted.

"What took you so long to ask?" Was Nathan's instant reply.

"Well you could have bloody warned me."

"What's the fun in that?" Nathan said with an obvious smile on his face, which Janus could easily pick up.

"Sol, you get down here too."

"On me way Boss."

"What about me?" Cyrus asked.

"Tell Peter to say where he is and then tell the guys to get ready to leave and for them not to interfere, they're good, but they aren't bullet proof, we'll handle this."

"Right fuckers, stand up." Nikolai told everyone at the table.

At the same precise moment, Nathan fell through the entrance doors, playing the part of a steaming drunk to perfection. Also right on cue, Solomon came clumping down the staircase.

"Stay where you are you fat bastard." Warned the man nearest Solomon.

"I'm only fat because each time I fucked ya Mamma she gave me a biscuit." Sol countered.

"Is this the right place for a shag?" Nathan slurred from the other end of the room.

"Where did you get such a foul mouth?" Janus asked Sol silently.

"Working with kids, I hear that kind of trash talk al the time, been looking for an excuse to use it. What do I do now Boss?"

"In case they haven't disabled the CCTV already, throw up some static and do it anyway."

"Doing it as we speak Boss."

"And me?" Nathan asked.

"When I give the signal, disarm arm, and don't be killing them, ok?"

"Aww."

Janus's instructions, took less then a heartbeat, and the commotion caused by the other two luckily allowed Ginny and one other enough sense to escape via a rear entrance, Janus breathed a little easier when he realized this, as he had no wish to see her harmed.

Janus didn't need this hassle or inconvenience, and the fact that one of the escapee's would surely call the police once they were safe, meant he had no time for fancy speeches or an elaborate show; time was against them, and he wanted everyone out before the authorities arrived.

"Nikolai, you despicable prick, I haven't got the time or energy to dish out my kind of justice, so I shall leave you in the capable hands of Peter, but I am sure he will make you pay accordingly." Janus was more than confident, knowing that Peter to get where he was, must have a ruthless side to him, and probably plenty of his own underworld connections, so appropriate and deserving consequences would befall Nikolai.

"Are you fucking blind?" Nikolai asked, still remarkably calm, although, taking the situation at face value, it did seem that for the first time tonight, he held the best starting hand.

"Everyone's ready up here." Cyrus transmitted.

"Nathan, if you please." Janus instructed.

To any casual observer, it would have looked like the inebriated Nathan just vanished, but in reality, Nathan moved at a speed that the defied the capabilities human eye, and in the less time than it would take the said eye to blink the casino contained twelve unconscious men, and their now empty weapons lay in a neat pile.

"How does he do that?" Solomon asked Janus.

"Fuck knows old friend, but I ain't complaining, and Janus, its safe to come down, bring Peter with you."

Nikolai just stood there, totally dumbstruck and confused; his plans, world and probably his future had crashed down around him, and he had no idea how it happened.

Janus soon appeared along with Peter, who now had a cold look in his eyes, he glanced at the comatose men, then at a deflated Nikolai, and a sly smile crept slowly onto his visage.

"Your employee named Ian Jones, tipped Nikolai off." Said Janus, after gleaming the information from Nikolai's mind.

"I knew I should have trusted my gut feeling when I hired him, there was something wrong about him. Is Ginny safe?"

"Yes. She managed to sneak out during the tumult, but due to the fact that she might call the police, do you mind if we make a hasty exit?"

"Phew, I am glad she is ok. It seems that now I owe you my life, first Cyrus, now you, I am a blessed man. Thank you Janus, Solomon and Nathan, this very evening has been a success, for I have gained three new brothers." Peter spoke with true passion, and Janus admired the way his mind worked, for what could have easily have been a disaster for Peter, he saw as a triumph merely because his family increased by three.

Also Janus now understood Peter's lack of surprise at what lay before him, he owed a debt to Cyrus, which meant, chances are, he had some insight into their capabilities.

"And yes Janus, you get away, I can handle things from here." Peter said, just as some of his own revived security burst in. "Get these men out of her, along with those." Peter spoke to his own and gestured to the weapons. "Tie them up, and I'll come over and deal with them when I have finished here, oh, and Ian is a traitor, he's probably long gone by now, but keep your eyes peeled and wits about you."

"You seem to have things sorted Peter, I shall bid you farewell, and please give my apologies to Suzie for not saying goodbye properly, and you can tell me all about Nikolai's fate when we next meet."

"I will, and once again, thank you and goodbye brother." Peter then embraced Janus, in a way that only close kin does, and whispered. "Thankfully, mankind is in the best possible hands."

CHAPTER 9

"Surprises Aplenty"

"That was fun." Nathan said happily, as they drove eastbound along the M4 motorway.

"Not for that Nikolai chap." Janus replied.

"Yeah true, stroke of luck we happened to be there though."

"Hhmm, not so sure."

"Not so sure about what?" Nathan asked.

"That it was luck."

"You've lost me."

"I don't know, I might be wrong, but Peter struck me as a very astute fellow, with plenty of his own connections and his ear to the ground. So I have a feeling if anything like last nights events was going down, he'd know about it." Janus mused.

"Hhmm, maybe, but surely us being there was a coincidence?"

"I'm not convinced that it was Nathan; Peter and Cyrus go a long way back and have history together, and something Peter said to me just before we left tells me he knows some details about us at least. If he sensed trouble ahead, I have no doubt that the first person he would have called is Cyrus."

"Ah."

"And if that was the case, it wouldn't have taken much for Cyrus to place a certain urge in the minds of the guys as he woke them."

"The crafty bastard." Nathan said smiling.

"Yeah, but I don't mind, I had an interesting evening and I am sure the guys did too." Janus laughed.

"Yep, even our Sol." Nathan joined in with the laughter. "On a serious note, we proceeding as planed now?" Nathan asked, but still giving the outward perception of laughter.

"I think so, Cyrus has three of his own planes chartered, just to add to the confusion, but I think the games are finished now." Janus answered, equally as silent.

"Lets hope so."

It didn't take long before the three vehicles reached the airport, and they entered via the route reserved for freight traffic only, all security checks were passed, although no paperwork was ever shown. Questions would be asked at some point at how this was allowed to happen, but by then the plane would have safely landed and its occupants vanished.

The men exited the coaches, all carrying large holdall's which contained items that in today's world would normally get them arrested, and most probably a long prison sentence would then follow. But due to the combined mental talents of four men, such things as passports and luggage checks would be strangely overlooked.

Janus turned off the engine of the Range Rover, removed the keys from the ignition and placed them under the sun visor. Nathan looked at him and raised one eyebrow.

"One of Peter's friends will be along to pick it up shortly." Janus explained.

"Ah, Cyrus set fire to his."

"That yellow contraption?"

"Yep."

"Why on earth did he do that?"

"I think he really liked it, and couldn't bare to see it fall into the wrong hands, so to speak."

"Fool."

"Oh, I don't know, I sort of see his point."

"You're a fool as well then." Janus said curtly.

"That's a bit harsh, people can become attached to material things such as cars."

"That's not what I am on about."

"What then?" Nathan was a little annoyed at being called a fool.

"In about a week's time, I intend to come back here and collect my car, your both talking like with have already lost and there is no hope."

"No, not at all."

"Yeah, whatever." Janus slammed the door; it was his turn to be annoyed, if his own closest friends didn't have faith, then what was the point.

Janus and Nathan joined their men as they walked across the concourse towards the waiting aircraft, both silent for their own reasons for the time being.

"I ain't getting on no plane fool." A voice could be heard from amongst the crowd.

"Shut up Percy." Janus warned, without having to look back to see whom the instigator was. "Just wait till you hear the bad news." He added, his annoyance already gone, he couldn't afford to harbor such negative thoughts.

"What bad news?" The voice this time was Solomon's.

"You haven't told him Cyrus?" Janus asked.

"Nope." Came the reply.

"Told me what?"

"You'll find out soon enough big guy."

"Hhmm, I don't like the sound of this." Said a worried Solomon.

"Can't say I am too happy about it myself." Janus laughed.

It didn't take long for everyone to board the plane and find a seat, but because the aircraft would normally handle twice this number and was devoid of the usual cabin crew, it seemed very empty and felt more like a hospital waiting room than a jumbo yet.

"Couldn't you find a bigger plane?" Janus asked Cyrus as the pair stood near the entrance hatch and waited for the guys to become settled.

"So what's the bad news then?" Solomon asked as he strolled over.

"Best you ask the Captain." Cyrus advised.

"Aye ok, where is he?"

"Standing right next to me."

"YOU?" Solomon screeched, looking at Janus.

"Did I detect a slight lack of confidence in your voice then Sol?" Janus asked.

"No, not a slight lack at all; a total lack. You're not serious are you?"

"Fraid so buddy, we are keeping everything in-house from now on." Cyrus added.

"But can you fly one of these monsters Janus?"

"First time for everything."

"Ya kidding me, right?"

"Nope, sorry bud."

"We're all going to die." Solomon muttered as he walked away shaking his head.

"But you have flown one of these before, haven't you Cyrus?" Janus asked quietly.

"Yep." He happily replied, and then added. "Once."

"Fuck."

"Don't worry old friend, with you as my co-pilot we'll be fine."

"I've only got a Private Pilots License remember, this is a tad bigger than what I am used too."

"It's like riding a bike, all be it a larger bike than normal, but all the basic principles are still the same, ish."

"Not the best choice analogy there Cyrus."

But before the duo could continue, they were interrupted by a huge roar of laughter coming from the cabin and seemingly from the whole gang.

They turned to see Percy, whom had somehow shoehorned his massive bulk into a stewardess's outfit, complete with lipstick and eye shadow.

"My name is Nancy, I am your flight attendant and I shall be looking after you for this trip." Percy said in a female voice worthy of a pantomime dame.

He then turned around so his back was facing everyone and bent down to pick up an obviously imaginary object. Of course the already straining dress couldn't take the extra forces put on it, and split from hemline to neck, revealing a spangly thong and stockings to match.

Those seated that thought it would be impossible to laugh any more or harder, were happily proved wrong, and the sight of over one hundred men doubled up with tears streaming down their reddened faces, made a proud Janus well up also; the men he knows and loves having such a good time, and in a couple of days will fight equally as hard and intensely, trying to protect the fate of mankind.

"Right, come on guys, settle down. Lets get this show on the road and bird in the air, so everyone sit down and buckle up. We'll let you know when it's ok to walk about again." Cyrus told everyone in a raised voice that quickly stopped the previous malarkey; yes the men were having a good time, but they knew when to shut up and be the professionals that they were when need be.

The Knights did as they were told, because although had had all flown many times before, each journey wasn't actually theirs, but one of Cyrus's many relayed experiences, and a memory can never compete with real thing, nerves and adrenaline fought for supremacy, and by the look of the varied faces from the men, it was a fifty-fifty even split.

The slow taxing brought a halt to any small talk, and the only sounds that could be heard were the low frequency rumble of the engines and various vibrations from around the cabin. The plane stopped, along with the breath of many of the seated. All could feel the impatient bird, straining with kinetic energy, her rising engine note, screaming, "Release me". Finally, the noise reached a deafening crescendo and the beast was let free, her outward appearance may be more like an elephants, but she accelerated like a greyhound leaving a trap. The cabin quickly filled with whitened knuckles and all manner of expletives possible.

"Fuck, that was fun, NOT." Percy said to a seated nearby Solomon.

"You didn't enjoy it I take it?" Sol replied, in a voice unable to disguise that he shared his friends' sentiments.

"What, you mean being sat in a thin metal tube, with a couple of wings attached and god knows how many jet engines strapped to them, pushing the tiny wheels at a stupid speed? Erm no."

"Hhmm, glad you didn't put it like that before we took off, I have never liked flying." Sol admitted.

"I have a question."

"Sure, Percy fire away." Sol felt important all of a sudden, it isn't often people come to him with any queries.

"Imagine the runway we just used was a giant conveyer belt, and it was traveling in the opposite direction at the same speed as the aircraft; now, would the plane take off?"

"I beg your pardon?" That wasn't the type of question Sol was expecting, and he wasn't entirely sure that he heard it right.

"I said, imagine the runway was a large conveyer belt moving in the opposite direction to the plane, but at the same speed; would she still take off?"

"Right, erm." Unfortunately Sol did hear the question right, and the answer would involve some thinking.

"No." Solomon finally declared.

"No? You sure?" Percy asked.

"Er, yes I think so, I'm no expert, but a plane needs moving air under the wings to generate lift, if the conveyer is going the same speed, then the plane would be stationary, and hence no lift." Said Solomon happily, proud at sounding intelligent.

"Your wrong." Percy added, after also thinking it through himself.

"Pardon?"

"Your wrong, I have just worked it out. The plane will still take off."

"Sorry buddy, I don't mean any disrespect, but I think you'll find I'm right." Sol replied, after imagining the scenario in his head many times.

"No, I am definitely right."

"How so? Explain then." Sol was still sure he was correct.

"Well, the way I see it is that the conveyer will have no affect on the forward motion of the plane, it will still accelerate and take off normally."

"But you said the belt would match the forward speed of the aircraft?"

"Yep, in fact, it wouldn't matter if the conveyer traveled at twice the forward speed, in the opposite direction."

"Of course it bloody would!" Sol was becoming confused and slightly annoyed now.

"No it wouldn't, remember the wheels are freewheeling and don't drive the plane, the engines push it forward."

"Eh?"

"The wheels will turn at twice the speed, but the plane would still move forward and take off."

"Bollocks."

"Imagine if you will, the same conveyer traveling up a steep slope at say two hundred miles an hour."

"Erm ok." Solomon said skeptically.

"Now, if there was a car near the top of slope, and the engine is turned off and the neutral gear is selected, the car will still roll down the hill, no matter what speed the belt is going."

"What have cars got to do with anything? You've completely lost me. But I think I am still right." Although he wasn't so sure now.

"Nathan, have you been listening?" Sol transmitted non-verbally.

"I have." Came the reply.

"So do you know the answer?"

"Yep."

"Great, so which one of us is right?"

"Not telling."

"Why not?" Asked a slightly peeved Solomon.

"Coz I'm a cunt." Nathan laughed.

"Fine. Cyrus, Janus?"

"Don't involve us, came their simultaneous reply.

"BASTARDS THE LOT OF YA."

Solomon's head filled with three laughing voices.

"Just you lot wait until you need an answer for something from me."

The laughter just got louder.

"Och, just piss off." He muttered audibly, properly annoyed now, as usual, he was the butt of everyone's joke.

The rest of the seven hour flight was uneventful, most men slept, some talked about the old days, especially when Cyrus and Janus joined them, leaving the plane to more or less fly itself.

It wasn't long before Cyrus's voice came over the tannoy.

"Ok guys, we'll be landing shortly, so make sure your all seated and buckled in. the good news is, I can see the runway, and it's definitely not a conveyer belt."

The cabin filled with discrete sniggering.

The landing at O'Hare airport in Chicago was surprisingly smooth and within fifteen minutes the plane was hooked up ready for the passengers to disembark.

"Nathan, you go ahead and steer any officials minds, so they don't give any of us a second glance or ask for paperwork."

"Will do Boss." Nathan said, and then left the plane.

"We'll give him five minutes before we leave." Janus suggested.

"Right people, just in case Nathan missed anyone, if you are approached or stopped by anyone, just pretend your Percy for a few moments and act dumb, until me, Cyrus or Sol reach you. Clear?" Janus told everyone.

"Boss." Was the affirmative chorus.

"Good men."

After about five minutes there was no news to the contrary from Nathan, so Janus surmised it was safe to leave.

"Here we go guys, I'll lead, Cyrus will bring up the rear, and Sol, you just mingle."

They must have been roughly halfway down the covered walkway when Janus received a message.

"Boss."

"What is it Nathan, is there a problem?"

"Possibly, might be an idea if you come ahead of the others."

"On me way." Janus replied. "Sol, you take over at the front. I'm going to meet Nathan."

"Is everything ok?" Sol asked.

"I hope not. Janus, have you arranged transport?"

"Already sorted Boss, got a bus waiting."

"Good, get the men straight on it, and wait for me unless I say otherwise."

"Will do."

Janus picked up his pace so he could meet up with Nathan and see what had him slightly troubled.

"What's up?" Janus asked a waiting Nathan as he entered the public part of the airport, which was full of people ready to great loved ones, all crammed up along a roped off area, desperately trying to make sure theirs was the first friendly face they'd see.

"See for yourself." Nathan said somberly, then stepped aside.

Standing in the area normally reserved for chauffeurs and taxi drivers, and looking surprisingly ordinary but most of all, human, was Ahriman, and he was holding up a large sign with the words written in bold black ink that read "The Four Horseman."

"He's having a laugh." Janus whispered before mentally transmitting. "Cyrus, Sol, carry on and don't stop, I'll leave my mind open for you, and if for any reason I lose contact, leave immediately and continue as planned."

"Without you?" Came Solomon's silent reply.

"Yes Sol, we're all professionals and have a job to do, but don't worry, I doubt very much that he will try anything."

"Shall I take him out?" Said a voice that was unmistakably Nathan's.

"How did I know you were going to say that?" A sly smile spread across Janus's face. "Thank you for the kind offer Nathan, but stupid is one thing he isn't, and so far he has held up his part of the truce, so we will do the same. You go and join the others."

"Sure you don't want me to hang about?"

"No, I'll be fine, I'm a big boy and don't need a baby sitter, you get going."

"Hhmm, ok boss." Nathan didn't sound convinced.

Janus left his friend and didn't turn back, just walked over to the somewhat smug looking Ahriman.

"Nice look." Janus said as he gestured towards Ahriman's appearance.

"Do you think it suits me?" came the reply.

"Undeniably." Janus admitted. "Right, enough of this crap. So, to what do I owe this pleasure?" He asked with a distinct growl in his tone.

"Just a chat, nothing more." Ahriman replied, in a voice that like his manifestation, was surprisingly affable.

"Lead the way then." Janus knew it would be a waste of time, but thought it might be wise to hear what he has to say, any Intel gained, however small might become important.

Janus followed Ahriman too a room, empty all be it for a table and a couple of chairs, obviously an interview room of sorts.

They both sat down, Ahriman lit a cigarette, for nothing more than dramatic effect of course; Janus didn't believe for a moment that the probable destroyer of all mankind was the type of being that needed to pop to the nearest seven/eleven just to satisfy his nicotine craving.

"Well?" Janus asked after a long and uncomfortable silence. "I presume this is the part where you offer me the chance of switching sides etc?"

"Yep, pretty much." There was no sarcasm and none of the earlier arrogance in Ahriman's voice.

"You've wasted your time then." Janus replied and started to get up to leave.

"Hear me out Janus." He paused then added. "Please."

Now that was the last word Janus was expecting to hear, so he took his seat once more, feeling half obliged to listen to what the ultimate wolf in sheep's clothing had to say.

"Your beloved Knights look like good men."

"The best." Janus answered truthfully.

"I don't doubt it for a moment, but you are leading them needlessly to their death."

"That remains to be seen." Janus said sourly.

"No Janus it doesn't, you know as well as I do, that you haven't got the faintest hope in succeeding." Ahriman paused once more and took another pull on his cigarette. "I will be the first to begrudgingly admit that your warriors are good, maybe even the best to have ever walked the Earth." Janus nodded his head slightly in gratitude. "But they are mere mortals Janus, and the majority of my fighting force isn't, but you already know that, plus the fact we outnumber you anything up two hundred and fifty to one. I don't care how good you and your men are, you quite simply don't stand a chance." Ahriman spoke honestly and without malice.

"Well, if you expect us to just give up, lay down and die without a fight, then you don't know me or mine half as well as you think you do."

"No, not at all, I wouldn't dream of insulting your intelligence by even suggesting that."

252

"What then?"

"Are you one hundred percent certain that your on the right side?"

"WHAT? Are you serious?"

"Completely."

"If trying to save mankind from unspeakable horrors and most probably extinction, is not the right side than I don't know what is. This isn't a fucking game." Janus spat.

"And you're convinced of this?"

"Of course, yes."

"And so am I."

"So are you what?" Janus asked.

"Convinced that I am doing the right thing."

"Oh fuck off, don't patronize me."

"I'm not Janus, believe me, but I'm as certain as you that my actions are the correct one. We both are following blind unchangeable logic, and that being the case, how can you be truly sure that yours is the correct path?"

"Because, how can your complete annihilation of humankind, even be remotely anywhere near the right path?"

"You're exaggerating." Ahriman replied bluntly.

"Really?" Janus said, not even trying to hide the sarcasm in his voice.

"Yes, very much so."

"Ok, convince me, that you are right and I am wrong."

"I may not be able to convince someone who is as blinkered in their reasoning as I am, but I will endeavor to best explain my thinking none the less."

"Please do enlighten me then." Janus said a little wearily.

"I am not as you put it trying to annihilate Man, I am merely going to free them."

"From what?" Janus snorted.

"From millennia's of suppression. All I am doing is releasing their prime evil instincts; they have had their emotions and true urges dampened for too long. They are like drugged up inmates of a hospital, isn't it right to stop their medication and set them free?"

"Not if the said inmate will then go out and brutally murder his whole family."

"But who are we to judge Janus? Man no longer needs a nursemaid, and even without my intervention will destroy itself and most likely the Planet and all that lives on it before too long anyway. At least I am giving them some chance at least."

"Like fuck you are."

"It will be survival of the strongest once more, Man can start afresh; cars, computers and mobile phones will be forgotten relics of the past."

"A return to the dark ages then?"

"But weren't those better days Janus?" Ahriman didn't expect an answer.

"The New dark age that you're proposing is entirely different to the one I remember." Janus said bluntly.

"Different doesn't mean wrong."

"It does in this case."

"And that's where our opinions differ; and it's for that reason as to why I am giving you the battle."

"You're too kind."

"I do have some sense of honor and value. If you win, then I am proved wrong."

"I see, so by your reckoning, outnumbering us by two hundred and fifty to one is called honor huh? Wow, forgive me, and I thought you were just a murderous beast, you have my sincere apologies." Janus had heard enough.

"I'm sorry you still feel that way; I didn't expect us to leave here seeing eye to eye, but I wanted you to understand my reasons and thinking that's all. And for you to realize that I am not quite the unreasonable monster that you believe me to be." There was even a touch of sadness in his voice.

"Yeah, well the jury is still out on that one. You're finished I presume?" The slight nod from Ahriman confirmed the question. Janus got up to leave and as just he reached the door, Ahriman spoke one last time.

"Goodbye Janus, and good luck."

Janus turned, but of course Ahriman's seat was already empty, and he was gone, leaving only a whisp of smoke and the strong smell of tobacco.

Janus left the airport in a somber and thoughtful mood, his friends waited outside in the longest articulated bus he had ever seen.

"Where the hell did you get this?" he asked Cyrus.

"The city of Chicago kindly donated it," Cyrus replied with a smile, "plus it's the only vehicle I could find that would seat over one hundred and twenty people comfortably."

"And this will get us across America?" Janus knew that buses such as this were normally restricted to the confines of the city.

"Erm, yeah." Then he sheepishly added. "Probably."

"Hhmm, right lets get going then." Janus added before finding a seat and sitting down.

Lost in his own little world; eyes closed, feeling the motion of the bus and listening to the rhythmic throbbing the engine, it was Nathan's voice in his head that brought Janus back to reality.

"You have to admit, he made some good points."

"I know."

"Bollocks, he's full of shit." Solomon answered.

"I have to agree with Sol, Boss. All he did was try to justify his actions, so we might think twice. Sounds like a worried man to me." Cyrus said his piece.

"He's not worried Buddy, just do the math, and even if he does have a point, it changes nothing, we proceed as planned."

"Amen to that." Solomon spoke for everyone.

It was a good while later, Nathan was happily watching the world go by and the coming dawn, when he noticed something was wrong, very wrong.

"Whoa, hang on." He said loudly.

"What's up Nathan?" Janus who was sitting directly in front of him asked without turning.

"We're going in the wrong direction."

"Not we're not." Janus replied.

"Yes, yes we are, I have only just noticed when I saw the Sun rise, we are traveling East, we should be going West." Nathan was about to stand up and quiz the current trance like driver, one of two brought along for the trip.

"Sit down Nathan; we are heading the right way, I can assure you of that." Janus replied calmly.

"But?" Nathan was annoyed and didn't like the idea of being kept in the dark and out of the loop.

Janus turned and smiled at his friend.

"Look into my mind now." He said simply, and Nathan did as he was asked.

"You bastards." He laughed, now he had access to a previously blocked area of Janus's mind.

"Surprise." Solomon joined in with the fun.

"You and Cyrus knew as well? But why are we going there?" Nathan asked.

"Well, we have a little time to kill, and we know how much that Croatoan thing has been bugging you, so we decided to take a slight detour to Roanoke, you never know, we might even find some answers." Janus said.

"I don't know what to say, why didn't you tell me?"

"Because you would have insisted we were wasting our time etc. and would never have agreed to it."

"Yeah suppose, still think it's a waste of time though."

"Told ya." Janus laughed. "On a serious note, are you going to be ok returning there?" Janus asked in a way that only Nathan would hear.

"Oh yes, completely, I've had my centuries of reflection, anger and mourning. Time does heal." Nathan answered truthfully.

"Good, I thought that might be the case. We'll be reaching Southport shortly, and we'll borrow a boat from there."

And as Janus had predicted, the coach pulled into the sleepy Victorian-esq. City of Southport, which ran along the banks of the Cape Fear River.

The hoard all got off the bus for much needed stretching of legs and the obligatory toilet break.

"Right guys." Janus spoke to everyone. "The four of us are going on a short trip, but we'll be back in a couple of hours, so when places open, get yourselves fed and watered. And most of all, stay out of trouble."

"Boss." Was the unanimous reply.

"Good men, I know that I can rely on you. Oh, and Percy is in charge." Janus announced with a smirk, and was rewarded with a barrage of groans.

Leaving their men in the probably not so capable hands of Percy, the four men found and liberated a small powerboat, and made the very short trip to Roanoke Island. They tethered the craft once the jetty was reached, and made their way along the paved walkway.

"Very different huh Nathan?" Cyrus asked.

"Strangely yes and no, of course it's unrecognizable from how I remember it, but yet, it's equally as familiar."

"I know what you mean; I have revisited old haunts from our distant past, and I used to get a similar feeling, everything is different but still the same, if that makes sense."

"Perfectly Cyrus." It's a sensation we have all experienced.

"So what are we looking for Nathan?" Solomon asked.

"I only wish we knew big guy, we'll just have a mooch about while it's still early and the aquarium is closed; whether or not we find anything, we'll leave before the public and visitors get here."

"Ok, you heard the man. Split up and if you find anything, don't touch it until Nathan's there, time is against us so let's get to it." Janus told them.

It was somewhat of an anticlimax when after only a couple of minutes, Solomon's voice transmitted to all.

"Hey guys, looks like I have found something."

Nathan was the last to arrive, and he found the others standing on part of the beach that was sadly very familiar to him, just down near the water line. Nathan looked down to see what it was that Sol had discovered and he saw the words "HOME", written in large neat letters in the sand.

"Could have been done by kids." Cyrus suggested.

"Kids would come up with something far more colorful. No, I know this area, and it's meant for us." Nathan replied.

"Does it mean anything to you Nathan?" Janus asked.

"Wish I could say yes, but afraid not, the conundrum continues."

"This may be an obvious question, but do you think it telling us to go home?" Solomon said.

"Your guess is as good as mine Buddy, but where the fuck is home?"

"Nathan's got a point Sol, when you break it down, we are nothing but Nomads, traveling from one place to the next. We have or have never had a true home."

"Suppose." Solomon answered glumly.

"Anyway, looking at the word isn't helping. The aquarium will be opening soon, which means the tourists will be along shortly, so lets spend another half an hour scouting about and then we'll make our back. That ok Nathan?" Janus asked.

"Yep, I think we have found what we were meant to find, but another thirty minutes wont do any harm."

"That's settled them, we'll meet back at the jetty."

As predicted, nothing else was found or became apparent, so the four men met back at the boat and made their way back to Southport.

"At least we found something." Solomon said, trying to sound upbeat.

"True, but we're leaving with more questions than answers." Nathan replied. "But, fuck it, I'm passed caring now, I've never been one for games, and now's the time to begin focusing on the task ahead."

"Spoken like a true warrior." Cyrus declared, adding his piece.

"What have we here?" Janus said to no one in particular, as he saw a nervous looking Percy waiting for them at the quay.

"Ok Percy, what is it?" Janus asked as he stepped off the launch.

"Erm."

"Come on man, I'm not in the mood for charades."

"Ah, three of the men are in the jailhouse Boss." Percy said sheepishly.

"WHAT?"

"It wasn't their fault Boss, but. ." Percy started to say.

"I don't want to hear. For Gods sake man, we have only been gone for just over an hour." Janus said, clearly annoyed, as he walked quickly down the pier, with a worried Percy in tow.

"Yes, I know, but. ."

"I still don't want to hear Percy, there is nothing open yet, so how the fuck can anyone get into trouble? Nathan, come with me. Cyrus and Sol, you make sure everyone is on the bus, and try and do it without incident." Janus didn't miss a stride or even slow down, he just carried on walking past the coach, everyone standing near it and directly to the jailhouse.

Less than a minute later the two men were in the sheriff's office come jailhouse, and faced a officious and humorless looking desk sergeant.

"I'm here to collect my men, which you seem to have in custody." Janus said, already not in the best of moods.

The sergeant slowly looked up, then back down at his paperwork.

"That'll be a Colombo, Magnum and a Mr. Michael knight I presume?" he replied without a hint of emotion, and merely raised an eyebrow at Nathan when he couldn't stifle a snort upon hearing the names.

"That's them." Even in his dark mood, Janus couldn't help but smile. "Now, Mr. Brunstrom, would you be so kind as to release them immediately." Janus asked after reading the man's nametag.

The desk sergeant made a strange hissing noise as he sucked in air through his teeth.

"Afraid I cant do that Sir, we have strict formalities and procedures to follow."

Janus wasn't in the mood or had the time for forthcoming paper trail to begin, so he leant over the desk and looked the man directly in the eyes.

"Now listen here you jobsworth prick, I wasn't asking for your permission; I said I want them released, and I want them now. So, fuck off in the back along with your petty tiny mind and get them for me."

"Certainly Sir, I shall fetch them right away." He had no choice but to do as ordered, so he turned his back and left the desk.

Janus and Nathan didn't have long to wait before Mr. Brunstrom returned accompanied by three large men, whom were afraid to make direct eye contact with Janus.

"Sorry Boss, but it wasn't our fault." One of them said as soon as they were outside.

"I don't want to know." Janus replied bluntly, before adding. "Actually, maybe I do want to know. Did you kill anyone?"

"Of course not." Came the reply, from a hurt sounding man, surprised at even being asked such a question.

"Good, in that case I still don't want to know then. Now get on the bus."

Cyrus waiting until every one had had settled down and the bus was well on the way before transmitting.

"Still in your pretend bad mood?" he asked Janus.

"Nah, did you hear the names that they gave to the police?"

"Yeah." Cyrus laughed.

"We should have taken them to Roanoke." Nathan said, joining in the conversation.

"What the fuck for?" Asked a now confused Janus.

"With Colombo, Magnum and Michael Knight with us, the Croatoan, Home problem would be solved in an hour, quicker in fact, since there won't be any commercials." Nathan said with a smile.

"Ho fucking ho." Janus replied, trying his hardest to keep a straight face.

The journey was well underway when Solomon announced excitedly.

"No way, I've just noticed, we're traveling along route sixty-six. It's something that I have always wanted to do, fantastic." He said to everyone but mostly Percy whom happened to be sat next to him.

"N'owt special, done the Mother Road a few times already." Answered a disinterested Percy.

"How and when did you that?" Solomon asked skeptically.

"Well Cyrus has done it, which in turn means all of us have done it also, in a sense anyway."

"When did you find the time to travel route sixty-six Cyrus?"

"Done it a few times good buddy, twice on a Harley in fact." Cyrus said proudly. "As you're already aware, I'm a successful and very much in demand businessman, but at the of a solid twelve months work, I always take time out to do something I want to, and during that period I am totally unattainable and don't give work a second thought."

"Really?"

"Oh yes, I have also climbed Everest, gone over Niagara Falls in a barrel, the list goes on and I have even built a boat."

"Built a boat? Bollocks, you're the most cack-handed person I have ever known."

"I agree, that's the reason why I attempted it." Cyrus answered.

"Attempted?" Janus asked, joining in the conversation.

"Erm, yeah, it was a slight disaster to be honest." Cyrus said, sounding slightly embarrassed.

"It sunk you mean?"

"I'll have you know, it floated perfectly." Cyrus boasted.

"But?" Janus asked.

"It would only go round in circles." Cyrus said quietly.

"You didn't build it straight did you?" Janus couldn't help but laugh.

"How was I supposed to fucking know?"

"Erm. Seems to be an obvious part of the build to me, but still, you live and learn huh? By the way Sol, I've done route sixty-six as well."

"You have?"

"Yep, in a Mustang many moons ago."

"Don't tell me you've done it as well Nathan?" Solomon asked.

"Yeah, sort of, in much the same way as the Knights experienced it, one of my hosts made the trip." Nathan replied.

"Fucking hell, so poor old Sol gets left out again." Solomon said unhappily and moved from his seat to sit alone and sulk.

Eventually, the bus slowed, maneuvered into a parking space, and stopped. A glum faced Solomon, still in a gloomy stupor looked up to see where they were now; his eyes widened, face lit up and his grin went from one ear to the other.

"The Big Texan Steak Ranch." He whispered, in a voice full of awe.

"Yep, we decided it was your turn for a surprise old friend, and we know that you've always wanted to come here." Janus said.

"The legendry home of the seventy-two oz. steak." Solomon said in such a manner that he could easily be confused for Homer Simpson.

"And the meal is free if you eat it with an hour."

"Walk in the park." Solomon declared.

"Yeah, yeah." Janus chided. "You did book in advance didn't you Cyrus?"

"I did Boss." Cyrus answered.

"Good man. So lets go and eat."

Even though they numbered well over a hundred, Janus and his gang barely filled one quarter of the huge eatery. Waitresses, wearing traditional cowgirl outfits bustled to and fro, supplying gallons of Budweiser and taking everyone's predictable order of the seventy-two oz. special.

"This is going to cost me a fortune." Groaned Cyrus, as he paid for all the meals in advance, a requirement of this particular establishment.

"I'll ya what." Janus offered. "You and I will hazard a guess as to how many of men complete the task in hand, the one furthest away pays the bill. How's that?"

"Sounds good to me, you're on." Cyrus replied, and then shook Janus's hand to seal the arrangement. "You go first."

"Hhmm." Janus thought about it for a while, and decided to go down the scientific route; the normal success rate for clearing your plates of the monster meal was about twenty percent, but his men were big with appetites to match, so he figured the ratio would be a little higher. "I say thirty five, but I am only including the men, none of us four count." Janus finally decided. "Your turn."

"Right, lets see." But Cyrus was half distracted by the surprising amount of very attractive woman present; the establishment was not as you would think, filled with overweight, three bellied, waddling patrons, but actually, its cliental seemed well groomed and pleasing to the eye. One woman in particular had caught Cyrus's attention, a stunning blond, wearing a skimpy t-shirt that was far too tight, but in Cyrus's eyes, it was a perfect fit. She looked at him, smiled and winked, then turned back to the bar where her drink must have been ready, it was then he noticed on the back of her sublime t-shirt the name of a collage and presumably a year of some significance, forty-four.

"Forty four." Cyrus said, already nearly forgetting the reason for choosing a number, and to make matters worse, he had lost sight of his briefly found cherub.

Then, right on cue, the monstrous meals started to arrive.

"What's the record time for eating one of these lassie?" Solomon asked the serving waitress.

"Nine and a half minutes sir." She replied with a smile.

"In that case, please bring me another in nine minutes, I'll have finished this one by then." Solomon announced proudly.

"Are you sure sir?"

"Sol!" Janus warned silently.

"Aww, but Boss." Sol transmitted unhappily back.

"You know the rules big guy. Any one of us could run the fastest hundred meters, lift twice the world record weight or be champion at virtually any discipline of our choosing. But A, it wouldn't be fair, and B, as you know full well, we do our utmost to stay beneath the radar."

"C'mon Janus, it's only a steak." Cyrus added coming to Solomon's aid.

"I know that, but then he gets his picture taken, and asked for his personal details, then gets challenged to eat the worlds biggest pie, etc etc. I may sound harsh, but we have to draw a line guys." Janus said, although he felt a little bad for laying down the law at such a grim time.

"Ok Boss I understand." Solomon transmitted unhappily back, before speaking verbally once more. "Nah, I was only joking lassie, thank you all the same."

"Tel you what old friend. On our return journey, we'll stop off here once again. You change your appearance and make up a name, and you can do it then. How's that?" Janus offered.

"Really?" said a beaming Sol.

"You have my word." Janus already felt better.

"Can I try and eat two within nine minutes? That is one record that will never be beaten."

"Don't push it buddy." Janus replied, smiling.

Ten minutes later, Solomon was just about to fork the last piece of Texan beef into his mouth, when he looked up and noticed, Janus, Cyrus and Nathan grinning at him, in front of them were now clean and empty plates.

"You're a bunch of dicks, you know that." He grumbled.

"Now, now Mr. Grundy, no need to be like that." Janus teased.

"Not sure I even like any of you any more." Solomon continued, although his pissed off façade was starting to slip.

But before the banter could continue, they were distracted by a commotion over near the bar area.

"Jesus Christ, you couldn't make this shit up." Janus whispered, once he realized the rumpus was due to what looked very much an ol' fashioned bar fight involving a handful of his men; of course, one of them had to be Percy.

"Sit down, I'll handle this." Janus said, as his three friends made to get up.

He reached the skirmish, and discovered it was six of his men against maybe twenty, and judging by their sizes, they were probably a collage football team; there to get drunk, have a good time and attempt the famous seventy-two oz special.

The rest of the knights remained seated, laughing and banging their glasses on the tables, wholeheartedly enjoying the mêlée; even though outnumbered, this was chicken feed for the half a dozen caught up in it.

"ENOUGH." Janus bellowed, and the fracas immediately ceased. "SIT." He then growled to his men, which they sheepishly did.

"And who the fuck are you? Their dad?" Asked the biggest and obviously the troublemaker of the others, whilst wiping his bloodied nose.

"You should be grateful, I just saved the lot of you from a arse whooping." Janus said calmly.

"Yeah right." Came the sarcastic reply.

"Anyway, this is an eating establishment and not a boxing ring."

"Well he was looking at me funny." Said the ringleader, and he pointed, but Janus didn't have to look to see whom he meant.

"Percy looks at everyone funny. Now grow up and go back to your tables, or if you want to be disgraced some more, take it outside."

"I'll fight where the fuck I want." He spat, but judging by the look on his companions' faces, they had had enough.

"Really?" Janus sneered, getting annoying at the idiots attitude.

"Try and fucking stop me arsehole." He continued, putting up a show because his friends were watching.

The unmistakable sound of one hundred and twenty chairs being pushed back as his men stood up, came from behind Janus; all but one of the two-dozen collage kids took a good few steps back.

"You're a big man when they are all stood behind you aren't you granddad?" He now taunted.

Janus raised his hand and his men sat back down.

"You're a mouthy little prick, aren't you? Just because you're big doesn't mean you can act like the way you do."

"I'll act and do just like how the fuck I want."

"Not in the same establishment as me you wont."

But Janus had now had enough, in a few hours time he would be fighting for the freedom and the lives of mankind, including distasteful lowlifes such as this, so he calmly stepped forward towards the still grinning hulk, and literally before he knew what him, aimed a powerful punch at the mans jaw, which offered no resistance when met with Janus's diamond-hard fist, and shattered with a satisfying crack under impact.

"Take him to the nearest ER to get his jaw rewired." Janus told the now unconscious mans companions. "And if any of you have any sense, you'll find a friend that wont undoubtedly one day get one of you killed."

The men unceremoniously lifted the limp body and carried him out of the eatery, trying their level best not to make eye contact with any of its patrons.

"Sorry Boss, but it really wasn't our fault." Said a worried sounding Percy.

"I know." Replied Janus, although sick of hearing that phrase, he knew he couldn't chastise his men for this instance.

He then sought out the owner, to make his apologies and pay for any damage done by either party, but was taken slightly aback when the owner thanked him. He said in an age where guns and knifes are readily available and used too often, a good ol' fashioned fist fight wasn't the end of the world and if Janus hadn't knocked the perpetrator out, then he surely would have. The two men shared a few glassed of bourbon and parted company as friends.

Now sat alone on the bus, Janus, forever the loner, couldn't help but realize in the last seven days he had made more friends than in the previous seventy years, and although he found it hard to believe, he enjoyed striking up the said friendships that had recently crossed his path. Another home truth struck him, even more incredulous than the last, but he decided there and then that when this was all over, he was going to live a lifestyle along the similar lines as Cyrus, not quite as extravagant maybe, but the days of the nameless office worker would be gone for good. He also couldn't help but smile when he imagined the look on the guy's faces when he would have to ask Cyrus advice on how to be more like him, a partnership even, now what an awesome team that would make. It's strange how a forthcoming catastrophe, often has a happy side to it, and this scenario was no different, bringing together four estranged friends, and once more sealing the bond of this adopted brotherhood.

But no matter how hard he tried or how much he wanted it, Janus couldn't keep the smile for long, although he knew he had to be positive, but not even someone with the enormous mental prowess that he processed could stop the distasteful tendrils of reality invading his mind. Lying to his men and friends was one thing, but lie to himself he could not, the odds were just too great, it was a battle with only one possible unhappy outcome; defeat.

"Penny for them."

Janus had no complaint at being interrupted during his current somber train of thought.

"As futile as it may sound, I was planning for the future." Janus replied, wondering how long Cyrus had been sat next to him.

"Don't be silly buddy, you have too, otherwise we might as well give up now, and I know for definite that none of us are going to do that." Cyrus spoke honestly.

"True."

"In fact, I was doing a similar thing myself."

"Really? What were you thinking?"

"Now, don't laugh, but I was thinking that when this is all done and dusted, I am going to try and be more like you."

Despite his friend asking him not too, Janus couldn't help but laugh.

"What's so funny about that?"

"Because old friend, I was thinking exactly the same about you."

"Piss off! You're joking right?"

"Not even remotely." This time the honesty came from Janus.

"So your going to start wearing designer clothes, drive sports cars and bed lots of women?"

"Well obviously I'll be more choosey and have better taste than you, but pretty much yeah, plus it's not just that."

"What then?" Cyrus's curiosity was piqued.

"Do you have many friends like Peter?"

"I have acquaintances and I have friends, too different thing, but yes, all my friends are like Peter, good people."

"Well I don't." Janus said in barely more than a whisper.

"You don't what?"

"Have any friends, apart from you and the others that is."

"None?"

"No."

"Why on earth not?"

"Because I knew I would outlive them, I never saw the point."

"No disrespect Janus, but that's the biggest load of bullshit I have ever heard. In school, collage, workplaces; people strike up friendships all the time, very rarely do they last until death, people move on, but the time spent together is never forgotten. I have lost count of the number of friends I have outlived, but I wouldn't have changed a single thing, and part of them always remains with me. It's how you learn, grow and mature."

"I know, you're completely right, and it has taken the last few days for me to realize this."

"See, I'm not just a pretty face. So starting next week, you and I are going to collage for a semester or two."

"You're not serious?"

"Damn right I am." Cyrus was clearly enjoying this.

"But I have never been to collage."

"Great, all the more reason to experience it then. I have done it five or six times now, and loved every minute of it. So you and I shall enroll as fresh face eighteen year olds, plus I am sure Sol will be up for it, and if we can talk Nathan into it as well it would be a blast."

"Every bone and sinew in my body is dreading the prospect and screaming that it just isn't me, so on the basis of that I am going to say, yeah fuck it, lets do it." Janus could hardly believe he had just agreed to Cyrus's proposition.

"Fantastic." Cyrus proclaimed, animated with excitement. "Sol?"

"I'm in." Was the simple reply.

"This gets better and better. Nathan?"

"My feelings mirror those of Janus, but I also have been without social interaction for too long, so a year or so can't hurt. Ok, I'll come."

"So, now we REALLY have something to fight for, fuck the fate of mankind, we battle for the right to go back to school, how can we lose?" Cyrus was of course joking, and his friends knew it, although he was sure that their resulting groans were genuine.

"Hhhmm, now fuck off and leave me peace for a bit, while I regret what I have done." Janus said, also joking with Cyrus.

"Ok matey, you wont regret it, trust me." And with that, Cyrus happily moved to another seat.

"What have let ourselves in for?" Janus asked Nathan in a way that was only for his ears.

"That remains to be seen, although its not like we have signed up for he foreign legion, we can leave any time we choose." Came Nathan's reply.

"Yeah suppose, but I'm surprised that you agreed so readily though, thought you had more sense than me."

"That also remains to be seen, but you and I have lived under our shells for too long, it's about time we poked our heads out."

"I'm still not convinced about that."

"You should be, the four of us in many ways have been equally cursed and blessed with our gifts, so lets look at them as a blessing for a change, and live."

"You already have changed, it's a different Nathan talking to me now than the one who turned up out of the blue less than a week ago."

Nathan merely shrugged mentally.

"Mind you, all this talk means nothing, we have to get the task in hand out of the way first." Janus tried his best to sound positive.

"At leas if we fail, we aren't going to around to worry about it."

"Fuck me, you even sound like Cyrus now." Janus joked.

"I'm not sure if that's a compliment or not."

"Neither am I old friend." Janus laughed.

But Janus's laughter was short lived as the unmistakable sound of air brakes engaging meant their long journey was at an end.

"This is it then."

"So it seems."

Janus paused briefly, gathered himself together before speaking to all three.

"Game face on guys, the end begins here."

Situated just north west of Furnace Creek, the normally busy settlement of Stovepipe Wells had taken the appearance of a dry land version of the infamous Marie Celeste. The visitor center was open, but un-staffed, the only greeting came from the public information film played on continues loop for the benefit of the tourists. Same at the diner, stewed blacked coffee bubbled away, but no one to pour or consume. A similar story could be told about every inch of the small village; life was here maybe even only a few hours ago, but something or more accurately someone caused every one to leave in a hurry, and four men standing there now, knew, that no one uninvited would be coming to Stovepipe Wells for at least twenty four hours.

"Considerate of him to make sure we're uninterrupted for duration." Solomon said to no one in particular as he surveyed the modern ghost town.

"That depends on the fate of the patrons." Nathan answered coldly.

"Ah."

"Sadly, what did or did not happen to the townsfolk cannot concern us right now. Nathan, are your men close?"

"Yes, I can sense them."

"ETA?"

"Two to four hours at a guess."

"Good, it will be nightfall by then, and it gives us plenty of time to prepare the men before yours get here." Janus paused briefly before calling. "Percy?"

Percy quickly appeared, the look upon his face was one of a man trying to work out what he had done wrong this time.

"It's ok Percy, you're not for a telling off, yet." Janus joked. "We'll be staying here until morning, so tell the men to prepare themselves ready for dawn. Also, we shall be having company in a few short hours, so make sure all newcomers are made welcome."

"Boss."

"One more thing, we want to meet each of our guys individually before others get here. We'll use the diner for that purpose, so I'll leave it in your hands to sort out which order you send them. I'll expect the first man in ten minutes prompt.

Percy nodded and left, knowing he'd been dismissed, already falling into the role of dutiful warrior.

"Why we seeing each of the men Janus? Do we really have to interview them when we know they've already got the job?" Solomon asked, half in jest.

"Oh they've got the job alright, but we shall be giving each man a small gift."

"Which is?"

"Essence of us."

"Eh?" Asked a now confused Solomon.

"We have to try and even up the odds a little somehow big guy. So we shall bless each of our boys with a small part of ourselves."

"And we can do this?"

"We can Sol, although it wont make the Knights anywhere near immortal, it will make them stronger, faster and a damn side harder to kill than anything else on the planet."

"Excuse my ignorance Janus, but wont that make the four of us less effective?"

"Not really Sol, the effect will only last twenty-four hours on our men, and by daybreak the four of us will have regained the little we lost."

"Sounds like a plan." Solomon admitted.

"I'm only sorry we cant do the same for your men Nathan, but the numbers are regrettably too great, if you know what I mean." Janus's tone was genuinely full of sorrow.

"Don't worry yourself Janus, our aid is not needed." Nathan said with a smile.

"Not needed?" Janus replied raising one eyebrow.

"No, the place from whence they came would have already blessed each with a similar gift."

"I really have to pay a visit to this wondrous location after we are finished here."

"And I will gladly take all three of you." Nathan replied, and then added for Janus's ears only, "It's quite urgent that I must speak to you about the garden in fact."

"After the battle is too late I presume?"

"Yes, as soon as we have seen the men if you don't mind."

"Ok buddy, but I'm not sure what can be so important at this late stage however."

"Please, trust me on this."

"Of course I do Nathan; with my life." And Janus meant it.

Two hours later, the men had been and gone; outward appearances they looked and felt no different, but come the morrow, a fire will burn inside them, giving birth to a rage unseen before on Earth.

"My people will be here very shortly, so if you can spare a few brief moments Janus, I would be grateful." Nathan asked.

"Ok, let us walk." Janus asked, but the melancholy tone of Nathan's voice troubled him.

"Where are those two going?" Solomon asked Cyrus, as they watched the other two walk off into the night.

"Who knows Sol, doing grown up stuff probably." Cyrus replied with a smile. "But don't worry, if it in any way concerns us, Janus will let us know."

As Janus walked with Nathan through the makeshift camp, he couldn't help but be slightly amused at the oddness of the scene before him. His faithful men, grouped off; some sparring, a few seemly sound asleep, but the majority polishing well used armor and sharpening immense two-handed weapons of various deadly descriptions, all this taking place amongst the bizarre backdrop of neon signs and rusted Chevy's.

Maybe twenty minutes later, Solomon and Cyrus were physically jarred by Janus's mental blow.

"NO NATHAN, ITS NOT GOING TO HAPPEN, END OF DISCUSSION."

Obviously that part of the conversation wasn't meant for the ears of the other two, but such was the anger of Janus that he couldn't keep it capped.

"Any ideas?" Solomon asked Cyrus.

"No buddy, my last statement still stands. We'll find out soon enough if it's of any importance to us." Cyrus replied, although he was as curious as his friend.

It was a full half an hour later when Janus returned to the camp, alone.

"Everything ok boss?" Cyrus asked the approaching Janus.

"Sure mate, Nathan's gone to meet his men." Janus replied, nothing in his tone gave anything away.

"We heard you know." Cyrus whispered mentally.

"All of it?" Replied a surprised Janus.

"No, no, just the shouty bit." Cyrus tried to lighten the situation somewhat.

"It was nothing."

"So you kissed and made up?"

"Yeah, but Nathan using his tongue worried me."

"That's just wrong, very wrong." Cyrus smiled, glad to see that whatever the earlier problem was, it didn't seem to be serious.

"Don't believe a word of it, it was him playing the tonsil tennis, not me." Said Nathan's voice, marginally before his form emerged from the darkness, his face painted with a strangely sly smirk.

"Enough of this hideous mental imagery please. And why that look on your face? Smugness doesn't suit you Nathan." Cyrus questioned for the benefit of everyone as well as his own curious self.

"It seems, I happily underestimated my brothers." Replied a smiling Nathan, still not giving too much away.

"Come on man, the suspense is killing us." This time the voice was Janus's.

"Well, remember the rough guess at numbers I gave you in the pub."

"You mean you've got the full five thousand?"

"My comrades have done slightly better than that and in the process have made me a very proud man."

"Yes, and everyone here as well as the whole of mankind will be eternally grateful, now please Nathan, how many?" The game had gone on long enough for Janus's liking.

"Ok, Ok, I've had my moment." Nathan laughed. "How does just shy of twenty five thousand sound?"

"You're fucking kidding?" Even Solomon had to add his constructive piece to the conversation upon hearing this astounding number.

"That's great news, please extend my gratitude to the masters of the schools when this is over Nathan. Looks like we have a fighting chance at least." Janus added.

"Of course I will my friend, but there is no need. They know the consequences of failure better than anyone, so they put the word out and sent every able-bodied person possible, no-one refused."

"And will your men be joining us for what's left of the night?"

"Your men Janus, and no, they shall spend what left of the darkness in meditation, and if you don't mind, may I join them?"

"You don't have to ask Nathan, yes please go, and we will see you all at dawn, geared up and ready."

Nathan nodded briefly, turned and dissolved into the night.

"That's a turn up for the books, have we really got a chance Janus?" Solomon asked.

"We will still be massively outnumbered by unearthly abominations Sol, but every extra pair of hands makes things a little more difficult for him." Was Janus's honest reply. "Also, on a side note, I wouldn't mind the last few hours alone with my thoughts, if that's ok with you guys?"

"Sure mate, catch you in the morning." Cyrus answered.

"Just the two of us then huh? Ideas?" Sol asked.

"I might have a rather nice bottle of Macallan twenty five year old hidden away, if your up for it that is." Cyrus said with a smile.

"Och, the night gets better and better." Came Solomon's eager reply, his Scottish accent returning and a smile to mirror that of his friends'.

Janus was aroused from his deep but meaningless thoughts by the unmistakable sound of high capacity diesel engines pulling into the makeshift camp. By the time he gathered himself together and joined his two friends, the sight of five large coaches and an only-in-America size immense articulated lorry pulling into the encampment greeted him.

"I'd clean forgotten all about these guys." Said an embarrassed Solomon, finishing the sentence with a loud hiccup.

"Have you been drinking?" Asked Janus sternly.

"Erm." Sol looked to Cyrus for backup, who in turn was inching slowly backwards with a huge cheesy grin on his face.

"I was speaking to both of you." Janus then added.

Of course it wouldn't have mattered if they had drunk a hogs-head size barrel of whiskey, but a bit of role-play and banter kept them sane, to a degree at least.

But all focus quickly changed with the hydraulic hiss of the vehicles doors opening.

As the newcomers streamed off the coaches, Janus had to admit that he was impressed by the make up of the men, all young, unmistakably fit and battle trained, and each had the same look in their eyes as his own warriors; each and every one ready to fight and if need be, die for the cause ahead.

On closer inspection however, one or two faces in the now gathering crowd looked distinctly out of place. Yes, the same hardened glint in their eyes was present, but although they did their best to hide in the crowd, there is one thing no mortal man can veil themselves from; and that is the unforgiving ravishes of time, and sadly, old age.

The Duke of Kent, realizing his human camouflage had been blown, stepped from the crowd, made his way towards Janus, then bowed his head and dropped to one knee, with all behind him following suit.

"At your service Sire." He whispered.

Janus had always been uncomfortable with such pomp and palaver, so he quickly motioned for everyone to rise.

"You of all people have no need to bow before me your Highness."

"I'll think you'll find, if there is any man that has ever lived whom deserves such formalities, it is you Sire, and I truly feel humbled in your presence." The Duke meant every word.

"Hhmm, on that particular matter, we shall agree to differ then. Times have changed, so please, just call me Janus."

"And would be honored if you call me Edward." And with that, the two men shook hands, as a new friendship was formed. "It was a tight squeeze, but we managed to cram in the full five hundred of our specially trained knights." The Duke said with more than a hint of pride in his voice.

"And one or two stowaways I notice." Replied Janus lifting an eyebrow.

"A mere handful of the old guard, which includes my good self, has tagged along yes. When we were in our prime Janus, we were trained for this eventuality, time pasted, and as it has been for hundreds of years, young blood took up the reins and we stood down. But the forthcoming events of the next few hours are the real thing, fire burns in our blood as intense as it does in the young-uns. Nothing or no-one will stop us being here and part of it." The Duke paused briefly before continuing his heartfelt passionate speech, one that he no doubt had rehearsed many times in his own head. "And before you say we could be a liability."

"I wouldn't insult your intelligence Edward by suggesting that." Janus said sincerely.

"Thank you, but the men are under orders which they are professional enough to follow by the letter, that if they see one of us fall or is wounded on the field of battle, they are to just step over our body without a seconds thought or concern. And if I and my handful of old fogies manage to take down just one of those bastards before we perish, then each of us will die smiling and happy."

"Edward, it will be an honor to have you and yours along side us. Now please return to your men and prepare them. We go into battle within the hour."

Once the Duke had left, Janus caught the key of the ever-ready Percy, whom immediately came over.

"Boss?"

"You and the others help our newcomers unload their stuff and make sure everyone is battle ready in sixty minutes."

Percy nodded and left.

"A remarkable man." Said an until now, silent Cyrus.

"Nah, Percy is just Percy." Joked Janus.

"You know very well I didn't mean him."

"Yeah, yeah, but yes your right, the Duke and his few are extraordinary, it's a shame that no matter what the outcome is, they wont be around to see it." There was genuine sadness in Janus's voice.

"Is there nothing we do for them?" Asked Solomon. "I'd be more than happily to give a wee bit of myself like we did last night."

"I'm sorry Sol, but no. Time is too short and we have to be at one hundred percent as it is, to even stand a chance."

"Aye, of course your right."

"Sadly yes. Now dawn is breaking, so time to dust off our own equipment."

"Erm, Janus, I foresee a slight problem."

"And you tell me this now Cyrus? Go on." Janus replied cautiously.

"Well, I can't see Sol fitting into his old gear, he's a wee bit, erm, rounder than he used to be." Cyrus winked.

"Hhmm, yes, I see you point buddy. Maybe you should sit this one out Sol." Janus said in the most serious voice he could muster.

A confused Solomon, taken off guard for a moment, looked Janus in the eye; upon seeing the look he got in return, the truth dawned on him.

"Ah, fek off, the pair of ya." And Solomon left, his muttering could still be heard even once he was out of sight.

"That was cruel Cyrus."

"Says the man that played along with it. Anyway, Sol knows we love him like the brother we never wanted." Cyrus laughed.

"I HEARD THAT." Sol transmitted mentally.

"Sorry buddy, only kidding." Cyrus replied in the same manner. "By the way, do you want me to come over and help you squeeze in. I'm sure I have seen a pot of grease somewhere."

But before Sol could counter, Janus stepped in.

"Ok guys, play time over. Game face on please."

His tone of voice lost all frivolity, sending a clear message to his friends.

From this moment on; humanity was living on borrowed time.

EPILOGUE

"The Last Dawn"

For someone that is used to, and prefers his own company, Janus had never felt so forlorn and alone at this moment, as he had ever done in his long existence.

Deep down, Janus never really believed that his current apparel would once more see the light of day and live and breath again, as it did now. Forged from the same unearthly materials as his legendary blade, his protective covering was far from inanimate. Janus risked a quick surreptitious look at his wrist brace; tiny tadpoles of light, played an unending game of chase the tail, hypnotically sucking in the unsuspecting and embracing them with uncontrollable nausea.

"Some things never change." Janus whispered, as he tore his gaze from the Siren-esq piece.

"Oh joy, he's wearing his sick suit." Said a jovial sounding Solomon as he came into view.

Solomon's own suit also differed from the norm: head to toe a brilliant pearlescent white, which, in a happy greeting to the first few virgin tendrils of the morning sun, would morph from one end of the visual spectrum to the other, first red, then violet but momentary pausing on each and every colour in-between.

"Looking good Sol." Janus had to admit. His friend had clearly shed a pound or two. Gone was the jolly giant, replaced by a walking man mountain.

"Not too shabby yourself buddy." Sol countered. "Now, where's Mr Vain?"

"You can't be talking about me, surely?" Came Cyrus's on cue reply. Somewhat predictability to anyone that knows him, his suit was cast from the purest gold and annealed with the hardest diamond.

"Gold is so last millennia." Sol chided.

"I've said it before, and I'll say it again. Fashion may change, but style always remains."

"Hhmm." Answered Sol, with a great deal of chin rubbing.

Then, the three friends stood in silence for a few brief moments; no words were needed.

Next to arrive was Percy, flanked by the knights, young and old, past and present.

"By your command Sire."

Janus nodded, then turned to the others. "Mount up."

If the twentieth century warriors were surprised at three immense warhorses appearing from nowhere, each armoured in the same fashion as their charge; none showed it.

"All we need now is Nathan." Janus said to no one in particular while he sat astride his huge snorting beast.

"I'm here."

Janus would never have thought that two simple words could be said with such coldness.

With Hollywood timing and effect, the nearby fog lifted; with so many men wearing plate and mail, even standing still, made silence an impossibility, but inconceivably, a complete stillness and hush filled the battle camp.

After what seemed like an age had passed, it was Solomon that finally broke the calm.

"Fuck." He murmured, the icy chill in his veins was shared by all present.

Sat astride a colossal horse, an obsidian coloured beast with burning embers for eyes and a mane of pure and living flame, was Nathan.

Wearing a near indescribable suit; fashioned purely from hate and anger, sadness and despair, it had no colour, other than being a swirling black vortex, darker than anything this world had seen. It fed on blood, and the more blood there was, the stronger it became.

Nathan's eyes, matched his demonic attire.

"I thought he vowed never to wear that here?" Cyrus said only for the ears of Janus.

"That suit is a big part of the reason we are here, so maybe it's fitting that he dons it now. Anyway, I am sure he knows what he is doing." Janus did his best to sound convincing.

"Yeah true, and he's brought ninja's." Cyrus added with half a smile.

Sure enough, in Nathan's wake, one hundred abreast and deeper than the eye could discern in the poor light, each with the constitution of the terra cotta army, stood his men.

No shiny plate adorned these guys however; black cloth was their battle attire, complete with hood and mask.

But in stark contrast to Nathan's doom filled orbs; their eyes shone with the brightness of a newly formed sun, a gift from their own benefactor no doubt.

"They are monks Cyrus, not fairytale warriors for hire." Nathan's chilling tone contained no hint of humour.

"Cyrus was joking Nathan, and you know it, so less of that tone please." Janus knew from bitter and unhappy experience that he had to reign in Nathan quickly, otherwise he got out of hand, and became uncontrollable, more than even the three of them could handle.

"So are you ok Nathan?" Janus said with genuine warmth.

"Yes, sorry, the suit needs feeding and is placing large demands on me." Nathan replied, sounding more like his old self.

"Well then, lets satisfy its appetite." Janus paused briefly. "Oh and Nathan, come and join us. The four of us should ride together once more."

"Agreed." Nathan responded.

"Agreed." Said Cyrus.

"Agreed." Followed Solomon.

Janus then turned to his troops and addressed them.

"Right men, the enemy awaits, so I think it would be rude of us to keeping them waiting any longer. So lets move out."

An old but instantly familiar cheer rang out, and even someone lacking such emotions as Janus, he had to admit, he felt a lump in his throat.

"I notice your men wear no type of armour Nathan, will that be a problem?" Solomon asked, as the horses ambled slowly along, keeping a steady pace for the soldiers on foot.

Janus answered before Nathan could speak.

"Sol, old friend, if you hand picked the best of our men against any random choice of Nathan's, I think you'd find our man would be dead before he lifted his sword."

Nathan nodded in agreement.

"That good huh?"

"Oh yes."

"So why aren't we ninja's then?"

The question was so Solomon like; childlike in many respects, but full of undisputable logic.

"You sure your horse is ok under all that weight Sol?" Was the best counter Janus could think of.

It was a short ride to the edge of the basin where the battle would take place. Janus halted his men, whom professionally fanned out, left and right.

Everyone took in the scene many meters below.

"What the fuck is that?" As usual, Solomon was the voice of reason.

Less than a thousand yards from their current position, in the flat desert basin was in immense translucent hemisphere, something akin to an eco-dome, but devoid of any flora.

"Nathan?" Janus asked.

"Insurance." Was Nathan's simple reply.

"Could you be a bit more specific?"

"Unless I am very much mistaken, that rotunda is a our one way ticket. Once any of us steps through its boundary, there is no way out, until our friend in the centre powering it is dead, that is."

"Hhmm, we knew this would be a one shot deal, so that changes nothing." Janus replied, and then adding for Nathan's ears only, "Well, that's your suggestion out the window."

"Don't be so sure." Was the instant reply.

Dead centre of the structure was a solid black ring, easily a quarter mile in diameter. Janus focused his vision to take a closer look.

The circle transpired to be Ahriman's extra terrestrial army; human in form, but that was where the similarity ended. Their make up consisted of part shadow and part flesh, constantly mutating from one medium to the other. A faceless army, without thought or reason; by far the worse type to come up against.

At it's hub, stood Ahriman, channelling a small part of his essence as a power supply for the surrounding bubble. As an extra precaution, his own personal protectors encircled him, at least ten deep; fathered by Incubus himself, ghastly forms, only normally present in the most terrible of nightmares, but as somewhat of a paradox, they mirrored Janus and his friends' very own infernal transmutations.

"Any idea of numbers?" Janus asked no one in particular.

"Two hundred and fifty thousand, near as damn it." Solomon answered hardly even giving Janus time to finish the question.

Janus knew well enough not to query Sol; he had an ability with numbers that could outshine anyone, alive or dead.

"And his bodyguards?"

"Seven hundred, I'd say."

Against a human army, odds of ten to one would mean an easy and quick battle, with his side of course being victorious. But against an army of undead, the battle would still be a swift one, unfortunately, even with men as good as his, triumph was an impossibility.

But what really saddened Janus, was the fact that every single man that stood with him, also knew the unhappy outcome. Yes, each and all were ready and prepared to die, but a battle fought with no chance of hope, would be every ones last and of course the most painful; physically, mentally and worst of all, emotionally.

One last glance at the brave faces of all present; Janus momentary considered sending them away, a futile thought because he knew none would go.

Sadly, mankind's bravest and best, would fail, badly.

"There is nothing more you could have done old friend." Nathan said to Janus, as if reading his thoughts.

"Bollocks! I could have been better prepared, brought more men, hunted Ahriman down and ended it."

"Yes silly me, you could have spent the last seven thousands years a nervous wreck, living on a knife edge, you could have hidden half the worlds population in underground caverns. Trust me Janus, you have done all you could, and all that was expected of you." Nathan spoke with genuine honesty and affection.

"But."

"No buts buddy, none of us knew when or if this day would ever come, or what we would be up against even. Where there is life, there is hope. So come on, lets give him a fight at least."

"Of course your right." Janus felt at last as if his fire was once again ignited. "Lets fucking do this."

Janus turned to his men, but a split second before he was about to issue his battle orders, the ground shook briefly and a blinding flash filled the surrounding area.

Everyone present was momentarily disoriented; Solomon was the first to gather his senses.

"What the?" He mouthed.

Janus wasn't far behind Sol.

"Well fuck me backwards and call me Mavis." Janus said with an uncontrollable grin.

For now, standing next to each man of Janus's outnumbered army, was what could only be described as a celestial Knight, wearing identical garb to Cyrus; all tall, proud and undoubtedly ready to fight.

"I always knew your suit was off the peg." Solomon laughed, brushing down his own unique suit and seeming less phased than anyone by the heavenly occurrence.

A stunned and still very much confused Cyrus, for once had no witty comeback. "Janus?" Was the best he could manage.

"It seems that worlds and powers well beyond our understanding, are somewhat concerned at the possible outcome of the battle, and as a romantic would say, have sent down a guardian angel for each and every one of us, to fight along side their charge and act as protector."

"Surely, him, them, it, cant be unduly worried at what the end of this day brings?"

"On the contrary buddy, if we fail, within a very short time, Ahriman's army of the dammed will conceivably number, billions."

"Then why not send more?" Cyrus asked logically.

"He probably cant or wont. Cant because; in worlds we know nothing of; there might be unwritten agreements etc. one guardian for one man sounds about right. And wont because; there are more people living now, than have ever lived on this planet, so he needs numbers to defend his own realm."

"Excuse me for sounding like an idiot, but isn't he meant to be all powerful etc?"

"A valid question, but being all powerful as you put it is all about a relative point of view. To an ant, a prowling cat is as godlike as we are to the said cat, and the relative ladder continues forever upwards."

Before Cyrus could ask any more questions, the ground shook once again and the earlier flash of light was replaced by a moment's darkness.

"You've got to be kidding." Cyrus exclaimed.

Another wave of soldiers had appeared, almost identical to the last except their armour was dull and tarnished.

"Was wondering when they'd turn up." Janus said with a smile.

"Your not telling me, you know who, has sent help as well?"

"Of course he has, his world is in just as much jeopardy."

"Sounding like a dunce again, but aren't Ahriman and co., his type of people, so to speak?" Cyrus was getting more confused by the minute.

"Wrong again old chap." Janus was enjoying this, now that his spirits had been lifted no end. "The way things work at the moment, are all about balance, and this world is a proving ground for want of a better word, to the next. Ahriman if he succeeds will upset the balance, which in turn will cause disastrous rupturing on many many plains."

"Ah, got it." Cyrus said half convincingly.

Janus turned to the two nearest newcomers, one from each faction.

"Are you under instruction to obey my orders?" He asked.

No verbal answer was giving, but Janus knew the answer was an affirmative one.

"Excellent, and thank you." He replied, receiving a slight head nod in return.

That made things a lot easier for Janus's strategy.

Janus turned this time uninterrupted ready to address his men, his voice would carry effortlessly to all, as though he was speaking to them personally.

"Listen up men." Janus paused, until he had everyone's attention. "Our enemy's below unique defensive ring will make my tactic's simple and easy to explain." He paused once more.

"Will he be listening to what I am about to say?" He silently asked Nathan.

"I couldn't say for certain, but somehow I don't think so. Rightly or wrongly I think he sees himself as a man of honour." Nathan replied in the same fashion.

"I draw the same conclusion." He told his friend before reverting to the more traditional fashion of communication.

"Imagine his circular stand off is a clock face, and beneath us is the six o'clock mark. Cyrus and Solomon will take Nathan's men and my Knights around to the twelve o'clock position and on my mark, attack hard and fast in an arrowhead formation. Our newcomers will engage randomly between one and four, also at eight and eleven o'clock. That will severely hamper his army as they shift to block the main attack. Are we all clear? This is a one shot deal guys, and our only goal is the demise of their leader, once he is gone, then it's all over, so focus on that and nothing else. If you have any questions ask now."

"What about Nathan and yourself?" Cyrus asked quietly.

"While all the action is taking place at the top half of the clock, when the time is right, Nathan and I will strike at 6 o'clock. Numbers there should be thin considering our whole army is at the other end, and with us now having nigh on seventy five thousand men, Ahriman has a fight on his hands and cant afford to hold many so low."

"But just you and Nathan?"

"And one or two of my canine friends to watch our flank."

It wasn't until then that Cyrus noticed, gathered nearby, was Janus's pack; dogs was a close description, but these beasts were the size of small ponies and had oversized teeth overfilling their slavering jaws, true hounds of hell in every sense, enough to make even Cyrus shiver briefly. His surprise and horror continued when he realised standing at the forefront of these monstrosities, like a pair of regal kings about to lead their men into combat, were his very own magnificent tigers, their white fur shining brighter than ever in the now full sunlight.

It seemed Janus also hadn't noticed them until now.

"Send your kittens home old friend, this is no place for them. I can't see many of my own pets surviving long, but they will serve an important duty." Janus said with affection.

It was a few moments before Cyrus spoke.

"Nope, they won't leave. Chong is a cantankerous bugger and insists on staying, his brother of course will do he same." Cyrus said with equal parts of pride and sadness in his voice.

"So be it, please thank them and they have my blessing."

"No questions then? Good. Ok comrades, move to your positions. And tonight I shall proudly toast our victory."

As the men started to make their way, Janus opened a channel to his three friends, speaking to Solomon first.

"You be careful out there ya big lump of lard, and don't be doing any thing stupid, like dying, you hear me?" Janus tried his best to sound light-hearted.

"Och, don't worry about me, I have Cyrus's big head to hide behind, besides, I cant die, coz without me there would be no Christmas." Sol joked, maybe not realizing, that if they did fail today, the apocalyptic infectious touch of Ahriman would plague the world long before December the twenty fifth.

"Same applies to you Cyrus, you and I have a lot of catching up to do."

"Catching up my arse, we have collage and cheerleaders to look forward too my friend."

"Oh yes, I had forgotten about that."

"Yeah, I bet you did." Cyrus said with a wink.

"And finally, Nathan." Janus paused while he unsuccessfully searched for the right words. "Ah fuck it, Nathan, you just do your thing and we'll be fine."

"Ready and waiting." Nathan's icy tone was returning.

"See both of you soon, ok?" Were Janus's final words as his two friends rode off to catch up with the moving army.

Not for the first time, Janus felt very alone and vulnerable, as he watched two of his best friends disappear in a dust cloud kicked up by the horses, he was briefly unable to shake the unwanted musing that they would not return.

"My plan sound ok?" Janus asked, feeling the need to take his mind off any negativity.

"It's spot on, hence you're the leader and we are mere grunts." Nathan tried to sound humorous, but was in obvious discomfort.

"Thank you, and don't worry, we go into combat soon enough." Janus said, realizing Nathan's internal struggle.

Time, mocked Janus, the ticking seconds while he waited for his men to gain their positions plodded wearily along; after ten minutes or ten lifetimes for one man present, finally the most significant epoch for the human race and beyond, was ready to begin.

"On your word." Cyrus transmitted.

Janus took one deep breath, opened his mind to seventy five thousand souls, no need for long romantic speeches, each waited on a knife edge for just one word; Janus had no wish to draw this out for a moment longer, so with a sense of final relief, he obliged.

"NOW."

The army immediately moved forward; not with the speed of an accelerating famished cheetah, but more the purposeful plough of an unstoppable colossal mammoth.

Without the slightest hesitation, the one-way barrier was penetrated, which in turn threw up the first of Janus's problems.

"Shit." He whispered, realizing he had lost all contact with his men.

"Don't worry, they are professionals and know what they are doing." Nathan reassured him.

The unexpected but welcome newcomers pealed off from their encroaching square and panned out left and right, making their way down the imaginary clock face, although no longer advancing closer to the target.

"What the fuck are they doing? Why don't they move forward?" Janus gasped upon seeing his army continue onwards, whilst the celestial and not so celestial warriors, hung back.

"Please, lets just see, ok old friend?" Nathan could feel Janus's distress.

Oblivious or unconcerned, the solid block of men moved ever forward, and from what must have been a signal from Cyrus, the square morphed liquid-like into a solid triangle configuration.

With his inhuman eyesight, Janus spirits lifted marginally.

"Good lads."

The V formation had Cyrus and Solomon still mounted and leading, the borders were made up of the armored knights, whom wisely switched from somewhat clumsy two-handed weapons to a shield and sword, hence making an impenetrable barrier, safely containing Nathan's cloth wearing army.

Just as things looked slightly more promising, Janus's world finally fell apart.

From his raised vantage point, but oblivious to the troops at ground level, Ahriman's circle darkened inexplicably once, then once again.

"You bastard." Were the only words Janus could find.

With the opposing army a mere five hundred yards away, Ahriman increased his own forces, first two fold, and then three. The result being once more, impossible odds and surely, a bloody and quick massacre

"Our numbers tripled at the eleventh hour, Ahriman's logic is that its ok for him to do the same I suppose." Nathan offered.

"You suppose? Is that the best you can do?" Hopelessness and anger often walk hand in hand. "First we are out numbered ten to one by an army that shouldn't exist here, then we have to pass a point where return or retreat is an impossibility, by the grace of heaven and hell we receive a welcome boost, although still very much the underdog, and even they seem to be content to stand and watch our men go to their deaths." Janus paused, blood at boiling point. "Tell me Nathan, what's the fucking point of this whole charade? We were never going to win this, ten thousand years of wasted existence. Played all along from start to finish. So this is the final punishment for our past deeds, well ha fucking ha."

"Enough!" Nathan intervened before his friend went crazy with rage and sadness. "I know you don't truly believe what you are saying, it's your emotions speaking. Here let me show you what we are fighting for."

Before Janus could protest, a new emotion washed over him, vehemence so strong that all others were instantly drowned; warmth, love, pride, ambition, and passion, all that is good in humanity filled him to his very core.

"I don't even have to ask where that came from do I?" Janus said humbly.

"Nope." Replied Nathan with a friendly smile. "Ready to give this our best shot?"

"I am now, and sorry buddy."

"No need mate, no need."

The two men focused again on the scene below, the battle was merely seconds away, but Janus was still at a loss as to why two thirds of his army had still not moved forward.

His troops were now less than two hundred yards away from combat.

"Here we go." Janus mouthed.

At that precise same moment the arrowhead surged forward, accelerating like a greyhound leaving its trap. Cyrus and Solomon were at full gallop; the unseen slipstream pulled the followers along at unnatural speed, keeping the formation tight and together.

When just inches shy of the dark army, the sprinting horses vanished, and without so much as one step missed, Cyrus, Solomon and all in tow, met the enemy at an astonishing velocity.

Steel met steel.

The momentum hardly slowed as the living plough advanced; Cyrus and Sol at its head, working in melodic synchronization cleaving a path forward, as one mans deadly sweep completed its arc, another began its brief and vicious journey, giving not a moments quarter or rest bite to all unlucky enough to be along this chosen route. The knights were doing an excellent job, attacking when their foe was in solid form, defending and parrying once they became shadows. Nathan's men were also unsurprisingly sublime; armed with two wickedly curved twin bladed swords, not much longer than a traditional dagger, tapering into a minute pin point (in skilled hands, an unparalleled weapon of death), they exuded liquid-like through invisible gaps of the impenetrable plate wall, dealing a tremendous amount of damage, then oozing back for another to take their place.

The so far immobile otherworldly watchers, at precisely the same moment all then disappeared.

Janus opened his mouth, about to fill the air with obscenities, but Nathan interrupted him before he swore.

"Wait, look."

The absent friends again materialized, this time however, their new locations was scattered somewhat randomly deep in the very depths of Ahriman's army; groups of four, dark and light fighting back to back with tattoo coordination, cutting huge swath's as the whirlwind of steel followed an invisible path.

The main bodies progress which had slowed considerably, picked up its pace once more now that the enemies reinforcements were being hampered considerably.

The lower part of the grim clock face, due to the major increase in numbers was never going to become as barren as originally hoped, but now at least, patches of desert floor could be clearly seen all be it in minute proportions.

"Now its our turn." Janus said to Nathan.

"Please don't flame me for this Janus." Nathan paused. "Put your emotion aside and please think this through logically. Would you consider staying here, because lets face it, an extra pair of hands wont make any difference, and before you say we are in this together, some things are bigger than us buddy, and if things don't go to plan, its vital that one of us at least survives." Nathan was sincere and honest.

He was slightly hurt, but Janus found himself unable to get angry at his friends suggestion.

"I realize you had to say it Nathan, but you know as well me, that its something I could never do."

"So be it." Nathan replied somewhat somberly.

"Enough of such talk. If we don't move now, we'll miss our only window of opportunity. Lets do this."

Janus kicked his until now, docile steed into action, not wishing to stay and ponder Nathan's proposition for longer than necessary, because not so hidden and screaming out for attention, in the back of his mind he knew his friend was right.

Janus rode at full gallop, Nathan was quickly alongside, their canine and feline troop in hot pursuit.

Upon passing through the translucent barrier, the first anomaly striking Janus was, silence: one medium that all battlegrounds share is noise, but this war, was all but silent. No primordial screams of humans in combat, no grating of metal on metal, and no howls of mortally wounded men desperately clinging on to the last throws of life.

Although the physical world appeared eerily hushed, Janus's mind immediately filled with clamor. He filtered out the chaff and concentrated on the two most recognizable minds.

"I am so sorry Janus, but it seems I misjudged their numbers." A solemn sounding Solomon was the first to make contact.

"No you didn't old friend, our nemesis increased his numbers three fold once it was too late to warn you."

"Ah, I thought that might be the case, see Sol, you have no reason for guilt." The voice this time was Cyrus. "Our army is dwindling fast Janus, and we can only last a few more minutes before we'll fall, but sadly, we aren't even close to the bastard. So no pressure dude, but the fate the mankind will be left solely in your capable hands, don't fail us you old goat." Such a poignant statement, and Cyrus still managed to lace it with humor.

Continuing at maximum gallop, Janus quickly surveyed the situation.

The arrowhead, still in formation, but now a shadow of its former size. Nearly all the Templar's had perished, although Janus couldn't help but a raise a small inner smile upon seeing the duke still standing, alongside was a completely out of position Percy, forever the protector.

"You're a good un buddy." Janus whispered, already feeling a prideful tear.

Nathan's army, now numbered hundreds rather than thousands, five would enter the melee, maybe one or two ever returned. The groups of four random warriors also had become few and far in-between; none contained the full quartet, but the remaining normally mortal enemies, fought and died valiantly as friends.

Janus briefly wondered why his two friends hadn't morphed into their hellish twins, but they obviously knew that the apparent battle was a hopeless one, metamorphosis would enable them to live a little longer, but being so far from their target, it would be a futile gesture.

They wanted to take their last breaths as humans, and die alongside their brave comrades.

Janus had to admit to himself that he would have done the same.

"Every single man has done an exceptional job, and I am proud of them all. Our job is nearly done here, and our time is limited. It's in your hands now Janus, goodbye and good luck." No humor from Cyrus this time, only sadness.

Janus had so much to say to his two oldest friends, but the right words just weren't there.

"Goodbye buddy." Was Solomon's last whisper, meant only for Janus.

Fueled by anger, Janus hit the first unsuspecting wave of evil like a monster possessed, his enchanted sword caring not if they were in shadow for or solid, they fell quickly and silently.

Nathan quickly passed him, already in the form of his horrific Alta ego; duel wielding swords at an impossible speed. His now invisible armored suit acted as a magnet for the unholy, sucking in all that are near and feeding on their deaths as Nathan cut them down.

Such was the speed and ferocity of his partner, Janus could do nothing more but run at full pelt, trying to keep up and pick off the very rare few that Nathan had missed.

There was then a piecing howl of emotional pain from directly behind Janus, telling him something that he already knew; Cyrus had died, and the cats felt it as strongly as Janus, Solomon followed moments later.

Cheech then accelerated passed Janus and Nathan, his tiny but loving mind filled with nothing but revenge for his master. The cat dodged and slipped its way through the never ending lines ahead, but even an animal as greasy and cunning as Cheech was devoured by darkness. Unsurprisingly, his ever-close sibling, went straight to his aid, but disappeared into the same abyss.

With the keystones of the main attack gone, the brave few remaining were quickly overwhelmed. With nothing left of the main assault, the hateful army in the northern end, still countless in numbers, become a focused tsunami moving at unimaginable speed, directly towards the only two men left standing.

The wave of death was only seconds away, the slim chance of victory they had at the outset, was now gone.

The world then stopped.

A confused and disoriented Janus felt as if he was trapped in a movie on pause.

"I can't hold this state for long."

Standing before Janus was Nathan; back in human form, gone was his battle gear and the distant look in his eyes.

"We don't have time to argue, but all hope is lost here. You have to do what we discussed." Nathan said softly.

"No." Anger answered for Janus.

"Yes Janus. I know it's the hardest decision you will ever make, but don't make Cyrus's, Solomon's and my death count for nothing. You owe it to the three of us, and to mankind, to live and fight again. While one of us breaths, there will always be a glimmer of hope."

"I Cant." Janus stuttered, but he knew his decision was already made for him. "But you said yourself that the dome covering us makes it impossible to leave."

"Don't worry about that, I have one trick left that will distract Ahriman enough to lower his defense slightly, and of course, IT will help you. Trust me." Nathan paused. "We only have seconds left, so give me your sword, and as soon as I am gone, engage every fiber of your being into concentration, and you will teleport to safety, but it will take the combined efforts of all parties involved."

"But holding my sword will kill you." Janus wasn't thinking straight, and realized as soon as he said it, that it was a foolish statement.

Nathan just smiled, and took the sword from Janus, he offered no resistance; all fight was gone.

"I wont say goodbye, because I know this isn't the end."

Nathan was once again in his hideous and deadly guise; there was a sickening crack, and Nathan become two, then four and finally six. Half a dozen bringers of doom, but only one wielded the legendary Excalibur.

Janus knew that each moment Nathan held the sword, his life would be draining away, but the effort it took for him to create the murderous doppelgangers would quickly kill him anyway.

"Go now, and find Croatoan." Nathan said calmly just as the world started once again.

Janus felt frozen to the spot as he watched the beasts' speed forward to meet the oncoming wave. Janus strangely then had the sensation of being watched from behind; he turned and through tear filled eyes he could make out a solitary figure standing at their original vantage point, observing the battle. His vision clouded by sadness and the haze of the barrier meant he couldn't make out who it was, but he knew it was a friend, and he could even feel a loving smile touch him. Without a doubt he finally understood that leaving was the right and only conclusion.

Janus turned back to Nathan, the six had become four as Ahriman's elite guard had been called into action to keep Nathan busy as the surge of the approaching army avoided him completely, Janus was their only target.

"Hurry." Said Nathan in a strained voice, just before his attackers overwhelmed him.

Janus closed his eyes, but knew that he had left it too late, the advancing faceless mob were only yards away. He tried his best to concentrate on the jump, but without knowing the contact point he couldn't do it. One last try as he put every inch of his essence into it, but failure would be only outcome; the army struck him, and for the first time in his impossibly long life, Janus felt pain, as a hundred burning swords were plunged into him.

Thankfully his world went black, and he no longer felt any pain.

BOOK TWO

Nemesis Child

Prologue

Janus regained consciousness, but hesitated about opening his eyes; uncertainty and the unknown scared him. He could feel no physical discomfort, but the still freshness of recent memory was agonising.

He curled his toes and clenched his fists, feeling for the first time, his soft yet strange bedding.

"Janus?" Asked a caring and comforting voice.

Tentatively and nervously, Janus slowly let his eyelids lift.

He genuinely hadn't realised that he was in open air, and the sunlight assaulted his eyes for a few moments; his surprised continued when he discovered his soft sumptuous divan was nothing more than the grassy floor on which he lay. As he propped himself up onto his elbow, he noticed the flora beneath him was brown and dying, a stark contrast to the myriad of life elsewhere; unbeknown to Janus, the said grass had happily sacrificed its own small life force to aid and heal someone in dire need.

Patiently sitting cross-legged opposite Janus was a friendly-faced young oriental man, in his early twenties, Janus guessed.

"Good morning Janus." He said with the warmest of smiles. " My name is Tenzin, welcome to the garden."

About the author

Jez was born in Cardiff, but has lived in Llandudno, North Wales, for the most part of his life.

He doesn't pretend to be particularly intelligent, or a professional author, but does enjoy a good book, and this project began as him attempting to write the book he always wanted to read, so he hopes you enjoy the voyage of discovery as much as he did.

He lives by the motto

"Don't trust the cheese."   Which has always served him well, apparently.

Please understand, that due to my limited budget, this book is wholly unedited, and for that I apologize sincerely (this will 'not' be the case with my next outing). Any comments etc are more than welcome via cyrusdraig@hotmail.com.

Printed in the United States
93108LV00007B/7/A